Animal Heart

Animal Heart

a novel

Brenda Peterson

SIERRA CLUB BOOKS

SAN FRANCISCO

The characters, places, and events in this book are either the invention of the author
or used in a fictitious manner. Any resemblance to real people or events is coincidental.

The Sierra Club, founded in 1892 by John Muir, has devoted itself to the study and protection of the earth's
scenic and ecological resources—mountains, wetlands, woodlands, wild shores and rivers, deserts and
plains. The publishing program of the Sierra Club offers books to the public as a nonprofit educational
service in the hope that they may enlarge the public's understanding of the Club's basic concerns. The point
of view expressed in each book, however, does not necessarily represent that of the Club. The Sierra Club
has some sixty chapters throughout the United States and in Canada. For information about how you may
participate in its programs to preserve wilderness and the quality of life, please address inquiries to Sierra
Club, 85 Second Street, San Francisco, California 94105, or visit our website at www.sierraclub.org.

Published by Sierra Club Books
85 Second Street, San Francisco, CA 94105
www.sierraclub.org/books

Produced and distributed by
University of California Press
Berkeley and Los Angeles, California
University of California Press, Ltd.
London, England
www.ucpress.edu

SIERRA CLUB, SIERRA CLUB BOOKS, and the Sierra Club design logos
are registered trademarks of the Sierra Club.

Book and jacket design by Elizabeth Watson
Front-cover photograph © Jos. Palmieri / The Stock Solution

Library of Congress Cataloging-in-Publication Data
Peterson, Brenda, 1950-
    Animal heart : a novel / by Brenda Peterson.—1st ed.
        p. cm
    ISBN 1-57805-108-8 (alk. paper)
        1. Human-animal relationships—Fiction. 2. Heart—Transplantation—Fiction.
    3. Underwater photography—Fiction. 4. Forensic pathologists—Fiction. 5.
    Women pathologists—Fiction. 6. Wildlife rescue—Fiction. 7. Photographers—Fiction.
    8. Dolphins—Fiction. 9. Oregon—Fiction. 10. Whales—Fiction. I. Title.

    PS3566.E767A84 2004
    813'.54—dc22

                                                                                2003061648

Printed in the United States of America on New Leaf Ecobook 50 acid-free paper.

First Edition

08 07 06 05 04

10 9 8 7 6 5 4 3 2 1

To Susan Biskeborn, friend and first reader, always

To my agent, Mary Ann Naples, and my editor, Linda Gunnarson,

visionaries who helped birth this book

Acknowledgments

FOR GIVING ME their invaluable scientific advice, I thank naturalists Susan Berta and Howard Garrett of Orca Network, naturalist and veteran diver Doug Thompson of Dolphin Works, wildlife biologist and botanist Robin Kobaly of Summertree Institute, author Donna Kelleher, D.V.M., and Jeff Blake, D.V.M.

For their dedication to marine mammal issues and cetacean advocacy, I acknowledge the extraordinary work of Joel Reynolds, Natural Resources Defense Council; Dr. Naomi Rose of the Humane Society of the United States; Dr. Lindy Weilgart, a sperm whale expert in Nova Scotia; orca expert Ken Balcomb of the Center for Whale Research; nature writer Leigh Calvez; Paul Spong and Helena Symonds of OrcaLab; Marsha Green of Ocean Mammal Institute; author Jim Nollman of *Interspecies Newsletter;* reporter Penny LeGate of KIRO/CBS television; and journalist Merritt Clifton of *Animal People News.* Praise is also due wildlife rehab volunteers Donna Porter of Free Flight Bird and Marine Mammal Rehabilitation Center, Bob Jones of Sarvey Wildlife Center, and Dianne Grob of H.O.W.L.

For courageous activism on primate labs, gratitude goes to Dan Lyons of England's Uncaged Campaigns for his groundbreaking Website "Xeno Diaries" and to writer Carla Bennett. For primate research, I also am so grateful to the remarkable books *Brutal Kinship,* by Michael Nichols and Jane Goodall, *Next of Kin,* by Roger Fouts, and *Rattling the Cage,* by Steven Wise.

For encouragement and for reading over this manuscript's many drafts, I am deeply grateful to publisher and editor Maureen Michelson of NewSage Press, Dr. Anne DeVore, painter and illustrator Christine Lamb, and my pod mates, the nature writers Sy Montgomery and Diane Ackerman, whose own work on dolphins is an inspiration. I also thank editor Judith Jones of Knopf, who inspired a revision.

For good counsel in the final stages of this eight-year project, I give heartfelt thanks to author Diane Johnson, author and animal advocate Dr. Marc Bekoff, author and inspiration Dr. Jane Goodall, and the Seattle Base Camp Leader of the Jane Goodall Institute and wizard of our writers' community Website, Literati.net, Gary McAvoy.

For helping me heal with his Taoist acupuncture, I thank Jim Dowling, R.N., and his assistants, Katrina Vegoni and Laura Zanieski. Also Catherine Englehart for her CST skills. For keeping my home and my cats, Loki and Tao, healthy during my many travels, I am so thankful to Vanessa Adams.

For remarkable editorial assistance, I praise the skills of Rebekka Stahl and Tara Kolden. Thanks to *Seattle Times* editor Jim Veseley for farsighted editorial vision. I am deeply appreciative of the generous yet rigorous copyediting by Bonita Hurd and the brilliant book designing by Elizabeth Watson. And my thanks to the staff of Sierra Club Books, including publisher Helen Sweetland and editor-in-chief Danny Moses, and the staff of the University of California Press, including marketing director Anna Bullard and publicists Amy Torack, Alex Dahne, and Joanne Skinner, who also worked on the dolphin anthology *Between Species*—your professionalism, environmental ethics, and heart are why I've chosen the gift of staying with a West Coast publisher.

Thanks always to my friends—my neighbors Bill McHalffey, Eve Anthony, and Joyce Russo, who help keep our beach, Rebecca Romanelli, Marlene Blessing, Kimberly Richardson, and my *taiji* teacher, Kim Ivy. I am also grateful to my students for our weekly dialogues about the writing craft and the natural world. And thanks so much for the lifelong support of my family and parents.

For a decade of friendship, travel, and creation, I will always be grateful to author Linda Hogan. And finally, I acknowledge in devoted memory Rachel MacKenzie of the *New Yorker* magazine, who always reminded me, "Keep your heart on your writing."

Animal Heart

chapter one

Kiwanda Beach Watch *15*

chapter two

Seal-Sitting *27*

chapter three

Eavesdropping *48*

chapter four

Underwater Volcano *69*

chapter five

Animal Heart *82*

chapter six

The Dead Zone *104*

chapter seven

Homecoming *124*

chapter eight

Stranding *139*

chapter nine

Perfect Empathic Pair *156*

chapter ten

A Dying Art *174*

chapter eleven

Blue Dragon Rising from the Sea *195*

chapter twelve

Deaf, at Last Listening *211*

chapter thirteen

Aquatic Apes *223*

chapter fourteen

Room 66X *242*

chapter fifteen

Family Cottage *253*

chapter sixteen

Silkie's Cave *271*

Epilogue *283*

"Whatever asks, heart kneels and offers to bear."

—Jane Hirshfield, "What the Heart Wants"

"The heart generates the largest electromagnetic

field of any body organ, several thousand times

more powerful than that of the brain."

—Michael T. Greenwood, M.D.

chapter one

Kiwanda Beach Watch

HIDDEN BEHIND A sea stack, Isabel Spinner sat on her haunches, keeping a careful eye on a tiny harbor seal pup who lay too still on the rock-strewn sand. Years of volunteer patrol for the local wildlife rehab center had taught Isabel that she must remain out of sight of both beached pup and swimming mother, who might not reclaim her infant if she saw humans on this beach.

Whistling softly for her well-trained Siberian husky to stay by her side, Isabel scanned the beach with her binoculars. Silkie helped Isabel divert other dogs and tourists away from the seal pup, whose speckled fur, which looked like a heap of stones and shells, was perfectly camouflaged by the mottled beach.

This evening Isabel was especially watchful. There had been a sudden intrusion of tourists this first spring of the new millennium because of a rare geologic revelation. One ebb tide, a two-thousand-year-old forest had eerily emerged from the sand. Petrified stumps stood like sentinels in the surf, and no one in the tiny beach town of Lawasskin, Oregon, knew what to make of this unearthing. Was it a premonition? Geologists theorized that this upheaval of what folks called the "Black Forest of the Sea" was convincing evidence of millennia of violent change.

"It's a mystery what killed these old trees," a state expert told the *Lawasskin Beachcomber.* "Most likely a massive offshore quake long ago sank these cedar, Sitka, and short pine, dropping our coastline almost ten feet."

Townsfolk said if such a killer quake submerged this old-growth grove once, it could happen again. Schoolchildren along Oregon's shores began tsunami drills in earnest. Hundreds of tourists made pilgrimages to stare at these ancient trees—last seen at the time of Christ. Touching them was like time traveling.

Only locals lingered here on Kiwanda Beach. Those, like Isabel, who had walked the sand as children hoped that this black forest did not foretell their fate. No one turned their backs to this ocean.

Through her binoculars Isabel couldn't tell for sure if the seal pup was in trouble, but she suspected he was. His skin was wrinkled, his small body shrunken from lack of nourishment or from dehydration. So far this spring, Isabel had stood guard over seven injured harbor seal pups, and all but one had died. She lost many of them because she followed the rules.

The rules of the Marine Mammal Protection Act insisted that humans not touch beached seals and instead call local government agencies and wildlife rehabilitation shelters, no matter how wounded the animal. The law required them to wait and observe for forty-eight hours, in case the mother returned, before taking any action. This last eight-hour shift was almost always Isabel's. She would make the final call for action. But so many times, Isabel had watched a marine mammal bleed to death from internal injuries before she was allowed to rescue it. Isabel clicked on her flashlight and tried to focus on reading the current *Science News* with its article on global warming, but she couldn't keep her eyes off the pup. If her younger brother, Andrew, or Grandfather Spinner were on the beach with her, he would have ignored the MMPA rules and run right over to help that struggling seal pup.

"Science is the job people choose when they're running away from life," Andrew often told Isabel, "escaping the messy stuff—like love." Andrew was a nature photographer and videographer who had won international acclaim for his underwater documentaries and photographs. Andrew had been particularly appalled when his older sister accepted the federal forensics job.

"But I'm working with what I love most," Isabel said.

"Dead animals, Isabel?" he interrupted on his latest call to her. His cell phone crackled with static. He was calling from the Amazon. "That's one more step away from real life."

"I'm not the one who's far away, Andrew. Are you ever coming home?"

"That's why I called, Sis. I'm going to be in Portland this weekend for that annual photography conference. Meet me there?"

Isabel hesitated and then, against her better judgment, complained, "I can't remember the last time you actually made it out here to our beach. Listen, I'll make a deal with you. If I come to Portland, will you take some time and come back to Lawasskin with me—maybe just for a few days?" When he said nothing, she added, "Oh, Andrew, there are so many seals this spring. You should see Silkie's Cave . . ."

Once when Isabel was eleven, she and five-year-old Andrew had gone beachcombing at low tide. Playing amid the craggy offshore rocks, they stumbled into a sea cave. Seals lounging on nearby rocks barked a warning, but still the siblings crawled deep into the dripping cave. Sharp shells pricked his palms, but Andrew seemed determined to keep pace with Isabel.

When Isabel leaned against the cave walls in the watery light, she heard Andrew catch his breath. "It's a silkie . . . ," he whispered.

The rare find of a molted sealskin that the children believed belonged to a mystical half-seal, half-human changeling was like discovering one of their mother's sheer evening gowns. Though most girls her age played dress-up in their mothers' fancy clothes, Isabel had never done more than shyly run her hand along her mother's silk dresses preserved in a closet. Isabel ran ahead of Andrew in the narrow cave. Lifting the sealskin from the rocks, she gathered up the gossamer gray skin. Though the sealskin was in tatters, the speckled gray fur was still dense and surprisingly luxurious. When Andrew tenderly draped the pelt around his sister's shoulders, it was heavy and warm, glowing like quicksilver.

Inside this second skin, Isabel had felt safe. "Seals belong to land and sea," Grandfather Spinner had taught them. He, like their parents, had emigrated from the Hebrides Islands. After their parents died in a sailboat accident, it was Grandfather who had raised Isabel and Andrew in his small beach bungalow just south of Lawasskin. "You children are from a long line of seal folk," he'd assure them. "You can go between the worlds, if you just remember how to change your skins."

Did Andrew remember? Or had he forgotten all the old stories? Now, Isabel recalled the last time her brother had visited. Four years ago, he'd come back on a diving assignment to photograph octopi off Coos Bay. If it weren't for the multitude of photos from his assignments that he sent his sister on-line, some showing him obscured by scuba mask or sunglasses, she wouldn't even know how he was wearing his hair, whether he'd lost or gained weight, if he was happy. Not that his marine photographs revealed much about his inner life. To understand Andrew's love life, Isabel had to ask instead about the state of coral reefs—were they bleached white and dying or still vibrant with fluorescent fuchsia and orange? Andrew's lavish photos of recovering coral reefs would signal to his sister that he was happily in love; his environmental despair would coincide with a broken romance.

"Seen any pups yet in our cave?" Andrew asked, his voice breaking up in the static.

So he did remember. "Quite a few. And last week I was snorkeling off Mallebey's Point when I startled these three harbor seals. Andrew, they were sleeping in the kelp forest, drifting up and down on the tide. It was surreal."

"I know, Sis," he said excitedly. "I've got a photograph like that of seals off the Azores. Isn't it amazing? I think they're dreaming, those seals. Or, is that not scientific enough for you?"

"Come on. Science isn't so dreary. I'll bet you didn't know that last year Russian scientists actually documented that gray whales dream . . ."

"Is that a fact?"

She could hear her brother's smile over the phone. "Yeah, and we also have evidence that some birds, when they sleep, have the same brain waves as when they're singing."

"Smarty-pants! So what's your favorite Amazon bird, Isa?" Andrew asked. "I'll bring you a photo from the rain forest."

"My favorite bird is extinct."

"It would be."

"Just bring me you, dodo bird."

"Meet you in Portland?" Andrew asked.

"No deal, then? You can't get out to the coast? You know I hate the city."

"Let's just see, Isa. Maybe I can pick up a diving assignment. Buddy of mine has a shoot near that underwater volcano erupting off your coast."

Your coast. With one pronoun, Andrew had betrayed his distance not only from their home but from his childhood. There was a time when her brother had still said *our* coast. No more. Even if he visited, he was not home here.

"Okay, you win, " she said. "Just hope you'll get home . . . I mean, back here."

Silkie let out a soft yodel and brought Isabel's attention to a slight movement on the beach. "Good boy," she said and focused her binoculars on the seal pup, watching his narrow belly rise and fall. This tiny animal seemed anything but restful as he flopped awkwardly on the rocky sand. Isabel sensed his pain. People who didn't live by the Pacific Ocean sometimes mistook solitary seal pups for orphans. Unknowingly, they'd kidnap a pup to a wildlife shelter in the wrongheaded notion they'd rescued it from certain death. But often the pup was simply napping onshore while the mother fished. Only a trained volunteer could sit vigil and then make the official call to the National Marine Fisheries Service for permission to move the pup to the wildlife sanctuary.

"Call it baby-sitting," the wildlife rehab center director explained to every volunteer. "When you sit watch over a seal pup, you create a protective circle against predators," she said. "For a few hours you're a guardian to some of our little mammal cousins."

Reassuring herself that the seal pup was not yet panting in distress, Isabel noted the time in her field log. Full moon. Midnight. Where was Marian?

As if in response, Marian Windhorse Gray appeared far down the beach. Isabel smiled, seeing the new silver rain slicker flash in the moonlight as Marian moved through the petrified snags toward Seal Rock. Isabel enjoyed watching Marian find her way with the subtle economy of her Oskeena ancestors. If not for the threat of sneaker waves, Marian could probably navigate this beach in her sleep.

As Marian approached, Isabel's hand flew guiltily to her hair. Marian would scold her for not wearing the new khaki rain hat she had ordered for her from one of her many catalogues.

When Marian silently sat down on the beach blanket, she cast a critical eye at Isabel's auburn curls tamed into a tidy braid and haphazardly stuffed under a bandana. "If you're not going to wear the hat, I'll give it to my cousin," Marian whispered.

Isabel noticed that Marian's own black ponytail was still perfect, even in the middle of the night. Her lipstick matched her red baseball cap. Compact and graceful, Marian crossed her legs in a full lotus position, as if this were a natural posture.

"That hat is really not my style," Isabel said apologetically.

Marian snorted and opened her satchel. "You don't *have* a style, Isabel. That's why you need me."

Isabel laughed, but very quietly so as not to alarm the seal pup. "No sign of Mom," she reported and handed her friend the field log.

Marian studied the log. "How many hours now?"

"Seven. You relieving me or waiting with?"

"Waiting." Marian smiled slightly. "And I brought food, even though it seems heartless for us to eat while that pup is so hungry."

Again Isabel raised her binoculars. She saw the seal stretch and shake himself from head to tail flippers in a mighty yawn. Isabel could make out the pink tongue like a festival balloon. "Good . . . ," she breathed. "Just one more hour."

The full moon, laced in gray-violet marine mists, was shining over the Black Forest of the Sea, a watery Stonehenge.

"Any injuries you can see?" Marian asked.

"Maybe an orca attack or gunshot wound. Hard to tell from this distance."

Isabel looked disinterestedly through the satchel Marian had packed. Marian frowned as she watched Isabel reject the baked beans and dill pickles. "Eat something."

"Don't be a nag." Isabel dutifully munched on a sandwich of home-made bread with artichoke hearts, cheese, and jalapenos.

Picking out the hot jalapenos and putting them in her plastic trash bag, Isabel checked her watch. They ate quietly, so as not to alarm the seal pup. At last Isabel lay back on the plaid beach blanket, studying the night sky. Stars above the beach always seemed closer. As children, she and Andrew could name every constellation. Now Andrew knew the pull of Cassiopeia and Orion's belt from other hemispheres. Sometimes Isabel wished she were not the one who always stayed here, that she also had been touched with their seafaring Scottish ancestors' wanderlust. But then who would keep their grandfather's cottage from slipping into even worse disrepair? And since neither Isabel, divorced and in her late thirties, nor Andrew had yet made a family, where would they find home but on this beloved beach?

Isabel sat up and leaned on one arm to better see Marian. Her friend was intently studying a dark starfish wedged inside the hollow of a petrified stump.

"My brother's coming home this weekend," Isabel said softly.

"Home, meaning here?"

"Well, Portland. He's guest speaker at an underwater-photography conference, but maybe he'll get some time to . . ."

"Better meet him in the city," Marian advised. "That's what he's asking, isn't it?"

Isabel shrugged. "Yes, as usual. But I'm hoping he might get out to the beach for some spring diving. It's his favorite time of year."

"And you're his only family," Marian said sharply. "If he doesn't make it to the beach again this visit, I'll personally get my ex to haul him out here on some legal excuse. Say, what's the opposite of a restraining order?"

Isabel smiled faintly. "An engaging order?"

"I think men were born to migrate." Marian shook her head. "Something in the DNA . . . speaking of which, I've got some news about that dolphin case."

In a DNA analysis that had landed at their federal wildlife forensics lab, they were trying to match the saliva from a cigar to a suspect turned in by an anonymous tipster—perhaps one of his fishing buddies or children.

"Can you believe that anyone would pour a can of beer down a dolphin's blowhole and then shove a lit cigar in it?" Isabel said.

"This is one of our lucky days. Two credible matches."

Most of their cases were more difficult, like the still unsolved crime of the poacher who preyed on elk in Nebraska, machine-gunning entire herds and taking only their valuable ivory teeth to sell in the international endangered species trade. Or the Bureau of Land Management mustangs rounded up in a remote Nevada canyon, hogtied, and shot execution-style, with one bullet to each wild head. So far the only break in the case had been a girlfriend who called the local sheriff in a tremulous voice and said, "I'm leaving him. He kills horses." But she gave neither her name nor his.

Again, Isabel studied the seal pup through her binoculars and checked her watch. "So what's the other DNA match?"

"Golden eagle."

Isabel nodded with satisfaction. "So the blood from the pocketknife *does* match the eagle's. Wesley something, right?"

"Wesley Wayne," Marian said. "Never did like that last name." Marian lay back on the beach blanket to stare at the nimbus of clouds shrouding the moon.

Isabel shook her head. "This pup looks really dehydrated."

"Well, we could lie and say it's already been eight hours . . ."

Isabel frowned.

"You know, dear," Marian grumbled, "one of these days you're going to rip up all those stupid rule books. I just hope I'm here to help you."

"Any dessert?"

Marian obligingly rummaged in her satchel for a Halloween-size Hershey's bar. Just then, they heard a voice hailing them. Marian peered down the beach toward Seal Rock and shook her head. "Now might be a good time to practice your martial art."

"Oh, I was praying Stewart had the night off."

"I think Stewart asks his NMFS buddies to radio him whenever you're seal-sitting on the beach. Poor guy."

"You'd think marriage to me would have cured him by now." Isabel grinned.

After knowing Stewart all her life and being pursued by him ever since they were middle school biology lab partners, Isabel had at last agreed to marry him on her thirtieth birthday. For five years they had floated along in a companionable alliance marked by its awkwardness whenever Stewart insisted they "act more like a real couple."

"But we *are* a couple, Stewart," she'd tell him, feeling the pang of guilt she always felt when he complained about their lives together. "I did marry you."

Yet somehow she had failed him. This Isabel knew, if she didn't know quite why. All Stewart could tell her was that, despite what he had expected of married life—their own closed set of intimacy—it had not given him the romantic security that he had awaited so long.

"You probably just don't know how to be married because you lost your folks so young," Stewart had told her. "Married people go places together. They eat supper together every night. They don't stay out all night with seals and take phone calls at 3 A.M. for strandings. Married people have routines, Isabel. They spend their weekends working on their houses or doing regular stuff together. You're not very . . . dependable."

"But we're good friends," Isabel tried to reassure him. "We've grown up together. This is our beach. We do the same work. You and I, we make sense . . ."

"I don't want to make sense with you, Isa," he protested. "I want to . . . oh, I don't know, maybe pretend like we've never met. Like it's always for the first time. Like you really *chose* me," Stewart said. "I mean, there were no other guys. Maybe you just kind of fell in with me . . . out of habit or something."

"You're jealous. How could there ever be any other guys with you always around?"

"And I never dated, either . . ."

"Oh, so that's it! You didn't have enough choice? Stewart, girls always ran after you. You could have had your pick."

"But I wanted only you, Isabel," he moaned.

"Oh," she said, bewildered. "So that's the problem."

"I don't know what the problem is," he concluded, as he always did. "But if we keep going like this, we'll end up . . . well, like my parents."

"You mean, having affairs?"

Stewart was quiet. "No, not that exactly."

"You know, Stewart, there's a difference between living in a small town and *being* small-town."

While it had always been her husband who routinely threatened to file for divorce, it was actually Isabel who did it, after five years of marriage. There had been rumors of Stewart following in his mother's footsteps and indulging in discreet affairs, always with passing tourists. But Isabel knew that, even if he had slept with other women, it was somehow her that he had imagined. He had told her as much.

For his part, Stewart Salk told himself that his youthful obsession with Isabel was at last doused by a failed marriage and familiarity, the way marine mists and steady Northwest drizzle muffled even the most intense sounds and sights. Yet he still believed that Isabel had held out on him—that there was some passion or devotion that, though his right, Isabel would surrender only to a stranger, a passerby.

Whenever Stewart slept with tourists, he imagined an elaborate fantasy: the tourist was in fact Isabel Spinner come to Lawasskin for the first—and last—time. She would recognize him as the one she had been looking for all those years, and she would help him escape this place, these parents who warred with and betrayed each other and remained locked together.

Stewart hailed Isabel and Marian now, his voice so loud it startled the seal pup, who glanced around in terror. "Don't you ever punch out?" he shouted, and Silkie growled low at Stewart. Though two years divorced, Stewart and Isabel still shared their wildlife work. Stewart was in the law enforcement branch of the National Marine Fisheries Service.

"Shhhh, everybody," Isabel cautioned.

Immediately her dog settled on the beach blanket, sitting so close to Isabel he almost forced her off onto the sand.

"Bodyguard," Marian said with a barely suppressed giggle.

"Sorry, gals," Stewart said loudly. He set down a large picnic basket that Isabel recognized as belonging to his mother, Maggie, the local deputy sheriff. Maggie Salk was often the first to receive calls about a seal pup on the beach. Isabel believed that her mother-in-law had been the best thing about her marriage to Stewart. Though she was a tough talker and did have that wayward eye for men other than her suspicious husband and son, Maggie almost replaced the mother Isabel had long ago lost.

Like Maggie, Stewart was extraordinarily good-looking, with his wavy, dark hair, uncanny green eyes, and lean, long body. Around her ex-husband, Isabel couldn't help but feel like a failure. Though everyone, especially Marian, said otherwise, Isabel believed their breakup was her fault, the result of some inadequacy within her that she couldn't quite understand.

"You weren't in love with him, Isa," Marian would tell her. "That's all. It's no crime. You just loved him. That wasn't enough for Stewart. Or for you. It shouldn't be."

Stewart sat down on the blanket. He leaned against Isabel while reaching into the picnic basket to take out the Tupperware container still warm with sour cherry cobbler.

"Yuummmm," Marian said and turned her flashlight on a work of art.

Maggie Salk's cobblers had won blue ribbons at state fairs, and she had once shared the recipe with her daughter-in-law. But Isabel could never make it like this: perfectly browned crisscross of crust, sweetly seeping small cherries, and bubbling red syrup.

"Tell your mother we want to make her an honorary member of our tribe," Marian said, "if she'll give us her recipe."

"You know my mother only gives her cobbler recipe to family," Stewart said.

"Will you serve the cobbler, Stewart?" Isabel hoped to head off the usual squabbling between her ex-husband and friend. If they were going to rescue this seal pup, the women needed Stewart to cooperate now and quickly give his federal permission to remove the pup to their Kiwanda Wildlife Rehabilitation Center.

Stewart sliced into the cobbler. "Divers' alert this weekend," he said.

Isabel closed her eyes. "Now Andrew will never come to the beach."

"It's just another tsunami drill. Not a big deal. But absolutely no diving on the beach from Friday through Monday. Tell all your people. We'll also post it."

Isabel nodded. As the beachmaster directing the Kiwanda Stranding

Network, it was her job to inform her volunteers of any red tides, research, or diving prohibitions. "Will do."

"You haven't asked about the pup, Stewart." Marian's tone betrayed some irritation.

Stewart uncrossed his long legs and stood up to take a look with his binoculars. In the light from the full moon, Isabel could see that Stewart cast Marian a baleful look. His behavior reminded Isabel that she shouldn't feel so much guilt about abandoning their marriage. She hoped she would never become as narrow as Stewart—that living in one place all her life would not insulate or diminish her. Of all sins, Isabel considered stinginess and lack of imagination the worst.

Stewart strode toward the stranded pup. "How long since you last saw the pup move?" he shouted.

At his voice, the seal pup startled sideways. Neither woman answered. The pup's dismay was answer enough. Vainly, the pup tried to flop toward the surf; but he fell back, head drooping.

"We've got to get that pup to the rehab center." Isabel stood up. Quickly, she packed up the uneaten cobbler and whistled for Silkie to stay.

"Sweet-talk Stewart, Isa," Marian urged. "Kiss him, promise him dinner, do whatever it takes to get this pup to safety."

Isabel very slowly moved toward Stewart and the seal pup, careful not to shine her flashlight directly on the pup. Isabel tapped Stewart on the shoulder, and as he nodded, she whispered a "thank you" lost in the surf.

A sign from Isabel, and Marian was up. "Come on, Silkie," Marian whispered, "let's try and save another one of your namesakes."

chapter two

Seal-Sitting

Anyone visiting the coastal branch of the U.S. Fish and Wildlife Service's National Forensics Laboratory might mistake it for a taxidermy shop, with its organized clutter of animal parts. Blue steel shelves were filled with the curved ivory of walrus tusks from a wasteful subsistence hunt in northwest Alaska, perfect sets of pearlized teeth from poached elk in South Dakota, and the wings of poisoned eagles and red-tailed hawks. Hanging from the rafters were the skins of deer, antelope, and buffalo, as well as several giant tortoise shells. There were also whole boxes of yet unidentified animal parts: tiny rib cages, crooked femurs, and mammal skulls. Scattered but meticulously tagged were the furs, talons, claws, and feathers of endangered animals from around the world. Several sections of blue shelves were devoted to projectiles—bullets and arrows the lab had proven to be murder weapons by detecting traces of their copper and lead in arrow wounds.

And then there was an entire back room filled with what Isabel always found the most heartbreaking of all—Asian medicines. Here were black rhino horn pills, tiger bone juice, and other potions that supposedly cured impotency and gave longevity. All that such medicines accomplished was the single-minded slaughter of endangered species—a bear bladder stolen and cubs left orphaned; a shark's fin sawed off and the ancient predator tossed half-alive back into the sea; a parrot plucked of its scarlet and green feathers.

Isabel and Marian were at home here in their lab. Just two days after

27

their midnight seal-sitting, they were working late under the bright lights, studying a single paw and a slim stretch of soft wolf skin.

"Whoever shot this wolf tossed the radio collar up into the trees," the investigating agent told them, "like in the old days when a guy threw a girl's garter belt after a big score." The agent from Idaho Fish and Game slouched at the end of Isabel's steel necropsy table. He watched as she sorted through the other evidence he'd brought: bits of fur, blood, and a shrunken leather collar.

"Did you know," Isabel asked him, "that wolf DNA is exactly the same as a dog's?"

"Makes sense." The agent nodded. But he was focused now on the woman's gray eyes, so like a wild animal's, and her unraveling braid.

Isabel smiled absently at the agent. She turned her attention to Marian. "Poachers?"

Marian didn't answer. Instead she turned to face the agent. Her dark eyes were direct but not unkind. "We better get to work on this."

"Right." The agent nodded and saw himself out.

Once the agent was gone, Marian said, "Poachers are the worst." She lifted the limp but still majestic wolf paw to examine it.

"Trophy hunters would be more humane," Isabel commented.

"Apparently, it was his hunting buddy who turned the poacher in," Marian said, reading the official report.

"Rancher?"

"No, salvage salesman. Most of the ranchers in that area seem okay with the wild wolf reintroduction program, since they get reimbursed at market value for any livestock lost."

Isabel nodded. "What else?"

"Well, according to the hunting buddy who was riding in the pickup with him, this Jeb Garfield guy just shot the wolf when she was crossing the road. No hesitation. Could have been somebody's dog."

"Target practice." Isabel frowned. "Ever notice how many road signs have bullet holes in them?"

Marian continued to read the officer's report while Isabel clipped fur samples.

The wolf was hunting elk or deer to feed her seven-week-old pups.

Fish and Game officers had finally located the starving orphan pups and were trying to nurse them back to health for eventual release into the wild. But without a mother, their survival chances were slim.

Even with an eyewitness to the shooting, Garfield insisted on his innocence. He claimed his hunting buddy was lying because of an old grudge between them. If the forensics lab's DNA analysis of the blood found on Garfield's camouflage jacket matched that of this gray wolf, it would be convincing evidence of his guilt.

Isabel was very careful when she smeared a streak of the wolf's blood onto a slide. This she handed to Marian, and they worked on in companionable silence until almost ten o'clock.

At last Isabel looked across at Marian. "Snow can't melt in a wolf's fur," Isabel commented, as if the two had been carrying on a long conversation. "The coat is too dense."

"Too beautiful," Marian said softly.

When they at last had finished their work, Marian suggested they drop by the Ocean Haven Tavern for some well-deserved coffee and homemade carrot cake.

"Can't." Isabel shrugged. "It's my turn for night shift at the rehab center."

Marian did not try to talk Isabel out of another sleepless vigil with the abandoned seal pup they had rescued from the beach. The pup was not expected to last one more night. Instead, Marian smiled and gave her friend a quick embrace. "Call me if you need company," she said.

Working alone on the night shift at the Kiwanda Wildlife Rehabilitation Center, Isabel tended the seal pup's wounds: gashes along his sides and a hole from the bullet that had entered and exited his tail flipper. Fishermen again. Fishermen tried to justify this casual target practice by blaming dwindling wild salmon stocks on marine mammals rather than their own overfishing. This pup showed a significant loss of blood and body fat; he was so undernourished that his fur fell around his tiny rib cage in wrinkles. But his fathomless black eyes fixed hers with a fierceness that made Isabel smile.

She would not lose this one, she hoped. The seal pup's eyes held hers. Isabel was reminded of the fact that seals in the open sea will locate a rock or person on land and navigate by them as if they are fixed points on a compass. Imagine trusting a human being to stay still long enough to find one's own way, she thought. Were people ever really like that—constant as true north?

For the first time during this long night in the wildlife shelter, Isabel pondered breaking the rules for this seal pup. She had named him Merlin, after the great Celtic magician, for surely this pup would need some magic to survive. Every volunteer was firmly taught not to bond with their wounded animals for fear of prompting them to imprint on humans, thus lessening their chances for successful rehabilitation and release back into the wild. With the eagles and red-tailed hawks, the raccoons and foxes, it was possible to simply feed and tend them with the kind efficiency of conscientious strangers. But the instinct for touch in many mammalian species was strong, especially among seal pups, who sometimes cried out in the night for their mothers, snuffling and trying to suckle any warm body. They were hungry for more than simply a feeding tube every two hours and the brisk pat-pat on the flanks that was all the wildlife rehab workers were allowed to give in faint imitation of the mother's reassuring flipper.

As Isabel worked to cleanse Merlin's wounds, the pup let out mournful, high-pitched cries and tried to suckle the nylon sleeve of her slicker. She allowed him this small comfort because she needed him to stay still and calm so she could examine and record some distinctive notches in his tail flippers. *Pinniped,* that was the scientific name for seals; it meant "winged feet." Merlin continued to suckle Isabel's slicker as she tenderly moved him across the cold, metal table and onto a nest of green towels still warm from the dryer. Their texture and touch would reassure the pup like a mother's body.

She felt guilty that she wasn't donning the handmade rubber costume a volunteer had patiently stitched out of old wetsuits into a makeshift illusion of a mother seal. But it was too difficult to nurse the pup's wounds while shambling around on her knees in the gray, ungainly rubber shroud of a seal-mother costume. The wildlife rehab volunteers had better success with the bright bird puppets they'd used for feeding baby eagles, red-tailed hawks, and a few peregrines to keep the birds from imprinting on humans.

Seals were more difficult to deceive, especially once eye contact had been made. And as Isabel settled the seal into his towels, trying not to touch him unnecessarily, she could feel his huge eyes seeking hers while he suckled her sleeve and whimpered. He was so desperate for mothering that Isabel allowed herself to stroke his gray snout several times, hoping this brief attachment might help save his life.

Still trying to avoid focusing on Merlin's exhausted, fear-filled eyes, she inserted a small feeding tube filled with a rich mix of nutrients into the seal pup's whiskered mouth. Accustomed to a warm-blooded seal mother's flanks and an inverted nipple, Merlin choked on the tube, his flippers vainly flapping against Isabel as she filled his belly.

"Merlin, do you really want to die?" Isabel asked. "Please . . . eat for me."

The seal struggled through the entire feeding and, when the ordeal was over, fell back wearily on the metal table. Gently she wrapped the exhausted pup loosely in a faded baby blanket also warm and fresh from the dryer and eased him back into his metal cage. Laying a palm on Merlin's shriveled belly, Isabel meant to touch him only for a necessary moment; but as if acting on its own, her hand lingered on the seal's dense fur. Warmth radiated from her hand.

With this warm hand. It was what her father had always whispered to his children when he gave them very special gifts—those rough fishermen's sweaters, hand-bound volumes of Gaelic poetry, and crumpled sepia photographs, heirlooms from his Hebrides childhood.

"I'm giving some of these to you while I'm still alive, little ones, because every one of these old things has a story, just like there's a spirit to every body. If you got these after I died, it would steal some of the life from them. Look, see how precious, this old horsehair blanket . . ." Isabel and Andrew had shied away from the sweet and rank smell of molasses, grain, and dust. "Your great-grandmother Morag McClelland made this from her favorite Eriskay pony, Glag."

Reverently Gabriel Spinner unfolded the beige boiled-wool blanket, woven with golden threads and embroidered with the fine Gaelic names. "Morag and her little Glag . . . ," Gabriel said softly. "Your great-grandmother named her pony after the old word for 'horse laugh.' Glag was always throwing back his head to show his great teeth. He'd just nod away every time Morag rambled off into one of her stories. She was a bit of a bard, your great-grandma," Gabriel said, watching his daughter study the blanket's primitively embroidered pony with a blazing shock of mane over small brown eyes, "not, mind you, an artist."

At first Isabel didn't like the blanket's musty odor, but the strange language and the texture of thick horsehair intrigued her. She had never been interested in ponies, preferring sea creatures. But one of her Kiwanda Middle School friends rode a Welsh pony with hot Arabian blood in the wildest surf. It scared the seals, but even so, Isabel couldn't help but admire the animal's pride, his measured gait against unpredictable waves.

"Morag's blanket is waterproof, you know," Gabriel smiled, watching Isabel run a slender finger along the round, raised outline of the embroidered pony. "Those native ponies from Eriskay Island belong to the sea. They come from such sturdy, ancient stock—Celtic and Norse—that their coats shed water. Even so, when Great-grandmother Morag was born, there was hardly a pony left to be found, even on her island. That's why they're so precious."

"Are they all gone now, like Morag?" Isabel asked, completely absorbed.

"No, dear girl, some good people brought them all the way back from extinction."

"Will you bring us one back from your sailing trip?" Isabel asked, even before realizing it was what she suddenly most wanted in the world—a pony from her great-grandmother's island, a survivor who belonged to the sea.

Gabriel laughed and turned to his son. "And is that what you want, too?"

"No," Andrew said solidly. "I want to go sailing away with you."

"Can't have that now; somebody's got to stay home with Grandpa Spinner. Keep the tide coming in right regular." He stood up, carefully folding the old blanket. "Isabel, this is yours now. We'll see about that pony. But if any horse has sea legs, it would be an Eriskay Island beauty. And guess what? Those little ponies just live to haul seaweed . . ."

Her father was teasing Isabel about her latest science project, a kelp forest display taller than any man; it was complete with painted papier-mâché replicas of sea lions, nearly extinct otters, and Dall's porpoises. In her backward-slanting penmanship, Isabel had written, "All these sea creatures depend on the kelp forest for food, shelter, and safety." Her father was helping her make a poster listing the many biochemical uses of kelp for people, as well. Competition for the state science fair was fierce, but Isabel was determined to win her second blue ribbon. Her biology lab partner at school, a surprisingly devoted boy named Stewart Salk, was beachcombing for Isabel in the hope of discovering a perfect, unbroken chambered nautilus shell. It would crown her kelp forest exhibit.

When her father gave Isabel the horsehair blanket and a vague promise to bring home an Eriskay Island pony after his next international sailing race, she considered changing her science project to "Practical Household Objects Made from Animal Hair." But she decided against it because she worried about what an animal might suffer for his coat, his fur, his pelt, his skin. So she kept the horsehair blanket to herself, a guilty pleasure.

Except for Great-grandmother Morag's blanket, Gabriel's old-country legacies were not the treasures Isabel and her brother longed for most. They wanted shiny new bicycles, a microscope, even their own fiberglass dinghy to row alongside their father's slim wooden sailboat, *Tighin*. But they never showed their disappointment when their father brought out yet another relic from ancestors who stared from their photos unsmiling, and whose names were impossible to pronounce.

Gabriel Spinner was a slight man who jogged along the beach without making deep marks in the wet sand. He skittered on lean, light legs like a sandpiper. Running, he let his mind rest on two things: the wind and his chemistry lab experiments. Gabriel was forever combining elements in his head—an alchemy of what he called the theory of forced relationships.

"Impossible things can come together," he lectured his children when he presented them with their first toy chemistry set, "to make something new, unexpected."

When Gabriel ran Kiwanda Beach, always far ahead of his wife and children, he raised his head to sniff the wind like an animal keeping its predators—and anyone who came too close—upwind.

But beachcombing slowly behind her husband, Diana Spinner stopped at every starfish and squirting sea anemone to ponder in her calm, curious manner the mysteries at her feet. She rarely watched the sky for weather, for wind or scudding clouds; she always kept her eye on the ocean, alert to sneaker waves. Though she was not a heavy woman, Diana's bare feet on the beach left deep prints that filled for a moment with sea-water, like tiny cisterns. Isabel measured her own growth by how many of her own handprints she could fit into her mother's beach footprints.

Diana Spinner also gave gifts from the Scottish islands. But these Isabel and Andrew marveled over: a single braid of black hair from a beloved sister, which still smelled faintly of lavender flowers; a fire opal without its wedding ring setting; and a tiny, battered world globe. Most wondrous of all was Diana's collection of chocolates from many countries, each wrapped in red, silver, or gold foil with foreign names and designs.

"It's like money you can eat," their mother would laugh each time she offered them a Hawaiian macadamia-nut cluster, a Swiss almond bar, a French champagne truffle, or a Belgian chocolate seashell. "Or like visiting another country, just for a moment, until the confection melts—and you're home again!"

It was another Spinner legacy, this love of travel, especially by sea in the tradition of their island ancestors. It was why Gabriel and Diana were often far away from their children, following the winds in Gabriel's racing sailboat. This was not a hobby so much as a "biological imperative," as Gabriel would patiently explain to his children, who eyed his wooden boat with the resentment of siblings recognizing a favorite child.

"If I were a whale or seal," he told them, "I'd migrate—the most natural thing in the world. Spinners can't help it. Did you know that gray whales have magnetite in their brains, little bitty iron particles that make them travel north along magnetic lines that we can't see, only feel?"

The idea that her father was somehow forced to migrate away from them by something metallic in his brain didn't seem strange to Isabel. Perhaps his leave-takings were like chemistry—the laws of attraction and chain reaction. Or maybe he was simply a sailor born to tack into a wind that could blow in from anywhere, and home was only a place where he was temporarily becalmed.

The problem was that their mother always sailed with her husband. "He needs me more than you do," she'd tell Isabel. "You and Andrew turned out so *sensible*. But your father is reckless. He's always taking silly risks if I'm not with him. Any wave could take him away. I'm his ballast."

When a wave did take both of her parents away forever, Isabel told herself it would not be so different without them. She could pretend her parents were on an around-the-world sailing trip. She and Grandfather Spinner would take care of Andrew, as always. At thirteen, Isabel was already self-sufficient. She had learned not to say goodbye—it had been her superstition that, if she ever gave her parents permission to leave, they might forget to sail back to her. Never would she echo the dutiful "love you" that Andrew always gave their departing mother, who would be looking backward from the bow of their boat—sorrow clear on her fine-boned face, but something else too: excitement. The smile was waiting there on her lips and would bloom as soon as she was out of sight of her children, their land.

That was the face that Isabel would remember the night Grandfather Spinner slipped into their bedroom and quietly woke them. With one wrinkled hand resting on the bunk beds he had lovingly carved from pieces of wrecked ships, driftwood, and his own old dinghy, Grandfather said, "I want to tell you this before you hear all these folks talking, phones ringing, strangers walking right into our house with their damn casseroles. They mean well, but . . ."

"What, Grandfather?" Isabel demanded. "Tell us what?"

He pulled the dead weight of a sleeping Andrew into his arms and patted him on the back as if he were burping a tiny baby instead of embracing a seven-year-old. "Such a terrible storm off the Island of Skye . . . ," he began, "gale-force winds in the Little Minch—she's taken so many of our islanders—and when most of the boats in the race turned back . . ."

Grandfather sat down heavily on Isabel's lower bunk. A short, compact man, bent by age and wind-wizened like those short pine trees along their coast, he rarely gave way to sadness. But Isabel could sense it in him now like a musty smell of something rotting and not quite hidden away.

"Your father . . ." Here his voice broke and Isabel clearly recognized rage. It occurred to her then that Grandfather Spinner had resented his only son, who had sailed away to a new world with a new wife and an old father. Had there been any other choice, once his own wife had died, but to follow in Gabriel's wake?

What had her father done now? Something silly and daring. He had perhaps forced together two things that didn't belong, that no one believed would ever mix. Maybe he had blown up their whole world.

"What's happened, Grandfather?"

He grabbed Isabel and pulled her close, his chin rough with white stubble. "Oh, dearie, dearie, they're gone, the both of them, gone back to where we all came from, where we all shoulda never left. She's greedy, our sea . . . I told your father it was bad luck to ever return for a race in those cold waters. The Minch took my brother when he was no more than your age, Isa. Stole him right off the bow of the boat when we were fishing. We found his sweater . . . the one Aunt Maudie knitted him . . . recognized all her knots. But her handiwork, all her praying, couldn't keep the sea away from him."

Grandfather rambled on as if talking to ancestors or ghosts in the room, as if continuing a running argument with his native waters. But Isabel was no longer listening. She escaped the old man's grasp, his rocking body, and her sleeping brother. Straight out the door of Grandfather's beach bungalow—it was where they stayed when their parents wandered—Isabel ran. Her footprints were flat and small on the beach as she fled along the winter surf. High tide and the sea stacks where she and Andrew played hide-and-seek would be flooded. Where to go?

She could climb to the top of Silkie's Cave and no one would follow. But Andrew could always find her there. It was all right if her little brother found her; he would need Isabel. But for now, she needed the solitude that was her most healing companion.

Hand over hand, Isabel climbed the sea stack, from the secret silkie cave and up along each craggy hold, until she stood at the top, balancing on a ledge. The full winter moon lent her light as she tunneled through a black basalt archway and huddled there away from the wind. Dawn was only a few hours away, but the beach was still a study in black and white—molten sea and pale-limned horizon. "These wee hours when the world goes quiet, that's the changeling time," Grandfather Spinner always told them. "Animal souls come ashore and change their skins, dance with us. They seem like humans, but they are not. Don't you know, we fall in love with them. Some of us follow them back to the sea. Don't call it drowning, call it returning."

Her parents had returned to the sea. Isabel rocked back and forth on the rocky ledge, only then realizing that she still had her horsehair blanket wrapped around her like a cape. Somehow she had knotted Great-grandmother Morag's small blanket around her shoulders as she ran from her bunk bed, from the terrible story that Grandfather told them—a true story. No happy ending. No changelings. Her parents were dead, drowned. They were never sailing home.

Far out at sea in the shining path of moonlight, several small heads bobbed in a circle. Harbor seals heading to shore, to rest after a night's feeding. Often they slipped in on the full tide to Silkie's Cave, stretching out on slippery ledges. Isabel and Andrew sometimes heard them snoring, short bursts of nasal breath and sonorous gurgles not unlike Grandfather Spinner's sweet and reassuring noise in the night.

The air was so cold her fingertips puckered; her jaw ached from clenching it against the biting west wind. If she'd had a boat, this gale would simply fill her sails and carry her to another world far away from here. But her father had never given his children a boat; nor would he bring home the stout Scottish island pony to carry Isabel's seaweed and shells the way her ancestors' ponies had diligently carted peat and fish back to their small farms. Generations of Spinners had navigated between tiny islands and the vast liquid landscape of the sea—water was perhaps where they really lived. Land was, as for the seals, a place for Spinners to rest, make children, sleep.

Why had her father and mother made children, if only to leave them? Isabel hunched inside the horsehair blanket, wondering if her great-grandmother hated a husband who left her for his sea. Or maybe it was the other way around. Maybe Morag was the one who left the family. Isabel wished now she had listened more closely to her father's stories of his ancestors. There was some mystery about Morag. She and her horse had run off, but with whom?

Was it possible that she dreamed, falling into sleep as if there she might find some warmth? Isabel looked for her mother's face inside her tightly closed eyelids, for her father's narrow back bent over his micro-scopes and his petri dishes that smelled astringent and acidic, as if their broth could burn through skin. Her skin was now too warm. But at last Isabel found her mother's face. Hazel eyes bright under dark, thick eye-brows, a nose that was long and graceful, a strong, full mouth. Diana's blue-black tangle of hair was always collected into one dense braid. It was the face her mother had passed on to her daughter. And now it seemed all that Diana had left her. It was not enough. It would never be enough.

Isabel was right. Andrew found his older sister high up in the sea stack atop Silkie's Cave. But not before she was lost in a fever, a sea sickness as Grandfather Spinner called it, unwilling to talk about the death as any-thing but a natural disaster, a shipwreck. There was no funeral, since Gabriel and his wife were buried on Eriskay Island in the Hebrides. Some of the Lawasskin townspeople were appalled that there was not even a local memorial service, if only for the sake of the orphaned children. But Isabel's pneumonia was so dangerous that she was under doctor's orders to stay at home until her fever eased and her scarred lungs cleared. Andrew and Grandfather Spinner nursed Isabel tenderly, but a secondary infection in her ears wrapped her in a moist, hot fog.

Isabel could barely hear the rapid flow of words rolling over her bunk bed. What did it matter? No one really talked about anything important around her, for fear of sending her farther away in her delirium. Mostly she caught snatches of talk about the weather as the round faces of the few, allowed visitors rose and set above her bed like familiar planets: Mr. Green, her seventh-grade teacher; her best friend, Matilda, who assured her that she didn't have to do any homework; her science lab partner, Stewart, who one day laid a gleaming chambered nautilus shell on her pillow, near one of her infected ears.

"Can you hear the waves?" Stewart asked, his cowlick falling over one green eye.

Isabel had never been this close to a boy's face, except her little brother's. She noticed tiny, thin hairs poking out from Stewart's chin. It shocked her to think that one day this boy she had grown up with might have to shave. "No, not yet."

"Maybe soon." Stewart backed away as if she were in a coffin, not a bunk bed. His smile was forced, and he seemed very brave because it was obvious to Isabel that he might cry.

She had never cried. Not once since she heard the news of her parents' drowning. Isabel had found Andrew sobbing in the kitchen as he stood on his tiptoes to stir the morning oatmeal; Grandfather Spinner wept often now, with the resignation of the very old. But Isabel dreamed her fever visions. She was drowning, too, but the sea was inside her.

One day her fever eased and more of her hearing returned, enough for Isabel to stay awake all day. And at supper, when Grandfather Spinner brought in her tray of fish soup and homemade bread, Isabel's ears opened to a sound she could not recognize. *Clop-clop-clop*. Something hitting hard against the wooden walkway to Grandfather's beach bungalow. In her wildest imagination Isabel could not have identified this steady sound, because her ears had never heard it; but her great-grand-mother's had, and by the time the clopping reached her bedroom window, Isabel was sitting up in bed, knowing that she would see the impossible, the longed for, the past.

"She came for you, darling girl. She sailed across all the seas to land here. But you must name her." Grandfather smiled.

Just like the woven gold image on Great-grandmother Morag's blanket, the island pony whose herds had almost gone extinct, this one stood on sturdy short legs, a sun-bleached shock of hair over mild eyes, a bay coat with its winter-soft thickness. The Eriskay pony leaned her head into Isabel's small window, her moist, dark eyes seeking out the girl. Andrew held the lead and, grinning, also leaned in Isabel's window.

"She's waterproof, you know," Grandfather reminded his granddaughter. He said the words as if he were saying, *She's proof against death.*

"Will she float, Grandpapa?" Isabel smiled with cracked lips, tasting a tint of blood. She used the old name she had called him when she was very little, and he beamed down at her.

"She won't drown, that's for sure. She has better horse sense . . . she won't nary go near a boat. She sailed here to you, Isabel, but it's the only time in her life she'll ever sail."

Isabel got out of bed and went over to rest her elbows on the window sill, where she buried her face in the pony's dense mane that soon she would learn to braid with wildflowers and even a few tiny shells. She breathed in the pony's smell of alfalfa, molasses, and salt. "She's been walking on the beach . . ."

And suddenly Isabel saw herself outside again, away from this shipwreck of a bunk bed, back on the sand, walking beside this small pony. "I won't ever ride you," she said, stroking the pony's thick coat. "I'll walk beside you."

"But she's a working pony," Grandfather insisted. "You have to give her responsibilities. I'll make you both a little cart that will be easy for her to pull—like in the old country."

Isabel suddenly jumped. "My science project!" she said. "What day is it? Have I missed the fair?"

Grandfather smiled. "Stewart Salk, that boy who dotes on you, he's almost finished it up for you. The fair is still two weeks away. But will you be ready?"

Isabel felt a little dizzy. "Yes," she said firmly. "I've got more help now." She raised a hand to pat the pony's sides. Dust puffed up. "Oh, she needs grooming. Can I brush her now? Please, Grandpapa?"

Grandfather considered this a moment and then grinned. "Some little girls you give dolls. This girl I give a good animal. As soon as you're up and about, dearie, you can groom her. But out to the boat shed she goes for now. By the way, what is her name?"

"What's the old name for . . ." Isabel stopped, coughing deep in her chest. "What's the word for 'dear' . . . 'very dear'?"

"Well, now, that would be *muileach*. It means 'beloved.' But you could just shorten it to *mol . . .*"

"Moll . . ." Isabel repeated the word, letting it roll off her tongue. "I like that best." She turned back to the pony, who was gently nibbling her pajama sleeve. "Hungry, Molly? Let's find some . . . what does she eat, Grandfather?"

"Carrots and apples, hay and alfalfa, grain and molasses, but she likes these best." Grandfather Spinner took out two small hard biscuits that looked to Isabel like fig bars. "They're called Mrs. Pleasure's Pasture Cookies . . . and they're just grand! Here you go, Molly girl . . . here's your little herd, your home. Now, I wonder just which one of you will be boss mare?"

With a backward glance at Isabel, the pony turned to the old man and delicately took the treats between her teeth. But just as quickly she turned back to the girl who would never ride her but would always walk beside her on the beach. The pony would carry seaweed, shells, and driftwood, even an abandoned seal pup in her shipshape cart the old man would make for her. But only once in her life would she ever carry Isabel's weight.

It was late the night Isabel decided to disobey Grandfather's direct orders not to go scuba diving without his supervision. Stewart Salk had come by to bring her a lifeless starfish he had found washed up on their beach.

"It'll be perfect for our kelp forest project," Stewart said, handing Isabel the scarlet creature with its five perfect points and suckers inset like ornate jewels. "A star for the top of the kelp forest canopy."

Isabel could never understand why this good-looking boy, whom every other middle-school girl had a crush on, seemed to prefer her company. She had never even kissed him, though she knew this was on his mind. It was evident in the way Stewart leaned lightly against her shoulder when they studied flowers in the biology lab, in the way he volunteered to carefully pin and dissect her frogs because Isabel could not bear to see their tiny legs cut open.

Animal Heart

"It *is* perfect," she said, receiving his gift as if it were a bouquet.

"But you know what's even better, Isa?" His smile was lopsided, teeth a little crooked, the only thing not perfect about him. If Stewart had had parents who could afford to fix his teeth and so give him the corrected beauty of the sullen young boys seen lounging in the clothing catalogues some schoolgirls pored over, Isabel would never have allowed him to be close to her. But she liked Stewart's lopsided grin and his chipped, crossed front teeth.

"What?"

"There's an octopus out by Seal Rock. She's huge!"

"Let's go, then."

"No, not at night. Your grandfather would . . ."

"He's at Widow Annie's cooking class." Ever since his son and daughter-in-law had died, Grandfather Spinner had taken on the kitchen work like a "galley slave," as he complained. But the truth was, he rather liked his weekly evenings with a doting coven of elderly women who hung a bright apron on him and revealed the mysteries of meringue and bouillabaisse, and who never stooped to casseroles. In turn, Roland Spinner taught the widows to make mango salsa and salmon chowder. "Listen, Stewart, we can do a dive and be home long before he's back," Isabel insisted.

"But you haven't gone diving since . . ." Stewart fell silent. In all his daily visits during Isabel's pneumonia, he had not once mentioned her parents' drowning. It was a silent pact between them. If they never mentioned it, it had not really happened. Her parents were simply, as usual, on a sailing trip.

This conspiracy between them had drawn Stewart and Isabel closer than even their science fair project had. Her little brother had unknowingly broken the illusion once by sobbing inconsolably at supper when Grandfather made Diana Spinner's favorite pumpkin and pecan spice muffins. Grandfather had only meant to try out the recipe, not haunt the children with memories of their mother.

"I'm well now," Isabel said firmly. "I want to see that octopus."

"What about all our scuba gear . . . your grandfather . . ."

"My Moll can carry it. In her cart."

Stewart wavered, studying her pale face, the shadows under her eyes.

42

It was too soon after the fevers, he knew this. But he also knew if he didn't dive with her, Isabel would go by herself. It was another secret they shared, her longing to dive alone at night with only an underwater flashlight and a full moon above. But Grandfather had told her she would have to be at least fifteen to dive at night. "You're trouble, you know that?" Stewart said, relenting.

"And you're sweet, Stewart." She touched his cheek lightly and his face flushed.

They followed the slim, athletic girl down the beach—the stout, nodding pony and the long-legged boy. There were no reins or bits or any visible attachments, but both the boy and the animal moved as if held by this girl's gravity—in an unpredictable orbit that still felt right and safe. To leave Isabel would be to veer off course into an unknown universe.

Isabel was exhilarated to fall backward into the surf, pull on her phosphorescent green flippers, and dip her mask in the chilly waves. It was the first time since her parents' drowning that she felt, if not happy, then normal. She was right where she belonged, diving off her beloved beach. And though it was her first night dive, she felt confident and serene. The sea had taken her mother and father, so it would be generous to her and not take any more of her family. Like people, nature had a kind of balance, she believed, a give-and-take that she could count on. Grandfather would have fiercely disagreed with her; he'd have been furious to know she was out here without his protection. After her parents' death, he had told his grandchildren the old Gaelic proverb *The sea wants to be visited,* then added grimly, "and she can just as soon murder her guests."

It was not the sea that claimed Isabel. With Stewart floating beside her, Isabel was careful not to shine her flashlight near the shell-strewn octopus den. As the children eased nearer the slippery rock, sudden streaks of fast silver spun them around—an exuberant clan of harbor seals surrounded the young divers, gliding and twirling. The seals' huge black eyes gleamed like obsidian mirrors in the soft haze of Isabel's flashlight.

She smiled, bubbles escaping her regulator, and reached out one hand—not because she wanted to touch the mottled sleek fur, but because she wanted to somehow tell the seals how happy she was for their curious visitation. One juvenile seal slid between Stewart and Isabel, arching his streamlined head to hold the girl's gaze. His tiny ears seemed tacked to his glossy head, his silken whiskers flattened against his snout by the single pulse of the sea. The seal swam figure eights around Isabel, careful only to spin her like a dance partner, not sink her in his whirling wake. She surrendered to the aerodynamic twirl of seals, so many of them, their curve of satin bodies rocking her almost tenderly as they at last dove down, out of the halo of her flashlight, deeper.

Of course, she would follow, not heeding Stewart's frantic hand signals. Of course, she would jackknife and propel herself after them into the dark night of the sea bottom, where no moon or human could reach her. Of course, she would listen to their eerie barks and calls until her ears felt like they would explode with the strange undersea melodies. She was spinning; that was her name, she told herself as if she spiraled downward through currents warmed by volcanoes and fiery vents erupting from the ocean floor.

But then there were ice pick stabs of pain in her ears. Again and again, so shocking this pain that it made her bend double with nausea. For a moment Isabel thought she might faint, yellow splotches like flotsam floating before her mask. But then there were weights against her body, buoying her up.

A seal and a boy. A seal who had seen Isabel Spinner on her beach since the girl was a baby on a horsehair blanket; a seal who had often fixed this particular human as a compass point by which to navigate his underwater descents; a seal whose head had bobbed up from the surf while a young girl searched for kelp and seaweed on their beach; a seal who had waited over a dozen years to meet this girl in his own element.

And a boy who had loved her since first grade, when he scuffed sand on her elaborate fairy fortress and she ran after him—the only other child who could ever catch up to Stewart—and then wrestled with him until he pinned her. And even then Isabel had not cried, but had challenged Stewart to another beach race, which she barely won. Only because he tripped on a piece of driftwood.

A boy and a seal—a boy she would one day marry, and one of the seals she would always protect. A boy and a seal who together swam a young girl to shore, where a pony knelt in the surf to take her weight. A pony with hooves that had never been shod, sturdy and fleet as she ran alongside the boy. And the girl, half-conscious, ears streaming blood and saltwater. The seal in the surf, barking, crying out to a girl who would never again dive down into the underwater world.

Months of silence, as if Isabel still moved underwater, her pony like a hearing ear dog leading Isabel. The schoolteacher even let the pony into the classroom, where she stood patiently in the back near the coat racks, her black eyes fixed on one girl, standing guard as the girl tried to memorize the way lips shape words. Isabel never considered learning sign language. She could not believe the sea would take away her parents and her hearing forever.

"It was too soon after the fevers," her doctor explained to Grandfather Spinner. "How could you have let her go diving when she was still so congested?"

"The same goddamn way I let her father and mother sink into the Sea of the Hebrides!" Roland Spinner shouted. He knew his granddaughter could not hear him.

Slowly Isabel's ruptured eardrums healed. By summer, her hearing was restored, but only in her right ear. Her left ear would always stay closed the way a chambered nautilus seals off abandoned chambers of its shell, like memory, and makes its many outer whorls, until one day this buoyant home is left behind.

Midnight at the wildlife shelter, and Merlin, the abandoned seal pup, grunted when Isabel lifted him from his cage once more, for the late-night feeding. Pectoral fins flailing and tail flippers thumping the steel table, Merlin used up so much energy in fighting her off that Isabel doubted he had anything left for healing himself. Certainly he would not last the night.

"Oh, Merlin," Isabel said, "don't go. Live a little longer . . . for me."

She was about to return to her station across from the seal pup, as required, when she found herself pausing to study the seal's gashed side, where she'd stitched up his wound. Looking down at the pup, Isabel was startled to feel a fluttering in the air like the beating of tiny bird wings. It was always like this, Isabel recognized, the death throes of an animal—a shimmering like nearby heat lightning as the animal's spirit took leave of its body and then was gone.

Merlin was diving down for the last time. The pup's dark eyes sought hers. Though all Isabel's training and scientific skills told her not to touch him, not to risk his future or her own, she knew she had to do something.

As the seal pup let out a rattling breath, Isabel laid her hand on his shrunken belly and began to rub him in small, calm circles around and around. It was how her parents had once soothed her as a small child; it was how she comforted her dog when he was agitated. It was as natural a touch as any in her life.

The seal struggled for breath, and Isabel noted with a frown the fresh blood pooling in each nostril. Shock and internal injuries were more dangerous right now than the pup's exterior wounds. Merlin fixed her with his large eyes and stared at her for what seemed like hours, as if she were that point by which he might navigate his journey—either back into life or on to death. With his eyes holding hers, Isabel began to sing softly under her breath:

Moan low, wild wave,
Drown not the seal's sad song . . . .

Give them sweet life
Until their day is done.

It was a silkie lullaby her grandfather had sung to her. As Isabel sang to the seal pup, she noted that his breathing steadied, as bleeding from his nostrils clotted; his eyes lost their frantic focus on her and softened. Was it the calming endorphins of near death she read in his expression? Whiskers trembling, the seal pup gave up a snuffle and closed his beautiful black eyes. Only when she was sure he was not dead, but lost in the sweet oblivion of sleep, did Isabel stop singing. She lay down beside the seal pup asleep in his blanketed cage, stretching her arm through the bars to rest one hand on the seal's belly. In rhythm to his steady breathing, Isabel also dreamed.

chapter three

Eavesdropping

IF ISABEL HAD STILL had hearing in both her ears, if she had not been wearing her noise-reducing padded headphones, she might have heard the spring storm outside their coastal forensics lab. But another listened for her. At every crash of the nearby surf, creak of corrugated tin roof above, and surge of wind through short pines, Silkie raised his head and let out his howls, snorts, and what passed for a wolf yodel. All these canine comments on the world around them Isabel understood. In fact, she relied on Silkie's sensitivities—a sense of smell and hearing that in humans would be considered extrasensory.

Now Isabel was listening to another world, another language, that she did not understand. Headphones plugged into her laptop computer, she leaned intently on her elbows, eyes closed as she tried to identify specific signature whistles from the A24 pod of northern resident orcas gliding past hydrophones in British Columbia. With her good ear, Isabel heard the high-pitched mewling, chirps, and rapid-fire bleeps of orcas vocalizing, their complex dialects swirling in her mind.

Isabel was a regular visitor to Orca-Live, a Website maintained by OrcaLab, where scientists living on a remote island in British Columbia and studying orcas had been recording their sophisticated vocalizations for decades. It was a marvel to Isabel that she would receive e-mail bulletins that announced, "There are NOW orcas near OrcaLab's hydrophones, and their voices may be audible. Listen in live!" Sometimes there was human commentary from as far away as Japan or Tanzania, where whale advocates, schoolchildren, or other Web surfers would chat about the passing orca clans as if they were distant relatives.

An eerie treble call rose and dove deep into sonorous clicks, and then, from farther away, an answer echoed the same rise and fall. For the first time in two years of listening in on orcas, Isabel thought she recognized a specific dialect. That these extraordinary creatures had created a language—or, according to the OrcaLab researchers, a "sound sculpture"— continually delighted her. She was determined to one day discern different pods by their dialects. Certainly she could learn to hear what harbor seals had already mastered.

Recently, she had read research reports about harbor seals eavesdropping on the orca chatter. Seals could clearly distinguish between the neighboring orcas, who preyed only on fish, and the mysterious transient orcas, who preyed on seals and other marine mammals. Oddly enough, the researchers noted, when they played the melancholy, downward-sliding calls from transient orcas the seals fled to the surface for safety; not so when they heard recordings of the "more upbeat" fish-eating orca neighbors, who meant them no harm. Distinguishing a predator from a neighbor— that was the power of hearing. That was what Isabel longed to regain.

She had other longings that she kept private. This spring she battled an unexpected restlessness, some insomnia. She had unusual yearnings to travel or at least try something new. This malaise was not like her. So far, no one but Marian had noticed Isabel's distraction, her polite retreat from other friends.

"Maybe I shouldn't have gone to the Hebrides to scatter Moll's ashes," was all Isabel had confided in Marian. "Things haven't been the same since then . . ."

Isabel couldn't admit to anyone except Marian that losing her beloved pony had somehow seemed more terrible than losing her parents. No one would understand; they would think she wasn't devoted enough to human beings. They would judge her for mourning an animal more than was acceptable.

"That horse was your protection," Marian had responded in her matter-of-fact tone. "Without Moll, you're at last an orphan."

When Marian said the words, Isabel felt a physical bolt of pain in her belly. Of course Marian would understand these things. She came from a people who believed that animal souls migrated between human and nonhuman bodies, shape-shifting. Marian came from ancestors who identified themselves by animal clans, whose songs and ceremonies were first given to the people by wolves and whales and ravens. The loss of an animal was as difficult as the death of a relative. Because they were kin.

"You were generous to bring Moll back to her island," Marian continued. "You know, that sweet little soul would have stayed here with you, even though it's more your home than hers."

"My home . . . ," Isabel repeated slowly. Yes, this mist-cloaked coast was her home; and yet when she had set foot on Eriskay Island, where Great-grandmother Morag had woven the horsehair blanket that Isabel draped over her own lap every night by the fireplace, she had felt for the first time in her life the pull of her ancestors. This beach, this bungalow made of driftwood and local pine, these daily tides were Isabel's anchors. They hadn't been enough to hold Andrew, but they still rooted her.

Yet when Isabel had stood in the Eriskay Island cemetery, where her parents were buried on a forlorn cliff overlooking the rocks, the flat, silver sea below, she had felt a stirring like a memory. This was the sea that had stolen her parents; this was the harsh, salt-scraped land that Great-grandmother Morag had fled with some secret that had not been passed down. This might be where she would one day return with a child of her own to explain the past, if only to again leave it behind.

A child of her own. Was that what Isabel really wanted? She had never expected to have children. Stewart made it clear he did not want any child to come between them. That had been fine with Isabel. It was all she could do to work in the forensics lab and volunteer at the wildlife rehab center, not to mention her service as beachmaster for the Kiwanda Stranding Network. And Stewart's demands on her attention had seemed like a full-time job.

But now in her late thirties and divorced, and now that her only link to the past—a humble pony who had followed her on the beach for over two decades—was gone, Isabel felt too light, as if she did not have enough ballast. Somehow she had lost some of her cherished stability. How could she, a single woman, take on raising a child?

What she talked about often with Marian was what Isabel called "personal versus impersonal mothering."

"It's not that women can't do both," Isabel would say, taking up the continuing dialogue that she and Marian engaged in as they worked in the lab. "I mean, having children of one's own and caretaking others or animals are not mutually exclusive acts. Look at other species and their allomothering." It was a scientific term that always touched Isabel, the proven fact that other cultures, such as the Hawaiian extended families of *hanai*, or adoptive, mothers, and especially other species, such as dolphins and elephants, gladly nurture infants other than their own biological offspring. "Allomothering," she said the word again, slowly rolling it off her tongue with pleasure, as if it were a word she was translating from a lost language.

"White people always think it's best to do everything alone," Marian commented one day as they catalogued a new inventory of incandescent parrot feathers poached from the Amazon. Once these feathers had soared, held aloft brilliantly colored birds rising from the burning forests like the phoenix; their tears, the Indians said, would heal all they looked upon below. "But native people have always known that parenting is tribal. What would I have done without my aunts and uncles and my cousins?"

"You *married* a second cousin," Isabel laughed.

"That was before I discovered the evils of buying from catalogues and knew I had to"—Marian did a brief, undulating dance—"shop, shop, shop around." Then she grew serious. "Besides, before we married, Buddy was really good to me. Kind. Protective. We were good friends."

"Marriage does seem to wreck even the best of friendships," Isabel commented and held up a scarlet feather, ragged at the ends.

"But mothering," Marian said. "You think a woman alone can do both—take care of her child and . . . well, the world?"

"Being a biological mother must be so intensely satisfying," Isabel sighed, then shook her head. "But it's also, well, maybe so preoccupying that a woman can't always see what else there is to take care of around her."

"She *sees* it, all right," Marian said. "She just doesn't have anything left to give. Unless somehow she has a lot of money or a lot of help. Men are much better fathers now, sure. More involved, hands-on. But how many marriages do you know that are truly equal? And how many women scientists do you know who've made it through this sexist field of ours to achieve something—in research *and* in family?"

"Did you hear that Susan Mecurio isn't coming back from her pregnancy leave? You know, she was going to be made director of research over in Portland."

"I rest my case."

Isabel fell silent for a moment and then added, "And single, working mothers, they're the real saints in this society. I don't know how Margie does it, now that her husband left her with the new twins."

"She does it by never sleeping, by trying to keep up with her forensics work even when she's sleep deprived. She does it by stealing into the morgue to get a damn nap when no one's looking. And after years of overwork, she gets one of those god-awful mysterious 'women's diseases' that they call chronic fatigue—something men don't seem to get."

"Men don't seem to get it," Isabel repeated with a wry smile. After a moment she added, "Does Buddy still want a child?"

"Not with me," Marian said firmly. "He was my child. And I already had a full-time job."

"You two will get back together; I know it."

"Your sixth sense applies only to animals, my dear." Marian looked at Isabel across the steel sorting table and asked, "What are you up to? You're thinking of adopting?"

"No, no, nothing like that. I'm just curious if it would be possible someday to do both."

"You're the best *impersonal mother,* as you call it, that I know, Isa. But I mean, think about it. Could you work all day doing this really heartbreaking stuff we do for the animals, and then go home and take care of children—and then stay out all night mentoring those young volunteers on a stranding alert or seal-sitting, and then take a shift at the wildlife center? I doubt it."

"Maybe when I'm older . . ."

"Maybe when you were younger!" Marian had snorted and returned to her work. "But then, being a teenage mother is like being *grounded* for at least eighteen years!"

Since that conversation, Isabel had not brought up the subject. Still, she had privately researched adoption programs for single mothers. And this she mentioned to no one, not even Marian.

Silkie suddenly leapt up and ran to the lab door. Wind from the coastal storm blew in, rattling in-boxes and ruffling feathers on a front shelf. There was a clatter as a small gust shook several other unsorted shelves of endangered ungulate antlers and hooves. But there was no need for Isabel to divert her attention from the Orca-Live Webcast. She already knew by her dog's wagging tail and yodel that it would be Marian.

"How's the family?" Marian swept into the lab carrying her huge red satchel. The warm scent of fresh French bread was immediately overwhelmed by the lab's smells of formaldehyde and disinfectant.

Everyone in the lab knew about Isabel's "underwater eavesdropping," as Marian fondly called her on-line listening. Some of the other forensics people also subscribed to the OrcaLab Website and had posted photos they had downloaded of the northern resident orca population. Every loss of a newborn or matriarch was cause for mourning; every birth a quiet celebration. It was good to be in contact with live animals in a lab full of broken body parts.

"Well," Isabel grinned. "Lots of vocalizations now, and so many people are tuning in that it says the orcas are playing to a full house!"

"I've also had an earful this A.M.," Marian said. "Maggie Salk was in the bakery this morning on her storm patrol. Seems the sheriff was out all night with a bad wreck on the Lawasskin Highway, and a Seattle yacht typically ignored local weather reports and is now run aground off Sargasak Point." Marian shook her head disapprovingly. "Out-of-towners . . ."

Deftly she unpacked her satchel; along with the two Tupperware plastic pie triangles and bright bowl of paprika-sprinkled potato salad, Marian unwrapped two foot-long submarine sandwiches, jalapenos dangling.

"Are you feeding an army, Marian? I can't eat that much."

"I ran into some friends. They'll be joining us for lunch."

"Who else is working this weekend besides us?" Isabel spun around in her chair and reluctantly took off her headphones. When she did, the rush of air and noise made her frown. Isabel always disliked this transition from the soothing sound waves of the speakers hidden in her high-tech headphones. Even with only one good ear, she found the daily world always too loud.

"It's a surprise."

"Oh, no, Marian," Isabel grumbled. "We've got too much work today, and I've got to get over to Portland tomorrow to see my brother."

"I think you'll be pleased." It was all Marian would say as she flapped open her handwoven lilac tablecloth, pushed aside Isabel's laptop computer, and began setting the desk for four.

"Not another one of your cousins . . ." Isabel stood up and fled to the back of the lab, almost toppling a display of raptor wings pinned to a bulletin board.

The last time Marian had surprised her with guests at their lab lunch break, it was disastrous. It was not that Isabel didn't like Marian's huge family; it was just that most of her cousins were, like Isabel, newly divorced. Unlike Isabel, the Windhorse clan was always scouting around. One would think that, with such an extended family, loneliness would not be a problem. The last luncheon, Marian's third cousin Darrell had descended on them for the whole week, insisting on taking Marian and Isabel to the Ocean Haven Tavern for nightly karaoke singing. While Isabel was a good singer, she hated the idea of chanting along with a box of music, a microphone, and bad percussion. She much preferred singing with another person, finding the perfect, delicate harmony to accompany another. Her favorite was hearing the unexpected harmony, the dissonant descant to any major melody.

"Is it Darrell again?" she ventured, afraid of the answer.

Marian's face widened with amusement. "Still sending you lovelorn e-mails, my poor relation?"

"No, I changed my e-mail account."

"Oh," Marian said wryly, "just for him. How sweet."

"Well, if you're not going to tell me who's coming for lunch, I'm disappearing," Isabel said, reaching for her lab jacket. "I'll be back in the morgue."

"Watch out, you'll wake Margie. Besides, don't you want to hear how Merlin's doing this morning?"

That stopped Isabel midstride. "How is he? Still taking his feeding tube?"

"Not only is he accepting nourishment, but he's also engaging with all the volunteers, not just you, Isa."

Isabel beamed. "Oh, that's the best news. Maybe I can get over to the shelter and see him again tonight."

She was about to leave the room when Isabel heard a voice that made her turn abruptly toward the door. Maybe it was a trick of her bad hearing? But no; when Isabel looked to Silkie, she saw him leaping up and down, howling his high-pitched wolf call. It was a welcome home to the dog's other love—her brother.

"Next year you'll come to Portland, Isa. Deal?"

Andrew squatted down to greet the husky he had gotten for his sister when he left for his first overseas photo assignment ten years ago.

"Deal!" Isabel crossed the lab to embrace Andrew. "Oh, I'm so glad to see you, little brother."

With his square, solid face and wind-tangled red hair, Andrew looked every bit the Scottish mariner. Lean and tall, her brother had taken on most of their father's features. Isabel's eyes blurred. How proud their parents would have been of Andrew's world-wanderings, his work. Would they have been as pleased with her choice to stay in one place and her odd career? Probably not. One thing about having no parents—there was no disappointing them.

Andrew let go of Isabel and turned to signal someone else. "Come on in, Marsh. She won't hurt you . . . much."

"The dog or your sister?"

"Silkie's a male," Andrew laughed. "Open your eyes."

Silkie sniffed the stranger, a short man with unruly black hair too beautiful, thick, and curly for a man. Isabel tried not to show her surprise. Of course, Andrew wouldn't come alone to see her. He was forever dragging friends around the world with him.

The man's smile was self-assured, as if expecting anyone, particularly a woman, would welcome him. He had a vaguely foreign look, his face wide, his skin a dark bronze, his nose flat, lips full. The careful way he tilted his head suggested that English was not his first language.

"This is my diving buddy, Marshall McGreggor."

The Scottish name stopped her. Perhaps he was from one of those strange outer islands Grandfather always told stories about, a place where the people spent very little time as human beings. Isabel smiled faintly to herself. The scientist in her was forever correcting the romantic.

"Come in," Marian said graciously, glancing at Isabel with some reproach. It was their old battle, with Marian, ever the extrovert, compensating for Isabel's shyness.

Unlike most visitors to the forensics lab, this man didn't hang back, put off by the strange animal scents and chemicals.

Isabel turned again to her brother, who now perched on her desk, twiddling a syringe between his fingers. "Why didn't you let me know you were coming out, Andrew?"

"Last-minute thing. Hooked up with Marsh here at the conference, and he's letting me tag along on his assignment to film marine life above that underwater volcano down the coast."

"Oh, I see." Isabel could not keep some regret from her voice. So Andrew was not here just for her, after all. "Well, the volcano is pretty exciting, especially to scientists."

"You're both welcome to come out with us on the research boat tomorrow." Marshall nodded politely to Isabel and gave Marian a wide grin. Then he focused intently on shelves holding tropical feathers, pink claws, and several furry legs. "Say, that's a really big paw," he said. "Is it from a gray wolf?"

Impressed, Isabel nodded. She discreetly took in the compact man in his waterproof, faded red parka. Dressed for the weather. Curious, but not too intrusive. Isabel was relieved that Marshall seemed more interested in her lab, and Marian, than her. It would serve her friend right, to be saddled with this stranger. Maybe then she could have her brother more to herself. "It's a case we've just solved," Isabel said. "This wolf's DNA matched the strands of fur caught in the poacher's wool coat."

"Good work," the man said. Marshall turned his dark eyes on Isabel. "Mind if I look around?"

His quiet appeal made her suddenly shy.

"As long as you don't sing karaoke, you're welcome here," Marian answered for her. "But don't get too involved," she nodded toward the tablecloth-covered desk. "I've made us all lunch."

"Oh, we should go out, Marian," Isabel said. "This is no place for them to eat . . ."

"I like it just fine here," Marshall said. "Thanks." With a nod at Marian, he disappeared into the back shelves.

Isabel thought it was odd that she could distinctly hear his footsteps on the tile floor—a sound Silkie responded to with narrowed blue eyes and a barely audible growl. Andrew was the only man this dog happily allowed near Isabel. But he seemed to tolerate this stranger. Taking up a position between Isabel and Marian, Silkie sat on his haunches and listened.

Hearing the man prowl through her shelves, Isabel was surprised. Marshall moved with a grace she hadn't thought possible in a man. And with such compromised hearing, how could she still track him so well? Maybe it was her imagination. But then Isabel noticed that Marian registered his movements, as well. Her friend gave Isabel a quizzical look as if to say, *Acceptable?*

Annoyed, Isabel shook her head. Why was Marian always trying to set her up? "You've been with only one man your whole life," Marian would remind Isabel. "You're practically a virgin. But don't worry. I'm looking out for you." Isabel dreaded her friend's matchmaking. God knows Marian's own marriage and recent separation were a mess. Besides, the stranger had obviously made his choice. And it was not Isabel.

Isabel sat down on the desk next to her brother. He smelled faintly of salt and neoprene. Had they gone diving here before coming to her? Andrew's tanned face and sun-bleached hair distinguished him; he certainly didn't look like he belonged in the perpetual rain shadow of this Northwest Coast.

When Andrew took off his jacket, she noticed he was already half-dressed for diving, with his sleek thermal turtleneck. It was one Grandfather had given him for Christmas years ago. Someone had patiently patched a tear in the collar. Isabel imagined a woman's hand, a woman who had left only this little seam on Andrew.

"If it's okay, Isabel, we'll be bunking with you in Grandpapa's cottage. Marshall can sleep in the boat shed. It's warm out compared to Antarctica. He's just been on a diving shoot under the ice . . ."

"But there's a big storm coming in," Isabel began. "And since Moll died, I haven't repaired the boat shed much. It leaks."

"Well, I guess we could both stay in Lawasskin at the Wayfarer, if you can't . . ."

"No, no . . . it's okay. We'll make space."

"Now that that's settled," Marian said, "let's eat." She called back to Marshall, "Hope you're not a vegan . . . We're having raptor claw and buffalo shank for lunch."

Stepping out from behind a shelf, Marshall grinned. "Call me carnivore," he said. "I can't help it. You know what my niece once said about animals? 'Every one of them is either my friend—or my food.'" As they all pulled up lab chairs around Isabel's desk, Marshall added, "And what's for dessert?"

"Pie," Marian announced. "You and Andrew are going to eat the pieces of pecan pie I brought for Isabel and me. If I'd had any notice, I could have baked you strawberry shortcake."

"Yuummmm," Andrew said. "We'll make it up to you. Marshall and I will take you gals out tonight to the Boondoggle Inn."

"Not that dive," Marian smiled. "Marshall, will you do the honor and cut the loaves and fishes?"

As the man delicately cut the two oversize submarine sandwiches, not into four equal parts, but finger-size pieces as if for a high tea, Isabel couldn't help but smile. He made a show of elegantly carving the long sandwiches into dozens of pieces.

"I need you at my next party," Marian commented.

"Speaking of party," Marshall said, "would you and Isabel also like to dive with us tomorrow out on the research boat?" He sensed sudden tension around him. Had he committed some faux pas? Instantly, Marshall fell silent and concentrated on his potato salad. It was delicious—tangy, with just the right hint of pepper sauce.

After an awkward few moments, Andrew said, "Isabel doesn't dive."

"I can't imagine not diving . . . ," Marshall began, but stopped, still sensing tension.

Marshall's first memory was of floating in water warm as blood, as his Native Hawaiian mother rested on her back with him on her soft belly. He looked up at a dome of a night sky splashed with stars. Constellations were all that weighed them down. Later, when Marshall first snorkeled along the Kona Coast off the Big Island, he looked down into an underworld studded with a multitude of marine life. The star-strewn universe had fallen into the sea.

"Anymore," Andrew finished. "My sister doesn't dive anymore." Andrew gave his friend a significant look, one Marshall recognized from years of diving and deciphering expressions obscured by a mask.

Well, obviously, he'd stumbled onto some family secret. This was exactly why Marshall had avoided the entanglements of marriage and sensitive relatives. He was a man who had endured enough of family for one lifetime, being the only boy among five siblings in a large Hawaiian clan.

Growing up in Hawaii in the seventies, Marshall had been teased by his father for being an "aquanut." A professor of astronomy at the University of Hawaii in Honolulu, Ian McGreggor was the grandson of a Scottish sailor who jumped ship from a whaling boat after a typhoon drove it aground off the Hawaiian Islands. Great-grandfather McGreggor had stayed in Oahu and married the island's most beloved singer, who was also a choral director at Kamehameha Schools. Ian McGreggor's own mixed-blood heritage made for an uneasy marriage with Lillian Pauahi Kane, Marshall's buoyant mother, who was also a composer of traditional Hawaiian choral music in her mother's and the Kamehameha tradition.

"Every other boy wants to be an Apollo astronaut." Ian often complained about Marshall's underwater obsessions. When Marshall asked for scuba diving equipment for every birthday, his father presented him with increasingly powerful—and unused—telescopes.

"Kai'e'e is from my *ohana*," Lillian would say quietly. She always called Marshall by his Hawaiian name. "He belongs to my people."

"Yes, dear," Ian would tell his wife. "What can you expect from people who believe their ancestors are sea turtles?"

By the time Marshall was in high school, Professor McGreggor was living at home only on weekends, preferring what he called the more "stimulating" company of other astronomers—and many student-mistresses—at his university observatory.

When Ian died young of a heart attack, his burial befit his wife's beliefs. In a flotilla of canoes, fifteen-year-old Marshall and his mother, along with their friends and family, paddled far out into the Pacific off the Nepali Coast, where his parents once had their retreat cabin on the island of Kauai. Rolling on languid swells, his mother opened the humble pine box and let the trade winds take her husband's ashes—bits of bone and fine white dust like so much sand scattered across sea foam.

Marshall kept quiet during most of the lunch. One innocent trespass was enough, especially since much unspoken communication obviously was passing between Andrew and his sister. Any more intrusion might be unwelcome. Marshall didn't much care about social etiquette, since it usually concerned only strangers. But he was cautious when it came to family, especially sisters. All his childhood he had stood bewildered when witnessing the changeable terrain shared by the three loquacious sisters and his mother. Marshall much preferred the dignified conver-stions with his deaf sister, Nohelani, with whom he spoke American Sign Language.

"She may not dive like the rest of us, but Isabel spends half her life on the water," Marian said loyally.

"I snorkel," Isabel said with a faint smile.

"So it's decided then," Andrew said after finishing his pie. "Marshall and I will go get Grandfather's Boston whaler ready for tomorrow's trip to the research boat, and tonight we'll meet you both at the dock. Meanwhile, you two women can . . ." Andrew grinned, "well, wait out the storm."

"Women don't wait out storms," Marian teased. "Here's a better idea. Marshall and Isabel can get the boat ready, and Andrew, you and I will go by my house and get us all some food for a floating supper."

"You're a diver, Marian?" Andrew asked. "Never knew that."

"I was diving when you were still blowing bubbles in your playpen and Isabel was changing your diapers."

"And you're sure the wind will die down for supper aboard the boat?" Marshall smiled as if sharing a secret with Marian.

"Ancient Native wisdom." Marian grabbed her parka and Andrew's arm. "I listen to the Coast Guard's weather report."

They disappeared so quickly that Isabel and Marshall were left a little stunned. This was all Marian's doing, Isabel fumed. She was the world's worst matchmaker. People all over town and even in her family complained about it. Marian had certainly misread this situation. Marshall was obviously not interested in Isabel.

"Well," Marshall said awkwardly after the others left, "Andrew has talked about you and his home and even his grandfather's old boat ever since I've known him."

"My brother talks too much," Isabel said.

She stood up and hastily wrapped the leftovers, placing them in the lab's staff refrigerator. Now that Marshall had made his thorough exploration, he seemed to take this lab and Isabel in stride. What Isabel didn't like about him was his habit of studying her without any attempt to hide his scrutiny. It was as if he believed himself invisible and could directly observe anyone around him. She dearly wished that Andrew had been more circumspect with this man and not babbled on about her or their lives.

Silkie also seemed to be showing less discretion than usual, allowing this stranger to lean down and fondly pet his white ruff. When Marshall got to scratching behind the husky's perked, black-rimmed ears, he gently turned one ear inside out.

"What's this—a tattoo?" he asked, referring to the faint turquoise lettering inside Silkie's ear. "CCI?"

"He was raised as a canine companion," Isabel explained softly, embarrassed.

"Oh, that's right," Marshall said matter-of-factly. "Andrew told me you're deaf in one ear. So's my little sister, Nohelani, in both ears. We speak ASL together. And I'm trying to teach it to your brother to use when we're diving . . ." Marshall turned back to Silkie. "So, you're a working dog, aren't you?" He glanced up at Isabel. "You know, some people think being raised from a pup to help people is hard on a dog. But these companion dogs go everywhere, see everything. They're never left alone." Silkie rolled over on his back to expose his blazing white underbelly. Marshall fondly scratched him. "Yeah, you got big responsibilities, don't you, boy?"

"He hears the phone when I don't," Isabel said, warming to the man. "Silkie's always looking out for me."

"Dogs are the world's best listeners. Who else would listen to us blather on about our bad love affairs or divorces over and over again?"

Isabel smiled a little nervously. Of course, Andrew had probably blurted out to Marshall all her troubles with her ex-husband. It was the last thing she wanted to talk about with a stranger. She whistled under her breath and immediately Silkie was up and racing for Isabel's pickup truck.

With Silkie between them, his eyes riveted on the road ahead, they drove the winding coastal highway, wind gusts rocking the small truck. Isabel was not surprised when Marshall relaxed, settled back in his seat, and stared at her. "I'll bet," he began good-naturedly, "that as a kid you won all the science fair prizes."

"Andrew tell you about that, too?"

"I also know that you have a moon-shaped scar on your right shoulder where Andrew's fishing line snagged you—and you almost died from a staph infection. I know that your grandfather raised you both when your parents died in that boating accident. I know that you work in that wildlife pathology lab because you can't stand to see animals suffering. I know that you have a sixth sense about animals that's so good that some people at your lab place bets on it. If you ever played the horses, you'd make out like a bandit . . ."

"Is there anything my little brother left out?"

"Not much," Marshall grinned. "He adores you." Marshall turned to study the bowed pine trees, the lush spring cliffs, and a few ramshackle houses along the winding road. "Now I can see why . . . ," he added softly.

Isabel blushed. "Do they really place bets on me at the lab?"

"Sure do. Anything else you want to know about yourself?"

"I don't know what's more irritating," she teased him. "Your know-it-all attitude or Andrew's gossiping about me."

"Men don't gossip," Marshall said. "We have conversations, big ideas."

"In my experience, it's really men who can't keep secrets."

"Had a lot of experience with the opposite sex, have you?" Marshall asked. "Field work? Must run in the Spinner family."

"Andrew maybe," Isabel murmured. She turned to glance at Marshall. "And are you like my brother and that silly song—a woman in every port?"

Marshall surprised her and himself by his serious answer. "Yes," he said. "You're right, I'm not a homebody. I'm as reliable as weather."

He had not meant to tell her the truth. Isabel was a very pretty woman, though she didn't seem to know this. Marshall especially liked her gray, lucid eyes and the long auburn braid down her back. The violet hand-me-down fisherman's sweater that Isabel wore without apology. But her friend Marian was more engaging and even beautiful. It had been Marian's flirtatious manner and inviting face that first caught his eye. Isabel seemed too serious. She was obviously a woman on a mission. Not that he didn't approve of Isabel's work; it was just that she was so passionate and even a little self-righteous for his taste. He was keen about protecting coral reefs and the oceans he loved, but looking out for the oceans was part of his job, not a spiritual calling. The way Andrew spoke about his sister, you'd think she was a modern-day Saint Francis. Saints didn't appeal to Marshall. But one did have to tell the truth to saints— and sisters. It was a matter of survival, not morality.

"At least you're honest." Isabel nodded and turned her full attention to the road. This close to the ocean below, they could hear the roiling surf. A blizzard of sea foam drove down the beach and draped the scrub and short pines that were already wind-sculpted into what looked like large bonsai forests. "If not loyal," Isabel added with a faint smile.

"Women make too much of a man's loyalty," Marshall said.

"Your women tell you that?"

"No, my four sisters." Marshall grinned. "Don't they have a support group for men who have survived so many sisters?"

"Somehow I can't see you in a support group," Isabel commented. It had been a long time since any man engaged her so easily. She understood a little better now why Andrew had chosen Marshall as a friend. He could be a pal. A brother. That's the way she would handle him.

"Me, neither," Marshall said. "This is beautiful country you got here."

He turned all his attention to the beach below as if he were photographing it. Isabel noted that Marshall was obviously quick to deflect another's curiosity. Like her father, he probably had an innate sense of when the wind had shifted so he could turn away from land. This man would never cling or demand much of a woman. But if the woman had her own life, that might not be so bad.

"So, Andrew tells me your grandfather was also a big animal lover."

"My grandfather had some strange beliefs about animals and humans."

"Like what?"

"Oh," she said, as she took another curve, "I'll tell you some other time."

"Tell me now. Your story couldn't be any weirder than mine."

Isabel glanced at him. "Will you tell me something about yourself if I tell you about Grandpapa?"

"You drive a hard bargain."

"A fair bargain," Isabel said, smiling. "Well, in the Hebrides Islands, where we Spinners always lived before Grandfather came here, they say my great-great-grandmother Finoola was a seal-woman."

"She hunted seals?"

"No," Isabel laughed, "she was supposedly a seal come ashore to shed her skin. But my great-great-grandfather Angus had other ideas. He fell in love with her and hid her sealskin."

"Oh, so she was a silkie," Marshall grinned, "and he was a typical guy. Possessive. The worst of us."

Isabel gave him a glance that was so open Marshall wished he had his pocket Nikon with him. Though he rarely took portraits, he wouldn't mind having a record of this woman's dark, delicate brows and gray eyes, of the way the misting coastal light framed her strong jaw line and full lips. Now that Marshall could study Isabel with his trained eye, he realized how much her features resembled Andrew's, even though her brother's coloring was ruddy and fair.

Suddenly Marshall recalled one of Andrew's photographs—a lithe woman doing t'ai chi on a beach. Slender arms rose like the suspended wings of a water crane. Only now did Marshall recognize Isabel from that portrait. Same long waist and grace, shapely legs. Funny, Andrew never mentioned it was his sister. Perhaps even a younger brother could be protective of his big sister. Of course, he wouldn't get involved with Isabel, but Marshall did enjoy looking at her. Maybe Andrew had his land camera handy, and Marshall could snap some shots of Isabel and Marian over dinner.

"Angus gave Finoola many babies and a fine house," Isabel continued. "That's how my grandfather always used to tell the story."

"Not enough for *our* Finoola, I'll bet."

"Would it be for you?" Isabel raised her eyebrows.

Marshall grinned. "Not every woman's dream?"

Isabel pursed her lips. "Three times every year on the full moon, Angus carried his seal-woman wife back down to the sea—tenderly, mind you. On the shore, Finoola changed back to her true self. Angus never knew if Finoola would swim back to him and her children." Isabel paused and said with satisfaction, "One day, she just didn't . . ."

"Is that why you left your husband?" Marshall asked.

Startled, Isabel frowned. "None of your business," she said. "Or has Andrew told you all about my marriage, too?"

"Andrew just said your ex never really understood you. He confused you with a wife." Marshall sat back, pleased with himself. "I like that silkie story. It fits you. Do you believe it?"

"I did, as a child—and after my parents died, it . . . it helped some." Isabel shrugged. "But I'm a scientist and . . ."

"And you still believe it, you just can't tell anybody," Marshall laughed. "Except me. Now, I'm a man who can keep secrets."

"So, what's your weird story?"

"Well, you Spinners haven't cornered the market on sea creatures. Seems my great-great-grandmother was one, too," said Marshall, settling in.

"What kind?"

"Almost extinct. Green sea turtle. And we still have our old Hawaiian songs about her . . ."

Isabel gripped Marshall's arm. "*Now* I know who you are! You're Andrew's friend who hums when he's underwater, who sings at sea—sings any chance he gets." She sat back and thumped the steering wheel.

"Andrew always talks about this diving buddy from Hawaii who's a great singer. Will you sing something for me? I love singing."

"Forget it. I'm not a great singer."

"My grandfather used to sing us to sleep every night. He told us his songs came down from the seals. He said silkies were once the lost Scottish kings of Lochlann caught in a spell. And we believed it because, every time Grandfather sang along the shore, the seals came to him. Once we even heard an old seal singing in a cave Andrew and I always hid out in as kids . . ." Without a trace of self-consciousness, Isabel sang a melodic scrap of ascending sixth notes in her soft mezzo-soprano.

To Marshall it sounded full-bodied and haunting, like one of his mother's traditional chants. Once when he was diving off the coast of Ireland, he had also heard an old bachelor seal singing on beach rocks—sonorous warbles and eerie arpeggios like a lonely fiddle tune. Local folk had told him that the seal's singing and the villagers' songs sounded so alike that no one could figure out whether it was seals who first taught people to sing or the other way around.

"Sing some more," Marshall said, when Isabel fell silent. "What language is that?"

"Gaelic," she said. "Grandfather would say it was even more ancient than human speech."

Marshall smiled and took a deep breath. "It's familiar somehow. Take out more of the consonants and it could be Hawaiian. Really beautiful."

"Just childhood stuff." Isabel seemed suddenly shy. "Now tell me your story. Or sing me a Hawaiian song. Please . . ."

"Oops," Marshall said as Isabel stopped the truck. "Looks like we're at the boat already. My story and my singing will just have to wait."

"Cheater!" Isabel said, but she was smiling. Not a trace of desire, like some women who smiled at him. Marshall leaned over and gave Isabel a quick kiss on the cheek. He didn't really mean anything by it—a dalliance, a sweet way to spend one stormy afternoon. Marshall was hoping she might turn those well-shaped, reserved lips to meet his.

Isabel did not. She sat back and, in a movement so graceful he would never quite remember how she did it, she rather tenderly pinned one of his arms against his back. Must be that weird martial art she practiced. He found himself helpless, but quite happy, in the passenger seat as she held him—not so very far from her.

She smelled of some strange chemical that must have come from her lab. It was astringent, but not strong enough to cover the faint, floral scent from her braided hair. Lavender? Lilac? He longed now to untangle that windblown braid and, as with all women, wrap his fingers in her hair. But Isabel still held him at a distance, not so far that he couldn't appreciate her beauty, not so close that he could do anything about it.

"While I was winning science fair ribbons," Isabel laughed, "you were stealing kisses from all the schoolgirls."

"No, " he said. Again that serious expression. Again telling her the truth. "I was underwater. Girls didn't like me much."

"Not then, perhaps."

Again, he didn't lie. "No, not then."

Isabel let go of Marshall and switched gears into reverse. Her wheels spun out on the sandy asphalt of the marina as she backed up and parked the pickup in the marina lot.

"If you ever give up on animals," Marshall said, holding on to the door handle with one hand, the other wrapped around Silkie's body, "you could have a second career in drag racing."

Isabel had to laugh again. "Silkie's used to my driving." She liked this man more than she'd expected. But she didn't know him. That would take time.

"Let's go get Grandfather's boat ready."

"So you don't want to sail out in the storm with me?" Marshall asked.

"Not this storm," Isabel said.

"You'll take a rain check?"

For a long moment Isabel hesitated, studying Marshall's face. It was a generous face, with a sympathetic arch to his brow. She even sensed that underneath his rather routine flirtation, there was kindness and true affection—especially toward women. The legacy of a childhood with doting sisters.

"It rains a lot here," Marshall encouraged her. "It never stops raining."

"Okay, I'll take a rain check," Isabel said. "Next time the wind blows you to my beach."

"You'll be surprised, Isabel Spinner, seal-woman," he said. "I'll come back." His sun-darkened face floated so near hers, his eyes obsidian, somehow ancient.

Isabel burst out laughing. "I *do* see it."

"See what?"

"Your family resemblance to sea turtles!"

"I'll take that as a compliment." Marshall grinned.

As he smiled, Isabel noticed small, imperfect teeth and cracks at the edges of his lips from too many hours clenching his diving mouthpiece. She had seen lips like these among the diligent boys who played trumpet and French horn in her middle school symphony, before she had lost her parents, half her hearing, and her conviction that her third-chair clarinet part was crucial to making music.

"And I won't ever hide your sealskin from you," Marshall added.

Isabel surprised herself by leaning over Silkie to kiss Marshall very lightly on lips that tasted of salt and balm. It was a tropical taste she didn't recognize. Maybe mango. She'd have to try that flavor herself sometime. But not now. Not him. Not yet.

chapter four

Underwater Volcano

THE GOVERNMENT RESEARCH boat twelve miles off the Oregon coast was bigger than Isabel expected. Its sophisticated video screen equipment, its diving gear, and a refrigerator-size submersible engaged busy geophysicists so thoroughly that there was no one to greet the divers and their guests when they came aboard off Grandfather's boat.

Isabel and Marian were gratified to note that several of the people directing this seeming shipboard chaos were women—one, Adriane Winthrop, Isabel had read about in an article in *The Oregonian*. Winthrop was a marine geologist well known for mapping the undersea floor and the midocean volcanic ridges along this Northwest Coast. Winthrop was not only one of a handful of oceanographers in the country, she was also an Asian American—a fact not lost on Isabel and Marian. And Marshall.

"She's from Hawaii," he leaned near Isabel and whispered with what she recognized as a note of pride.

"I know. I've followed her work, too." Isabel let Marshall's hand rest on her forearm. There was no pressure, only a sense of shared adventure. "Her major influences are . . ."

"Jules Verne and Herman Melville," Marian finished. As was typical of her, Marian made off for the ship's control room and engaged Dr. Winthrop in conversation.

Isabel turned to Marshall with a smile. His wide face was inviting. "I don't know what I'd do without Marian," she said. "She's not afraid of people at all. Just walks right up and talks with anyone."

"And you stand back, studying everyone as if you can read people's minds," Marshall commented.

"I'm not the only one," Isabel said. "I saw you watching me when we first met. Figure me out?"

"Nope," he said. "But I will."

"It may take more time than you have."

Had they met at the lab only yesterday? Last night's dinner on board Grandfather's boat had been a delight, with Marian and Marshall sparring good-naturedly and Andrew settled into the captain's chair as if he'd never left these waters. To have her brother home, to get to know his diving buddy, and to share it all with her closest friend—how long had it been since Isabel had felt such connection? All those years fettered by Stewart's possessiveness, his dislike of any person or community that took her away from him—it had taken a toll on Isabel that she hadn't really reckoned with, not until last night. Perhaps some of this spring's restlessness had been simple loneliness.

Coming home from their floating supper, Marshall had unobtrusively made his bunk in the boat shed, leaving Isabel with Andrew in their old kitchen, where they sipped Grandfather's favorite peppermint tea. Picked by French monks from pristine gardens, this tea, and his ritual for preparing it, was the closest Grandfather Spinner ever came to the Church. Every night, he had brewed the fragrant loose tea leaves, releasing the sharp, sweet scent of Himalayan and Ceylon mint.

"Cold?" Marshall asked Isabel as a brisk breeze rattled equipment on the research boat's deck. "Here, take my down jacket. I'll be underwater."

"I'm fine," she said and shivered. Though the Pacific was unusually calm, the late spring mists billowing in from the west felt chill, biting.

"Oh, I forgot. These are your waters." Marshall began to strip off his jacket, knit watch cap, and boots. Underneath he was already suited up with his first layer of thermal underwear and neoprene. But he would need a dry suit for this dive.

"Of course, we can't dive as deep as those robot submarines can," Marshall said. "They call the one on this ship Albert."

"That robot is probably as good with a camera as we are," Andrew said, as he too began suiting up and checking his regulator and tanks.

70

"Yeah." Marshall pulled his black cowl over his head. It constricted his round face—the diver's comically pinched expression. He glanced at Isabel. "But not as good-looking."

Then both men turned their full attention to their camera equipment. While Marshall worked mostly with still, underwater photography, Andrew was more of a generalist, and these lucrative video jobs shared between diving buddies supported the photographic art that each produced. The equipment looked too heavy for any two men to carry, except in the underwater world, where gravity surrendered to buoyancy.

Isabel longed to be diving with them. She could hardly remember, except in her dreams, the pulse of the ocean pulling her down with her weight belts, the bubbles like a visible blessing rising up from her regulator, the undersea caves and the alien creatures who made their own bioluminescent light. Snorkeling was not the same. Never again would she be able to join her brother as she had when they dived as children. Never would she hear what Andrew and other divers often marveled over—the sound of a bass heartbeat mysteriously echoing up from the abyss of a submarine canyon. A heartbeat not made by anything mechanical or electromagnetic, or understood by science. No wonder she never wanted to leave her coastal home. Where was there to go if she had to stay on land?

Isabel shoved her hands deep into her parka and shivered again. She really wished she had dressed more warmly for the boat, especially now that the wind was picking up, unsettling the horizon with the suggestion of whitecaps. Marian was forever teasing Isabel about the many layers of silk and polypropylene she wore. "I don't think I've ever seen you naked, Isa," Marian often commented. "You're like an onion. Some poor guy will have to peel back layer after emotional layer to get down to the real you. And most men just don't have that kind of patience."

"Here, Isabel, you look like you need warming up." Marshall handed her his cast-off jacket. Isabel changed her mind and accepted the loan of his coat. The warm down stilled her shivering. "Thanks," she said, smiling.

In her left jeans pocket, Isabel fingered one of her favorite talismans from her personal fossil collection—the golden swirls of a Moroccan ammonite. This ancient, coiled shell was related to the modern-day chambered nautilus and was an ancestor to octopi. She loved the perfect symmetry of ridges that traced the many chambers circling the shell. In the Mesozoic era—before comets changed the earth—this sea creature was plentiful, moving easily up and down different depths in the sea with the grace of its own buoyant gases. Grandfather had given Isabel this fossil when her kelp forest project had won only an honorable mention at the state science fair. "You live long enough, things come back to you," he said softly and placed the golden shell in her open palm, closing her small fingers around the fossil. "Some folks don't stay around to see this." Of course Grandfather meant her parents; but rarely did he criticize them aloud. "But you, my Isa, you'll have a long life. You'll be a living fossil, just like your old Grandpapa."

It became a ritual, Grandfather giving her fossils every year around the anniversary of her parents' death. When she had shown Marian her fossil collection, her friend said, "We call those magic stones. Our elders say that if you meditate on fossil ammonite a long, long time, you can get a glimpse into the origins of all life." Isabel Spinner had one of the finest collections of ammonites on the West Coast, and everyone who knew her well understood that she could not have too many fossils.

Isabel lifted the shell from her pocket and tenderly studied it a moment; then she turned to Marshall, who was bent over his tanks. Brief blasts of oxygen shot out into the chill air as he tested his regulator. "Here," Isabel said in what she hoped was an offhand tone. She felt anything but nonchalant. Her heart was floating a little too far up in her chest. As she handed the fossil to Marshall, she felt what other people would describe as sea sickness. Was she really going to give one of her treasures away to someone she hardly knew?

The delicate, golden spirals seemed to mesmerize Marshall. For a long while he held the shell up in his bare hand. "Amazing," he said at last. "How old?"

"Oh, ammonites became extinct a little more than seventy million years ago."

Marshall laughed. "But who's counting, right? I mean, besides you scientists?" He scrutinized the chambered shell as if discerning exactly the right angle at which to photograph it. In his hand, the golden ridges captured the faint sunlight, gleaming. "Now, these little guys really knew a lot about equalizing pressure at whatever level of the ocean they traveled. They could teach us divers a thing or two." Carefully, he offered the fossil back to her. But Isabel did not take it.

"Did you know that the logarithmic spiral of a chambered nautilus has the exact same configuration as the Milky Way?" Isabel said.

"Too bad I'm not an astronaut." Marshall grinned and continued to hold out his hand to her with the shining ammonite in his open palm.

"Well, you are an aquanaut."

Marshall seemed visibly moved. "That's what my father used to call me."

"Does he still call you that, now that you can actually make a living diving?" Isabel asked.

"No," Marshall said quickly, as if recovering himself. "He died young. And actually, I think the term he used was 'aquanut.' He never approved of my diving. He preferred astronomy."

"Well," Isabel said firmly, "I approve. And you never know when an ancient map of the heavens *and* the seas, like this little ammonite, might be the best guide. Take it down with you."

His face was very still, his gaze holding hers. "Thank you. I will." He looked away, as if confused. "Do you want me to leave it in the sea?"

"No," she said quickly. "I want you to always keep it with you." Isabel stepped back from him at least an arm's length, as if he had come too near. "For luck."

Marshall nodded, noting the distance she had put between them. He seemed no longer confused; he seemed pleased.

That was the worst thing, his easy pleasure. Maybe women gave him presents all the time. Of course they did. How could she have given away something that meant so much to her to a man who obviously already had his own collection—of women?

Then Marshall surprised her. Unzipping his dry suit, rummaging through awkward layers of neoprene and tight thermal, Marshall pulled out a golden chain hanging around his neck. On it was a worn leather pouch. "Look, Isabel," he said and unknotted the tiny drawstring around the pouch to reveal a jagged shark's tooth, a polished piece of green sea turtle shell, and a Tahitian black pearl. "I always wear this when I'm diving."

Isabel tried not to show her disappointment. Her gift would be just one of many.

"All these I've collected myself on my dives," Marshall explained. "Yours is the only one given to me to *help* me in a dive."

He crossed the rocking space between them and held Isabel as close as he could in such heavy gear.

"It's really beautiful. Thank you."

"My pleasure," she answered. And it was.

Marian joined them now, giving Isabel a faint smile. Then she turned away to pull on her dry suit. Marshall helped her with the long zipper up the back. As Andrew, Marshall, and Marian hoisted their heavy tanks, they all cast Isabel sympathetic glances. "Sorry, dear," Marian said. "Hate to leave you up here with all these science geeks."

"Well, at least I'll learn something," Isabel said with a shrug. "Give my regards to the thorny heads and eelpouts." Isabel grinned mischievously over at Marshall. "Watch out for sharks."

"And lava?" He arched his eyebrow. Marshall's face mask was pushed back on his forehead at a jaunty angle. "Ciao!"

Something about his expression was disturbingly familiar. That was the way her mother had looked leaving land, leaving her. Except with Marshall there was no sorrow. Only excitement. No, it was more than that. Pure, undisguised happiness. Did any of it have to do with her?

As Isabel watched her brother, Marshall, and Marian clamber over the side of the boat to balance on the large metal ramp rocking up and down with the waves, she felt a punctilious tapping on her shoulder. A tall man glared down at her. Though he didn't wear a uniform, Isabel knew, merely from his perfectly creased pants, that he was no civilian.

"What is the military doing here?" Isabel surprised the man by asking.

"I was going to ask the same of you. By what authority are you aboard?"

"I'm with the divers, not the military."

Irritated, the man snapped, "I'm not, as you say, military. I'm a scientist here assisting the Volcanic Vents Program. Dr. Alexander Sharp." He nodded curtly to her. "Darnell University Bioacoustics Lab."

Marian and Isabel had a favorite game: Name That Ph.D. It was like playing poker with doctorates. "I'll raise you that one and call," Marian would say whenever they had to deal with the most arrogant scientists visiting their lab. Though Isabel herself had a doctorate in veterinary medicine and pathology from the University of Washington, and Marian was working on hers, what helped them most in the closed set of federal lab and bureaucratic policies were skills that most Ph.D.'s might find remedial: courtesy and openness.

Isabel fell back on these skills now, correcting herself for her earlier gaffe about this man's obvious military connections. "Hello, Dr. Sharp. I'm Isabel Spinner, with the coastal forensics lab in Lawasskin. My brother and friends are diving to shoot marine life above the volcano for a television documentary."

"Hmmmmm." The man nodded, impressed. Isabel could now see, along with his pride, the man's youthful inexperience. Darnell University. It had the most ambitious acoustics department in the country, long known for its government contracts for controversial auditory experiments on laboratory animals. Isabel had read somewhere that the Defense Department was funding 90 percent of marine mammal scientists in the United States. Was this one of them?

"Well, you're welcome to stay on the upper deck here." Sharp's tone was more moderate, but it was still an order. "The control room is off-limits to civilians."

"I *was* hoping to watch some of the video from your submersible," Isabel pressed. "Dr. Winthrop invited my friend and me to . . ."

"I'm sorry, but we can't allow civilians . . ." Sharp stopped as soon as he said the word. To his credit, he actually blushed.

So he was working with the military. Why keep it confidential? The once top secret system of hydrophones was positioned along seafloor volcanoes and on continental slopes. This sound surveillance system, with which the navy used to listen in on Soviet submarines, had passed in this post–cold war peacetime to seismologists and other scientists studying and acoustically mapping the many undersea ridges and faults along the Pacific Rim. Some oceanographers regretted the collaboration with the military, even though their equipment was often far more sophisticated than university budgets allowed. Recently, up in Seattle, there had been a major protest, one that included concerned scientists, when navy divers had routinely killed thousands of endangered fish during training exercises in which they detonated underwater mines.

Though Isabel was skeptical about the military funding so much ocean research, she tried to take a more collegial tack with the man. "I've read that there have been over four thousand quakes along the Gorda Ridge this spring. It must be gratifying to study and map this firsthand."

For a moment Dr. Sharp hesitated. "It is," he admitted. "It certainly is."

Studying this well-groomed young man, Isabel estimated him to be in his mid- to late twenties. Sharp was impeccable in his brown slacks and polo shirt under an expensive tweed-lined raincoat. Among the slicker-clad Oregon scientists, he looked like a newly minted professor leading a field trip of more mature graduate students. She had seen his type before at the lab, and now Isabel felt a moment's sympathy for him. He knew he was out of place, even if his military funding might place him higher in the chain-of-command hierarchy. In the more exacting calculus of "pure" science, he was tainted. More an outsider than she.

Isabel noted that several other of the technicians and scientists pointedly excluded Sharp from their conversations. He was obviously a military observer, a necessary part of the state-of-the-art equipment the researchers had borrowed. That's why he had time to talk to her. No one needed him here.

Isabel smiled faintly when Dr. Sharp actually took out a pipe and lit it slowly. "Everyone was intrigued at Mount Saint Helens exploding so dramatically," he said. "But an underwater volcano is invisible, so no one even thinks much about it, except us. We have so much information to gather while she's still erupting." He went on to lecture Isabel on the volcano Axial, which had been spewing lava since its first eruption in 1998, to the delight of oceanographers. While assured that this active volcano wouldn't disturb coastal life or shipping, townspeople were not ecstatic that an unpredictable volcano was awake off their shores. It could trigger earthquakes. "Its basaltic lava first erupted at 1,190 degrees Celsius," Sharp explained to Isabel, who had read all about it. "Or about 2,175 degrees Fahrenheit."

Dutifully, she listened. How she wished she could dive with her friends instead of enduring a new doctorate's lecture.

"You know, we're eyewitnesses to volcanic history, seeing just how the seafloor is formed," Dr. Sharp continued. "This volcano stretches eighty miles by thirty miles at her base. She stands twenty-six hundred feet above the ocean floor. Her summit is forty-six hundred feet below the ocean's surface. Imagine . . ."

At last Isabel could not help but interrupt. "Why do you call this volcano *she?*" It was more like something Marian would do, baiting this young pedant.

For a moment, Dr. Sharp was silent. Then he looked at Isabel, as if seeing her for the first time. He surprised her by laughing, not only with her but also obviously at himself. "Touché," he said. "But wouldn't you rather we call something in this world so powerful by the feminine pronoun?"

Isabel nodded good-naturedly, but before she could respond, she and Sharp were interrupted by Dr. Winthrop, hailing them over to the control room. "Come see these shots!" the oceanographer called. "Unbelievable!"

"Okay," Sharp said unnecessarily, "you can go in and watch."

Inside the darkened control room were rows of computers recording seismic data from the plumes of roiling, chemical-rich water along volcanic ridges. But what the researchers were focused on now were the rows of video screens—images sent up from the deep-diving robot Albert, now nearly two miles beneath the ocean's surface; others, from much higher up—at the usual 130- to 150-foot depth limit for such divers—came from Marshall's and Andrew's video cameras. They were documenting the effects on vegetation and marine life caused by the volcanic activity far below. Beneath Marshall's and Andrew's cameras, Albert's eerie sonar images of seafloor geology were revealed: pale lava pillows squeezed out from hydrothermal vents, where giant tube worms swayed, and the black clouds of superheated waters spewing out hot, metal-rich fluids from the seafloor chimneys. Rose-tinted sulfide deposits were now being revealed by Albert's remotely operated cameras. It was a world no human diver had ever descended into, a world once thought uninhabitable, but where bizarre new creatures were now being discovered every day.

Even though Albert's revelations were astonishing, Isabel preferred keeping her eyes on the images relayed by Andrew and Marshall. She watched a blizzard of translucent moon jellies undulating through black water. Isabel could not keep her eyes off the fragile lace of this surreal ballet, as if the jellies were dancing for her.

How Marshall wished he could dive farther down, follow the whirring, gangly Albert with its mechanical hands, scoops, shovels, and many camera eyes to the very bottom of the ocean, where bright hydrothermal vents pulsed and pumped out seawater and lava. How he wished he could be the first man to photograph this undersea volcano reshaping the earth's crust.

Andrew let go of the dive line, signaling this was as deep as they and their equipment could safely go. Hoisting his video camera on his shoulder, he pointed it toward a rocky ledge of sea cucumbers and brilliant red sea stars. The mucus from these thousands of sea cucumbers could damage a diver's eyes, even through a mask, so Andrew kept his distance, signaling to Marian to do so as well.

Amid passing schools of hagfish and flat-bodied halibut, Marshall drifted, his whole attention now focused on finding that exactly right shot of parachuting jellyfish or, if he were lucky, an inky squid. A little jab to his chest distracted him. Something sharp inside his first thermal layer. Now he remembered, that fossil Isabel gave him had some rough edges. He should have waited to put it in his leather pouch until after he had found time to file it down. But only a diamond saw would smooth the ancient ammonite shell. So there it hung, tiny uncut edges probably tearing through his worn leather pouch, scratching his bare skin. If the fossil tore a hole in his pouch, he might lose it and all his other treasures.

Irritated by the distraction from his work, Marshall shook his head, bubbles cascading upward toward the surface. That surface where a woman might be watching this undersea world he was filming. In the past, the pressure as he dove underwater was never as hard on Marshall as the pressure of a woman waiting for him on shore. His mother said he was born with ears that could equalize any descent, a heart that could slow its pulse in synch with the sea, and lungs so expansive that as a boy he could hold his breath twice as long as his father.

Another little jab to his chest. It should have irritated Marshall again, but for some reason he could not fathom, it didn't. Remembering Isabel's tight braid, the remarkable gray eyes so like the violet mists of this Northwest Coast, he smiled. Some oxygen escaped his regulator. Isabel wouldn't wait for any man. Why would he imagine she was watching his video when the robot submarine was probably sending up once-in-a-lifetime footage? No, she didn't have an eye on him; she was just being gracious to her brother's friend.

Isabel had a full life, a fascinating life, really. Her problem would be fitting anybody else into her schedule. Andrew was always saying that his sister had run first him, then her poor husband, ragged with all her science projects and animal rescue plans. Passionately curious, that's how Andrew had described his sister's style. Marshall liked Isabel's passion; he understood her curiosity. He even liked this little fossil scratching his chest. Maybe he would find an excuse to come home with Andrew again on another visit.

Delicate globes of moon jellies, called *Aurelia*, fringed with luminous lace, throbbed in Marshall's viewfinder. Within its orb, each jelly carried a cluster of eggs that, once fertilized, would grow into flowery polyps. Once the eggs hatched, the larvae would search for rocky crags and attach themselves; there they would reproduce, splitting into white, spidery new species.

A faint pulsing of the video camera echoed in Marshall's ears; tiny moons orbited him. Whenever Marshall watched the pulse and slow-motion parachute of jellyfish, he imagined music. Maybe they did move to music, only humans couldn't hear it, like so many of the ultra- or subsonic symphonies that whales and dolphins sounded out through undersea canyons. Maybe other creatures mapped their underwater world with songs.

Moon jellies, with their miniature sex organs shaped like four-leaf clovers on top of each translucent dome. Perfect shot. Marshall hoped Isabel was at least watching this one, as if he were sending her an undersea bouquet.

Why did he care so much about whether she was seeing this splendor? It was always enough that he and his camera were watching. Another sharp pain to his chest, but this one wasn't Isabel's jagged fossil. This one felt like a thud, a mule kicking his sternum. Once. Twice. Over and over. Then came molten heat and ache as lava erupted along his left arm. What had hit him? A shark or a barracuda outside his viewfinder?

Marshall bent double, one hand clutching his chest, the other vainly trying to hold on to his video camera. Where was his breath, his oxygen? What were all those bubbles doing escaping when he needed every bit of that air to stay down long enough to finish his filming? And why was he closing his eyes, just when he needed to see what predator was attacking him? But instead of fighting for his life, Marshall somersaulted slowly, scattering moon jellies in his wake. He was like them now, moved by tidal currents and the moon, not his own will. He was a dead planet too far below the sun to shine on his own. He was a man, much like his father, leaving life too soon.

Floating now just a little above his own body, Marshall saw a man in a bulky diving suit clutching at his chest. Something there keeping him conscious. Scratching him, just when he thought he was free. Something so much older, like the ocean floor, a golden shell, a creature who swam at many levels, who made its own buoyancy, who spun intricate chambers and sealed them off—like his own heart.

If only someone had been there to save her parents, as Isabel was here now for Marshall McGreggor. Isabel had been the first to notice the odd fluttering on the screen as moon jellies seemed to lurch and then disappear into blank ocean as if the camera were dropping, sinking. Everyone else was focused on Albert's astonishing footage of a seafloor thermal vent spewing scarlet lava.

But Isabel's alert sent people scrambling to the side of the boat, where soon Andrew and Marian and another diver were lifting a limp Marshall over the ramp. An onboard medic ripped open his dry suit, flat hands pounding his chest.

"Medevac is on its way to airlift him to Portland." Dr. Winthrop directed the rescue as surely as she had her ocean research team.

"Let me fly with him." It was Andrew, his face almost as pale as Marshall's, looking to his sister in case he needed her help in convincing whatever authorities that he was close enough to accompany the unconscious man.

"Fine," Dr. Winthrop said. Then she turned to Isabel. "But only one of you can fly in the helicopter with him. Choose."

Isabel knew that she was more competent in emergencies, but Andrew was Marshall's friend and who was she? An acquaintance. All that mattered was that Marshall survive what the medic said was a massive heart attack.

"Thank God someone else was watching," Marian said as she pulled off her heavy dry suit and embraced Isabel. "Your brother and I were in a cave. We never would have known if we hadn't seen the diver come down to rescue Marshall." Marian stood back, still holding Isabel's shoulders, as if to brace her. "It may be too late, you know that?"

"I know."

When the helicopter arrived, Isabel nodded to her brother. "You go!" she called to Andrew. "Godspeed."

"I'll call from the hospital." Andrew looked terrified.

Even Marshall noticed this, floating in and out of consciousness, the helicopter blades too loud. Why wasn't he still in the ocean filming those moon jellies? What happened to his camera, his dry suit? Why were there tubes dangling here and there, an oxygen mask constricting his face? Why was his diving buddy staring down at him, clutching Marshall's leather pouch as if it were important? Nothing was important now. Not this friend. Not his odd but interesting sister. Not even this life. Nothing was important except getting back to that place of perfect equipoise where he floated in a celebration of moon jellies.

The emergency medical technician was smiling at Andrew as the helicopter banked wide and flew inland. "Leaving his oxygen tanks on until we got here was probably what saved your friend's life."

The EMT's smile and the thought that even in an emergency Andrew Spinner could attract a woman's eye were the last things Marshall remembered before he swam into darker waters. It was like night diving, except there was no strobe light.

chapter five

Animal Heart

I HOPE I DID the right thing," Andrew's voice was uneven on the cell phone.

"What?" Isabel said. "I'm losing you."

Andrew shifted from the plastic red waiting-room chair to a hospital window overlooking a courtyard. Bamboo swayed in a wind he could not feel, but his eyes rested gratefully on the slender green trees that reached as high as this surgical floor. "I mean by giving the go-ahead for Marshall's new heart."

"Didn't his mother give permission for the transplant?" Isabel asked. By his strained and weary voice, she could see her brother's face—the family shadows dark under each eye, the rumpled red hair, and Andrew's particular sign of fatigue, bloodshot eyes. She wished her brother could close those eyes that were always trained to watch, to document, to memorize.

It must have been awful for him, getting hold of Marshall's mother so she could fly to Portland after Marshall's heart attack, then the shock of the doctor's discovery that Marshall's heart was damaged beyond repair. The grief of letting him go, then the tragic miracle: the death of a young man at a nearby hospital after a motorcycle accident and the consequent donation of a heart that matched a very rare blood type. Marshall's blood type. Marshall's mother telling the surgeon before she boarded the plane to the mainland, *Do whatever it takes to save my son. Anything.*

"Yes, Isa, his mother did give permission. But then . . ." Andrew fell silent. Static on the line.

"Andrew . . . ?" Was he gone?

"I'm here." Silence again.

"Then *what*, Andrew? What's happened? Tell me."

"I don't think I can tell you, Isabel. Especially not you."

"Why not?"

"There were . . ." Andrew's raspy voice betrayed more than exhaustion. "There were what the doctor is calling . . . extraordinary circumstances."

Isabel knew this voice. Something was terribly wrong. "What circumstances?"

"Just get here, Isa," her brother said. "Soon."

It was a plea she had not heard from her brother since they were children. A brother asking an older sister for help. What Andrew had to tell her would only be said when she could embrace him, somehow soothing him. "Of course, of course. I'll leave now and be there in Portland this afternoon. Have you had any sleep at all?"

"No," Andrew admitted. "And the surgery . . . well, it's still going on. It would help a lot if you could pick up Marshall's mother, Lillian, at the airport on your way to the hospital. She's on the noon plane from Kona."

"How will I recognize her?"

"You'll see Marshall in her," Andrew said simply. Static. Then he added, "Love you, Sis. Drive safe."

In the Portland Memorial Hospital operating room, there was the shocking glare of fluorescent lights. Marshall floated above a steel table where a man below lay splayed out, his chest cavity wrenched open by saw-toothed metal retractors like instruments of torture. And inside this scarlet red, gaping gash was—emptiness. No pulsing muscular heart, as complicated as the heart's emotions. Nothing. Marshall saw his body as blank and vacant as any dead body. Worse. It looked as if he were being harvested organ-by-organ while still alive. At last, drifting farther away from the pale body on the surgical table, Marshall gazed down with calm detachment. If he felt anything for the man below, it was a surprising tenderness.

Then there was a strange physical surge, and suddenly he no longer floated painlessly above his own body but was harshly anchored back inside that unconscious man. Marshall's chest felt raw, split open like a melon, though voices assured him that he was meticulously stapled tight. Marshall's last memory of the transplant surgery was one of a surgical nurse commenting wistfully, "Sometimes I still wish they sewed them up with those delicate stitches, like mending lace."

For several days after the transplant surgery, his body fought to reject his new heart. He wandered between worlds, uncertain. Awakening one midnight in a sweat, he heard his mother chanting in her native Hawaiian. Tenderly she lifted her son's head so he might better see what she'd brought close to his bedside, sacrificing the space usually taken up by several intensive-care-unit machines. It was a small aquarium with a bright-pink rock bottom, ragged green algae, and tropical fish—tiger-striped oscars and pretty, pale gouramis. Like a tiny castle, his mother's favorite red coral bracelet was wedged between plastic fronds so the fish might hide from the unnatural glow of hospital fluorescent lights.

Because there was a tube down his throat, Marshall could not tell his mother that within days the fierce oscars would devour the dainty gouramis.

He let her hold his hand and sing to him. "*This* is your home. All sea animals are your *aumakua*. They belong with your spirit, boy," his mother whispered as they both watched the gouramis flicker through her bracelet at the bottom of their miniature world. Lillian reached out and lay a small hand on her son's arm. "When you were born," she told Marshall, "there was a great wave wash over in Hilo. Your sisters wanted to name you Tsunami. Remember?" She smiled. "Rise up, boy. You rise up now."

Marshall turned away and then slowly nodded. For the first time, he felt a steady, slow heartbeat thudding in his ears.

The day Marshall was moved from the intensive care unit to a private room on the critical care floor, Dr. Lamb swept in unexpectedly, without his usual entourage of medical students and attending doctors. It was the first time since the operation that Marshall could remember being alone, without what he called the "obnoxious caretaking." His mother had been there, of course, and Andrew with his sister, Isabel, and her pretty friend, Marian. It was too much fuss, distracting him from his underwater dreams.

"Don't try to talk too much at first," his surgeon said softly as he finally eased the tube from Marshall's esophagus. "It'll hurt your throat."

"My heart . . . ?" Marshall's voice was hoarse, and he could barely swallow.

"I'm sorry, Marshall, but your own heart was really damaged—beyond repair. It was amazing that we found a donor. Your rare blood type makes you a lucky man. Moved you to the top of the waiting list." Dr. Lamb stopped and took a plastic chair near Marshall's bed. "Listen, I don't want you to be worried or afraid. But I have to tell you what happened during the surgery."

Marshall fell silent, watching the light refracting off Dr. Lamb's glasses. A pair of magnifying loupes still hung on a chain around the man's neck. These surgical loupes caught the glare of fluorescent hospital lights above and scattered it into tiny prisms that bounced crazily around the pale green room. Marshall was so distracted by the fleeting miniature rainbows that he could hardly focus on the doctor's words.

"Are you listening?"

"Yeah, yes . . ." Marshall reluctantly focused on the surgeon. "God, these drugs are intense."

"I know, but you'll get used to them over time. You'll be taking some three dozen pills a day—for the rest of your life." Dr. Lamb took a breath. "Marshall, I have to tell you—there was a problem with the donor's harvested heart."

"Problem?"

"God knows how it happened, but somehow in transit your new heart was bruised. Ruined. There you were on the operating table with an open chest cavity, three hours into the procedure, with no heart." The surgeon leaned forward. "Either we put another heart into you—and fast—or, we let you die." The surgeon laid a hand on Marshall's shoulder. "I know you'll agree that we made the right call to go ahead with the transplant."

"How long . . . ?" Marshall's throat burned terribly. "Until I can dive again?"

"First things first," the doctor said. "You need to know something about your new heart." He sat back and was quiet a long moment. "It wasn't taken from a human."

"Not human? What is it? Plastic?"

The surgeon signaled to the nurse who had come into the room. She added a tranquilizer to one of the dangling IVs. Dr. Lamb waited a moment, watching the dripping tube before cautiously continuing. "Your friend made a difficult decision, with your family still en route here from Hawaii . . ."

"What friend?" Marshall demanded.

"The man who brought you in."

"Oh, Andrew." Marshall sank back. A surge of inexplicable grief. "So . . . what kind of heart *do* I have?"

"It's a baboon heart."

Marshall sat straight up in his bed. "You mean, like from an ape?" Now he saw yellow blotches floating before his eyes. The window outside wavered. He must be hallucinating all this, especially the doctor's crazy story.

"Baboons are monkeys, actually. Highly intelligent, and their DNA is so close to ours . . ."

When the doctor spoke, his sky-blue surgical mask billowed out like a puffer fish. To Marshall, he looked somehow clownish, this tall man stooped from many hours in surgery. In fact, everybody around him in the operating room had been indistinguishable in their paper scrub clothes, caps, and masks. They seemed a circus act, juggling long wires, beeping machines, and high-tech instruments.

"This is not real . . ." Marshall slurred his words. He closed his eyes and saw parrotfish spinning in black and yellow circles.

"It may seem like the stuff of science fiction, Marshall. But it's true." Dr. Lamb continued, "Of course, we'll keep you on the list for a human heart. Baboon heart transplants have not been ultimately successful in the past. But recently a baboon bone marrow transplant has been extraordinary in extending the life span of an AIDS patient." The surgeon grew more comfortable as he warmed to his scientific explanation. "Bone marrow is the beginning of all life, and when we perform a cross-species transplant, the baboon cells help regenerate not just the person's immune cells but also their red blood cells . . ."

"Where in the world did you get a . . . a baboon heart?" Marshall interrupted groggily. If he kept his eyes open and didn't look at the prisms cast by the surgical loupes, he could focus better.

"We're really fortunate that our hospital is fifteen minutes away from Roseland Research. It's internationally known for transgenic research on baboons. Their work in cross-species organ research is the future. I've got an . . . arrangement with Roseland, having a background myself in xenotransplantation. You were a good candidate for this rather unorthodox transplant because, except for your heart, you're in excellent physical shape. And the baboon's heart is strong and unusually large."

"So I'm not only part baboon," Marshall murmured. "I'm also a guinea pig."

"Well, xenotransplantation is such a new, unpredictable science," Dr. Lamb began. "Your heart is from a wild baboon captured in Africa. There may be some simian virus we'll have to watch out for. And there is no guarantee that your body will not reject this heart . . . as usually happens in these cases."

"So I'm not the first?"

"No. There have been a very few other baboon-to-human heart transplants. Remember Baby Fae in 1984? But then, in the early nineties, Dr. Starzl gave us more hope with his baboon liver transplants . . . cutting-edge, before he stopped." Dr. Lamb rushed on, "I've never given up, nor has Roseland. They've got a baboon colony over there and were just waiting for the green light and the right recipient. And, as I said, recently we've had baboon bone marrow research that is most promising. The recipient is still alive!"

"Did those other people with animal hearts survive?"

Dr. Lamb fell quiet. "Well, no, they didn't. But you and I could change all that. Our research has advanced so much, and after this current lapse in official support, more clinical trials should be imminent. Why, look at the success rate of pig valve transplants. And now they're grafting pig hearts into baboons." The doctor turned to his nurse and whispered something. "Listen, Marshall, yours is an undocumented transplant. Not for the record books—unless we succeed. We might just make medical history, and you'll pave the way for others."

"So I'm still going to die," Marshall said flatly.

"Or this baboon heart could just be transitional until you get another human heart. You know, we're successfully using baboon livers during surgery to temporarily cleanse a patient's blood during short-term liver failure."

"But why did you do it?" Marshall demanded. "And why me?"

"We do it," Dr. Lamb said simply as he walked toward the door, "because we can. And why you?" Dr. Lamb shrugged. "Because frankly, you were dead on the operating table, anyway."

"Can I ever dive again?" Marshall called after him.

"You can keep living. That's all we ask." At the doorway, the surgeon paused. "We'll have to be on the lookout for any signs of infection or rejection. You'll stay in Portland for rehab and transplant group sessions."

"No way," Marshall murmured.

"Now, just settle in. Rest. And, man, you might try to be a *little* grateful."

As the doctor strode out, Marshall noted that in his small aquarium the oscars had indeed devoured the gouramis.

The nurse frowned and then squared her shoulders. "Dr. Lamb would like you to attend group sessions to help you through this post-transplant phase."

"Forget it!"

"Oh, come on, Marsh." It was Andrew sweeping into the room with a good-natured grin at the nurse, who seemed very happy to see him.

"You two dating already?" Marshall commented. If he hadn't almost died, if he hadn't heard that his heart wasn't human, if he hadn't lost all sense of control over whatever life was left him, he too might have engaged with Andrew in their usual friendly competition over a good-looking woman. But suddenly it all seemed so pointless. Stupid, really.

"Mr. McGreggor, you've been through a lot," the nurse continued. "You need to rest." She turned to Andrew and brightened. "Maybe you'd like to go with him to the first group meeting. It's next Monday, upstairs on the rehab floor."

"We'll be there," Andrew promised and then reached down and swatted Marshall on the leg. "Won't we?"

"If I live that long," Marshall growled.

Closing his eyes, Marshall pretended to doze. He could hear Andrew's chair scrape the hospital floor as his friend settled in for yet another afternoon visit. Vigil was more like it. Didn't Andrew have a diving job somewhere far away? And Marshall wasn't going to stay here in Portland with these crazy doctors and their freakish experiments. He'd go back to Hawaii with his mother, rest up a little, and then get right back to diving. "I'm going to check myself out of this goddamn place. Baboon heart . . . it's creepy."

Marshall listened to the whirr, bleep, and click of machinery and the softer whoosh of his aquarium. Again a school of parrotfish danced before him, then a slow-motion tornado of flashing blue-green mackerel. He dove until at last the trance of tranquilizers and immunosuppressant drugs eased him into a fitful sleep.

Deep grass, and he is sitting at the edge of a group of baboons peacefully preening each other, as if they had all the time in the world. Two juvenile offspring are grooming their mother, a mature baboon whose expression is open and relaxed, her head thrown back in pleasure. It is a ritual full of familial fondness and contentment, as if this were all the communication ever needed between primates. But he himself is sitting just outside the group, still a supplicant. This older female is regal. She has raised many infants to adulthood; they sit in a circle around her with their own newborns in this close-knit family troop.

He, too, wants to claim this mature matriarch and, by doing so, gain acceptance into a new family. But he must move slowly, befriending her offspring and lesser baboons of the troop, until she decides he is worthy of her notice and patronage. At last, as he quietly waits, she does glance his way, while her daughter delicately grooms her head. She seems to take him in without effort or much interest. In that brief glance is her name: Hara. It is all she gives him—and it is enough. It is everything.

Marshall thrashed in his hospital bed. Tubes like dangling scuba equipment clattered to the floor. A piercing alarm buzzer sounded, and his nurse ran into the room.

"You're okay, Mr. McGreggor—just lost some of your IVs," the nurse said soothingly.

He tried to remember who this woman was. "Am I in Africa?"

She stood near his bed and put a hand on his chest, as much to comfort as to hold him still. "You're in the hospital in Portland, Oregon. Under heavy medication. You need to be very calm now and rest. You had a heart transplant."

"I saw . . ." Abruptly he stopped. "Nothing," he said and closed his eyes tightly. No savannah, just blackness. "Nightmare."

Isabel and Andrew were silent as they drove up to Portland Memorial for another visit. Andrew was staying with his sister in their old cottage, and the two commuted every other day to visit Marshall in the hospital. Andrew had brought in a hospital television and VCR and insisted on playing endless tapes of his underwater videos. These beautiful and bright pictures of tropical fish, sharks, underwater caves, dolphins, and manta rays seemed to interest Marshall more than any of his visitors.

"Go ahead, say it, Sis," Andrew frowned. "You're appalled that Marshall's got a baboon heart."

"I never said that."

"You don't have to; you've always been transparent to me. Besides, I know how you feel about this kind of stuff. Even when Grandpapa had that pig valve replacement, you made the whole thing into a moral dilemma. Well, I think it's simple. You can save a life, you save a life."

Andrew was right about her uneasiness over Marshall's new heart. But her brother didn't know that Isabel's deepest dismay was not only philosophical; it was personal. Yet inexplicable. Even as Andrew first told her about the unexpected animal-to-human transplant, Isabel had sensed something was terribly changed in Marshall. The moment she placed her hand on Marshall's arm as he lay in the ICU, Isabel had felt her own chest constrict. Dizziness and that familiar dread she usually sensed only when an animal was in danger.

Isabel heard an odd heartbeat—*whoosh-whoosh, whoosh-whoosh*—in waves through her body. Maybe it was just her bad hearing or the stress of seeing this unconscious man—to whom she had found herself strangely drawn—so depressed after his surgery. She shook her head to clear her hearing, but the phantom sound, an audible pulse, echoed inside her. It was as if she were listening through an esophageal stethoscope to an animal's heartbeat. A frantic animal.

As Isabel had stepped back from Marshall's bedside, she realized she must somehow be hearing the new heart beating inside this man. But how could that be? She told no one, not even Marian, about the unsettling experience. But Marshall's mother had perhaps also intuited something troubling about her son. As they shopped for the aquarium equipment that Lillian hoped would cheer Marshall, she said, "My boy is not happy to be here. Maybe it's not right what they did, putting a wild animal inside him." She turned plaintively to Isabel, her dark eyes so lustrous, like her son's.

Isabel had not told Marshall's mother of her misgivings. But now in the hospital parking lot, she turned to her brother and argued with Andrew. She knew she shouldn't. "You do have to wonder what all this costs the animals. So many lives sacrificed, and these cross-species transplants always fail. Besides, there are terrible dangers of a simian virus leaping species and . . ."

"You're not just a goddamn scientist in this," Andrew snapped, his eyes shadowed from sleeplessness. "Really, Isa, I know you liked the guy. Isn't Marshall worth a few apes?"

"Monkeys, actually . . ." She stopped. She knew she sounded like a prig, but she couldn't help it. It was all too chilling. "That doctor is not supposed to be doing xenotransplants now, not since last year, because a virus from a baboon liver infected the patient and . . ."

"Oh, come on, will you?" Andrew slammed the car door and strode ahead of her into the hospital lobby. He punched the elevator button. "Whatever you do, don't get into one of your philosophical debates with Marshall. He's in no shape for it."

"Of course not," Isabel promised. But no sooner had they sat down in Marshall's hospital room, no sooner had he languidly greeted them and quickly turned his attention back to his aquarium, than Isabel broke her own promise.

"You don't approve of all this, do you, Isabel?" Marshall demanded, his eyes suddenly fixed on her. "You think it's creepy, too, and that my life isn't worth all this animal suffering."

Isabel wished she hadn't hesitated. "It's very . . . very risky for all involved," she began. "It's scary stuff."

"If you'd been in the operating room with me," Marshall said with satisfaction, "you wouldn't have let them do this to me. You would have let me go."

"Anyone who cared about you might have made the same decision . . . ," Isabel said. She noticed that the fossil ammonite she'd given Marshall was lying at the bottom of his aquarium. Isabel fell silent.

"I doubt *you* would have." Marshall pushed himself up in his hospital bed. "You'd have thought of the whole picture, Isabel. The animal, the person, my future."

"Honestly, I don't know what I would've done," Isabel said. She could not believe how keenly she felt disappointment at seeing her precious talisman discarded. She sat back in her plastic chair and stared at some place right behind Marshall's head. "I do know what science is capable of doing—and how little we think about the consequences."

"Yeah, well, our Grandpapa had a pig's valve replacement that gave him five more years with us," Andrew interrupted, scowling at his sister. "We were both really grateful for that—weren't we, Isabel? Besides, this animal heart is transitional, isn't it?"

Her brother was plainly glaring at her now, and Isabel was about to nod when Marshall burst out laughing. It was the first time they had seen even the suggestion of a smile since his surgery.

"I have to say that right now you two are a better show than my aquarium!"

Andrew was up and patting Marshall on the forearm. "So glad you think we're good for something." He turned to open his backpack and take out sandwiches and several videos. "We've brought you the Kenyan coast dive. Remember our last trip to find aquatic ape evidence?" Andrew excitedly slipped the video into the VCR.

"I remember," Marshall smiled, though his lips were still cracked and swollen from the intubation during surgery. "How could I forget your discovery of a hominid bone fragment that turned out to belong to a big tuna!"

Andrew laughed and told his sister, "One day we'll discover aquatic ape evidence, and you'll help us prove it, Isa, with all your DNA expertise."

"I'm sure I will," Isabel said indulgently.

"Turn out the lights, will you, Sis?"

Isabel obliged, and the hospital room was illuminated only by the turquoise waves of watery light from the video. Everyone settled into companionable silence. Marshall kept only one eye on the image of manta rays soaring through the sea. The other eye he kept on Isabel. She seemed collapsed in the plastic hospital chair, her fatigue evident in the shadowy lines around her eyes, her hands unconsciously fiddling with an uneaten sandwich. This afternoon she was not that strong, confident woman in charge—as she had been in her lab and on her beach—ensuring the well-being of those who needed rescuing.

Maybe that was the problem. Isabel had a need to nurture, even to nurture a man like Marshall who might leave her to wander the world. Here was a woman who sat vigil on the beach for seals, and who might wait for Marshall, the pull of her hopes worse than gravity for a man who loved the weightless orbit of water. Even though he might need a care-taker right now, Marshall did not want Isabel to watch over him like she would some wounded animal. Isabel not only would have all the burden, she would also have all the power. And that, he would not allow. If there were ever to be anything between them, Marshall would have to come back to Isabel when he was well.

"Isabel," Marshall blurted out, "you need to eat. You need to take care of yourself as well as you do me or any of your other stranded animals."

She turned to him in surprise and then dutifully began eating a crust of her sandwich. Marshall knew that if he weren't laid up in this hospital, Isabel would have told him to mind his own business. More than ever, he realized he didn't want Isabel to see him so dependent. If he could not escape her right now, he must send her away. He must heal.

"Do me a favor, will you both?" Marshall looked at Isabel. "Don't keep visiting me. You have to get back to diving, Andrew, and Isabel's lab needs her . . ." He studiously avoided meeting Isabel's eyes. "I've already got one mother watching over me, and we'll be heading back to Hawaii soon."

"Forget it, Marsh. I've taken a couple weeks off. Besides," said Andrew, reaching out an arm to pull Isabel close to him, "Isabel insisted on coming to see you."

It was a false gesture; Isabel could feel it in Andrew's awkward grasp. He was never awkward with women, except if he didn't want them near him. Ever since Marshall's transplant, there had been this tension between the siblings. Would Andrew ever forgive Isabel her misgivings? Would Marshall?

Of course, to Isabel she seemed to be the very last thing on Marshall's mind. All he wanted was to get out of this hospital, perhaps out of this world. Though she was hurt, more than she could admit even to herself, by his request for solitude, she would honor his wishes.

"All right, Marshall," she said, coming up alongside his hospital bed, only close enough to lay her hand lightly on his. There was hardly any place to touch him, for all the wires monitoring his heart rate and blood oxygen levels. Isabel noted that Marshall's skin was warm. Good circulation. Maybe the poor primate's heart would not be rejected and Marshall would actually be the first to survive long-term such a disturbing xenotransplant. Or maybe he would be lucky again and a human heart would soon be found for him. She sincerely hoped so. "You take good care of yourself. And please keep in touch."

He did not meet her eyes. "Yeah, you, too."

"Well, *I'll* see you tomorrow," Andrew said, leaning over Marshall, demanding his full attention.

"No, buddy." Marshall looked up wearily at Andrew. "No more visits." Then Marshall directed his next words to Isabel. "In a few weeks I'm going to Hawaii to recuperate. I just need time. Please, listen to me." He smiled faintly. "Even with only one good ear."

Isabel turned away, stung, angry that the blur in her eyes might betray her. She knew how to say goodbye, just as well as he knew how to leave. They both had a lot of practice. And she, at least, was a survivor.

"You'll heal faster here with your family, Kai'e'e, you'll see." Marshall's mother took his arm as the jetliner eased through layers of evening vog—that sea of volcanic fog rolling in waves down emerald mountains. "We'll take you to the ocean and lay your feet in the water like the old ones used to do when the smallpox came to the islands. Missionaries thought that was primitive, but it was the only way to wash away a white man's disease." Lillian gave her son a sober look. "You got a white man's disease, Kai'e'e. You lost your heart."

Below, a black, hardened splash of lava lay over the land, the legacy of a fiery tongue that found the sea, which at last stopped and cooled the fury. As Marshall stepped off the plane, he was embraced first by moist heat and the scent of white hibiscus, pakalana, and plumeria that lent a fragrant lightness to the air. He loved this smell and this lava land that he'd first photographed before he dove down into underwater worlds. Now, as long as he couldn't dive, Marshall would again photograph this Big Island and perhaps even take pictures of his family. Portraits were not his strong point, but the work would satisfy him for now.

"First we feed you—not that poison the hospital calls food," his mother said as they walked toward the small airport terminal. "Your sisters are fixing fresh opah in honor of you tonight. Then, Kai'e'e," she said firmly, "we make a big celebration."

"No, Mama," Marshall groaned. "No big fuss tonight. I just want to be . . . quiet . . . and alone."

"Too quiet, you!" Lillian burst out and leaned over to look directly at him. "Too alone. That's how you lost your first heart." Her dark eyes were fierce with a fire familiar to him.

It was a look Marshall dreaded more than her tenderness. He could not seem to resist his mother's care. It was why he was here with her, landing after six hours of turbulence over the vast ocean, at the small

Kona airport, where tourists were easy to distinguish from the locals. Some tourists and tour guides wore leis made of tuberose and pikake. His mother had draped an amulet, a sacred *o-mamori*, around her son's neck in the hospital, its pungent herbs and incense a daily offense to the nurses and their sterile smiles. "This good heart, you keep," his mother had commanded as she massaged the slight edema in her son's feet and calves.

Her touch, as always, was skillful and kind. Since Marshall had sent Isabel away from the hospital, he had not worried about betraying his reserve by a display of the volatile emotions that swept over him, the recurring nightmares that stranded him, somehow between species, on a strange savannah. He could endure his mother's daily affection and concern. No one but the nurses and Andrew, with his determined visits, had witnessed Marshall's uncontrollable mood swings and drug-induced hallucinations.

"Kai'e'e always has some trouble in him," Lillian had explained to Andrew. "But the sweetest nature."

That sweet nature was about to be sorely tested. Marshall spotted his entire extended family waving and shouting behind the terminal gate. There was his older sister Iolani, whom his mother had hopefully named after the greatest dancer of the hula tradition; but Iolani had forsaken dance to become, in her late twenties, a passionate advocate of the Native Sovereignty Movement. The whole family dreaded the day she might be arrested or worse. Iolani and her husband envisioned the day when Native Hawaiians might rise up and destroy the intruding tourist hotels that so trivialized their sacred traditions. To her, even the many Japanese and Chinese here in the islands were haole.

There, too, were Marshall's twin sisters, Flora and Nani, jumping up and down in unconscious symmetry; and his favorite sister, Nohelani, who stood very serious and a little taller, holding up one hand to welcome her older brother. Nohelani's hands usually talked for her; but now she was quiet.

It was only Nohelani and her silent world that Marshall longed to be with now. Not his huge, gregarious family with their mixed blood and even more mixed politics. Every family gathering was exhausting, with its endless food and fighting and gossip and singing. It was no wonder his father had spent most of his time in Honolulu at the university, having an affair with only one woman at a time. The complicated kinships that Professor McGreggor had left behind on the Big Island were so much more unpredictable and passionate than the simple intrigue of his marital deceit.

"Whoa," came a voice from behind them. "I see what you mean, Marsh. There sure are a lot of them."

It was Andrew, leaning over to help Marshall and his mother with their baggage. His friend had insisted on coming to Hawaii with them, even though Marshall had protested. Andrew stood quietly, his hazel eyes taking in the throng barely contained behind the airport gate.

"You watch," Marshall muttered. "They'll break through airport security any minute and take over the runway."

"I guess I didn't need to order ahead for that wheelchair. They'll probably carry you!" Andrew exclaimed.

To Marshall's amusement, Andrew seemed uncharacteristically subdued. He, too, was overwhelmed by Marshall's family. "I told you, Andrew, there was really no need for you to come."

"I taught you better manners, Kai'e'e!" Lillian burst out. She turned to Andrew, with whom she had obviously grown close over the last month at the hospital. "You saved my son's life."

"Actually, Lillian," Andrew said, "it was my sister who saw Marsh was in trouble and first . . ."

"Isabel did not tell me this." Lillian was surprised. "We sat together all the time in the hospital and she did not tell me this."

"Yeah, so Isabel gets the credit, not me."

"But Kai'e'e keeps you near him," Lillian concluded. "So, Andrew, you are part of our family. Tonight we make you welcome. We make you one of our own."

Andrew grinned and gave Marshall a look of triumph. It struck Marshall that maybe this was how a younger brother might behave toward him. He didn't really know, having had only sisters. Sisters who now fell all over him with tears and a language that took him only a few seconds to remember. All his sisters' kids were speaking the rolling vowels of his native Hawaiian.

And then Marshall was lifted up, before he could take his only unmarried sister, Nohelani, in his arms or talk Sign with her. His sisters' husbands hoisted him on their shoulders and carried him as if he were a returning Polynesian king, lost at sea and now found.

Their joy was so unabashed and possessive that for a moment Marshall was breathless, as he had been at first after the transplant surgery. But then a strange sensation surfaced: gratitude. It was the first time he had really felt it, although most of the other transplants in his mandatory group sessions had made an obnoxious mantra of their daily thankfulness for their new, alien hearts.

"My God, Kai'e'e, we thought you were a goner when Mama left to be with you in the hospital," Iolani said, grabbing her brother's dangling feet with a possessive tenderness.

From his vantage point, Marshall looked down at Iolani and smiled. "Here I am, a miracle of science, a freak of nature."

Nohelani was reaching, trying to touch her brother, too. One of the husbands noticed her gesture and plucked the lithe Nohelani up from the crowd to place beside Marshall on the other men's shoulders.

Nohelani looked at her only brother and her face was somber. Marshall's trained eye took in a new image of Nohelani to replace the precious one in his memory: The tiny snail-shaped scar from a snorkeling accident high on Nohelani's tanned cheek, the misty blue eyes—so rare in his family—now a shade darker. Marshall was shocked that his young sister had become a woman in his absence. He would always think of her as a little girl. He read her beautiful, slender fingers, a dancer's eloquent hands, a deaf girl's voice.

Nohelani was the only sibling with a father other than Ian McGreggor. No one knew her father. No one cared. Nohelani was theirs, just as surely as if she had one morning crawled out of the sea like her turtle ancestors. Everyone belonged most to the mother in these islands.

Now Nohelani met Marshall's smile with a grave expression, as if considering whether he were still her true brother, now that he had another's heart. She laid a delicate hand lightly on Marshall's chest. The long scar underneath his silk shirt did not interest Nohelani as it would everyone else. She listened, eyes lowered, until at last she was satisfied that

Marshall was the same soul she had loved all her short life. Marshall believed his little sister, all of them, would outlive him. She would remember him best. She knew how to listen.

Nohelani also knew how to sing. Marshall had taught her to sign the words, and her sisters had taught her the ancient dance of hula—that slow, undulant wave that begins not in the hips but in the earth. Traditional hula was a warm energy rising up in the body, circling calves and thighs, a swirling in the belly that pulsed upward, along the spine, until it found release and flow in the fingertips.

It was Nohelani who that first night finally convinced her brother to sing again with his family. No one said it was what he most needed to bring him back to them; no one spoke about healing or blood or traditions and gods so old they were not all human.

After a dinner of fresh opah and mango salsa, taro, and their mother's coconut custard, it was time for family singing. All his sisters and mother did was stop midsong and turn to Marshall expectantly. "We need your part here, Kai'e'e," Lillian said softly.

"Let the husbands sing it," Marshall replied. He glanced out to the spacious veranda of his mother's sprawling house. At any given time, depending on the state of their marriages, one or two of his sisters might be living here. They said it was because Lillian's house was right on the water, its airy pink and turquoise wooden frame built on stilts and walled with screens so trade winds cooled the two stories. "I'm sure you've bamboozled the other guys into singing my parts, Mama."

"They cannot sing your *kauna*," his mother said, frowning. "We need your falsetto part here or we do not respect the song."

It was the first time Marshall had seen his mother truly irritated with him since his transplant. And it took him aback, just as it always had when he was a child. Her criticism was so rare; she had seldom showed any disappointment in her children's choices or disasters. But for her son not to sing with his family, not to give voice to the gift that was his heritage—this was cause for her severest judgment.

Lillian looked around at the gathered husbands and Andrew, who had positioned himself at some distance from the singers, perched on a stool at the border of the kitchen and the veranda. "The husbands cannot sing your part, Kai'e'e. This is your *mele,* your song. Or did you lose your song, along with your heart?"

A tremble in his sisters' voices quivered like a disturbance in some electrical field, as they hesitated and then sang on without their brother. Lillian turned away from her son to continue a particularly complicated harmony on the traditional "Mauna Kea"—a song celebrating the glacier-clad volcano, Hawaii's tallest. As a boy Marshall had hiked near this most dormant of island volcanoes. Called White Mountain by all those on the Big Island, Mauna Kea was revered as much as her sister volcanoes, Hualalai, Mauna Loa, and Kilauea, all alive and erupting whenever the gods awakened them to rise up and birth their fiery lava fountains and molten lakes—the newest land on earth.

It was during the chorus of this song that Nohelani appeared beside Marshall, one hand resting very lightly on his arm. It was the touch of a butterfly—delicate and undemanding. And then she was singing with her sisters, her hands fluttering, their gestures half words and half dance.

For a moment Marshall could not understand his little sister's graceful words; then he realized she was signing in Hawaiian. He had taught her American Sign Language in English. Nohelani's hands were trying to sing *his* part, his syncopated descant sung in the mysterious and extraordinarily rare falsetto tradition. Along with diving and capturing the splendor of an underwater world, Hawaiian falsetto was an art that had come effortlessly. Why shouldn't he sing with them? He had always sung his part, even after his voice broke; he was still able to raise his natural tenor to vibrate astonishingly high to create that pure, eerie grace of Hawaiian falsetto tradition.

If he had forgotten how to speak sign language in Hawaiian, perhaps he had also forgotten his falsetto part? Before Marshall could stop himself, at the exact moment the song called again for his falsetto, his voice rose up to mingle with those of his sisters. He could hear their startled smiles in their voices as he joined them in the proud, slow pacing of the lyrics. Then their chorus fell back to support him as Marshall's voice glided between registers. His song echoed in the chambers of his chest where once his own heart had been. A voice almost not his own, borrowed perhaps from his ancestors, stretched his vocal cords thin and taut as he reached for that high G above middle C.

Soaring, his voice was a brilliant island bird—rare and no longer endangered, because the people remembered this ethereal melody, as Marshall remembered. This time, changing registers, he exaggerated his breathless and beautiful *ha'i* break like a bright ornament set off from all the other sopranos by its strangeness, almost a yodel, so high was he, so happy. Home.

As he sang the second verse with his sisters, Marshall saw his mother's quiet smile. This is the way she must have looked at her son when she first saw him, or when he floated on her belly in the ocean, or when his body did not reject his new heart in the ICU. Now he sang on for her and for his family, wondering why he had always run so far away from them.

It was what his father had done. Marshall had hated his father for his emotional abandonment, his betrayals, but he saw now that he had become very like his father. And yet he also understood his father now, more than the child in him ever could. Sometimes it was just too much for a man—all these complicated and shifting feminine alliances, like a harmony almost out of reach of a man's range. While Marshall was growing up with his sisters, the family dramas had often seemed like the machinations of a royal court. Who's in? Who's out? No wonder his father had fled.

But when Marshall sang this falsetto, he wanted only to follow his sisters—his pure, silky voice ranging between his sisters' harmonies, their voices woven like an acoustic tapestry. When Marshall sang falsetto, he felt purely Hawaiian. No longer mixed blood. He found himself—or maybe it was the music, the ancestors, and the sea finding him.

As Marshall sang on, someone else found him, too. The woman he had come here to escape seemed to cross the room to embrace him, her face angular in a sea of wide faces. "Here," Isabel Spinner said and opened her palm to reveal a golden, chambered fossil shell. "I want you to keep it with you always."

Where was that ammonite fossil Isabel so prized? Had he misplaced it? Just as he had lost his way? Where was Isabel? He saw her sitting across from him again as she drove the winding coastal highway near her home.

She was singing to him in an old language that also belonged to seafarers—Gaelic songs she had inherited. Why had he not repaid the gift and sung for Isabel?

Maybe for the same reason it had never occurred to him until now that he could simply settle down here in his islands with his family. Marshall closed his eyes and listened to his sisters' sweet voices and wondered: What if he stayed? What if he never left them again? Would he be happy? Or did this longing for daily society and family belong more to the heart of another primate? Suddenly his reverie was interrupted by his oldest sister.

"You're on my part!" Iolani snapped at one of her sisters and stopped the song only seconds before the family finished. "Next song, Nani, you stay on your alto," Iolani insisted.

"I was on my part. You're the one who got confused when you tried to sing Marshall's tenor."

A squabble, a squall of sisters, blew over them, and Marshall sighed but kept silent.

It was Andrew who made the mistake of jumping in. Having had to reckon with only one sister, he obviously didn't know he was not only outnumbered but also insignificant. "Gosh, I thought your singing was gorgeous, like angels.'"

Marshall's sisters turned on Andrew. "You don't know about our singing," Iolani explained with an obvious show of patience.

"Well," Andrew said, standing and taking a step backward, tilting his stool. "I know it's beautiful. And Marsh here sounds just like a . . ." Andrew fumbled. "Like a Hawaiian Aaron Neville . . ."

"Haole music," Iolani suggested.

Marshall burst out laughing. "Aaron Neville is a black man. And my voice is nowhere near as fabulous as his." Marshall considered stopping there. It was against his better judgment to further join in the feminine fray. But he owed it to Andrew. "Besides, Iolani," he teased, "you're half-haole."

"No, I leave that part to you!" Then Iolani turned to Andrew and continued as if she and he were suddenly confidantes. "Our papa's haole blood is definitely *not* Kai'e'e's better half."

"Enough!" Lillian interrupted. With one wave of her hand, everyone fell into respectful silence. "This night is for celebration. Your brother is alive. He is home . . ."

"Yes, Mama, but for how long?"

"How long am I home?" Marshall asked simply. "Or how long am I going to live?"

There was a silence so fraught with subtext that it almost made Marshall smile to imagine the unspoken words. Isabel had told him that dolphin family pods were believed to carry on at least three conversations in different dialects simultaneously—and that was only what researchers were capable of monitoring.

"Kai'e'e is always home," Lillian concluded firmly and gave her daughters a warning look.

No one said a word until Nohelani laughed out loud and plopped over onto Marshall's lap from where she had been poised by his chair.

"We just sing Kai'e'e's part whenever he is away from us," Lillian said and turned back to her son. "Another song, you!" It was not a request.

Dutifully, the sisters took up the complex harmonies, weaving and waiting for Marshall's falsetto entrance.

"I can sing your falsetto now, too." Iolani leaned over and embraced her brother. "The women are learning it nowadays."

"I'd like to see you just try," Marshall teased.

The oldest sister and brother took off on the same part, singing way above the others, their voices rising, reaching for that elusive falsetto, that place between the worlds, together.

chapter six

The Dead Zone

It was the first time since his transplant that Marshall had fallen into this world, which was more his own than any other. His cardiologist was so shocked that Marshall was still alive that he barely protested Marshall's scuba diving again, a year after his heart transplant. The three months of rehabilitation in Hawaii and weekly checkups, the required transplant group sessions, the daily medications—all this Marshall left behind on land. Floating weightlessly now, he felt free from the anxious care of his family and friends.

Hand over hand, Marshall descended the dive line. At eighty feet, he let go of the taut line, and the strong currents propelled him between two reef gardens embellished with scarlet and orange staircase sponges, chartreuse grape weed, and feathery gorgonian fans with their bright yellow branches. So glorious these colors, as if freshly splashed by some Poseidon-Picasso using phosphorous paints. Here in the Flower Garden Banks Marine Sanctuary south of the Texas-Louisiana border, Marshall, Andrew, and a few sanctuary researchers photographed a diver's delight—constellations of translucent star coral in full spawn. Bubbling, pearl-like bundles of egg and sperm swarmed the reefs, whole colonies cross-pollinating in such a bright storm it seemed that Marshall swam through glowing green galaxies.

Eight nights after the August full moon, Marshall had flown to the underwater salt domes of Flower Banks to meet up with Andrew to photograph the lush coral spawn. Last year, they'd teamed up to photograph whale sharks and even a rare loggerhead turtle here. Every year when they visited this marine sanctuary, they hoped for the Holy Grail—to find and film a manta ray in its watery nursery. It would be the photo that Marshall needed to finally complete his one-man show scheduled for next summer at Honolulu's prestigious Oceania Gallery. But their diving destination this afternoon, after the marine sanctuary, was the real reason Marshall was risking his health. Before his heart attack, *National Geographic* magazine had given the two men an assignment to photograph the expanding Dead Zone in the Gulf of Mexico, in Louisiana waters near the mouth of the Mississippi River.

"Weird isn't the word for those waters," Andrew had told Marshall a month earlier, never expecting that Marshall would insist on keeping this assignment and making their production deadline. "Man, this is one dive I don't want to do."

"I'll do it myself."

"Wait a minute, Marsh, this is an especially tough assignment, and should you really go diving so soon? I mean, it's the size of New Jersey, but *nothing* lives there."

"I know about that," Marshall said. "I'm coming."

"Over my dead body!"

"No. Over mine. Besides, I'm a medical miracle. I can survive anything."

Marshall could picture Andrew's stubborn expression even though his friend was calling from Australia's Great Barrier Reef, a world away from Marshall's daily drudgery of rehab. But diving the Dead Zone now felt like the most important thing in his life.

"It's our job," Marshall finished firmly. "I'll be there."

Andrew relented. "If you're sure it's okay . . ."

"But before the Dead Zone, we dive the Flower Banks. As usual. Deal?"

"You make deals just like my sister," Andrew complained, but his tone was good-natured. "You two always get the best end of the bargain."

"Do we?" Marshall stopped himself.

He did not really mean to be argumentative. The truth was that Marshall was anxious about meeting Isabel again the following week, when he and Andrew would attend another underwater photography conference in Portland. It would be the first time he'd seen Isabel since the hospital and his severe postoperative depression. They'd kept up a courteous e-mail relationship—she sent notes full of stories about her forensics work, and he sent her his favorite underwater photographs. He'd even invited her to attend the opening of his new show—sometime in his unreliable future. But when Marshall really thought about it, he knew more about the weather on the Oregon coast than he did about Isabel's life. Was she seeing anyone? He had not wanted to ask Andrew for fear his diving buddy might misinterpret his interest. But what was his interest?

"So, how *is* that sister of yours doing these days?" Marshall asked, hoping his tone was not as confused as he felt.

"She's good. Working too hard, as usual." Andrew stopped. "You're looking forward to seeing her again?"

Marshall was quiet. Yes and no, he wanted to say. Yes, Isabel still moved him as little did now: the memory of her singing old silkie songs, holding him just at arm's length, her pale face floating above his in the ICU like a translucent moon jelly. And no, she was probably the last person Marshall should reach out to when his life seemed day-to-day. Isabel deserved an equal. Even if he liked her—and he did, with a new tenderness that he attributed to his having lost his own heart—he would not be good for her. Anybody could see that. Even Andrew. Especially a brother.

"Sure, sure. But not like you're worried about. Don't worry. Your little sister is safe from me."

"She's my big sister. And it's not really Isabel I'm worried about."

Marshall ignored the comment. "Listen, I'll buy you both dinner at the Heathman. How's that for gratitude?"

"Now, that's a good deal all round," Andrew said. "See you in the Flower Banks."

As Marshall adjusted his waterproof lens now to capture green brain coral studded with spawning clusters, he was all but lost from sight. Hidden in this spawn of life, he felt the throb of his new heart—strong and steady.

Marshall raised his camera to shoot the beautifully dangerous, bone-colored dorsal spines of a crown-of-thorns starfish. Suddenly a human arm scattering a funnel of star coral spawn in a million directions intruded on his private rapture.

You okay? Andrew signaled with his gloved fingers. They used their rudimentary sign language underwater.

A blast of bubbles shot up from Marshall's regulator. *Yes, fine, fine,* he nodded. Then as politely as possible, he gestured for Andrew to let him have space to take his shot. Satisfied, Marshall stretched from shoulders to powerful stroke of flippers. Breathing easily, he drifted, arms outstretched. A school of parrotfish encircled him in a blue-green cloud. He surrendered to the stillness and the safety he always felt underwater. Raising his camera, he captured a reef ledge bright with jade algae whose tubular branches lent life to the crackling coral. Without algae, coral lost its energy source and drained of color into bleached archipelagoes—miniature, abandoned civilizations. In the shallower waters of the sanctuary, creeping starvation threatened this northernmost coral reef in the United States.

Marshall photographed schools of Caribbean reef fish and invertebrates—from sea urchins to mollusks to the delicate pulse, parachute, and play of jellyfish. Always he had an eye out for a silky shark or a ray.

Someone at his elbow, a nudge from one world to another, and Marshall knew it was Andrew again, thumbs up, gesturing to his watch and waving him to the surface. Out of time. Time. It was what every underwater photographer longed for, more than color, more than the perfect shot. Never enough time in this submarine world. Marshall inhaled and slowly propelled himself upward into a shaft of sunlight. Diving was like his life—it was over just at the moment it got interesting.

"Thought we lost you two there for a while," the skipper was saying as he hauled first Marshall, then Andrew, from the high waves. Whitecaps, unpredictable currents, and wind at the surface crazily rocked the small boat.

Gravity and the harsh, humid air hit him at once. Marshall was breathless for a moment as he slid out from under the burden of his tank.

"Too long for your first dive back?" Andrew was next to him, helping him with his heavy gear—a tentacle-like assortment of cameras, cases, and extra lenses that awkwardly swung around his body. "You look just like an octopus." Andrew laughed and clapped him on the back, but carefully.

Andrew's restraint irritated Marshall, and so did the skipper's insistence that they take a quick pulse reading "just for the hell of it."

"Good, strong, stable . . ." The marine sanctuary skipper nodded. He returned Marshall's wrist to him and looked up from his waterproof watch. "Seventy-two beats per minute. Shipshape."

Under the glare of the sun, Marshall unzipped his lightweight underwater vest with its myriad pockets.

"Who needs tattoos?" the skipper commented dryly as he caught sight of the raised reddish pink surgical scar slashed from sternum to belly.

Busying himself with his camera equipment, Marshall ignored the skipper. Then he reached into his photo bag for his afternoon doses of cyclosporine and prednisone. He should have taken his temperature to make sure he had no fever after such a dive. But no fussing over his health in front of his friends. "How long until we can get to the Dead Zone?"

The skipper hauled back hard on the outboard engine rope, and the boat scudded across the warm waves, splashing everyone aboard. "You just work on your tans, boys. We've got to motor almost to the mouth of the big ol' Mississippi River."

Above the engine roar, Andrew leaned near Marshall and shouted, "Good idea." Andrew, his red beard already woven with golden highlights from the sun, flopped back onto the deck to sun himself some more.

Marshall smiled. He had missed his friend, even if Andrew was irritatingly cheerful at times. What Marshall liked most about him was that bit of sorrow around his eyes and the rare times he was truly still, listening to the surf or the underwater chatter and click of coral. Marshall's thoughts returned to the coral he'd just seen—those tiny animals who begin as almost microscopic larvae, drifting amid ocean plankton, vagabonding all their lives, until the chemical signal of the red algae tells the coral to stop, anchor to a foundation, and then transform into the tiny, funnel-shaped polyps that will form a future reef. Andrew was like coral larvae that had never heard the call of the red algae. He was perhaps as damaged as those immature coral whose wandering was not yet put to an end.

After a long lunch and an afternoon boat ride, the skipper at last cut his engines. "Okay, boys, Dead Zone straight ahead. Don't get spooked now."

Marshall gazed down through the Gulf of Mexico's unexpectedly clear waters. He set out the small buoy with its red-and-white-striped flag. After defogging his face mask, he pulled on his fluorescent green flippers and fell backward into the warm waves. Floating on his back, he quickly tested his regulator and then held the mouthpiece above the mild swells.

As Marshall stretched his full length, floating, he felt a sudden quickening of his pulse. No pain in his chest, but something foreign. Fear. The bitter bile of adrenaline and his heart pumping crazily. Was it another attack? He cursed, struggling inside a body that suddenly seemed alien to him. How could he be afraid when he was in his element? For a split second he had an image of hot sun over a sea of endless grasslands—that landscape of his recurring, post-transplant nightmares. His pulse raced.

Floating on his back, he gazed up at a sky with pink cumulus clouds like phantom clipper ships. He had a job to do here. If he could just focus his mind, his body would follow—even his heart. He could train it, like any frightened animal.

Small, sudden movements caught his eye as Marshall saw a tiny horseshoe crab clinging to his diver's buoy. The crab's struggle calmed Marshall. By summer the crab's springtime urge to haul up on shore to spawn was over. So what was this ancient creature doing here on the surface?

"You can thank the horseshoe crab. That little guy's blood saved your life," Marshall remembered Dr. Lamb, his heart surgeon, telling him in those hallucinatory post-op days in the ICU. "That crab's another deep-sea diver, Mr. McGreggor, like you."

The surgeon had explained that the blood of the horseshoe crab is used in biomedical research because it contains a clotting agent that aids in detecting dangerous toxins. This borrowed blood of the crab is actually blue; the crab is bled alive, then thrown back into the ocean.

"The clotting agent from crab blood is used to tell if the new heart in your chest and the new transfused blood pounding through your veins are free from contamination," Dr. Lamb said.

"Horseshoe crabs are in trouble, too," Marshall had murmured and then fallen back into his drugged, twilight sleep.

Awaiting Andrew's dive, Marshall lay on his back and let the waves lull him. His heart slowed. Fear eased into watchfulness. Eye to eye with the sickly crab, Marshall wondered if this ancient creature had crawled up this past spring on Maryland shores to lay those thousands of eggs that would hatch with the high tide. Taking a quick photo of the familiar domed shell and tail spike, Marshall thought he might bring the image to Isabel Spinner. She probably knew who was studying the recent decline in horseshoe crabs along the East Coast from overfishing and the biomedical industry. Marshall considered saving the creature by lifting it to the safety of the motorboat. But he decided against it. Why not let the creature die at home, at sea?

It was what Andrew should have done. Isabel would have been more scientific, more sanguine: she would have let Marshall go. He liked this about her. Isabel had also honored his request to stop visiting him in the hospital. It was bad enough that Andrew had dragged him to those first hospital mandatory group sessions, where everyone seemed to vie to see who could produce the most anguished confessions and weird theories about why they had been "chosen" to live on.

One day a new member had entered their session. At twenty, Irene Feinstein was the youngest of the group and herself the recipient of a pig's valve to repair her congenital heart defect. She bounded into the group with such energy that everyone scooted their straight chairs backward as if to make more space for such exuberance.

"Yo," Irene addressed the startled group. "Brave new world . . ."

". . . that has such creatures in it." Marshall finished for her. He noted Irene's shoulder tattoo. Still healing, it was an elaborately coiled, scarlet-and-black king cobra with Egyptian hieroglyphs. Irene's delicate nose was pierced with a turquoise stud and her hair was pale gold with electric blue streaks.

To Marshall she was like a bright, flickering tropical fish. He couldn't help but grin at this boisterous girl. "Welcome to the fish tank," he informed her.

"You mean, the future," she shot back.

The group seemed just as startled by Marshall's sudden participation as they did by Irene Feinstein.

"Welcome, dear," George, the group leader, said heartily. He was a former parole officer. Patting the empty chair next to him, he said, "Why don't you take a seat next to me and we'll begin."

"Forget it, Pops." Irene flounced down in an easy chair next to Marshall. "So, I guess you and I are the only two animal-parts people here. I'm part pig." She turned to the group and said, "Marshall here is part baboon."

"How do you know so much about me?" Marshall asked her, startled.

"Talked to your night nurse." She shrugged. "Nurse Ratched thinks you have a bad attitude."

As if on an impulse, George added, "We've all noticed, Marshall, that you're a little . . . depressed. It's perfectly normal after a heart transplant. Some of us have felt it, too, kind of an unexpected letdown when we should really be happy."

Irene burst out laughing. "Lazarus had a right to be depressed when he got raised up from his grave. But Marshall must feel like Frankenscience . . ."

Abruptly Marshall stood and walked out the door. As he strode down the hall, Irene caught up with him.

"Hey, I'm sorry if I came on a little strong. Blame it on my newfound health. But really, Marshall, let me make it up to you."

"And how are you going to do that?" He slowed down, allowing Irene to slip an arm through his.

It was the first time since his transplant that anyone had touched him without concern, with a kind of playfulness.

"I'll take you on a field trip with me. Let's go to the zoo!" She now took his hand and swung it as if they were in the schoolyard at recess.

In spite of his earlier irritation, Marshall felt responding warmth in his belly. He glanced down at Irene and noticed how fair her skin was, except for the smattering of freckles. He must be at least fifteen years older than she.

"I hate zoos," Marshall snapped, but he let himself be led to the city bus, which ran along the Sunset Highway to the Portland Zoo.

Past the pregnant elephant, whose keepers worried about her weight, past the reptile house, with its stately python and massive Amazon boas, past the endangered wolves exhibit and the aviary with exotic birds, Irene propelled him to the primate center, which she insisted they visit first.

They heard the baboon exhibit before they saw it. Howls, screeches, and chattering voices of six guinea baboons oblivious to the people staring in at them in their rocky habitat of concrete cliffs and acacia trees. In a blur of glossy fur and long arms, two infants scampered, one after the other, in playful pursuit. With their tiny, wrinkled snouts and huge, pink ears, they looked quizzical and comic as they swung and shrieked in their frenzied chase. Below them, in perfect calm, as if peacefully perched on African sleeping rocks far removed from the fray, a small male tenderly groomed a female. Amid the din of screaming infants, the grooming pair was lost in a ritual as old as evolution and as immediate as pleasure: he preened her silky cinnamon fur as if spinning it between his fingers.

Behind the grooming pair, eyes intent on their every move, hunched a male whose posture suggested age. A smaller female was foraging for rotten fruit on the concrete hill. Another male sat atop the highest tree, as if waiting to be recognized by the others. Not one of them looked up at him. This last, smaller baboon was so obviously a supplicant, following every move with his dark eyes. His longing and isolation were palpable.

A young girl pulled on her father's shirt. "What's wrong with that one? Nobody plays with him."

"Maybe he's the new kid on the block, honey."

"You're right, sir." A tall, plain-faced woman with a name tag smiled at the father. Then she addressed the small gathering outside the baboon exhibit. "That's Senegal being groomed by the juvenile male we call Lion-Heart. Senegal is the matriarch, the highest-ranking female in this troop. Everyone vies to groom her."

Irene whispered to Marshall. "Senegal is kind of like me, don't you think?"

Marshall laughed and took out his smallest pocket camera, the one he always carried. "Well, your hair's too sticky to groom."

"Senegal is very protective of her infant up there playing in the trees," the docent continued. "We call him Cape. He's chasing after Savannah, an infant baboon whom sanctuary workers in Africa rescued when poachers killed her mother for bush meat."

As the two tiny baboons streaked along the branches, Marshall waited for his shot. But Cape and Savannah were never still—*Running shapes, shaggy, screaming across the tall grasses.*

Marshall shook the images away, his heart quickening. Focusing now on the grooming baboon pair below, he trained his camera on Senegal, her head thrown back, relaxed, eyes half-closed. Her posture and obvious sensual satisfaction steadied Marshall. How long since he had wanted to touch and be touched by another person?

Snapping a roll of film, he focused on the matriarch's lovely snout and Lion-Heart's deft fingers as he untangled strand after strand of Senegal's long fur. Marshall was soothed to see the deep, physical contentment of their grooming.

"Let's sit down," he told Irene and led her to an iron bench in front of the exhibit.

"No hurry to see the other animals?"

"Nope," Marshall said. "This is a good spot."

It felt easy and right to stretch his arm around Irene's sun-warmed shoulders. Like her cheeks, her bare arms were dusted with freckles, which gave texture to her warm, sunburned shoulders. Marshall thought about running a finger along her slender forearm to feel the delicate raised knit of her young skin. He might trace the many constellations, the stars and dots of her freckles, like reading Braille.

Marshall drew Irene closer to him. He knew it was ridiculous, but force of habit made him ask, "I know you're too young for me, but maybe we . . ."

"And you're going to die too soon for me," Irene said quietly. She turned to look directly at him.

"Right you are." Marshall noticed for the first time that the young woman's eyes were hazel.

He felt his chest tighten. In the humidity, Marshall felt clammy rivulets running down his chest, following the raised staple marks and indention of his surgical scar. The surgeon had said it would take several years for the bruised and angry red scar to grow pale. But it would never look like real skin again.

A whoop and screech above as the infants wrestled on the highest tree branch. Marshall intuited his shot and disengaged from Irene to reach for his camera again. Fast clicks as Cape swung from impossible leap to leap in a treetop chase. When Cape pirouetted into a back flip and missed a branch, falling and screaming, Marshall was ready for the photograph: midair, arms flailing, tiny teeth bared, eyes huge, the baboon infant falling toward the concrete slope.

Without missing a beat in his grooming, Lion-Heart, sitting below, reached up and caught the somersaulting infant with one long arm. Not one of the baboons seemed surprised by the casual grace of this rescue or the fact that Lion-Heart held the infant aloft in one palm, as if he'd simply plucked ripe fruit, not a baby baboon, from the trees above.

Lion-Heart was rewarded for his solicitude by Senegal, who turned to cradle Cape with one arm and, with the other, began grooming the young male in return. At her long breast, Cape instantly fell into lip-smacking suckling and sleep. Lion-Heart shook his shaggy shoulders and settled into his well-earned preen.

The docent's clear voice carried to Marshall and Irene on the bench. "Friendship between male and female baboons like Senegal and young Lion-Heart here is what makes their societies so stable," she explained to the crowd. "It's not about paternity; it's about trust. In the wild, while the bachelor-boy baboons are off hatching their war plans, the females and their friendly males like Lion-Heart are making sure the next generation survives. Did you know, scientists now say baboons are capable of abstract thought, just like us?" With a respectful nod to Senegal, the docent concluded. "That's nothing new to the ancient Egyptians. Long ago they believed baboons were sacred. Toth, the baboon god, weighed the soul of a dead man."

Marshall was very still, keeping his camera on Senegal and Lion-Heart. How natural they seemed in their solicitude for each other, how careful and attentive their intimacy. By comparison, the human families strolling by this zoo exhibit seemed chaotic, their attention on everything except one another.

Squinting, Marshall turned his trained eye on the matriarch. The slope of her snout was unexpectedly elegant. In the dusky sunlight, her reddish fur was shot through with golden highlights.

From deep within Marshall, an unexpected longing: *Look my way, look my way . . .*

Gazing out now through the bars, the baboon let her brown eyes meet Marshall's. For a long moment, Senegal stopped grooming Lion-Heart and turned her complete attention to Marshall. Those level eyes, so familiar.

An explosion inside his chest and Marshall coughed, bending double. He hadn't felt a deep ache like this since just after the transplant.

Irene leaned over with him, whispering, "It's okay, Marshall."

Only then did he realize that Irene had her fingers on his wrist, unobtrusively taking his pulse.

"Your pulse is fine," Irene said.

Marshall shook her off and rummaged in his shirt pocket. He had forgotten his medication this afternoon There it was. He swallowed two prednisone pills and noticed that Irene took steroids of her own. What a sight they must be, downing drugs while tourists strolled by curiously.

"It's not the animal parts that will do us in," Irene said. "It's all these damn drugs."

"I didn't expect . . ." Marshall found it hard to breathe. "Didn't expect them to be so . . ."

"Beautiful?"

Soon he steadied himself, and they watched the baboons. Senegal had turned back to her nursing infant and Lion-Heart.

"I've been to the zoo only one other time in my life," Marshall said. "I'm not big on captive animals. But when I was a kid, my dad dragged us to the monkey cages . . ."

It was winter in Honolulu, and Professor McGreggor had insisted on taking his son and daughters to the zoo. Marshall's mother had refused to go along. Outside the rhesus monkey exhibit, the professor immediately became absorbed in taking Super Eight home movies of the animals.

The crowd had blocked Marshall's view. "I want see. I want see!" he'd screeched and run toward the monkey cage.

His eldest sister, Iolani, had lifted her little brother up and hadn't protested when he fiercely gripped the bars with two small hands. Suddenly a baby rhesus monkey ran over and reached between the bars to grab the boy's T-shirt and jerk him up against the bars. Again and again, as Marshall wailed, the small monkey tried to pull the youngster inside the cage, banging him against the bars.

"Daddy, what do I do?" Iolani screamed.

"Nothing! It's a great shot!"

As Marshall's father filmed the struggle, a zookeeper finally appeared and hastily separated the tiny monkey from Marshall. "Movie's over," he told the professor. "No harm done."

"Come here, son." Ian McGreggor could barely contain his grin. "Be a big boy. It's okay. Here, you can play with my camera. I'll show you how. Look through the viewfinder. See how easy it is? They're far away. They can't hurt you. Nobody can get to you."

Marshall never again went to the zoo. For many years, he woke up with nightmares—the grasp of the rhesus, those desperate eyes boring through his, the rank smell of the cage, those five fingers on his T-shirt as if the animal would never let go. Whenever Professor McGreggor showed that home movie and all the adults howled with laughter, Marshall left the room. When he was eight, his father gave him a camera. Marshall immediately sealed it in a clean plastic bag and carried it with his snorkel gear. His first pictures focused on the underwater world he most loved.

"So . . . ," Irene said encouragingly, "you don't like zoos?"

Marshall forced his attention away from the baboons and faced Irene. "I can't believe you really like it here, either."

Irene grinned. "Don't really know what I like now. I mean, me, a strict vegan, a card-carrying PETA member, animal rights activist, sitting here with a pig's heart valve inside me. I don't even know who I am anymore."

"Nothing's really changed. You're just going to live longer."

Irene's eyes widened. "You really believe that, Marshall? You really believe that our lives aren't totally different?"

He hesitated. "I don't know." Looking at the baboon exhibit again, he noticed Senegal watching him as she nursed her infant. Sepia tones, he suddenly realized. That's how he would shoot her, backlit with the fading light, Cape's soft, sleepy eyes unfocused.

"You know," Irene said, "your night nurse also told me about the nightmares . . ."

"It's the drugs."

"I've had them, too," Irene said, pushing on. "And bad feelings. Premonitions, like. I've read that DNA has memory—that every cell remembers who it belongs to. Listen, I've read that when researchers put one throbbing heart cell next to another in a separate petri dish, they beat independently, solitarily. But when scientists put several heart cells together in the same dish—even if the cells are not in physical contact, and without a brain to tell them what to do—those heart cells fall into the same rhythm. So, you and I have animal parts living inside us, Marshall. Doesn't that make you wonder about things—for us? Maybe even for them?"

"No," Marshall said quickly. He kept his eyes steady on Senegal behind the bars. But in his belly there was a swirling as he tried to push down another moment of physical panic. He shifted his gaze to the maple trees above the baboon exhibit, which were hung with moss like a kelp forest strangled by seaweed. He loved the patterns of plant, wind, and light. It was the same movement underwater, except no breeze, just currents.

"Well," Irene blurted, "I've kind of gotten into some activist things."

"Radical?" he asked, distracted. Once his mother had told him that every tree had a different song as the wind moved through the leaves.

"An underground group, ALL, Animal Liberation Lifeline . . ."

Marshall turned to look at her and saw a girl not much more than half his age, with weird hair and even stranger notions. "Let's go."

Irene stared past him, her jaw clenching. She seemed so dejected that he had to rejoin her on the bench.

"Sorry," he said. He again put his arm lightly around her narrow shoulders.

Irene faced him, her eyes fierce. "Will you ever really level with me?"

Marshall hesitated, and then said slowly, "Okay, okay . . . I've had . . . well, some strange feelings, too. Dreams."

"Like what?"

"Oh, Africa, I think, grasslands, steep cliffs . . ."

Irene sat up straight on the bench and leaned toward him. "Marshall," she said excitedly, "those might be cellular memories. It happens with heart transplants. Recipients can get the temperaments and certain personality traits of donors. Maybe your heart is trying to tell you something."

Marshall held up his hands. As much as he didn't want to disengage from this young woman's body, he did. He walked away from her to stand in front of the baboon exhibit. For a long time, he stood there alone, trying not to notice his racing pulse and the tightness in his chest every time Senegal paused in her preening to study him.

When at last Irene ventured near him, Marshall was studying the female baboon to figure out the right angle of light and speed to take a photograph. Not sepia, he decided now. Full color.

Irene did not touch him. "Did you ever read about the pot-bellied pig whose human companion had a heart attack? Well, that pig unlocked the front door and went right out into the street to play dead. Tried to stop passing cars. Three times the pig did this. Three times the cars just ignored her. But finally someone stopped and then followed that pig into the house. There was the woman, unconscious on the living room floor. They called nine-one-one, and that woman was saved because of her pig."

"So does this mean you're going to get a pot-bellied pig as a companion?"

Irene was quiet a long time. She and Marshall, like the baboons, were now gazing at the big-eared newborn in the crook of Senegal's arm. Cape stared through the bars, pulling on his mother's long nipple and lazily studying the two-legged, pale-skinned people outside his cage.

"Nope," she said. "I already live with an animal. Inside. Always inside."

When Andrew plunged into the gulf waters to join Marshall, he, too, noticed the horseshoe crab clinging to their diving buoy. "Here you go, buddy," he said, lifting the crab up gingerly and reaching over the side of the support boat to hand the creature up to the skipper. "See, something's still living here in these waters."

"For how long?" the skipper said.

Holding his regulator out of the water, Andrew swam back to where Marshall was treading water.

Marshall was fuming. "You didn't even give it a moment's thought—saving that crab."

"What's to think about?" Andrew was irritated and fiddled with his face mask. "I mean, isn't that the bloody point, Marsh? Isn't that why we're here? For the living?" Andrew scrutinized Marshall. "I know it must be, well, weird to be back in the water."

"Oh, for God's sake, shut up and dive!" Marshall snorted and slapped Andrew's oxygen tank. But he felt a sudden surge of excitement. The fear he'd first felt on entering the water was gone now as the steady swells lifted them.

Marshall clenched his regulator between his teeth and dove. He let his weight belt lower him through water that was clear and rich with marine life. Now he was in his element. Sinking down, his tank and camera gear no longer adding any weight, his flippers stroking the liquid life embracing him. But about fifty feet down lay a murky layer obscuring all in sight. Diving into this turbid cloud of stirred-up sediment and dead sea creatures, Marshall lost any sense of his surroundings. A flaccid jellyfish floated on the flat current. Marshall gave into panic again. It was like losing consciousness, swimming through these tiny corpses. He steadied his breathing, felt his heart strong and stable.

At last he settled onto the white sand bottom. Here, at least, he and Andrew had sunk beneath the worst muck of the Dead Zone. On the bottom, the waters were gray and terrifyingly empty. Gazing at this underwater world emptied of all life—no coral, no fish, no algae, nothing but the noxious oily streaks of red tides and lethal plankton blooms—Marshall felt the same blank horror as he had during the transplant surgery, when he seemed to float, gazing down at his own vacant chest. Andrew was right; it was unfathomable that everything in this seven-thousand-square-mile zone had died from hypoxia, or lack of oxygen. It would be as if every person in New York City were suddenly sucked dry of air and had suffocated together. Except this death had been agonizingly slow for the fish, the algae, the marine mammals, and his beloved coral.

Nearby on the ocean bottom, Andrew was agitated; he waved his long arms as if to say, *See, I told you.* Then he began to use the signs that Marshall was teaching him for underwater communication. *Look around. Nothing!* He shook his head.

The Dead Zone was seasonal, forming each spring and intensifying during the summer as the nutrient-rich runoff from overly fertilized farms and other chemicals, such as pesticides, flowed into the Mississippi River, which drained farmlands, cities, and prairies from the Appalachians to the Rockies. Farmers still protested the scientific proof that their agricultural runoff was partly to blame; but commercial fishermen in the gulf who were responsible for catching almost half the country's fish were alarmed and outraged. It was as if the Dead Zone foreshadowed a future war between those who farmed the land and those who fished the sea.

What works on land can poison the waters. Marshall wafted through this disturbingly quiet, dense sea. Only autumn and winter storms would bring any relief and new oxygen to these starved waters. Without any marine life, there were none of the landmarks or acoustic maps by which he usually navigated. Coral didn't pop and crackle, because it was dead; there was no visual flicker of danger from a hammerhead shark, no curious companionship of a loggerhead turtle. No swarm and flutter of clown fish or ugly, saw-tooth smile of a moray eel.

Marshall hummed to himself to offer some life to this forlorn marine world.

When a brown speckled eel
gets a-hold of your heel,
'at's a mor-aaaay!

This diver's ditty was a favorite joke between Andrew and Marshall, ever since they'd heard the famous oceanographer Dr. Sylvia Earle sing it during an otherwise serious lecture on endangered oceans. Marshall's fierce hum caught Andrew's hooded ear. Andrew abruptly stopped and stared at him quizzically until he recognized the tune and realized this was no diver's alert.

Nodding, but not grinning as he usually did when Marshall hummed underwater, Andrew led the way through the Dead Zone. Everywhere they looked it was the same barren wasteland of pallid, lifeless waters. Marshall could only imagine this once abundant coral garden slowly suffocating. How long did it take the algae to die and droop, becoming this rotting, ragged refuse, wisps of which straggled by in the vast emptiness? How long before the star coral paled into silence? How long for the storms of eddying orange sponges and delicate jellyfish to drift without pulsing?

Marshall reached for his underwater flashlight and the one camera he always carried that was loaded with black-and-white film. In a world drained of all its color and all life reduced to such a bleak, wavering blankness, that was how this Dead Zone should be photographed. No distraction of color film. He cast around for some object to focus on for his shot, but the world was a pale, empty canvas. He had never seen such an image—liquid, gray *nothingness*—in his viewfinder.

His heart began pounding erratically. A rush of terror much stronger than before. His teeth began chattering, and suddenly his wetsuit was a constricting vise tightening on his chest. *Not again.* Marshall checked his own pulse. Racing. He tried to breathe deeply but his air supply seemed too thin. Yellow splotches again flickered before his eyes, and a cold, clammy sweat broke out inside his neoprene skin.

For a moment Marshall thought he might lose consciousness, and he waved his arms wildly, as if to keep from fainting. He cast about for any signs of life underwater to focus his mind. But the Dead Zone's blank world disoriented him, and he found himself spinning crazily. Where was Andrew now? Marshall closed his eyes to blot out the sight of this gulf emptied of all life except his own—

Rocky cliffs standing straight up from grassy plains. It is evening and the savannah below is backlit by a scarlet sun sinking behind sparse trees. Tightly knit families of baboons sprawl lazily across these sleeping cliffs, socializing. A touch of skilled hands, a tender pull of fingers through thick fur of back and shoulders. After his three years of longing, the matriarch, Hara, now allows him to groom her. Now that Hara is his friend, he has found another family. A family to fight for and protect, a family to die for, if necessary.

But there is no threat now. It is another long day of hunting and foraging for fruits, tubers, and acacia buds. This year, there is no drought. He belongs here on these steep cliffs surveying the world of open veldt and savannah. He baby-sits Hara's newborn son, stroking his shiny pink face. The infant's fingers as slender as sweet grass.

His heart is complete. He has not been preened for so long, not since leaving his mother's troop to embark on his own journey. At last, on this long, lovely evening, it is Hara's touch he feels. It thrills him. Her hands are strong and sure, as are her powerful shoulders. Her massage at the small of his back eases an old wound inflicted by one of the other strong males in her troop, Namib, who once slashed him with his razor teeth.

The family is just settling down for the night when he hears a sound he has experienced only once before. It is the ringing voice of a man-animal as he thrashes at a scrubby thicket on the rocks below. Then there are other loud voices and a circle of men with dart guns. Chaos as the family scatters screaming. He does not scream, though he wants to. Nor does Hara as they gather up the babies to their bellies while trying to climb down the sleeping cliffs to run for safety in the tall grasses below.

The baby slows him down. He must climb very carefully for fear of dropping this special one, Hara's favorite son. But it is this burden that makes his descent so difficult. He is the last to drop down to the grass floor. And when he runs, the infant screams in terror, so he must slow down and cover the soft head with a comforting hand.

Sharp pain in his shoulder, and blackness pools in his eyes. But he must not drop Hara's son. Hara's newborn must be saved at all costs. So when he falls on his back, the baby safely clutched to his belly, his posture goes against gravity and his body's instinct for self-defense. The last image he sees is Hara clutching her daughter, teeth bared, trying to protect her as the men with guns circle them—

Someone gripped Marshall's shoulder, ripping the regulator out of his mouth, grabbing the backup buddy breather from Marshall's oxygen tank, and putting it in Marshall's slack mouth.

Like a goddamn pacifier. Marshall thrust Andrew away with so much force he sent him spinning backward in slow somersaults.

When Andrew tried to approach again, Marshall held up his arms.

Surface? Andrew spelled in sign language with some difficulty. *Heart?* he signed. *You need hospital?*

No! Marshall signed back. Though his breathing was still agitated, and his pulse racing, he had gotten hold of his mind. *I'm trying for a shot here. Leave me alone.*

Still trembling, Marshall managed to raise his camera and focus his entire being into the small square of the viewfinder. Black-and-white was the most difficult to shoot, especially underwater. He had designed and built his own waterproof camera. At least it, and his trained eye, would not fail him.

The tiny square of the viewfinder completely righted Marshall. Now he was in control again. And the vision? It was a hallucination. Maybe hypoxia. Marshall put the intrusive images out of his mind.

Focusing on what was left of a floating, shredded branch of star coral, Marshall waited until the black and white and gray of this Dead Zone was its most haunting. Click, click, click. Slow film. Clarity.

chapter seven

Homecoming

Of course he would be late. Isabel watched elegant travelers fill the Heathman Hotel's historic bar, long renowned as a Portland landmark. Andrew had even been born late. Sometimes her brother seemed like a man permanently mired in adolescence. Tapping her high heels against the immaculate floor, she was not only cross at Andrew's tardiness but also annoyed at herself. Why had she let Marian talk her into buying high heels and a silk suit from that catalogue? It wasn't as if this was a date. Marshall had made it clear that he and Andrew would be passing through Portland on business, attending this underwater photography conference. Then they were off to Seattle and Africa on diving assignments. Business—it was what they all could fall back on when there was little else to draw them together. Busyness.

Nearby, two men lounged in the bar. The elder man, silver-haired and impeccably dressed, was giving counsel to a protégé.

"Just because he's a friend doesn't mean you can trust him in business."

The younger man nodded. "Of course, sir," he said with just the right deference. "I won't trust anyone with this."

"Except me," the older man intoned with a laugh and then opened a gleaming gold case to choose cigars, which both men then sat rolling and licking unlit. The Heathman was a nonsmoking bar.

If Isabel had been in some Tanzanian rain forest doing primate studies, she might have written in her field journal, "Obsequious behavior, younger chimp. Submission to dominant male. Cigar as tool-making."

But instead, she ordered her favorite drink, a margarita. When Andrew had attended his first photography conference in Portland, he'd taught his older sister to drink these fizzy frozen concoctions with lime and salt on her hand. But here at the stately Heathman, Isabel would have to settle for a salt-rimmed glass. She tried to ignore the continuing lesson on power and success between businessmen.

One of the reasons Isabel had chosen marine mammals as her field of study was that the incessant hierarchical struggles of primates wearied her; she was much more fascinated by cooperative, altruistic cetacean societies such as that of the great orca whales. Their matriarchs held sway over their clan, called "killer whales" because of their skillful, focused group hunts. Yet the lack of competition or aggression within orca pods was still a scientific puzzle. Isabel always marveled over these cetacean cousins—from dolphin to gentle gray to humpback—whose bodies held such strength, yet who glided so kindly through troubled seas.

As Isabel watched the men at the next table order another round of martinis, she noted that the formal boundaries between the two were loosening. The protégé actually reached out and touched the elder man's elbow in a collegial gesture. If they had been chimpanzees, the leader might have registered this touch as an attempt at dominance and reacted violently with a screech and a calculated slap. But the senior businessman frowned and shifted in his seat away from his young companion.

Isabel settled into her cozy chair. It was so like her grandfather's long-ago lap. Except that this chair smelled faintly of wood polish and the musk of men's cologne, not the comforting fragrance of sea salt, cigarettes, and the lime-scented aftershave her grandfather splashed on after a day of fishing. In the long summer evenings, he'd call his grandchildren to his lap and together they'd read everything from seafaring novels to *National Geographic*.

World maps, imaginary islands like lost Atlantis, and sea monsters were what most fascinated Andrew as a child. But when Isabel was young, real, endangered animals mesmerized her. At seven, she was obsessed with dugongs. Cousins to the manatee and leatherback sea turtle, dugongs were predicted to be extinct in Australia and the Persian Gulf before

Isabel was old enough to help save them. Throughout her elementary school years, Isabel assigned herself the mammoth project of making a picture book devoted to extinct animals. She'd titled it *Noah's Lost Ark*, and by the time she'd reached sixth grade, its increasingly accomplished watercolor sketches of Badlands bighorns, silver trout, and Atlantic gray whales were famous among the other schoolchildren. As if to counter his sister's preoccupation with what was being lost, Andrew took up photography as a hobby at the age of twelve, using his grandfather's old Kodak.

"It's your hope that's your biggest gift—and your curse," Grandfather used to tell Andrew as his grandson spread *National Geographic* maps across the floor, even then plotting his travels. "Your unending hope."

"And it's your heart." Grandfather would give Isabel his most contemplative smile. "So be careful, my girl."

A man's purposeful steps sounded behind her, and Isabel turned expectantly. It was only the waiter. "Will you be having the salmon hash, then?" he asked, as if he had read her thoughts or recognized her.

At the Heathman, Isabel usually broke her moratorium on eating salmon. Even though farm-raised salmon were abundant, they were driving out the wild salmon, just as the huge factory trawlers had overfished oceans, bankrupting her grandfather. If it had not been for a small stipend left by his son, Grandfather, like so many of his Hebrides ancestors, would have "drowned in a sea of debt," as he said, "the only waters I can't sail."

"No, thanks," Isabel answered. She was ambivalent. The Heathman was famous for its rich smoked salmon, potato, and sweet leek hash, and she knew that Marian was expecting a to-go box upon her return to the forensics lab that afternoon. But the federal government had just announced this week what the Northwest had long dreaded—several legendary runs of wild salmon, this territory's totem, were now officially listed under the Endangered Species Act. Isabel jotted a mental note to make it up to Marian by bringing her a to-go box of another Heathman favorite—whiskey-drenched bread pudding. "I'll wait to order in the restaurant when my companions arrive."

"Oh, yes, Ms. Spinner," the waiter said with just the right mix of courtesy and recognition. Everyone at the Heathman knew Andrew Spinner was coming here for the photography conference. Not only was Andrew a Northwest native son who had made good, but he was also the photographer whose painterly portraits of Oregon coast sea stacks and mist-shrouded orca pods greeted guests in galleries around the world. Portland had been the first to recognize Andrew's talent; now he belonged to the world.

"Isabel!" Andrew called her from across the room as if he were hailing her from across the Pacific.

Isabel shrank farther into the sheltering armchair as everyone in the bar turned her way. She frowned. How like Andrew to announce himself *and her* to strangers.

But when she saw her brother decked out in his khaki slacks, bright African shirt, and pale pink "vest-of-many-pockets," as she called his trademark safari camera vest, she shook her head. Just once, couldn't he dress in the rain-diluted colors of his homeland—gray windbreaker and washed-out plaids?

"You don't have to scold me for being so late." Andrew leaned down and kissed her on both cheeks. Isabel noticed this new dramatic touch to his public persona. It was the way highly civilized men greeted each other in foreign movies. "I already see the annoyance on your face."

What did her face betray? "So where's your diving buddy?" Isabel asked, trying to keep her voice casual. "I just can't believe he's still alive."

"He'll be right here." Andrew sat back and studied his sister. "You still keen on him?"

"What a question, Andrew. We hardly know each other."

"Yeah, that's what Marsh is always saying."

"He talks about me?"

Suddenly Andrew frowned. "Be careful, Isa. He's not the same guy you met. He's . . . changed."

"Of course. It's amazing what he's been through . . ."

Andrew fell silent, fiddling with a cocktail napkin. "But . . . well, you think he'd be grateful to be still alive after all . . ." Andrew faded off, evading Isabel's scrutiny. "Maybe it's all the drugs they have him on— dozens of them. That's probably enough right there to change his moods a million times a day. But he's just weird, Sis. The things that used to make him laugh don't anymore. And then other things set him off . . . well, you'll see."

Andrew hesitated a moment and then nodded reluctantly. "Diving is the only time he's really happy."

"But he shouldn't be back diving so soon after . . ."

"Isa, you remember when Grandpapa took his boat out three weeks after his heart surgery? The fog, how long it took him to find his way home . . . ?"

Isabel remembered that night as if every hour were indelibly etched in her skin—a tattoo of terror. Grandfather had insisted the only way he could truly recover from his surgery *and* reckon with what he called "this little piggy" inside his chest was to get out on the water as soon as he was "seaworthy."

"I'm not like your folks," he'd promised his grown grandchildren. "I'll come back to you."

That night, the siblings had sat at the chipped green Formica kitchen table. Isabel brewed endless cups of peppermint tea, and Andrew studied a world atlas. When, at 2 A.M., Isabel called Maggie Salk at the sheriff's office to report a missing boat, her voice had quavered uncontrollably. It was Andrew who had to take the phone and make the report.

"Our grandfather," he'd said, "fishing off Blakeley's Point, the last he radioed in. Please. Find him."

At dawn, Isabel lay slumped over the table where she had fallen asleep. She awakened to the persistent scrape of spoon against porcelain as her brother beat pancake batter until it was too thin. "Rise up now and shine, sleepyhead!" Andrew said. It was how their grandfather greeted them every morning of their childhoods.

Grandpapa was sitting quietly across the kitchen table from her. His face was pale, grizzled. "I didn't need no Coast Guard," he growled good-naturedly at Isabel. "Seals steered me home in that fog."

When Isabel had leapt up and run over to embrace her grandfather, she slipped in some splattered pancake batter and fell down laughing and crying. It was the last time she could remember feeling such unfettered joy. Grinning, the old man had let her drape Great-grandmother Morag's horsehair blanket around his stooped shoulders.

"Yes," she told Andrew. "How could I forget?"

"Well, Marshall is a lot like Grandpapa. He just needs to get his sea legs back. Diving does it for him."

"But he could die at any time from complications, like all the others."

"Give it up, Isabel." Andrew shook his head. He reached across and took his sister's hand. Directly meeting her eyes, he said softly, "Give *him* up."

Her brother's hand was warm. She held on to him, able to take in his concern. "I have, Andrew," she said. Maybe it was the truth. "I have."

Arm in arm, Isabel and Andrew left the bar and strolled into the hotel restaurant. By the time Marshall found them, they were deep into the elegant menu.

"Are we having dessert first?" Isabel asked. "I recommend the whiskey bread pudding with caramel sauce."

Andrew sat back and laughed. "We'll make it two."

"Or three."

Both of them looked up, startled to see Marshall standing at their table. Without Silkie along, Isabel was often startled by someone's approach. But usually she tried to be more alert in public places.

In spite of herself, in spite of all her plans for an aloof and offhanded friendliness toward Marshall, Isabel felt her stomach dropping. She had expected to see a pale, weakened man, an invalid. Instead, Marshall's skin was sun-darkened, his demeanor confident and even playful. What was Andrew talking about? Marshall seemed transformed by good health, radiant even.

Where was that animal pain she had sensed in him the last time she'd been with him in his hospital room? Perhaps he had made his peace with the unsettling procedure. Simple, as Andrew had once said. Simple living.

Isabel cast a confused glance at her brother as Marshall leaned near her. She expected a brief hug, but instead Marshall held her close. His hair was scented of coconut. Must be from the shampoo his mother made for him. "Good to see you, Marshall," she murmured.

"And I hear it's you, Isabel Spinner, I have to thank for saving my life." Marshall let go of her to take his seat. He shot her a raised eyebrow. "Or blame."

There it was. The edgy bitterness Andrew had warned her about. But somehow it didn't put her off. Why not? Of all things Isabel most disliked about people, it was cynicism. Personal despair was an indulgence when so much around was endangered. What took real courage was hope. She couldn't figure out whether Marshall had given up on hope. Maybe he was simply living day to day without much expectation. Perhaps his uncertain future gave him a kind of buoyancy and bluntness.

"Blame?" she asked.

"Sure," he said. "Because you noticed something wrong on the video screen. Now I owe you."

"No, no, anyone would have noticed. You owe me nothing. Please, forget it."

Marshall eyed her a moment, then shrugged. "Okay. Forgotten. Now, what's good to eat here?"

He was so unexpectedly breezy. Maybe it was part of his way of coping with his "afterlife," as Marshall called his unexpected survival. Or maybe, as Andrew said, it was the effect of all those drugs. Had Andrew mentioned he was on an antidepressant? Enough. Isabel held up her menu like a small shield for some privacy to recover herself. Who cared what was going on with this man? He was, after all, still a stranger— attractive, likely doomed, and passing through. He was also probably, like some heart transplant patients, indulging in numerous affairs—just as couples often fall into frenzied lovemaking after attending a funeral.

"We're having dessert first," Isabel said, trying to match Marshall's light tone. "It's a Spinner tradition when we're in the big city."

"I'll have whatever you two are having," Marshall said.

"So you and Andrew are off to Africa again?" Isabel asked. "More aquatic ape research?" Her brother had been obsessed since childhood with that maverick theory of evolution and its hope for the undersea discovery of "missing link" fossils.

"Yeah." Marshall smiled. "Andrew tells me you have quite a fossil collection of your own."

Stung, Isabel looked down at her menu. Didn't Marshall remember the ammonite shell she'd given him? "Yes," she said shortly. How could she expect him to remember anything that happened the day of his heart attack? Still, she regretted having parted with such a precious golden shell, especially when it meant nothing to Marshall. Turning to Andrew, she said, "You want to split the shitake ravioli?"

"Nah," he said. "Something spicier."

As Isabel and Andrew bantered about what to order, Marshall pretended to study the Heathman's lengthy menu. The abundance seemed overwrought to him. But Marshall was quite pleased with himself. He had managed just the right lighthearted, friendly tone. He had taken an extra dose of that damned antidepressant the doctor was always pushing on him. "Think of it as a mood stabilizer," Dr. Lamb had said. "Just until you get the hang of things."

Getting the hang of it, that was a full-time job. Insomnia, those recurring nightmares that now sometimes happened in broad daylight. Handling himself, his inexplicable new yearnings for companionship, and these fierce emotions that washed over him like weather—now, that was as overwhelming as the fact that he was defying all odds and surviving.

But he had not betrayed himself yet to this woman who somehow still mattered to him, when not much else besides diving did. Isabel obviously had no idea that he had dreaded and dreamed about their meeting—that at the sight of her, his heart had actually quickened. Just like in those sentimental movies. Shameless and somehow lonely, this other primate inside him. Fortunately Marshall had some practice in evading intimacy.

A sudden distraction as his eyes strayed to Isabel's finely shaped fingers. Only a simple silver ring on her left forefinger. It was a silver Northwest Coast design of a stylized orca. As he squinted to see it better, Marshall noticed a splinter in her thumb. The skin was irritated, with little red streaks, and looked as if it had been unsuccessfully probed with a needle.

As if of its own volition, Marshall's hand moved to touch that splinter embedded in Isabel's thumb. His own gesture startled him so much that Marshall reared back in his chair. "Sorry, sorry," he muttered to Isabel, who smiled uncertainly.

"Splinter," he tried to explain, but shook his head. What was wrong with him? For a split second he saw another face before him—*gold eyes and sleek slope of snout. Cinnamon fur. Savannah sunlight and flat rocks.* Marshall closed his eyes.

"You all right, buddy?" It was Andrew, leaning to take his arm, his face concerned.

Marshall shook off his friend. "Sorry, sorry . . . ," he muttered and stood up. Fighting nausea, he made his way out of the restaurant. On the busy street, as bellmen navigated around him with their gleaming luggage carts, Marshall struggled to regain his calm. He felt his forehead. No fever. When would these panic attacks stop? Maybe he should call Dr. Lamb and adjust his medications. Maybe he shouldn't have self-prescribed that extra pill.

"This happens sometimes . . ." Andrew seemed torn between explaining to Isabel and following Marshall out of the restaurant. "I warned you." Abruptly Andrew stopped. "Just a minute." He jumped up and trailed after Marshall, almost tackling him as a taxi swerved to the curb. "C'mon, man," Andrew said and took Marshall's arm. "Where you running, Marshall?"

Marshall relented. "Sorry, just needed some air. I'm okay now."

The two men headed back into the hotel. Isabel had remained seated. Even from across the restaurant, Marshall noted her professional detachment and careful observation. He used to be like that.

"Should we worry?" Andrew asked him as they walked back to the table.

"No," Marshall said as they took their seats again at the table. "It's just a bad spell." He turned to Isabel and explained. "It's like the bends— sometimes I surface too fast."

"I understand," Isabel said politely.

She was more attractive than Marshall had remembered, and the shade of gray silk she was wearing perfectly matched her eyes. Marshall wished she had betrayed more pleasure in their meeting again. But then, he'd have to get used to women regarding him differently now. Damaged goods. Even Irene had told him as much. Embracing Irene had been the closest he'd come to sleeping with a woman since his transplant surgery. It was the first time in his life that he'd had no romantic offers and made none. Well, he'd attempted something with Irene, but she had insisted on them becoming friends.

"*Lifelong* friends," she'd emphasized. "Don't worry, Marshall. For you that's not really much of a commitment."

Friendship with a woman was something new for him. It was an intimacy a little like his teasing familiarity with his sisters. But with Irene there was the added dimension of shared experience—they both sometimes looked "askance and strangely," as Irene often said, at themselves.

Irene had shocked him six months ago by showing up on the Big Island, where he had gone home with his mother and sisters to recuperate after his transplant.

"Group therapy wasn't the same without you," Irene explained, as if it were the most natural thing in the world to fly across an ocean to take her wicker chair alongside him for the outpatient therapy sessions at Kona's community hospital. "We animal-farm people got to stick together."

That began a routine between them. Three times a week they attended transplant group therapy at the community hospital. Irene was living with her animal rights activist friends, and Marshall lived at his mother's sprawling house on Kealakekua Bay.

At first Marshall had half hoped this young woman was here with him because of some romantic notions. After all, to a twenty-year-old, privileged child of professors who had spent her life practically bedridden, reading instead of living, Marshall might have seemed intriguing.

But Irene set him straight when she picked him up in her rental car—a red Mustang convertible. "It's an understatement to say I haven't been out much," she grinned, honking and waving at a minivan loaded with surfers. "But you, Marshall . . . you've never really been in, have you?"

"In?" He was amused, noting with pleasure that Irene had put on a little weight and, in this tropical climate, her pale skin was soaking up sunlight like a plant leaning into light. Marshall was glad she had come to find him. But how had she figured out where he lived? He hadn't returned her calls or e-mails. Knowing Irene, she had probably wheedled it out of some nursing assistant. He had never met anyone quite so devious and yet honest as this young woman. She would make a formidable spy, if she weren't so left-wing.

"Inside yourself, I mean. Guys are like that, of course . . ."

"How would you know?"

She ignored him and then happily shifted into a grinding fifth gear to pass an elderly couple in a Cadillac. "Tourists!" she cursed.

Marshall grinned. "The minute the doc gives me permission to drive, you've going to take some lessons from me, kiddo."

"Don't call me that," Irene snapped. "If you had a kid, Marshall, she'd be way more messed up than me."

The comment hurt him more than he would have thought. "Why do you say that?"

"Because you've got no heart!" Irene burst out laughing and Marshall noticed suddenly the tiny wrinkles etched around her eyes like spider webs. "No, no, I don't mean that. Well, I do, kind of, but what I mean really is that you're like Teflon Man. You don't stick to anybody for long. That's why somebody just has to stick to you."

"And you're that somebody?"

"Yup. I figure I can teach you more about love by being your friend than by being your lover."

Taken aback, Marshall had turned away and watched the strong waves. At high tide, the surf on this point rose to the two-lane highway. Any day, another tsunami. "And you know a lot about being a lover?"

"All right, mister. I'm a virgin. Get over it. It's a condition I can always remedy now that I have more hobbies than just breathing. But that's not what you and I are about. You know it!"

"Yes," Marshall said slowly. "But I don't know what we're . . . about, as you say."

"We're different now. We have responsibilities. Our lives are not just our own."

Marshall snorted. "You've been in the transplant group too long."

"I'm going to live a long time," she corrected. "And I want to give something back, after what was sacrificed for me. Don't you ever feel that way? Not one bit?"

Marshall was silent. The fact that he'd been researching and planning a trip to Africa for more aquatic ape research and to document a recovering coral reef for a grassroots conservation group—he told Irene none of this. What he told her instead was, "Not one bit."

"Well, then, I'll tell you something," she said heatedly. "I'm not just here for you. Although you're partly why I came. I'm here to help out in some undercover research at a primate lab in Honolulu. My friends in ALL, the animal rescue underground, are helping me check out reports of horrible conditions at . . ."

"That's enough," Marshall said. "I'm driving from now on."

"There's nothing wrong with my driving. And you can't yet."

"There's everything wrong with your driving."

"I get it. You don't want to know anything about my real work here."

"Your real work is getting well, Irene. Getting a life, a boyfriend, maybe a family someday. That's what's important."

"Oh, I see how important it is to you."

Marshall shook his head. "Listen, Irene. I'm glad you're here. The transplant group without you would be worse than my nightmares. But let's make an agreement. I don't ever ask to sleep with you. You don't ever tell me what nonsense you're getting mixed up in."

Irene swerved to the side of the road and stopped the car. She turned to him with an expression so full of regret that it startled him. Had other women looked at him this way and he'd never really seen it, or felt it?

"I may be younger than you, Marshall, but I know more than you do."

"Oh, you do, do you? Like what?"

"I know how to love, damn you. Why else do you think I'm here?"

"For the animals?"

"Idiot! Don't you think that includes you?"

For a moment he could say nothing. Irene was right. Perhaps he was more animal now than human. "You've made your point," he snapped.

"Listen, Marshall. There's more. We're different. You've always been healthy, until your heart attack. And now your heart is strong again. But I've always been sick, until now. Before this surgery, I was sentenced to a contemplative life."

"I know it's been tough for you," Marshall said. Now he realized those wrinkles around her eyes were premature. He suddenly saw Irene as a young girl sitting in bed, propped up by pillows, her bed piled with books. Here was a girl who had never run on a playground, wrestled with a sibling, run full tilt through the woods. "I'm sorry about all that. I'm glad you're going to have a better life now. It makes me . . . happy."

Irene's smile was so suddenly exuberant that it broke his heart. "Do you know what I can do now? I can go to Greece and study the Eleusinian mysteries. I can go to India and hope to meet the Dalai Lama. I can volunteer to live way up high in an ancient redwood tree and protect her from loggers. I can rescue animals imprisoned like I was for twenty years. I can make sure they have a place to run and play again and be wild. I can learn to scuba dive. Will you teach me?"

"Yes, " he said and did not embrace her.

Instead, Marshall met her hazel eyes and felt an opening within his chest. He would take her to his favorite diving spots, warn her not to go near the barracuda or snaggle-toothed moray eel, show her the brilliant clown fish and electric blue-silver schools of anchovies. He would introduce her to his sisters and maybe ask Nohelani to teach her sign language so they could talk underwater. "I will teach you."

"And I'll teach you, too."

"Okay . . . but what?"

"About yourself. You know, Marshall, you're really pretty perceptive about other people, but not about yourself. You're clueless."

"So what don't I know about myself that you think you do?"

"That you are capable of great . . . devotion. You're generous, but you're just so afraid to get hurt or left that you haven't ever fully given yourself to anyone else. Have you? Well, if you have, tell me." Irene sat back and studied him with a grin. "Make my day."

Marshall was quiet. Was it true what Irene saw in him? He didn't know. Maybe he should ask his sisters if they saw him that way. It occurred to him that he had always relied on his sisters, his mother, and their sprawling family to be his emotional compass. They and these islands were so much his home he'd never needed to risk settling down. Even now, he could retreat to his family home and heal. Because of them, he had never believed himself truly alone. But what would his life have been without them? Would he have extended himself more? Would he have married and made his own family?

Marshall reached out a hand to Irene. "Friends," he said. "Lifelong."

The young woman studied him as if searching for signs of hesitation or dishonesty. Then she nodded seriously. "You'll beat the odds, Marshall."

He knew exactly what she meant. The odds against the immunosuppressant drugs devastating his immune system and causing cancers, the many side effects of chronic organ rejection, the life-threatening risk of this trial xenotransplantation. "Hope so."

"Your heart will take. You won't reject it. I'll help you."

For a moment he thought he might weep—a rising in his belly like grief or something else he did not recognize. Gratitude? Hunger? "Drive," he said suddenly to hide his feelings. But Irene had seen his emotion. "Drive and dive," he said. "I know a little shop that has shrimpy wetsuits to fit you. And I know a beach with green sea turtles who still like to swim with the likes of us people."

It became their daily routine. During the mornings, Marshall taught Irene diving, emphasizing safety and the beauty of the tiniest undersea life. Sometimes she was mysteriously unavailable. Marshall didn't ask. Nor did Irene ever tell him about the details of her undercover work in a nearby primate lab.

She did tell him when she had to leave Hawaii. Her work had helped expose the plight of a dozen medical lab chimpanzees who were, amid much public outcry, at last being released and retired to a primate sanctuary. Now that the chimps were safe, Irene was headed to Ellensburg, Washington, to do some volunteer work at the renowned Chimpanzee and Human Communication Institute. "Don't you think I'm putting my trust fund to good use?" she'd teased Marshall. "I'll even buy you a ticket to come visit me there."

"I'll get my own ticket, thank you kindly, ma'am," he'd said.

Marshall had promised to visit Irene after the photo conference in Portland. Now in the Northwest, he looked forward to seeing her again, just as he had been excited to see Isabel. It was the last thing he had ever expected—to be seeking out women as friends, to be keeping in touch with Andrew for more than just diving. It was not what he used to do; it was unfamiliar and risky. And right now, at their elegant hotel table, it was not going so very well.

"So, Isabel," Marshall said, not knowing exactly what he might do to reach out across her polite distance. "You want to come to Africa with us to find aquatic ape fossils?"

He could not tell which of the three of them was more shocked—himself, for betraying anything deeper than a passing attachment to Isabel, Andrew for his friend's unexpected suggestion, or Isabel for his sudden offer.

Each of them was stunned into silence. And before Marshall could make light of his invitation, there was a melodic beeping from someone's cell phone. They all searched in their satchels and pockets.

"Excuse me," Isabel said. Taking the call, she listened for long minutes without saying a word, and when she did, all she said was, "I'll be right there."

Isabel stood up from the table and announced, "I'm really sorry, but I've got to get back to the coast. You two enjoy your lunch—and the conference." With a distracted frown, she embraced her brother and explained in a worried voice, "Mass stranding."

"We're coming with . . . ," Andrew began. "Oh, I forgot. I have to give a speech tonight."

"I'll come," Marshall stood up, his body again acting against his will.

Dubiously Isabel glanced at him. She seemed to be judging him. "All right," she said at last. "It's really bad on the beach. We need all the help we can get."

chapter eight

Stranding

As she drove the winding roads along the Oregon coast, Isabel couldn't help glancing at Marshall. He had barely said a word during the two-and-a-half-hour drive. She didn't mind his silence; what distracted her was his obvious inner turbulence. She had been wrong to allow Marshall to come with her, especially when she needed her wits about her. Isabel noted that he had taken several doses of pills—the lifelong ritual of any transplant patient. Andrew was right; they probably affected Marshall's moods—and his stamina.

"Listen," she told him, "a stranding might be too much for you. Let me drop you in town. I've got to pass by the tavern anyway on my way down to the beach."

Marshall was quiet for so long that Isabel interpreted his silence as acquiescence.

"Okay, I'll let you off at the Ocean Haven Tavern."

"I don't drink anymore." He turned to her and surprised Isabel with a smile. "You and your brother have a lot in common."

"Like what?"

"You both have a need to nurture," Marshall said. "Animals. People . . . me."

"That's hard for you?"

"It's sweet, Isabel," he said, and then added, "but it can be . . . well, a little obnoxious."

Stung, Isabel resolved that she would just drop him in Lawasskin. Let

139

him be alone. How could she have ever imagined that she and Marshall might be connected? Besides, she had far more important things to deal with right now.

At the last stranding, in 1998, they had successfully rescued half the forty-odd pilot whales that washed up on her beach. Isabel hoped the many drills she'd run her stranding network through had prepared them for whatever was going on now. Mentally, Isabel calculated how much heavy equipment she could count on—Daniel McHalffey would bring his large van, and Marian's brother had his flatbed truck parked at the marina, in case any cetaceans needed to be hauled to Newport Aquarium for medical treatment. But would it be enough for the dozen whales Marian said had already washed ashore?

As if sensing Isabel's withdrawal, Marshall shifted uneasily in his seat. He propped a boot up on her dashboard, as if he was only now settling in.

Isabel frowned. Just ten more miles to Lawasskin and she'd be free of him. It wasn't worth any more tension.

"Listen, Marshall, I've got a lot on my mind right now with the stranding. Can we talk about this another time?"

"Sure, sure." He fell silent.

Another five miles and Isabel felt a pang of relief and something else—loss. It irritated her, the part of her that would remain open to Marshall. It was what Grandfather had both praised and cautioned her about—her heart. Sometimes it was just plain unrealistic.

"Isabel," Marshall reached over and touched her arm lightly. "Sorry if I hurt your feelings."

Isabel seemed to consider his apology for a moment and then nodded. But she said nothing more.

Marshall knew she was exasperated with him, but since his transplant he had so little control over his impulses. Like now. All he wanted to do was help out with the stranding, talk about something safe like the time he'd been on a New Zealand beach and helped refloat a dozen whales. But no, every time Marshall opened his mouth, he blurted out exactly the wrong thing. Like now.

"I don't know why I'm still alive," he said suddenly. "My mother says it's because, when I was home, she lay me in the surf like the old ones healing the smallpox from our people. Dolphins came near, sounded me. Maybe, she said, they accepted my heart for me."

Isabel turned to him. "Marshall, I can't imagine what it's been like for you this past year, not knowing if you're going to live from day to day. But I'm so glad you're still here."

Marshall felt warmth in his chest, almost as if someone had placed a hand against his sternum. His gaze again rested on Isabel's thumb and that festering splinter. "I'm so different. I'm really not myself anymore."

"You'll figure it out with time."

"Time . . ." he echoed.

For a moment Isabel seemed to come close, but then she turned her attention back to the road. Yet her glance still held him somehow. Marshall was surprised at the sensation of warmth spreading now from his chest to his belly and groin. His legs pumped blood as if he were getting ready to run for his life.

"You know, the last time we drove this coast road together, you and I talked about our family myths—my sea turtle ancestors, your silkies . . ."

Isabel turned to focus her pale gray eyes on him for a moment. "I'm surprised you remember."

"Of course, I remember," he said. Then he turned to stare at her profile. "But, it's one thing to talk about animals and humans living so close together. It's another thing to have part of some other creature actually living inside your chest."

"What's it like?"

"It's so goddamn *strange*." Marshall threw up his hands and turned away. What was he doing? And why was he confiding in Isabel, of all people? She would probably be the most judgmental of all. She believed his transplant was a waste of a wild animal. Maybe even a crime.

"It's not scientific, doesn't make sense," Marshall blurted. "But sometimes I really think I get memories that don't belong to me . . ." He stopped, staring out the window. "It's just crazy."

Isabel pursued him. "Memories? Not yours? Tell me . . ."

For a moment Marshall felt trapped, claustrophobic, and his heart thudded with a surge of fear. He tried to pull in the deep relaxing drafts of air his doctor had taught him to inhale whenever he endured what the medical world called panic attacks, common after a heart transplant. *Breathe into your belly,* the cardiologist had advised. *Breathe out through your mouth . . . slowly, slowly.*

"Another bad spell?" Isabel asked.

"No," he breathed.

"Any other . . . sensations? Strange symptoms?"

"No," he lied.

"Maybe you'll tell me more about it, Marshall," Isabel said simply and focused now on the beach below. "Another time." She fell quiet and speeded up.

Marshall turned back to the window. He noticed that they had passed the Ocean Haven Tavern without stopping, without her abandoning him.

As they descended toward Kiwanda Beach, the road's shoulder was dangerously washed out in places. Far down the beach, Marshall saw flashing red and orange signal lights from emergency vehicles and dark shapes running. From this distance it was a pantomime of pandemonium. He counted at least ten sloping whale bodies like small mountains on the white sand.

"Looks bad on the beach," Marshall said.

"I know." Isabel leaned into a curve and took it on two wheels. "We've got to get down there."

Wheels bouncing along barnacled rocks and sliding on seaweed, Isabel drove fast down the long beach. They were halted at a roadblock manned by a young agent from the National Marine Fisheries Service. He held up his hand to stop Isabel's truck and wave them toward a detour route.

"I'm with the stranding network volunteers," Isabel told him brusquely.

The young man recognized her. "Oh, right," he said politely, "you're Stewart Salk's wife. Come on through."

"*Ex*-wife," Isabel informed the young NMFS agent firmly and drove past a caravan of official trucks and heavy equipment. Activity was frantic all around them as they raced down the beach. A crowd had gathered, some of them in wetsuits braving the treacherous surf.

Isabel turned to Marshall and saw him studying the water. It was high tide. Marshall's forehead was deeply creased with concern. She briefly touched his hand. "Are you sure you're up for this?"

"I'm sure," he said.

A uniformed man brought them to a stop on the wet sand. "Oh, no," she groaned. It was Stewart at his most officious.

"You should have been here hours ago," Stewart began, and then noticed the stranger in Isabel's passenger seat. "Who's he?" Stewart demanded.

"Stewart, this is Andrew's friend Marshall McGreggor," Isabel said. "He's a trained diver." Isabel cast him a quick glance. "He's here to help. Now, let's get to work."

Without a word, but with his all-too-familiar frown of blame and longing, Stewart waved his ex-wife through the maze of machinery and rescue equipment.

Marshall grinned. "Are all your exes this jealous?"

"He's not dangerous."

"No," Marshall said, "of the two of you, I'm sure *he* is not the dangerous one."

Before Isabel could respond, she saw a wild churning in the surf and the heartrending sight of the mass stranding. Fifteen or so whale and dolphin dorsal fins of all sizes and shapes waved crazily in the waves, while a chain of rescue workers stood unsteadily in the sand.

"Hold the line!" Everyone was shouting encouragement. "Push them back to sea!"

But whales surged forward with each wave, their bodies turning in the undertow.

"Keep them floating! Keep them off the beach!"

More than a dozen whales had already run aground. They lay helpless on the sand, their grace and buoyancy gone as their massive body weight painfully crushed their bones and internal organs. Around each of the beached whales was a circle of volunteers passing pails of seawater hand-over-hand in an attempt to lower the whales' body temperature and cool their exposed skin. More than fifty trained volunteers and tourists stood waist-high in the surf, pushing the whales back to sea. Others attended already beached animals. Schoolchildren drenched bedsheets in seawater; then they ran to lay this scant protection over the whales' and dolphins' sun-blistered bodies. Isabel heard exhausted blasts of breath from many blowholes, high-pitched whistles, and the rapid clicks of distress calls as the whales and dolphins cried out for their pods.

From their strained and despairing faces, Isabel knew that her stranding volunteers had been rescuing animals since she got the call in Portland. Several of the thinnest volunteers were so cold that, when she stood near them, she could hear their teeth chattering. But she knew not one of them would go home, even if she told them to rest.

"At least the tide is in," Isabel told Marshall grimly. "We have some time."

"God, I hope we can help them!"

Isabel and Marshall leapt from the pickup and began rummaging in the bed for their wetsuits. Neither glanced at the other as they stripped quickly and layered on underwear and neoprene and waterproof boots. Marshall was the first to finish and ran off to join a group of volunteers in the surf surrounded by flailing fins.

Isabel grabbed her veterinary bag and sprinted straight toward a shuddering whale encircled by shouting rescuers. It was a minke whale. Isabel immediately recognized it by the broad white stripe on the pectoral flippers. At only thirty feet long, minkes are among the smallest whales, and until this century, commercial whalers had passed them by in favor of larger, more lucrative whales. But now the minke was the world's most hunted whale. Every year the Japanese hunted minkes for "scientific research," even though the valuable whale meat mostly ended up in Tokyo fish markets. This minke's body was already curved from too much time lying on the sand. Even if they could lift her back into the surf, she might not be able to swim straight.

When Isabel appeared, the crowd parted to let her through. She knelt down with her medical bag and placed a practiced hand on the minke's side. With concern she noted that the skin, usually cool and the texture of silken rubber, was already hot and dry. A volunteer wept as she poured seawater over the whale's heaving side.

"Oh, Isa, you're here," Marian called out as Isabel approached. She was tending a trembling Dall's porpoise whose brown eye was rolling backward as she labored for breath. "Body temp is swinging hot and cold. Now she's burning up!"

"Blood test?" Isabel held the porpoise's fin as if it were a patient's exhausted hand. She felt the fragile finger bones inside the fin. Evolution had padded a perfect skeletal hand here inside buoyant blubber. "Any infection?" she asked Marian.

"Not yet," Marian answered, "but my last blood test was an hour ago. God, there are so many whales and dolphins, I haven't had a chance to stay with one for long."

"I'll take another blood sample and we'll see." Isabel expertly swabbed the porpoise's fin with alcohol and pulled scarlet blood up into the syringe. She noted that the porpoise was female and still smelled of brine and kelp. Downwind, the scent of death gave even more urgency to Isabel's work, though her actions were careful and skilled.

"How's her circulation?" Isabel asked Marian. The two women spoke in the quiet, respectful voices they used in their forensics lab.

"Not so good," Marian said. "Slowing down."

The even tones of the women's voices seemed to calm the Dall's porpoise somewhat. Isabel fought off the empathy that always seized her when she was too near animal suffering. Instead she concentrated on keeping herself steady and reassuring so the porpoise might stop flopping and settle enough for Isabel to listen to her heart with her stethoscope. Like muted thunder, the porpoise's heart beat erratically. Isabel stood up, calling out, "Get me more ice to pack her tail flukes and flippers!"

The Dall's porpoise's soft, unblinking eye fixed on Isabel's every move, while Marian helped several others splash and sponge cold seawater along the length of her. To an untrained eye the porpoise might be mistaken for a baby orca, with her black-and-white body. Isabel saw skin cracking along the animal's pectoral and dorsal fins. This was not the time to remember that the skin of whales and porpoises was twenty times more sensitive than humans'. It was as if the porpoise were enduring an earthquake from the inside out, her tender skin ripping open along fault lines. "Is her whole pod stranding?" Isabel asked.

Marian shook her head. "That's what's so strange. There are all kinds of cetaceans on the beach, not just one pod stranding with its leader. So far, we've identified several minkes, a goose-beaked whale, this Dall's porpoise, and some white-sided dolphins. Whatever's wrong with these animals is cutting across species." Marian hesitated. "I've never seen a goose-beaked anywhere, much less here in these waters. Can't imagine what could disorient and strand so many different species swimming at different depths." Her face was streaked with sand and blood. "What in the world is going on here?"

Isabel briefly embraced her, then leaned again over the porpoise, looking for any signs of boat propeller slashes or possible pollutants, such as oil or paint. In a soothing voice Isabel spoke to the terrified creature, whose primary sense was hearing.

"Shhh . . . the water's not far away from you. It's okay . . ."

She examined the porpoise's vaginal and mammary slits. "This is a lactating female," she called out to Marian. "She's just given birth. That means she's got a little one out there somewhere." Isabel tore off her surgical gloves and ran toward the surf, calling back to her friend, "Stay with her. I'm going to go see if I can find her calf!"

In the turbulent surf, Isabel barely kept her balance. Punishing waves crashed over her shoulders as she reached out and embraced a flailing calf. It was a tiny Dall's porpoise calf driving headlong toward the sand. "I've found the calf!" Isabel yelled, but her voice was lost in the surf. Other rescuers called out, encouraging one another as they successfully pushed at least three whales and a dolphin back into the sea. But the larger whales languished on the shore. No one could lift them.

"We're losing these guys!" a volunteer shouted helplessly and heaved against the goose-beaked whale's dark purple body.

"Oh, God, there must be thirty of them!"

"And more coming in! Look!"

A wall of whales, like a tsunami of dark, twisting shapes, surged toward shore. Some of the rescuers scattered to escape being crushed, but Isabel stood her shifting ground and held on to the thrashing calf.

This calf had almost zero chance of survival without a mother. In all her years studying cetaceans, Isabel had never once seen an abandoned dolphin calf. The bond between cetacean mothers and their offspring is so strong that the only reason a calf would ever be left alone is if the mother is dead. And if a calf died, the grief-stricken mother would carry the corpse with her pectoral fins until it decomposed.

Clutching the yardlong calf to her own belly, Isabel held the trembling calf as securely as she imagined a mother might. Sometimes she even had to clamp hold of the tiny black-and-white dorsal fin to keep the calf's breathing blowhole above water. A species known for its exuberant bursts of speed, this little Dall's frantically thrust his tail flukes against Isabel's grasp.

"Calm down, buddy," she said, trying to soothe the calf. "I've got you safe."

Isabel kept all her attention on this one calf, trying to stay clear of the roiling whales stranding all around her. In her bones, Isabel could feel the echo of bleeps, frightened ultrasonic chirps, as the dolphins signaled vainly to their pods. Their vocalizations were usually above her human hearing, but now many of the dolphins had tuned their pitch lower, so their lost calves might hear. This lower sound frequency made it possible for Isabel to hear more dolphin vocalizations than ever before in her life. And it was terrible. So many voices calling out for so many lost.

As she counted the juveniles and calves washing ashore, Isabel was shaken at the sight of all the abandoned offspring. In fact, it seemed that most of the stranding whales were juveniles or calves. How had they gotten separated from their mothers and pods? Why were there so many *different* kinds of cetaceans here? This was not a normal stranding. Isabel felt a chill that had nothing to do with hypothermia. She'd never heard of anything like this. What had driven all these whales and dolphins to die on the beach?

As soon as she asked the question, Isabel regretted it. Some memory or sensation rose up inside her body. It began as an ominous humming like the far-off grinding of a generator that groaned, growing louder until it thundered in rolling waves of pressure—and pain. It felt like someone repeatedly punching her in the belly. Painful pulses, and then a loud noise penetrated her chest and head. Inside her body was a shuddering, and she felt her lungs vibrating.

Breathless, Isabel bent double, barely able to hold on to the calf. She endured the porpoise's pain as her own. Nauseated by the noise imploding, Isabel struggled against the horrible sound. It was a sound that nature never made. It was not the sonorous, subsonic bass voice of blue whales and volcanoes, of thunder and earthquakes. It was not even the howling roar of a tsunami rising up midocean. The sound had no harmonics, no natural melody or range; this unbearable wave of pinging, piercing pressure and metallic shrieking must be human-made. But who would make such a horror—and why?

On an instinct, Isabel managed to turn the Dall's body sideways to check the pinprick ear hole right behind each eye. Porpoises and dolphins had no external ears to slow down their streamlined bodies. Through a complex evolution, cetaceans had developed an ultrasound sonar and echolocation that let them see with their ears. Often Isabel had marveled as she witnessed dolphins expertly find fish in murky waters or use their sensitive forehead, or melon, to send out short bursting pulses, click trains, to accurately scan the ocean bottom.

A rivulet of blood ran from each tiny ear hole. Scarlet bubbles gurgled from the calf's blowhole. The calf was twisting not just in terror but also in pain. *A deaf whale is a dead whale.* Isabel considered letting her little Dall's porpoise mercifully strand along with his dying mother. But someone was shouting to her over the waves. It was Marshall. She called to him.

Isabel's grip on the small, slippery calf tightened. "I've got an abandoned calf here! The mother may be the one Marian's tending up on the beach."

"Hold on!" Marshall yelled and made his way toward her.

It was hard going for Marshall with all the whales tumbling dangerously near him.

"Disoriented, shock . . . ," Isabel said. Marshall helped her hold the calf above the waves. "So many others are dying on the beach . . . Got to get this calf to the aquarium."

She pointed to her pickup on the beach. It was already filled with ice surrounding a Pacific white-sided dolphin calf. "Can you help me get him into the truck?"

Marshall and Isabel struggled to hoist the Dall's completely out of the water. Isabel figured the three-foot-long calf weighed just a little over twenty-five pounds, but he was thrashing about in such panic that it took two of them to tenderly carry him over to the truck bed.

"One, two, three!" Marshall counted, and they carefully lifted him into the ice. In this makeshift cradle, they packed the Dall's porpoise so tightly he couldn't move.

"Marian says we've got nine already dead on the beach," Isabel said. "Five of the smaller whales got pushed back into the sea. At least for now. Don't know how we'll save the others still washing in . . ."

Marshall scanned the horizon. "When's low tide?"

"Six hours away." Isabel placed a hand on the Dall's porpoise to check his heartbeat. "But at least we can get these two calves to Newport Aquarium. Can you come with me? Or do you want to stay here?"

"I'll come along with the calves."

"I think I saw Marian euthanizing what might be his mother up on the beach. Not a lot of hope for this little one. You know that, Marshall."

Marshall soothed the tiny Dall's porpoise and splashed it with a bucket of seawater. Isabel listened to the Pacific white-sided dolphin's heartbeat. She intended to drive the truck like a demon the two hours to Newport. Ever since the aquarium had returned the famous killer whale Keiko to his Icelandic home waters, there had been an empty pool. Someone had already radioed ahead to have the aquarium tank filled and ready for any possible stranding survivors.

"You ever seen anything like this?" Marshall asked Isabel as they both stripped out of their neoprene wetsuits on the beach. She had seaweed caught in her hair and wrapped around one leg. Marshall bent down and untangled kelp from Isabel's bare foot.

"Never," she said grimly. "When we first checked most of them for injury, the animals appeared healthy. Except that some of the animals have a little bleeding around the ear holes and eyes. Could be an internal rupture or hemorrhage."

Isabel turned her attention to the abandoned calves again. With her stethoscope she listened to the Dall's porpoise's wildly erratic heartbeat. If they didn't get these cetaceans to the aquarium and medical help quickly, they would both die from exposure and dehydration. "I'll ride with the calves in the back of the truck to keep an eye on their vital signs," she said. "Can you drive?"

"Sure."

As Isabel and Marshall jumped into her truck, they heard Marian calling from far down the beach as she ran toward them.

"Stop!"

Jumping down from the truck bed, Isabel met a breathless Marian.

"You can't leave!"

"Marian, you're more than capable of taking over for me as beach-master," Isabel said, holding her friend steady in the sinking, wet sand.

"I know, but there's some guy on the beach doing necropsies, Isabel. Nobody's ever seen him before. Refuses to give his name. Got some badge he flashes around . . . says it's official business."

"Tell Stewart," Isabel said, and was about to jump back in the truck when Marian held her back.

"Stewart is telling everybody that this guy's legit. *He* won't stop him. It's not like the guy is doing a good job of his necropsies. He's moving so fast from whale to whale, more like he's *stealing* than collecting samples."

"That's not right," Isabel said.

"There's something else." Marian lowered her voice. "There're some whales also stranding up the coast near Vicente. And we're getting radio reports from fishermen out by Seal Rock who say they saw a minke whale so agitated that she was skimming across the water like she was trying to outrun something."

"I've never heard of a minke porpoising fast like that," Isabel said.

"And then we got a shortwave call from a whale-watching boat. They had their hydrophones in the water and heard this insistent pinging, really loud. The transient orcas they were watching tightened into a defensive group around a newborn calf. When the pinging got so intense that people could even hear it *above* water, the orcas exhibited extreme escape behavior."

"Must be some kind of acoustic stress or harassment," Isabel muttered. She looked at Marian suddenly. "You know, I've read about something like this happening before. I think it was in the waters off

Greece recently . . ." She grabbed Marian's arm. "Let's see what the hell is going on here."

Isabel started off down the beach with Marian. She called over her shoulder, "Marshall, can you get volunteers to keep an eye on the calves until we can drive them to Newport? Then come help us?"

Immediately Marshall leapt from the truck. He ran over to a volunteer, filling her in and telling her they'd be right back. Then he caught up to run alongside Isabel and Marian. Stranded whales lay everywhere.

As they ran together down the beach, Isabel listed the strange symptoms. "Bleeding, disorientation, agonistic behavior . . ."

"What does *agonistic* mean?" Marshall asked.

"When you were first in the water with them," Isabel asked him, "did you see the whales and dolphins thrashing among themselves? Sometimes defensive, sometimes violent? Confused, as if they'd . . ." Isabel stopped and then suggested, "As if they couldn't navigate, had lost their bearings. Did you notice any injury to their heads or their ear holes?"

"Yes," Marshall said. But before he could say more, Isabel was stopped midrun by a man she didn't recognize.

"Far enough, lady," the man commanded. He looked like a plainclothes policeman.

Stewart and another man were beside the stranger, scowling at Marshall. "Isabel . . . get out of here!" Stewart ordered.

"Stewart, if we're going to fight about who has the most authority here, you do," Isabel said. "But it's my job to necropsy these bodies." Isabel took a long look at the whales and dolphins thrashing on the beach. So many. She'd never seen a stranding like this. "You know," she said, "we should declare this a possible crime scene." Isabel noted that Marian had avoided the men and run on ahead of her to where the stranded and dying whales lay. She sealed off the area with wooden stakes and the official yellow crime scene tape she always carried in her forensics bag.

"You're relieved of jurisdiction here . . . Ms. Spinner, isn't it?"

Isabel focused on the stranger next to Stewart. She vaguely recognized the man, and then it came clear. This was the young scientist she'd first met on the seismic research boat last year when Marshall had his heart attack. What was his name?

"Dr. Alexander Sharp," the man reminded her with a formal smile. He clearly remembered her, since his manner was collegial yet still slightly controlling.

Unlike at their last meeting, Sharp was now obviously in charge, and he was directing whatever was going on here on her beach. Was his a rescue operation? Isabel couldn't ever recall the military involved with stranded whales before. But perhaps she could persuade them to assist.

"Are you here with Dr. Winthrop's team?" Isabel asked, trying to open a dialogue. "Are you helping out with the stranding?"

"Dr. Winthrop has moved on to the South Pacific," Sharp told her. "I'm in charge now."

"Of what?" Isabel asked, confused. Then she suddenly remembered reading of the deaths of two whales connected with acoustic sonar mapping of undersea faults off California. Was that what Dr. Sharp was doing here? Some kind of underwater acoustic testing?

"Of all . . ." The young scientist hesitated. "All rescue operations."

Beyond Dr. Sharp lay the large bulk of a whale. It was the rare goose-beaked, or Cuvier's, whale. For a moment, Isabel was so awestruck at the sight of this rare whale that she forgot everything else. Quickly, she sidestepped Dr. Sharp to kneel down beside the twenty-foot whale, one hand on her cool, still supple skin. Stretched on her side, barely alive, this beaked whale showed a mammary slit and long scars crisscrossing her sides. By her gently sloped forehead and short beak, her apparent smile and slender, sharp teeth, her unique coloring—white dorsal fin and slate gray belly—Isabel recognized this rare deepwater whale only from textbooks of strandings. No whale biologist she'd ever known had actually seen a living Cuvier's whale. In fact, Georges Cuvier, a French anatomist who believed he was creating a new genus for an extinct whale from fossil evidence, first named this species in the early 1800s. Fifty years later, it was discovered that this highly elusive beaked whale was in fact still a living species.

Deciding to encourage Sharp's help rather than engage in a turf war, she asked him, "Will you help me euthanize those animals who are suffering the most?

"No time," he said brusquely.

"No time for what?" Isabel demanded. "No time to do your job properly?"

At this, Sharp turned again and his face betrayed irritation. "I'm a scientist, not some animal rights activist, Ms. Spinner. And we've got more important issues here. I'll have to ask you to stop hindering our work or else the lieutenant here will escort you and your entire stranding network off the beach."

"Lieutenant?" Isabel asked.

"U.S. Navy," he snapped.

As the lieutenant took her elbow and moved Isabel away, she called back to Sharp, "Could this stranding have anything to do with your *military* acoustic tests?" Isabel raised her voice and resisted by digging her heels into the sand. Some of the volunteers ran over to gather around her. "Any *real* scientist would recognize that these necropsies you're doing might be a conflict of interest!"

With a frown, Sharp turned away from Isabel, the volunteers, and the stranded Cuvier's. He strode down the beach where another, smaller whale lay barely breathing.

With the ease of a decade of training in the martial arts, Isabel slipped away from the lieutenant's grasp. As if they had planned this distraction, Marshall easily shoved the lieutenant aside so that Isabel could move away from him. Running free down the beach, Isabel called to several volunteers working on the Cuvier's whale, "Don't let Dr. Sharp do any more necropsies!"

"But you have no authority here," Sharp shouted at Isabel as he ran after her. "You're just a lab technician."

Isabel nodded to a few of the burliest stranding network volunteers as she sped past them. "We'll make a citizen's arrest then, won't we, boys?"

With a shout and a pounce, several of the strongest volunteers tackled Sharp and threw him down onto the wet sand. They did the same to the lieutenant, who had followed after him. In the commotion, Marian quickly drew out a syringe from her medical bag and euthanized the whale before she suffered any more. For a moment, she watched the goose-beaked whale's dark eye fix almost gratefully in death.

Far down the beach and away from the fracas between the volunteers and military men, Isabel took stock of her beach: Dark shapes lay like debris all along the sand. The hand-over-hand seawater brigades worked endlessly to keep the whales cool. Near her, several schoolchildren were sobbing, their hands patting a small, still dolphin.

Isabel walked over and stood next to them. "You did your best, kids," she said, soothing them.

Coming alongside, a little out of breath from running, Marian took Isabel's arm. "Maybe there's some hope," she said. "Remember that stranding in Ireland?"

Isabel had read about it on the Internet. Somewhere off the coast of Ireland, a small pod of dolphins had stopped stranding after one of their pregnant matriarchs gave birth on the beach. This birth seemed to signal the pod to reverse their decision to follow an ailing leader and die together on the beach. The call of a new life had summoned them back to sea. All but the leader and a few of his most devoted brothers had chosen to live.

"There *is* a pregnant female on the beach," Marian said. "You know, we could induce labor and maybe . . ."

"What if it's not any safer out there in their ocean than it is here on shore?"

"They're *dying* here, Isabel."

"I think there might be more of them dying at sea, where we can't keep count."

Marian eyed Isabel. "What's out there in the water that's worse than sure death here on the beach?"

Isabel remembered the agonizing sound she had intuited when holding the thrashing calf. "I don't know"—she looked at Marian—"yet. But I have some ideas."

"Uh-uh, Isabel. We're way out of our territory," Marian sternly reminded her.

If Isabel hadn't been so exhausted, she might have smiled. "I've got to get to the aquarium. But tomorrow night—you, me, one of these bodies—in our lab."

"And the other animals we can't save?"

"Ask Daniel to get one of the smaller, dead lags"—she used the simplified scientific name for the Pacific white-sided dolphin—"to his home freezer. He's a surgical nurse—maybe he knows a sympathetic CAT scan technician who can x-ray a carcass to check for hemorrhaging in the inner ears and brain."

"That's a lot to ask . . ." Marian began, but she stopped when she saw Isabel's frown. "Okay, okay," she said, holding up hands streaked with blood from the dying cetaceans. "This is more important than any rules, any U.S. government. My ancestors taught me that."

Before Isabel could thank Marian, her friend was off and running down the beach to Daniel and a group of volunteers standing over a Pacific white-sided dolphin. The circle of volunteers with their bowed heads looked just like mourners at a funeral.

chapter nine

Perfect Empathic Pair

WAIST-DEEP IN the Newport Aquarium pool, Isabel kept a close eye on the Pacific white-sided dolphin and Dall's porpoise calves floating languidly near her. She and Marshall were exhausted after today's stranding, but both knew their fatigue was nothing compared to the calves', who still showed no sign of an animal's startle response or will to live. Would they last the night?

"They're still disoriented and in shock," Isabel told Marshall. He pulled on his wetsuit and flippers to enter the pool and steady the calves while Isabel drew more blood and checked their vital signs.

Marshall gently held what now felt like his own calf as Isabel took a quick blood sample from the animal's listless tail flukes. At the tiny prick of the needle, the slender male Dall's porpoise did at least slap his pectoral fins against the water, splashing them both. Good sign.

"It's all right," Marshall said to soothe his orphaned calf. "I've still got you."

"He's bonding with you." Isabel was cautiously heartened. It was good to have Marshall here to help her, since almost the entire aquarium staff was still at Kiwanda Beach with more stranded whales and dolphins. "Can you stay in the pool with the calves, Marshall? Just swim with them?"

"What do you think is going on out there?"

"I have some ideas," Isabel said, frowning. "But I have to do the necropsy tomorrow on this little porpoise's mother, and ask Marian for some research, before I can really begin to say . . ."

"Aren't you suspicious? My God, Isabel, the beach was crawling with military. Something big is going on."

"All the more reason to find sound forensic evidence."

In the shallow end of the pool, Marshall studied Isabel's face. It was weary and drawn. "I understand," he said. "Now, what else can we do to help out these calves?"

Marshall knew that close, physical contact was what dolphin and porpoise calves needed to thrive. If they could encourage these two survivors to form an empathic pair, the bond might save their lives. But he was uncertain how to encourage such empathy.

"You did a wonderful job on the beach," Marshall said as he held up his Dall's calf so Isabel could measure the small porpoise from beak to tail fluke. Three feet, four inches. Weight, twenty-six pounds. If he survived, the life span of this speedy little Dall's would be half the more than forty years a Pacific white-sided dolphin usually lived in the wild. If the two cetaceans were kept captive, those life spans would not significantly increase, despite the absence of predators and pollutants. If they could heal their injuries, these calves might be successfully reintroduced to their home waters, like the many seals Isabel's animal sanctuary had rehabilitated.

As she examined the Dall's, keeping an eye on the female Pacific white-sided calf, Isabel said to Marshall, "So did you. Thank you."

For a moment she met Marshall's gaze. Isabel's eyes were bloodshot from saltwater and sand but still so clear, level. Marshall smiled at her, and though the pool was quite cold, he felt warmth flowing through his body.

Isabel seemed a little flustered as she turned back to her physical examination of the Dall's porpoise; the other calf swam shyly a little nearer to them. "Okay, Marshall," Isabel said, "you can let go now."

"We should name them both," Isabel added, watching the two calves exploring the small pool. "It'll give them a better chance of survival."

Marshall pulled on a small, yellow oxygen tank and swam to the center of the pool. "I suppose that's scientific, and not because we're both already so attached to these little calves."

Isabel gave him one of her rare smiles. "It's not very scientific," she said. "But wildlife rehabilitators always name their animals."

"I know, let's call them Mack and Molly."

Calling each calf by name, Marshall quickly adjusted his mask for the fifteen-foot dive at the deepest end of the tank. He hoped to encourage the calves to follow him, which would increase their sluggish circulation. Isabel would be able to determine if their hearing and sonar were still intact only by watching them swim.

The Dall's porpoise was soon somewhat roused by Marshall's playful dives. His stream of brilliant bubbles seemed to also engage the female calf. Molly let out the first vocalizations they'd heard from her—a click train of ultrasonic chirps that sent Mack into a seemingly joyful leap above her.

"Did you know, Marshall, that cetaceans are the only animals besides humans who naturally call each other by name?"

"Primates who are taught sign language do, too," said Marshall, smiling.

"Yes, but dolphins do it without human training. It's already part of their cetacean culture." Isabel also smiled, her eyes following the two calves as they explored each other underwater, swimming slowly, almost touching. After circling the pool several times, Mack sped up and veered off to Marshall, who had returned underwater and was inviting the Dall's porpoise to do what dolphins spend three-quarters of their lives doing: play.

Engaged, Mack dove down to explore this flippered man, who was no match for the month-old calf, despite Marshall's agility in the water. It had taken Marshall a lifetime to learn some of the underwater ballet that any cetacean calf could master in several weeks. The only time a dolphin is ever awkward is right after birth. Newborn calves spend their first days perfecting the elegant arch and dive of conscious breathing. The unpracticed newborn gulps air through its blowhole and then, in an attempt to arch, he belly-flops. Mothers and aunts, guardian juveniles, and male escorts, all devote themselves to any newborn calf. Marshall knew that now he must somehow continue the nurturing of these orphaned calves. While there was little he could teach them about swimming or breathing, he could give them the affection they needed to keep choosing to live, to breathe.

Moving and breathing together in synchronicity, like dolphins in their traveling position, is an art form that humans can't endure for long. It is too intimate. Certainly Marshall had never managed to breathe in rhythm with another human. But in the chill pool, he now paced himself perfectly in synch with Mack, at times tenderly touching the calf's black-and-white side to reassure him.

Suddenly Mack zoomed around the cement pool, his echolocation sounding off the cement walls. This pool was like a house of mirrors for the calf, to have his own vocalizations echo back to him endlessly and to hear no call and response from any member of his pod. Vocalizing in such a confined space was perhaps a painful step for the Dall's, but it was a big step toward his survival and eventual release back into the open ocean. Now, if only Mack could just keep from falling into the lethal depression that usually killed any orphaned calf.

Turning to swim on his back beneath his calf, Marshall mirrored Mack's powerful underwater circles. Though the bleeding from his ear holes had stopped, Mack did indeed seem disoriented. Perhaps his hearing was only temporarily disturbed. Perhaps he and Molly had survived because they were much farther away from the source of any acoustic harassment.

With another rush of bubbles and some high-pitched noises of his own, Marshall dove down to the cement bottom as Mack followed him. Porpoises love acoustic stimulation. When Marshall pulled a mesh bag full of clanking camera gear from his dive belt, the new but intriguing noise caught Mack's attention.

So Mack was not completely deaf. Again the calf zoomed toward Marshall, who let go of the mesh bag of gear. A sudden idea struck Marshall and he took off his diving gloves, using his fingers to make signals for *Come. Leap. Go.* Mack learned these typical training hand-signals in minutes.

Marshall knew that dolphins are particularly adept at understanding the most sophisticated and subtle hand motions. Researchers in Hawaii, near Marshall's home, had long studied dolphins' ability to perfectly interpret hand signals as a visual language. Both man and calf surfaced simultaneously to breathe.

Catch! Marshall made a tight circle with his thumb and forefinger and threw his mesh bag high in the air. Mack let the bag land on the water's surface and then carried it on his sloped snout. He zipped over to Molly to show it to the disinterested dolphin still floating quietly.

"It takes him only once to learn my hand signals," Marshall marveled. "Now, you try to get Molly interested in something besides floating."

Isabel sang softly to attract the Pacific white-sided calf's attention. Molly stirred slightly and swam a little closer to Isabel, but still kept her distance. Marshall followed Mack in the pool and engaged the calf in a game of tag. And then something amazing happened: Mack initiated physical contact with Marshall. As he probed the man, a small, smiling mouth searched somewhere around Marshall's knees for mammary glands.

"He's trying to nurse," Isabel said softly.

It moved Marshall that this little calf sought his body for nourishment. All he could give was affection; the only food that awaited Mack, with his restored appetite, would be a plastic feeding tube and rich milk fat to imitate the lost mother's. He was hungry. He needed to know he was not alone.

With a whistle and bleep, Mack leapt over Marshall's back and then probed his small oxygen tank. The stream of sonar clicks sounded like a rusty door creaking shut. Marshall glanced over to the opposite side of the pool. There Molly lay listlessly. The stark difference between the growing liveliness of the Dall's porpoise and the lassitude of the Pacific white-sided dolphin on the surface pulled Marshall in two directions. One part of him wanted to go help Molly, but Marshall also needed to keep Mack engaged. With a thrust of his flippers, Marshall propelled himself over the water's surface, pleased that Mack accompanied him. Careful not to come too close to Molly, who was slowly circling Isabel, Marshall swam in exhilarating figure eights with Mack following. Would their play so nearby be enough to engage Molly?

Marshall felt the slightest touch along his side as Mack slid past him and then turned his head sideways to make strong eye contact through his mask.

"Oh, that's good, Marshall," Isabel called out. "Mack's looking at you. He's really attaching."

Isabel's musical voice echoed above him in the aquarium as she sang. He thought of her singing to him in the pickup, an old sea chantey from her grandfather's people. Perhaps somehow the calves heard the haunting music in Isabel's voice and found solace, again found the sea.

Eye to eye, Marshall and Mack swam. Then with a careful lift of his arm, Marshall let the little calf lodge his small, thick body under his arm the way a mother dolphin or baby-sitting aunt might protect a newborn calf. After a few close circles, Marshall changed his swimming style—his belly undulating, his legs fused together so that he came close to imitating the strong arch and curve of a dolphin. Mack grew excited and wriggled against Marshall's side as he might seek physical comfort from an adult in his own pod. To keep the awkward man alongside him, Mack slowed to accompany Marshall. Together they circled around the cement pool as if they were enjoying the most pristine tropical lagoon. With Marshall's arm still loosely embracing the calf, the two fell into a timeless rest pose—a slow float at the quiet surface.

So calmed and mesmerized was he by their swim, Marshall did not notice that Isabel was treading water nearer them. But Mack noticed and veered away to greet her. Leaping over Isabel, Mack made a breach, flying straight up out of the water and then back-flopping in a splash that rocked everyone.

"He's jealous of me," Isabel laughed. "Mack wants to keep his human float toy to himself."

Marshall smiled at Isabel, noting how lovely she looked in her sleek wetsuit with its stripes of blue along the legs. How he wished she could dive with him. "Isabel," he told her, "I don't think Mack is deaf. He heard you singing."

Mack slowly swam toward them, careful to keep at a distance.

"We'll have to do more audio tests," said Isabel, "to see if his hearing is completely intact and to make sure there's no internal damage."

Turning her full attention now to the drifting Molly, Isabel treaded water, studying the dolphin calf several feet away. Molly's black body, with its characteristic gray "suspenders" running from head to tail, was leaner than Mack's, and her spirits were subdued. In the wild, Molly would be zipping through and leaping the surf of a boat's bow wake. In this pool, she seemed barely able to keep herself and her breathing blowhole righted in the water. "She's suffering," Isabel said softly.

"How do you know that?"

"I can see it." After a moment's hesitation, Isabel added, " I can feel it."

"Do you feel her pain in your body? Is that how it works, this empathic stuff? Is that why they place bets on you?"

"No," Isabel said. "I get just an echo of her pain."

"It's enough," Marshall said softly. "Maybe it's your human form of echolocation."

"You could call it that." Isabel seemed relieved that he understood. Very cautiously she approached Molly. "Let's hope she's just in shock." Isabel reached out one hand to touch the calf, who made no response. "If this little lag really is completely deaf, then I want to euthanize her quickly. She would never survive, and it would be cruel to continue her suffering."

Isabel was right. It might be the most humane thing to do. But Marshall couldn't bear to think of these calves not surviving. The images of all those stranded whales and dolphins dying on the beach haunted him. He should have taken photos to document the devastation, in case there was something besides an algae bloom or sick pod leader responsible for the stranding. It was really suspicious that the military was crawling all over the beach. Maybe that's why Isabel had declared the beach a possible crime scene.

But he was an artist, not an activist. Someone else could do that work. He might send an e-mail about the unusual stranding to Irene Feinstein; he would be seeing her soon on this trip.

"I didn't hear you call Molly by her name yet," Marshall said to Isabel.

For a long moment, Isabel, gently resting her hand on Molly's side, did not respond. "I'm afraid . . . I'm afraid to name her. She might not make it."

"All the more reason to name her."

"Moll . . ." Isabel's voice caught on the name, a name she had loved for so long, the name of an animal who had saved Isabel's own life. Maybe the name still carried the power to heal. Isabel gathered herself and said in a calm, firm voice, "My beautiful Molly . . . We're here. We're right here with you."

Isabel ran her hand along Molly's pectoral fins, skin so sensitive and as smooth as cool melon.

"You both look beautiful," Marshall called out.

He felt the tap of tiny pectoral fins along his ribs as Mack again sought refuge underneath his arm. They swam several fast circles around Isabel and Molly. Isabel gently struck a metal tuning fork that she had brought into the pool with her and held it to one of her calf's pinprick ear holes. After only a few seconds, Molly did respond slightly to the ultrasonic hum of the vibrating tuning fork by turning her head to one side.

"So she does have some hearing," Isabel said, relieved. "But we don't really know how well she can navigate acoustically. Her blood tests looked pretty good, no infection, and her heart rate is normal again. So, if the injury is only to one ear, we might be able to save her—that is, if she has the will to live."

In captivity, but also in the wild, grief could kill a dolphin as fast as any shark. Losing their pods and their mothers, orphaned calves also lose all hope. They simply stop breathing. Knowing how sensitive dolphins are to human moods, how they can even read a human's emotions by the tumult of stomach gases, Marshall tried to summon up an image that always gave him pleasure, maybe one that he could somehow communicate to Mack. Some of his mother's family said dolphins were the most telepathic creatures in the sea. Sorting through pictures in his mind, Marshall realized with a start that he couldn't remember the last time he was truly happy. How could he help Mack find pleasure in surviving if he couldn't?

In spite of himself, Marshall gave way to an overwhelming grief. It began in his chest and descended to his groin. Oddly enough, diving into his own despair didn't seem to harm his calf; instead, Marshall's emotional turmoil seemed to fascinate Mack, who could discern the man's moods by echolocating his inner body. There was no hiding one's true feelings, one's heart, from a dolphin's acoustic scan. Mack leapt up, vocalizing in excited whistles, and then splashed down gracefully, close to Marshall. Rolling around in the water, he suddenly stopped, his brown eye inches from Marshall's face. As the dolphin's unblinking eye held his,

Marshall felt the fury of feelings in his heart grow stronger. He couldn't even name them all. A memory flooded his mind.

Once as a teenager diving off the Kona Coast photographing humpback whales, Marshall found himself alone, floating above a male escort and a female-calf pair. Marshall had listened to the bass rumble and high-pitched mewling of the male humpback beneath him. The mating songs vibrated up through his leg bones, out his arms, eerie arpeggios swirling inside his bones as if his body were simply a tuning fork responding to this ancient singing. Trembling, Marshall had let his waterproof camera float free.

Only then did the shot that had always eluded him appear: hundreds of spinner dolphins, silver streaks below him, alongside him, leaping and splashing above him. He could not count them all. They swam upside down, white bellies just below his, gleaming as the small spinners glided close. Brown eyes glimpsed his. The dolphins' echolocation sounding his body, bouncing against his skin, seeing inside him, they accepted his presence in the middle of their superpod. Marshall was a boy and he wept like a boy, his mask filling with his own saltwater. But it was joy he felt. He had absolutely no desire to take a photo. Always he would remember this. He was part of their spinning, twirling, traveling pod. They shared the same sea.

When Marshall told his mother about the spinner dolphin pod encircling him, carrying him, he asked her, "So, why do they spin?"

"Because they're happy," she'd said. "And like you, Kai'e'e, they want to get a really good look around."

As if reading his mental images, Mack now swam belly-up right beneath Marshall, who drifted face-down in the pool. Trust. It was the way a calf would swim tucked under a mother's belly for protection. Then the calf's sophisticated sonar scanned Marshall's body again—that ping-ping-ping tingling along his bones and ricocheting off his organs. It felt so good, little electric zings. Mack's echolocation focused on Marshall's chest—rapid bleeps and clicks as the calf probed along the thick scar with his sensitive, short beak. A blast of the calf's subtle sonar went straight into his heart. Marshall inhaled and felt a piercing ache, then inexplicable pleasure. Did the dolphin know his heart was not human? Did it matter?

Dolphins had long ago demonstrated to researchers their ability to easily recognize through their sophisticated echolocation any anomaly in the human body—from tumors to metal implants. Why not another animal's heart?

The calf seemed compelled to repeatedly scan and then probe Marshall's chest. Then the calf did something utterly unexpected. Vertically in the water, the calf positioned himself chest to chest, belly to belly, against Marshall's body. Laying his tiny pectoral fins against Marshall's sides, the calf—a far stronger swimmer even at half the man's length—spun Marshall in a slow, corkscrew spin.

As they both rose, breathing together, and broke the surface, Marshall heard Isabel gasp, then say very tenderly, "Take off your mask, Marshall. Let Mack really see you."

"He has. He already has."

Treading water alongside Isabel and both calves, Marshall took off his mask and tank, letting them float away. He felt such exhilaration when Mack scooped up his scuba gear as if this were yet another game. Surprising himself, Marshall began to sing the old Hawaiian chant that his mother had always sung to him: *"O Ha'iha'ilauahea 'O na wahine I ka puoko o ke ahi."* The words were full of rolling, mellifluous vowels.

Mack floated in perfect stillness, attentively turning his body toward Marshall's low, sonorous voice. Marshall continued the rich chanting, unaware that his face was streaming tears. Unexpectedly, Molly lifted her pectoral fin to ever so briefly turn toward Marshall and his calf.

"Keep singing," Isabel urged. "She's responding."

"O 'imi'imi, 'o nalowale a loa 'a," Marshall sang on in a sweet falsetto. *"Loa 'a ho'I ka hoa e."*

Without warning, Molly splashed with her tiny tail flukes and dove straight down. When she surfaced again, she burst out with rapid-fire whistles and chirps.

Isabel recognized the vocalizations as being exactly the same as those of one of the Pacific white-sided dolphins as she lay dying on the beach, calling futilely for her offspring.

"Molly's naming herself," Marshall said softly. He swam over to Isabel as Molly repeated her signature whistle, at first weakly, and then with more force.

"Every dolphin inherits the mother's signature whistle," Isabel added.
"Like me," Marshall said. "My mother gave me my first name ... Kai'e'e."
"What does that mean?"
"It's the Hawaiian word for 'tidal wave.' "
"A wise mother," Isabel said, smiling.

Mack followed Marshall to Molly's side and encouragingly swam around the dolphin calf. This interested Molly, who turned on her side to study Mack before allowing him to swim up alongside her, his pectoral fin tracing a subtle line along her body. It was a reassuring touch, a playful invitation. After a few more passes, Molly joined Mack in exploring the pool. It took only seconds for Molly to adjust her breathing and body to the other calf's speed, and they swam in perfect synchrony, their little dorsal fins rising and falling together.

"Beautiful," Isabel breathed. She floated near Marshall. "She's no longer in shock. You called her back from the dead."

"I know what that's like."

Who knew which of them initiated the embrace, but the two humans in the deep end of the pool wrapped their arms around each other and would have sunk, except that their flippered feet kept them afloat.

This embrace seemed to intrigue the dolphins. The two calves veered toward Isabel and Marshall and swam around the entangled couple, vocalizing in clicks and chirps.

"A perfect empathic pair," Isabel said, still wrapped around Marshall in her long-limbed embrace. "Now, they can simply rest and socialize together. It's what will heal them most."

"And us?" Marshall smiled. "Can we rest and socialize, too?"

Marshall's strong, stocky body made a lovely buoy. Her legs wrapped around his waist. They bobbed together, his flippers now treading water for the two of them.

What most moved Isabel was that, when Marshall's face was this close to hers, when his dark eyes with their surprisingly thick lashes gazed deeply into her own, he hesitated. Isabel had spent so many years being pursued by a relentless suitor. Stewart's every touch had been a demand, his lovemaking invasive, as if by fiercely claiming her body he might possess her.

But here was Marshall, who held himself back from her a little, waiting for Isabel to want his touch. His lips were generous, his light brown skin was sun-darkened, and his black hair fell over his forehead. Marshall's touch was as light as his long, tapered fingers. These were the skillful hands of an artist. He was not so caught up in his own passion that he blundered against Isabel. Marshall simply waited, treading water for them, as if they were out in a vast sea. They were not shipwrecked humans—as Isabel had so often felt with Stewart. Instead, she and Marshall seemed to belong in the water, like these little calves now swimming circles around them, turning on their sides to better study the humans.

"My little Dall's porpoise likes us together." Marshall smiled.

"Of course . . . ," Isabel said.

For the first time, she noticed, along Marshall's jaw, a slight scattering of tiny freckles almost invisible beneath the day's stubble of his beard. She wrapped one of his black curls around her finger and pushed his wet hair away from his forehead.

In a graceful movement, Marshall balanced Isabel's body on one hip and reached to pull off one of her diving gloves. "You need that splinter taken out of your thumb before it *really* gets infected," he said softly, still treading water.

She burst out laughing. "Why did you notice that silly splinter?"

"I notice everything about you," he said. "Trained eye."

She laughed again. "I got that splinter off my old bed. Andrew probably told you all about that, too."

"Nope, he didn't."

"Well, Grandfather made us bunk beds from one of his old boats—it broke up on Spinnaker Rocks down the beach from our cottage when Andrew and I were still in elementary school."

"You still fit in a bunk bed?"

"It's more like a boat than a bed," Isabel said. "You'll see for yourself . . . sometime." She smiled. "You can sleep in Andrew's bunk."

Marshall gently kissed her thumb and then examined the splinter more closely. Isabel had to admit there was more infection around that splinter than she'd noticed before. "It's all right," she said. Then she wrapped her arms around Marshall's sturdy chest and laid her head on his shoulder.

She hadn't quite recognized how strong her attraction was to Marshall. She realized suddenly that it was the middle of the night.

"Would you like to go home and rest?" Marshall asked. With one hand, he stroked her hair, untwisting her braid. "I can stay here with the calves all night."

"No." Isabel lifted her head off his shoulder. Unwinding herself from his loose embrace, she used her own legs now to tread water next to him. She should be doing a better job of watching over these abandoned calves; after all, the first twenty-four hours were crucial. "I can't leave them."

Mack and Molly circled the pool, rising and diving, their bodies held in the shallow arch characteristic of resting behavior. Marshall smiled. "It would be great if we humans didn't need to sleep, like these calves don't actually sleep. I'd also like to rest just one side of my brain at a time, as dolphins do. Keep floating through my days and nights." Marshall lay back on the water and floated as if feigning sleep. He even gave out a few false snorts and snores.

This intrigued the calves, who traced a wider circle and curiously came over to check out this noisy human. It also heartened Isabel to see Molly responding accurately to airborne sound. Dolphin hearing is as acute above the water as below, though air is such a slow conduit for sound compared to water. Did their human voices seem unsophisticated after what the calves were used to hearing underwater? Isabel reminded herself that, at birth, cetaceans hear about the same range of sound that humans hear; as they grow, so does their ultrasonic frequency range.

Isabel was grateful to Marshall for helping her with the calves, but suddenly she felt shy and a little too open for her own good.

"It's my job to watch over these calves all night," Isabel said. "You don't have to stay with us."

Marshall rolled out of his back float and again treaded water next to her. He touched her face, lightly traced her strong jaw line. "You're too used to people leaving you, Isabel," he said. "Andrew doesn't have it in him to stay." He paused and then at last admitted, "Neither do I . . . But I don't know if I could always keep leaving someone like you."

Without a thought, without knowing what she was about to do, Isabel again wrapped her arms and legs around him. She deeply kissed Marshall's warm, chapped lips. He tasted of salt and mentholated lip salve. He returned her kiss with a tenderness and restraint that drew her to him even more willingly.

This was desire, Isabel knew in the way her body fit against his, their slick wetsuits like skin on skin. His ribs were wide and sturdy, not those of a barrel-chested man so much as a man who had spent much of his life breathing carefully to conserve his air supply and linger longer under-water. Isabel ran one finger down his chest, tracing from memory the hidden scar.

Marshall nuzzled her neck. Again she caught that scent of coconut. Maybe it wasn't his mother's homemade shampoo. Maybe it had belonged to another woman. Isabel felt a bolt of jealousy through her own body. She, who had never been jealous one minute in her life, who had never lost herself enough to any lover to fear loss. Marian was right—Isabel hadn't had much experience with other men. But the thought of losing Marshall, now that she had him in her arms, was disturbing. She fought against such unexpected possessiveness, even as her body embraced him more tightly. Fiercely she accepted his delicate, lingering kisses along the ridge of her brow, her eyelids, and the nape of her neck, a light tongue in her ear—everywhere Marshall kissed her felt like virgin territory. Isabel would have let him strip off her wetsuit and make love to her here underwater. She felt his own growing excitement, but Marshall's movements were still slow, unhurried. Being with him was like being able to dive again.

"Rest," he said and leaned Isabel away from him. Swimming slowly, Marshall moved them to the shallow end, where he could stand up.

He laid her body back on the water's surface. Isabel lay stretched out full, floating in his hands. Cradling the small of her back, Marshall rocked her with a tender rhythm.

It was this rise and fall of her body that called the calves to circle them again. Mack and Molly also floated in the human-made waves. "It's what they like most about humans," Isabel whispered. "When we can finally care about each other."

She knew that Marshall was keeping a close eye on Mack and Molly, as well as on her, as he took up his song again.

"O 'imi'imi, 'o nalowale a loa 'a," he chanted softly. *"Loa 'a ho'I ka hoa e."*

Did she sleep? Isabel drifted in this watery reverie, upheld by Marshall's wide hands. For the first time tonight, she heard other sounds—nearby barks of sea lions, good-natured grunts and gigantic splashes of walruses in another tank, seagulls cawing—and around them the *whoosh-whoosh* of dolphin exhalations as these surviving calves swam in slow circles. She felt their quiet swells and, even with her eyes closed, saw their arch and dive. Isabel allowed herself to hope for the first time all night. Maybe Mack and Molly would live. Maybe they would be returned to the sea.

Through sleepy eyes, Marshall gazed down at her, this strong woman who could rest in his hands. By her alert reverie and the way she listened intently to his singing, Marshall knew it took all Isabel's courage to surrender to him. It was the way an animal rests, her body utterly relaxed, yet ears tuned to catch the slightest sound of a predator.

With Mack and Molly circling, Marshall continued to rock Isabel back and forth slightly. Gazing down at her face, he noticed again how similar the small, delicate nose, the arch of brow, and full lips were to Andrew's. His friend was fair and redheaded and had freckles speckling his body; Isabel was auburn-haired and had wild, kinky curls. Marshall liked that Isabel's hair seemed slightly rebellious, even when she twisted and braided it. Only her lovers or a brother or friends would ever see her hair so undisciplined. And perhaps only he might see it like this, floating out from her suntanned face in sweet, drifting tentacles.

It occurred to him as he let Isabel drift that he had been holding another in his arms for hours and hours now. First it was Mack, and now it was this woman. Isabel was so lovely; she called him dangerously far out of himself.

Even before his transplant, Marshall's emotional range had been more like that gray, suffocating sense of loss he experienced in the Dead Zone. How many years had his heart been deprived of oxygen, of love, and he had not realized it?

Tenderly he lifted Isabel to the side of the aquarium pool. She barely stirred as he covered her with a light wool blanket from a nearby supply shelf.

In the pool, Mack and Molly breathed together, their small blowholes opening and closing like the strong valves of a heart. Isabel murmured, "We need to feed them in another hour."

"I'll do it."

"Don't leave," she yawned.

"Shhhh," Marshall said. "Try to sleep."

She vaguely reached out to him and he obligingly lay down beside her. "Stay," she said, before her breathing deepened and she dove down into a deep rest.

Marshall dove with her, closing his eyes. But he did not sleep. Pictures floated through his mind: blue-green galaxies of spawning coral; barracuda circling in a tight turquoise tornado, a bright ball of fish; swaying kelp forests of green leaf and translucent bulbs. These were his favorite underwater images and often flowed through his mind when he was most relaxed, or sometimes when making love.

These images were familiar and calming. But as he rolled over to embrace Isabel, other pictures flooded him.

Sleeping cliffs high above a grassy plain. Savannah again, and he must not sleep. He must watch and guard the others, the matriarch and newborn. A dignified face. Hara. A female with cinnamon fur. And then a large, high-ranking baboon. Namib, with his Hara. The matriarch and Namib are reaching out to him. It is his naming ceremony.

Sol. They name him. Young son. Sun.

His heart expands, aches, races so fast, running exuberantly through wild, sweet grasses. This is the power and freedom that comes from any naming ceremony, animal or human. He is given back to himself. Forever he is bound to his family, who at last, through Hara, accept him. He is no longer alone.

Early in the morning, Marshall awoke, agitated and spooked by yet another weird dream. These drugs, these necessary and lifelong companions. He was very careful to untangle Isabel's long legs from his shorter legs and ease away from her. As he always did after he slept well with a woman, Marshall left a brief note with the number of his cell phone. *I'll call from Portland,* he scrawled. *Please keep me posted about Mack and Molly.*

Lifting his gear, he was about to leave the aquarium quietly when the arc and dive of two dorsal fins caught his eye. Where was his camera? Rummaging noiselessly in his camera bag, trying not to disturb Isabel, Marshall found his small Nikon. It was the only camera he used out of the water. It was digital, though nothing too fancy, since he rarely took photographs except underwater.

Marshall crept to the water's edge and whistled softly. Leaping and zipping to the side of the pool, Mack answered Marshall's call. Marshall was pleased to see that Molly was not far behind, though much shyer.

"Steady, little guy," he soothed Mack. Marshall snapped an entire roll of film before he knew it. "You two get better so I can meet you again out in the open ocean."

As he was turning away, Marshall felt his chest constrict. How could he hesitate or feel a moment's sadness? He had to get back to the conference and on to Seattle with Andrew for a diving job, then visit Irene, and then head on to Africa and another diving assignment. A busy, nomadic life— just what he had always loved about his work. As he gathered his gear, his mind swam with images of stranded cetaceans—especially the larger Dall's porpoise, Mack's mother, flat and still, suffocating on the beach.

He glanced back at Mack, who had turned his head sideways to better make eye contact with Marshall. Almost hidden behind Mack, Molly also turned her head to make eye contact with him. Good sign. "Okay, okay . . . ," Marshall promised. "I'll do what I can."

Maybe it was still early enough to get back down to Kiwanda Beach this morning and at least document some of the stranding. Then he could drive back to the conference in time for his panel. He would send a few digital photo files of the stranding over the Internet to Irene and her animal rights contacts. Let them have a go at it. At least get the word out.

As he tiptoed past Isabel, her deep breathing distracted Marshall. After a night sleeping alongside this woman, hearing the calves' steady inspiration and exhalation, Marshall felt a lingering tenderness toward them all.

Quickly, he searched again for his small camera. As he snapped a photo of Isabel curled up as if he were still there beside her, her hair tangled, face scrunched in sleep, Marshall grinned. She would hate this photo. But Andrew would like it. Of course, he could not show Isabel's brother such a shot without betraying this night together. Better to keep it quiet. Better to keep moving, diving, in an element he understood.

"You understand that, don't you?" Marshall asked Mack and Molly. He spoke in a whisper, which he hoped the calves could hear. Believing that Isabel was asleep, Marshall very quietly closed the door behind him.

Isabel lay beside the pool, her eyes open, steadily fixed on the symmetry of two tiny dorsal fins rising and falling—the perfect empathic pair.

chapter ten

A Dying Art

O N THEIR CLANDESTINE night shift, Isabel and Marian were careful not to discuss exactly what they were doing. They knew this unauthorized necropsy of one of the stranded dolphins might cost them their jobs. Since the stranding the day before, the NMFS had collected the carcasses of the dolphins and whales that had sustained the worst injuries and moved them to an undisclosed necropsy lab. The frozen bodies were awaiting an official, closed necropsy. Stewart had informed Isabel that she was not allowed even to observe the procedure. "NMFS will announce the necropsy findings next month, after we've had a chance to call in experts and do CAT scans on the dead animals."

When Isabel pleaded with him to intercede on her behalf and let her necropsy at least one of the stranded bodies, he'd flatly refused. "We'll do a fair and honest job," he'd said.

"But will you tell the truth" Isabel asked, "if the evidence is clear that the navy is responsible?"

"Of course," he said, and would not meet her eyes.

Tonight, this dolphin, one of two removed illegally from the stranding by Marian and some other volunteers, provided their only chance to discover the truth about all these deaths. Isabel was anxiously awaiting a call from Daniel about the CAT scan results from the other dolphin their stranding network had unofficially taken off Kiwanda Beach.

"Well, one good thing," Marian began, as if sensing Isabel's uneasiness, "looks like your seal pup, Merlin, is going to make it."

174

"Oh, that's wonderful, Marian. We can release him with the other rescued pups."

"And maybe he'll be back," Marian said, as they donned clear plastic autopsy aprons over their scrubs and pulled on knee-high rubber boots to prepare for lab work.

"Merlin?"

Marian looked up from her tray of stainless steel tools and gave Isabel a level look. "Don't even try that with me. I know how you feel about Marshall McGreggor. I saw the way you watched his every move on the beach during the stranding. Never saw you so mindful of any man."

Isabel nodded curtly. "You know everything."

"A Native tradition," Marian said.

Isabel kept her eyes on the dolphin. "I'm very curious, you know, especially about his heart . . . about his transplant."

Marian was thoughtful a moment. "Our elders tell us that the soul migrates between animal and human bodies," Marian said. "Only with Marshall, it's a heart that does the traveling."

"You know, science makes up all these new technologies just because it *can*. Then, it's up to us to figure out how in the world we're supposed to live with them."

Marian shot Isabel a wry smile and then concentrated on counting their sterile tools. "Oh, Isa," she said, "don't make this into one of your soapboxes. This really isn't about science. Admit it—you're just falling for the guy."

Isabel gathered her courage. "This is . . . new for me, this feeling."

"I know, dear," Marian said. "Your experience with men is so limited. And Stewart wasn't exactly Mr. Sensitive. Now, take my Buddy—he was a smoothie. He had that reputation—Mr. Native American warrior-lawyer, always working for his people—but at home, I was the one who did all the work. Sometimes, I swear, I came to the lab just to get some rest!"

Isabel smiled sadly. She had seen her friend through a marriage that had seemed so right in the beginning—Marian Windhorse Gray and Buddy Whitewolf Hamilton, each the pride of the Oskeena Reservation, both destined to navigate between the traditional worlds of wild Indian ponies, berry picking, salmon fishing, and the labyrinth of federal grants and government jobs. Marian's great-great-grandparents were from the original Oskeena tribe. In the late 1800s they had been forcibly moved from their Columbia River homeland onto the arid, sagebrush steppe of north central Oregon. In this seeming wasteland disparaged by white people, the nomadic Oskeena had been settled on a reservation, given plows and seed grain, and expected to farm. Instead, they fought back.

Marian's Windhorse grandparents had led the struggle for reparation for their lost Columbia River fishing rights. In the 1930s, the federal government had finally settled the suit for millions, giving the Oskeena an economic base, which they used wisely, investing in timber, fisheries, horses, and education. But it was tourism and the tribal-run resort that brought the Oskeena Reservation the most visibility and income. During her high school years, Marian Windhorse alternated between pursuing her traditional dancing on the powwow circuit and working in the tribe's spa. When the tribe fully funded her studies at the University of Washington and then medical school, the Oskeena elders hoped Marian would someday bring her skills home. Many young people never returned.

Dropping out of medical school had been a difficult decision. Fearing that she had failed her own people, Marian knew she must bring back something to give the tribe. So she completed veterinary school with a specialty in pathology. Her family was known for their bond with wild ponies, but later generations had learned to round up the wild horses freely roaming the reservation, selecting the most high-spirited for rodeo. Marian distrusted the rodeo tradition, considering it the white man's final conquest of the wild horse *and* the Indian.

In her quiet crusade to care for and keep as many wild ponies away from the rodeo circuit as she professionally could, Marian met Buddy Whitewolf. Under Marian's influence—what Isabel fondly called her "sweet-talk nagging"—the man she loved had been maneuvered away from the bull- and horse rings and into law school. Buddy wrangled law as well as he did wild horses. He was a self-proclaimed expert at "hog-tying white bureaucrats in their own red tape." Because of Buddy's acumen, the tribe was now negotiating for its own million-dollar hydroelectric plant on the Columbia River.

But one effect of all this success in the white man's world was the fact that both Buddy and Marian were sometimes considered outsiders because they had left the reservation. "Even though Buddy and I came back, even though I still go back to the rez every damn weekend," Marian had told Isabel, "there are some people who still don't trust us."

It was this distrust by people she had grown up with that most pained Marian. When a tribal council member accused her of sabotaging their lucrative wild Indian pony roundup in order to expose the cruel treatment of animals on the rodeo circuits, Marian had at last resigned her job as the tribe's veterinarian. She took on a different kind of activism— investigating crimes against wildlife.

It was a federal job, and the federal government had been responsible for almost every lie, crime, and incidence of abuse against Indian people. But the irony was that, here in the pathology lab, Marian believed she might do more good in the long run for animals and her own people. She hoped the next generations might one day reject the cowboy hats and rodeo ways of the white people and return to the spiritual alliance with the wild ponies that had given her Windhorse family their ancestral name.

After Marian had married Buddy Whitewolf, they waited for a child who never came. Sometimes Marian heard the spirit of their child in the heat and the dark as Buddy lay sprawled across her body. The sound of her unborn child was a lament, a hesitation, haunting like the far-off cry of a night owl.

Isabel knew all this about her dearest friend. She also knew that Marian still waited not only for that wandering child's spirit to find her body but also for Buddy to abandon his willful pride and come find Marian again—even though she was the one to leave.

Buddy Whitewolf Hamilton was one of the most graceful men Isabel had ever met. His long, lean limbs were slightly bowed from his early years riding rodeo, his black hair disciplined in one elegant braid under his cowboy hat, his lawyer skill in defending his tribe's substantial resources all but legendary.

The marriage had fared well until Marian landed her forensics lab job on the Oregon coast and began commuting the three hours inland to her

Oskeena Reservation and an often empty home. Buddy spent so much time fighting cases in Washington, D.C., that, when the two were together, they were exhausted. The marriage could not survive.

"How *is* Buddy these days?" Isabel asked, trying to keep her concern from her voice. Marian always fended off anyone else's compassion, though she was the kindest-hearted person Isabel knew.

"Oh, Buddy has finally got a woman to cook for him—morning, noon, *and* night. Maybe Buddy likes her better in the kitchen than the bedroom. He used to be a man just born to make Levis look like a work of art. Now he's got to wear one of those big, awful silver belt buckles to hold up his belly." Marian shook her head and gave Isabel a grin. "At least when I was cooking for him, he was a long tall glass of water. Now, I'll bet he's forgotten how to fancy dance."

Marian grinned. She threw her head back, her long black ponytail swaying like a horse's tail as she sidestepped around the necropsy table. Even though hidden under an apron, scrubs, and a paper hat, Marian moved gracefully. She swept her arms out and stepped high in soaring imitation of a raptor's winged dance. Then she twirled so fast that Isabel had to close her eyes to keep from getting dizzy.

Marian stopped abruptly next to Isabel, who said, "Buddy is a damn fool. And I'm hungry. I'd love a midnight snack. Margie left an entire coconut cream pie in the small fridge. Her way of saying thanks for so many good naps in the morgue."

"Was that pie from the shower today?" Marian grinned. "How come they have showers for weddings and not divorces? That's when we really need the Martha Stewart Brigade to come to our rescue."

"Okay, okay," Isabel said. She peered into the personal refrigerator at the sugared waves of coconut meringue. "It does look good." Pulling out the leftover pie, Isabel cut two slim pieces.

"Don't dissect it, Isabel," Marian called. "Make the pieces bigger!"

When Isabel served the pie on two gaily colored plastic picnic plates in the shape of a salmon, Marian beamed. "Good girl," she said. "The pie's homemade." Marian studied Isabel from head to toe. "You know, Isa, in Britain, they have this reality television show called 'What Not to Wear.' Women hand over their fashion-impaired best friends to professional style experts for an intervention, a total makeover. Another month of your green scrubs and faded jeans in public and I'm turning you in to the fashion police, too!"

"Oh, please, not that!" Isabel said in mock horror.

"Another thing . . . how come I'm going against my better judgment—and risking my paycheck—by doing this necropsy with you?"

Sitting down together at the forensics desk, the women took up the blue plastic forks they had each long ago written their names on with a black felt-tipped pen. "I'm really glad you're here tonight, Marian."

"I'm always here."

But Isabel knew Marian was not as put-upon as she pretended. If Isabel hadn't wanted to do this necropsy, Marian would probably have taken it upon herself to find out exactly what had killed so many whales and dolphins. The difference between them was that Marian would have done the necropsy alone and, if caught, taken the blame, whereas Isabel would always ask for Marian's help. The thought of how much she had come to depend on Marian sobered her.

"Thank you, Marian."

Marian waved a hand, spooning up the generous stiff froth of meringue atop the coconut cream pie. "Buddy was always talking about independence," she said between mouthfuls, "like he had bought into the whole American Fourth of July thing. But there's a hell of a lot to be said for *interdependence*," Marian said. "*And* a good piece of pie."

"Doesn't Buddy want you back?" Isabel teased. "I've heard rumors . . ."

"Wanting and asking are two different things."

"So what will you say—when he does ask?"

"What will you say when Marshall begs you to leave town and go traipsing all over the world with him—you, who can't even dive?" Marian parried.

"I won't leave here, you know that, Marian. I'm just trying to understand why the man seems to matter to me. It was only one night. And we didn't even make . . ."

"Love?" Marian laughed sharply. "It's not about how long you've known him. And it's sure as hell not a hypothetical problem you can solve."

"No," Isabel said softly, the shadows under her eyes deepening. "I guess it's not."

"Listen, Isabel, if you were indigenous, you'd know that even a heart or a liver remembers where it truly belongs." After a moment's thought, Marian added, "If Marshall would listen to the part of him that still belongs to his mother's people, he'd at least have an elder—a *kahuna*, or medicine person—to show him how to cross over into the animals' world. Shamans were the first healers. Their medicine is much older than Western science."

Maybe Marian was right. Marshall was lost and trying all on his own to find a place in which he now belonged. *Maybe he belonged with her.* Instantly Isabel put this notion out of her head. He was somebody she wanted to understand. His search might parallel hers. They might travel together for a time. But Isabel knew that, like her nomadic brother, Marshall would never stay long with her. Hadn't he already proved that by leaving Isabel to wake up alone at the aquarium?

"Will it be easier if we pretend that Marshall *is* just a specimen—someone we can dissect?" Marian set down her empty picnic plate and eyed Isabel's portion. "I can't believe you don't like pie crust. What kind of American are you, anyway?"

"Be my guest," Isabel grinned. She passed Marian the hollowed-out shell of her pie. She couldn't help but add, "Pie crust is pure lard, you know."

"Don't be a prig, Isabel. We're not on a diet . . . not yet!"

The two howled, and this startled Silkie, who was distracted from his solemn duty of guarding the forensics lab door. Silkie trotted down the hall toward their lab room, eager to be part of the fun.

"No, no, Sil, go back. We're working here." Isabel fondly patted her dog and then walked over to the sink, where she washed her hands. Then she pulled on latex gloves.

"If they'd transplanted a canine heart into your man Marshall, there would be no question," Marian teased, dropping the empty pie plates in the sink. "You'd totally devote your life to a dog."

"Well, of course. Dogs are too loyal to leave you."

"Some dogs." Marian grinned. "Reservation dogs wish they *could* leave." Scrubbing their plates, Marian sighed. "God, sometimes I wish I was just your standard-issue Wal-Mart American. No trying to figure out how a Native and a Native American can coexist in one psyche . . . one history." Marian dried her hands and pulled on a pair of surgical gloves. "Of course, Indians practically live at Wal-Mart. It's our trading post. It's all many of our people can afford of the American dream."

"So," Isabel asked, "what's Buddy done lately?"

Every month or so since Marian's recent divorce, Buddy had "borrowed" another kitchen appliance, because Marian "never used it anyway and he needed it." Marian cooked only for her friends now that Buddy was gone.

"He stole the stupid Crock-Pot." Marian grinned mischievously. "His mother gave it to us as a wedding present. As my own protest against Western civilization, I never used the damn thing, not once."

"I believe it." Isabel laughed. "First we get rid of our bras and finally our Crock-Pots. That's liberation."

"Well, if we're such liberated women, how come we're slaving away here at midnight?" Marian countered. "And talking about men who leave us?"

"Because we're trying to distract ourselves from the fact that we're doing something illegal."

Together they walked over to the steel lab table to begin their work. As they leaned over the body of the dolphin on the table, both women grew serious, each silent as she assembled her instruments.

Perhaps it was all for the good that Marshall was gone, Isabel told herself as she worked. Yet she did let herself remember his hands steady beneath the small of her back as she floated, encircled by Mack and Molly—calves who seemed to be surviving, twenty-four hours after the stranding, because of something more than science. Mack and Molly seemed to be nourished more by human affection than by any tube feeding from round-the-clock volunteers. But what about the human pair who had come together in those chilly waters with a warmth and affection that had startled them both? Would they survive so well without each other?

Such absurdly romantic notions made Isabel wince. This was not about survival. She was fine. Watching Marian prepare her instruments,

Isabel frowned. She had already confided enough to her friend. Ever since finding Isabel at the aquarium in her morning-after reverie, Marian had treated Isabel solicitously, as if she had just discovered her friend had a wasting disease.

Offering love and devotion solely to one person always laid waste to human hearts—this was Isabel's theory. Look at her parents, drowned together because one of them—who knew which?—had wrapped a safety rope, like unyielding arms, around the other while giving up on everyone else. The truth was that her parents were a closed set—a father who was nomadic and a mother who was so afraid of losing her husband that she abandoned her children.

Isabel had spent many years of her childhood imagining her parents' last hours together. What did they say to each other? Had her mother at last seen her ancestors' silkies in her sun-blistered and hallucinatory hypothermia in the Sea of the Hebrides? Had her father or her mother surrendered first to the slap and rise of salty waves? They had apparently died of exposure to cold waters.

But Isabel had found out something more about her parents' drowning. No one, not even Andrew or her grandfather, knew what Isabel had searched out her second year in medical school. Through one of her professor's colleagues—a Scottish cardiologist at the South-Uist Island community hospital where the authorities had taken her parents' bodies—Isabel had discreetly been shown a copy of the official autopsy report. It revealed this anomaly: The cause of her father's death was not drowning, as was her mother's. Long before he was found bound to his wife's body, her father's heart had simply stopped beating.

Isabel had pondered her parents' deaths in a new light, one that helped her decide to do what she already suspected she must: leave medical school. There was another emotional legacy of her parents' deaths that Isabel had not resolved, one she would not find any satisfying answers to by studying simple anatomy. It was a mystery of the human heart.

After she left medical school, Isabel followed her lifelong devotion to marine mammals; she entered veterinary school with a special focus on pathology. But as much as she focused her energy on animals, questions of the human heart still haunted her.

Had her father suffered a coronary while caught with her mother in the storm? There was another theory, one that Isabel tried her best never to admit. Had her father died aboard the sailboat during the race? Did his wife then tack straight into the storm's maw with the despair that drowned her? Had she given up not only on herself but her children too? That terrible theory might explain the fact that her parents, who were both strong and safety-conscious sailors, wore no life preservers when at last they were found.

Isabel turned her attention back to their necropsy. She did not like dwelling on a mystery that would never be solved. Not when some mysteries could be successfully examined. She carefully studied the small dolphin from rostrum to blowhole, noting the girth, fluke, and body width. What had killed all these sea creatures? Or was the stranding a natural event?

"By the way, Mack and Molly are swimming so close together now that their pectoral fins are touching," Isabel said.

"I'm so glad. I hope we can release them back into the ocean soon."

As the two women carefully measured and documented each healed scar, tooth rake, and other injury to the dolphin that could possibly indicate a death by natural causes, Isabel couldn't shake the memory of this afternoon's argument with her boss.

"I'm telling you, Isabel," Trevor Franklin, the director of the forensics lab, had said this afternoon, "don't get hung up on this." Then he ordered her to dispose of the two Pacific white-sided dolphins that Marian and the stranding network volunteers had managed to transport from the beach on a flatbed truck with little bruising or postdeath trauma.

This particular dolphin carcass was one of the few with internal ears still intact after all of Dr. Sharp's on-site necropsies. Was he destroying evidence or collecting it?

"But why not at least do a preliminary investigation?" Isabel had asked her boss. "You know these are two of the few animals from the crime scene that were not tampered with by the military. They're perfect specimens. They're evidence that might explain why many of the animals suffered ruptured eardrums."

Trevor held up his hands as if to say, I'm not arguing with you. "Yes, I know, Isabel. And in any other case, I'd be pleased as punch to get a full body—not just jigsaw pieces of animals we try to identify." He stepped back, shoved his fists in his denim pockets, and cursed under his breath. "But this is not any other case." He paused, then blurted, "And finding out what's deafened and killed these cetaceans is not going to bring back your hearing, Isabel."

Shocked, Isabel glared at him. "Is that all you think this is? Something personal? It has nothing to do with that. It has everything to do with the fact that this is our home, our responsibility . . ."

"No," Trevor snapped. "You're too involved. You're losing your scientific detachment. Besides, this job has been taken away from us by D.C. officials. Don't you remember how many decades it took to get federal funding for our lab? No, you were just a bright kid in school at the time. And you're still just a bright kid in a small town, Isabel. Let NMFS handle it now. We'll be in way over our heads if we pursue this."

Isabel was bewildered to see a man she had so long admired compromising himself and his life's work. "So," Isabel said, "we're just a *little* wildlife lab, way out in the sticks? We're not 'the world's only forensics lab to bring to justice those criminals who victimize animals'?" Isabel couldn't help but quote Trevor Franklin's well-known professional boast.

"We don't know that any violation occurred here!" Trevor turned his back to her.

"I'm sorry, Trevor." Isabel softened. "I'm sorry we don't agree."

Her tone unmanned him, and Trevor walked toward the door without looking back. "Just don't let me see what you do, Isabel," was all he said. "Don't let anybody see."

Isabel had taken his words for tacit support of what she and Marian were doing tonight in the lab. As was their habit, Isabel and Marian paused before beginning their dissection.

With a slight bow of her head, Isabel rested both gloved hands on the body of this female Pacific white-sided dolphin and said very softly, "I am so sorry for the violence of your death." Her words were formal, almost an incantation.

Be gentle, Isabel's anatomy professor, Dr. Grayson Elliot, had taught his first-year medical students in basic human anatomy. *Every body once belonged to somebody.*

Now, in their work with animals, Isabel and Marian practiced this same professionalism, even reverence, first taught by Dr. Elliot. In medical school, Isabel and Marian had met while studying in the Willed Body Program at the University of Washington.

Our work is a dying art, Dr. Elliot had taught his students. First of all, he said, they must respect the human being naked before them on the stainless steel table. They must never make jokes or ridicule the dead person who had given his or her body for their higher knowledge. Dr. Elliot suggested his first-year students give their cadavers proper names and an imagined personal history, so they could not dismiss and detach from the bodies' own humanity. At the same time, so identification would not be personal, Elliot made sure that all the cadavers for his first-year anatomy students were at least sixty years old.

Before professors like Dr. Elliot, with his more humane and respectful anatomy courses, human cadavers were routinely fished out of vats of formaldehyde with large hooks and plopped down unceremoniously on the table. Often students were simply presented with a severed arm wrapped in plastic, sometimes even with a wedding ring on one finger. In the same callous spirit, students would sometimes revile their cadavers. Isabel had heard of medical students who, while practicing dissection of the skull, indulged in a mock war using human brains as their weapons.

But with anatomy professors like Dr. Elliot and the increasing number of women in medical schools, that had changed. Isabel had been particularly moved by the collective memorial service that administrators of the Willed Body Program held in gratitude for their donors' families. One of the first donors had been her grandfather. Grandfather Spinner had given his survivors two choices: donate his body to medical science or throw him, without cremation, into the Pacific Ocean.

Both Isabel and Andrew had argued with the old man about the illegality of a body buried at sea, and both had decided to do it anyway if that was what the old man wanted. But in the end, their grandfather made his own decision. "You don't need another body lost at sea to haunt you. Let me do some good after I'm dead."

The old man had often said Isabel would make a fine doctor.

At the collective memorial service, Isabel had looked around at other families of donors. When the medical students stood up to read poems or letters from donors, Isabel recognized that here was science *and* compassion.

Isabel had bowed her head, tears spilling as she heard her grandfather's familiar voice in his letter: *I can't leave money, but I can leave my body. Let it make some surgeon's hand sure.*

When Isabel finished her ritual, Marian said a prayer in her native language. After Marian's prayer, Isabel turned on the official tape recorder to document their findings.

Isabel carefully examined the dolphin. Except for the bleeding around the eye sockets, this appeared to be a normal, healthy Pacific white-sided dolphin. Probably no more than four years old. Frowning, Isabel leaned over to more closely study the still, wide-open eye.

She spoke clearly so the voice-activated tape recorder would document her notes. "Conjunctival hemorrhage . . . perhaps indicative of some kind of trauma."

With her scalpel, Isabel very slowly cut twelve-inch rectangular blocks in the dolphin's flanks, creating a precise patchwork of skin. These squares of flensed blubber Marian carefully laid out on the steel table beside the dolphin.

"Let's discreetly send some specimens to another lab," Isabel suggested. "Maybe we can get some other wildlife pathologists involved."

"I know a few who might help us."

Marian placed several pieces of the flensed skin into plastic evidence bags. Other specialists would puzzle over whether this blubber betrayed disease, parasites, or malnutrition. Marian labeled and photographed each square of pale gray and black skin.

As Isabel continued her work on the dolphin, her mind roamed back to the aquarium, where a miniature version of this beautiful Pacific white-sided dolphin, Molly, was playing with Mack. The species was among the liveliest of all dolphins, so active and demonstrative, always splashing and spinning midair to delight each other and any swimmers who were lucky enough to be nearby.

Once while seal-sitting several years ago, Isabel had seen dozens of

Pacific white-sided dolphins surfing and riding the wake of huge spring-time waves. There must have been thirty of these exuberant acrobats twirling within that one wave, playing together. And when the big waves subsided, the dolphins changed their game to one of chase and race, traveling side by side so fast that their tail flukes set off the luminous sprays of water that scientists called "rooster tails."

To see these same tail flukes lying so quiet and flat on the stainless steel table as Isabel now measured them caused her a moment's hesitation. Her scalpel was still as she took a deep breath. The pungent smell of blood and blubber was nothing compared to the sorrow. Isabel was accustomed to the smell; she would never get used to the grief. Would Molly also end up on her table?

"It's hard with this little lag, isn't it?" Marian asked softly.

Though she used the scientific name, it didn't seem to make Isabel feel any more detached while doing the necropsy. This was personal. This was their beach. This was their responsibility, in a way that their forensics work had never been before. This was one wildlife crime that would not go unsolved.

Isabel did not have to say any of this to Marian, who was now helping her dissect the area around the scapula.

"Here's something," Isabel said, leaning over the dolphin and intently studying the blubber. "Look at this pattern of deep bruising along the shoulder. You wouldn't expect it to bleed like this without some trauma or impact."

"You think it could be postmortem?" Marian asked.

"No, definitely not. It's a recent event, but not postmortem. There's a shearing effect here, see? As if the tissue imploded outward against the hard bone of the scapula to cause this internal contusion."

"That would be consistent with the effects of a pressure wave, wouldn't it?"

"Yes, it's compelling evidence of some trauma, since blubber doesn't tear and hemorrhage without an intense force. This is a hemorrhagic pattern I've never seen. Have you?"

"No, never."

Isabel stopped her dissection and looked intently at Marian. "Let's go to the lungs and then the other organs and see if this hemorrhage pattern repeats."

It took almost another hour of careful work, but diligently the two women dissected down into the rib cage to reveal the deep-red lobes of the lungs.

"Oh," Isabel said, trying to keep her tone neutral for the tape recorder. But what she saw was so disturbing that she could not keep an edge from her voice.

"Yes, I see it," Marian echoed.

There were dark bands of bruises circling each lung that exactly matched the pattern of the rib cage.

What Isabel saw convinced her now that she was speaking not simply to Marian or other pathologists but to the tape recorder and the world. She knew now that this evidence would become part of a document that must be understood by laypeople and perhaps a jury. So, very clearly, Isabel explained, "Tissue is so democratic. It responds the same way to all traumas. Tissue has physical limits of expansion and compression, especially shown in the lungs here and internal tissues. When tissue is impacted, say by an acoustic blast or pressure wave, it will explode outward and hit against bone, thus leaving these telltale bruises. It's like what occurs in a brain injury: when the head is traumatized, the brain will hit the skull contralaterally, that is, on the side opposite from the impact. The hard surfaces of these ribs have profoundly bruised the dolphin's lungs in a pattern that clearly reveals intense trauma. If the injury is from an acoustic blast, the dolphin's inner ears and brain will tell us."

Marian snapped off the tape recorder. "Okay," she said firmly. "We're entering the real evidence stage. Do we want to continue with this?"

"How can we stop now, after what we've found?"

"You know what this will mean." It was not a question.

After a long silence, Isabel said, "Yes, I know." She gave Marian a pleading look. "Leave. Leave now and let me finish it. I'll take the blame. We can't both lose our jobs. Somebody has to stay here . . . for the animals."

"And who will stay for you, Isabel," Marian demanded, "if I don't?" Before Isabel could protest, Marian pulled out the small bone saw. "I want to see the heart, liver . . ." Marian muttered and her voice was drowned out by the buzz of the saw.

Isabel watched her friend, shaking her head. She was too moved to say anything more, except, "Thank you."

Marian didn't reply, pretending not to have heard above the drone of the saw. But Isabel knew by the clenching of Marian's jaw that she had not only heard but had also fiercely decided to share Isabel's fate.

At last lifting the small heart in one hand, Marian almost tenderly presented it to Isabel to dissect. As Isabel cut into the heart, there was an unexpected popping sound as gaseous bloody bubbles frothed forth, revealing spongy tissue inside. Neither woman had ever heard or seen such a thing. It so startled them that for a moment they could not speak. But their eyes met and they each looked down again. Only then did Isabel notice that Marian's hands were shaking. Isabel felt it, too—a mixture of dread and despair—as she leaned against the table to steady herself.

"This is terrible," Isabel whispered.

"Truly terrible."

Inside, the heart's tissue was so lacerated and so savagely sheared that it looked as if a grenade had ripped it loose. Only an unfathomable shock could cause such astonishing injury. Isabel couldn't imagine what it must have felt like to have one's organs vibrating horribly and then, at the most intense blasts, rupturing.

Once she had heard Daniel McHalffey tell about a heart surgery in which he'd seen a heart actually explode from aortic pressure, right there on the table. "It was like a little bomb bursting," Daniel had described it. "That heart just blasted open and bloomed right out of the chest like a tiny red geyser."

This dolphin heart's injury was more appalling because it was not made in any effort to save a life. Now Isabel made the disturbing connection: it was a calculated trauma inflicted by a device that could later be used as a weapon. Now, the victims were cetaceans; someday would they be humans?

Isabel snapped on the tape recorder again. "It is probable," she said in a loud voice that echoed around the small necropsy lab, ". . . probable that we are seeing evidence of intense injury due to acoustic blast trauma."

Then Isabel, with Marian's expert assistance, continued dissecting the other organs. Liver, spleen, pancreas, kidneys. As they cut into these organs, as when they cut into the heart, there was that eerie, audible pop of gaseous, bloody bubbles and the spongy, ruptured tissue inside.

"You know, I've read about this kind of tissue damage happening once before, in the Canary Islands," Marian said, after they had weighed each organ and placed them in specimen bags. "The stranded cetaceans also had organs just like this after the NATO acoustic tests off the islands. It was all over the Internet . . ."

Isabel had also read several citations of the U.S. Navy's research circulated on the Marine Mammal Network. In studies on lab animals sponsored by the U.S. Naval Undersea Warfare Center, their new low-frequency active sonar had clearly induced dizziness, vertigo, and lung hemorrhage in the study animals. But the damage to this dolphin was so much more extreme than what she'd read about.

"What we'll be looking for next in the inner ear tissue," Isabel said to the recorder microphone above their table, "is evidence—which the pending CAT scans may also clearly reveal—that there is massive sub-arachnoid hemorrhage . . ." Isabel's voice dropped in pitch. "We do not know why some animals in the stranding suffered so and others had lesser injuries. Perhaps it has to do with how close they were swimming to the source of the sound blasts. What we do see here is undeniable. Unimaginable acoustic trauma." Then she reached up and snapped off the recorder.

"Someone has imagined it," Marian said softly. She walked over to her desk in a corner of the lab. "There's this Website I stumbled on once . . . ," Marian said, clicking the keys on her computer. "Think I saved the file . . . Yes, here it is on the International Environmental Alert Website. Listen to this." Marian read aloud, "The U.S. Navy is developing a dangerous new underwater acoustic weapon. Concerned critics are calling it 'Water Thunder.' The military maintains that this sonar device is designed only to detect enemy submarines, of which there are few since the end of the cold war." Marian fell quiet, scanning. Then she resumed reading. "In peacetime there is less and less for the military to do except research and development. In the midnineties, the U.S. Navy began seriously developing this low-frequency active sonar. In 1998, the navy performed sonar tests off the Big Island of Hawaii—right in the middle of the humpback calving and mating season. International scientists are vocal in their fears that this sonar is responsible for mass strandings off Greece and the Canary Islands. In March of 2000 there was another mass stranding off the Bahamas."

"Yeah, I read about that, too."

Marian continued reading aloud, "'Eight whales died of cranial hemorrhaging. The navy has been slow to admit any cause-and-effect relationship between the whale deaths and their concurrent sonar tests. But at a congressional hearing, the navy, under international pressure, has at last accepted responsibility. Still they continue conducting the dangerous sonar tests . . .'"

"Is there someone to contact on that Website?" Isabel asked.

"Dr. Nathan Siestina—he's a marine biologist off the Bahamas. There's an e-mail address and Website for contacting him."

"I can send him some tissue samples. We have to get corroboration. I know this damage isn't from any natural causes. Do we have any confirmed reports of the navy conducting sonar experiments off Kiwanda Beach?" Isabel heard her own voice. It was steady and sure, not at all the way she felt inside. "That might explain why these whales were so disoriented, why there were so many highly unusual separations of mothers and calves."

"No confirmed reports," Marian said. "But NMFS *did* issue another divers' alert for this weekend. Said they were doing seismic testing for earthquake faults. Remember those two gray whales killed last year off the coast of California during the seismic tests?"

"I don't suppose Stewart will tell us anything?"

"Ask him for cobbler, ask him for a date, ask him to come running back to you, and he'd say yes." Marian shook her head. "But that man won't risk his job—or his authority—for you."

"I know," Isabel said. "I just keep hoping that Stewart might still become his better self."

"Stewart's better self is *you*, Isa," Marian said. "Without you, he's clueless."

Isabel fell quiet, gazing down at the dolphin before them on the table. Sorrow overwhelmed her.

"If this death is from deep-sea experimental acoustic tests," Marian said quietly, "you know they'll use this sonar on humans someday as a new weapon. Whales are just guinea pigs. It's all practice for future wars when a submarine can sneak up on an enemy sub. This sonar may acoustically annihilate those living on board. Then they can simply take the sub hostage, without messing around with any living prisoners of war."

"That's monstrous."

"Remember the plans for the neutron bomb, which would vaporize people but not buildings?" Marian asked. "Entire cities without people could then just be taken over. Well, this sonar will be the same thing, but underwater. We've seen what it can do to tissue . . ." Marian held up a spongy piece of heart tissue. "The military made the atom bomb out of a nucleus. This is the result of what they're making out of sound."

Isabel turned her tape recorder back on and dictated, "Severe hemorrhaging in heart, inner ears, and lung tissue. Cause of death, acoustic trauma. Possible military source: high-decibel, low- to mid-frequency active sonar."

Marian came around the stainless steel table to place her hand on Isabel's shoulder. "Water Thunder," Marion said. "History will judge this weapon harshly."

The ascending trill of a phone interrupted them, and Isabel snapped off the recorder, scrambling for her mobile. She noted the caller ID and the time on her cell phone: 3 A.M. She was too troubled to feel at all sleepy.

"Daniel," she said tersely, "do you have any CAT scan results yet?"

"Yeah," he answered. "We got a neurologist to come in and read the X rays in the middle of the night. A real trooper . . ."

"And . . . ?"

"Massive hemorrhaging in the brain and especially in the inner ears. The doc has never seen anything like this kind of damage. Does this help?"

"Yes, it's absolute confirmation," Isabel said.

"So, you now know the cause of all these deaths?"

"Acoustic blast trauma," Isabel said flatly. "With this evidence, we can clearly link it to some kind of sonar the military is using off our coast. But I need something else from you now, Daniel."

"You got it. What?"

"Please be very careful not to tell anybody about this, or that we have two cetacean carcasses that NMFS doesn't know we took off the beach. From this moment on, we have to do things by the book, even though the CAT scans and this necropsy are unofficial. But before we can call in any media, we'll send tissue samples to another scientist who's done necropsies on stranded cetaceans. And . . . and I've got to try something else myself, first."

"What? Don't do anything dangerous . . . or alone," Daniel said.

"I'll ask for your help as soon as I can. Agreed?" She knew now what she must do. "Thanks, Daniel. Now get that poor dolphin back into your freezer for safekeeping. It's evidence."

"Will do," Daniel said and hung up.

Isabel did not have to explain her conversation to Marian. All she did was turn back on the official tape recorder and dictate, "CAT scans confirm our findings."

Marian nodded, and the two women continued the necropsy, though now it was Isabel's hands that were shaking. And for the first time ever since she began pathology work, she felt faint.

Marian took the lead, as if sensing Isabel's vulnerability. Expertly, she cut off the dolphin's head, and they began the delicate dissection of the skull and brain. Neither woman was surprised to see ganglia of ruptured vessels and sheared tissue, as well as dark bruises and extreme swelling in both hemispheres of the brain—as if the brain had been mercilessly bounced around inside the hard, curved bones of the skull.

"Can you imagine what it must be like to endure this kind of pain and noise?" Marian said quietly.

"Like acoustic bullets in the brain."

"No wonder these little guys fled right out of the water to die onshore. Even suffocating on the beach would be a better death than imploding, blasted over and over with those hideous sound waves."

Both women fell silent, and then Isabel said, "I can't fathom a mind that could create this acoustic weapon." She was thinking of Dr. Sharp, a scientist whose necropsies on the stranded animals were certainly a conflict of interest. Was he still on the beach with the navy?

"I know you're planning something," Marian said wearily. "But I'm not going to ask—not now. You wouldn't tell me, anyway."

They finished the necropsy in the usual way. Carefully Marian disemboweled the dolphin with a surgical sickle. They tied the bright red intestines and purplish stomach with strings for later analysis and put them in freezer evidence-storage bags. At last, around 4 A.M., the women cleaned the stainless steel necropsy table and drained the remaining blood into a bucket below. Then they completed their necropsy notes. Finally, very gently, Isabel pulled up a blue plastic tarp to cover the creature. Then she and Marian wheeled the dolphin back into the cold morgue.

"We should get some sleep," Marian said wearily, watching Isabel. "Don't do anything without me. Promise?"

chapter eleven

Blue Dragon Rising from the Sea

AFTER SHE AND Marian left the lab, Isabel did not head to her beach cottage to sleep. The most important thing now was to somehow find Dr. Alexander Sharp. Surely, as a scientist, Sharp could be reasoned with, especially given the shocking results of their necropsy on the dolphin. Isabel hoped she could convince Sharp that the navy's sonar tests were the probable cause of the stranding deaths as well as the deaths of countless animals who may have died at sea unseen. She also hoped that the young scientist would not harbor any hard feelings after his scuffle with her loyal stranding network volunteers. They had not, in fact, made a citizen's arrest; instead they had been escorted off the beach by the military. Many had simply returned under cover of darkness to help the stranded cetaceans. By then, the military men and Dr. Sharp had disappeared.

Isabel knew she was risking her job, but she couldn't ignore the evidence. Still, some part of her wished she could just go home, crawl into bed, and fall into sleep like Nepenthe, forgetting all she had discovered. Was this the way Marshall had felt when he left her on the side of the aquarium pool? Could he just pretend that things were the same as before the stranding, before their night together? Could he simply go on without changing his life? Of course he could. He had.

As Isabel drove the coastal highway, she noted the navy boat far out near Sail Rock Point, its mast-strung lights gleaming like an ominous constellation. Were the tests still going on? A frown creased her forehead, and her lower back ached. Below, on Kiwanda Beach, shone the headlights and flashing red lights of her stranding network crew still trying to rescue the few whales and dolphins yet alive. Horrible images of the deep-scarlet rivulets in hemorrhaging lungs and brains drove Isabel on.

She checked her watch; it was almost dawn. Not a decent time to rouse Dr. Sharp from his slumber, whether he was out on the navy boat or here on land. Glowing an eerie green, her cell phone looked like some bioluminescent deep-sea creature in the darkness of the truck's cab. Isabel pondered the consequences of her next move, then punched speed dial.

"Salk," came the gruff, sleepy voice. "What is it?" Stewart was especially cranky when abruptly awakened. Isabel wondered why he used to insist on accompanying her on her late-night stranding calls. He'd followed Isabel's lead ever since middle school biology lab. Isabel had been somewhat surprised when, after their divorce, he kept his job at the National Marine Fisheries Service. She had always believed he'd chosen wildlife management as a way to be with her. There had been some rumor, never proven, about Stewart accepting kickbacks from offshore oil companies trying to get federal permission to drill off the Oregon coast. Stewart had personally assured Isabel that he cared for their native beach as much as she did.

"Stewart, I'm so sorry to wake you . . ."

"Isabel?" His voice softened, and he sounded vulnerable.

She was again lying in bed with a young husband who was as confused as she was about their failing marriage.

"But we belong together," Stewart had said, rising up on one arm and kissing her ear—the one that had long ago lost its hearing. He could never remember which ear was silent. Stewart's body had smelled of her lemon cleansing cream; he was always borrowing it. "You keep forgetting that."

The cell phone buzzed static in her good ear. "Stewart, I need your help."

"You got it, Isa," Stewart said, then added, "always."

His tone was so earnest, almost grateful, that Isabel felt an uncomfortable pang of guilt. Under ordinary circumstances, she would have kept her own rule not to ask Stewart for anything. Whenever she had, she'd felt such obligation and pressure to give Stewart yet another chance at reconciliation. Still, these were not ordinary circumstances.

"Do you know where Dr. Sharp is right now?"

A pause, then a voice full of disappointment. "What do you want with him?"

Isabel couldn't tell Stewart about the illegal necropsy, nor did she want to lie to him. "I've got to speak with him in person, Stewart. I think I know what might be causing this stranding. I have . . . some evidence in this case that . . ."

"There is no case!" Stewart snapped. "This is way beyond your authority." He added in a more conciliatory tone, "I told you that on the beach, Isabel. I was trying to protect you."

"Your job is to protect the beach and wildlife, Stewart." She knew the minute the words were out that she would lose him, unless she found a better way to ask for his assistance. As Isabel took a curve on the highway, she changed gears. "Stewart, I know you were trying to look out for me on the beach. But I'm doing something . . . well, dangerous—and I need your protection now."

Without a word from him, Isabel knew he was again with her. By the shuffling sounds on the phone, she also knew he was hastily dressing. "Tell me where to meet you, Isabel. I'm there."

"Where is Sharp?"

"Him again?"

"Just trust me, Stewart. Please."

"Dr. Sharp is still out on the navy boat. No one is permitted out there."

"You are."

Grudgingly, Stewart admitted, "Yes, I am."

"Will you take me out with you? I just want to talk with Dr. Sharp. It won't take much more than an hour to reach the boat. And we won't stay long. I promise, Stewart . . ." Isabel shook her head. "I promise I'll make it up to you."

"And I'll hold you to that."

"I know."

"Meet me at the dock. We'll take out an NMFS boat so we can get past the military guards."

"Stewart, why are there all these military people on our beach? Do you know what's going on with the divers' alert and . . ."

"That's not for me to tell you, Isa." There was real regret in his voice. "But I will take you out to the boat."

"Thank you."

"I'm not such a bad guy, Isabel," he shot back. "You know I always try to do the right thing."

"I know, Stewart."

"It's just that . . . ," he said softly, as if someone else were listening in, "it's just that sometimes it's hard to know what the right thing is."

In that moment, Isabel loved him again and remembered the awkward lab partner who, without complaint, endured days on Kiwanda Beach to support her science fair projects. It was not Stewart's idea of a date, he would tell her, but never once did he stand her up.

"I knew I could count on you, Stewart."

"For better or for worse," he said. "See you in a sec."

When Stewart met her at the NMFS patrol boat, his hair was sticking straight up, uncombed. Isabel smiled and smoothed it with her hand, then briefly embraced him. "What a sweetheart," she said. And she meant it.

Grinning, Stewart put on his NMFS cap and revved up the twin motors. "I'm the arresting officer on this beach," he said. "I should be arresting us for trespassing."

"Divers' alert still on?"

"Much more than that," he frowned.

"Can't you tell me . . . anything?"

"Better not, Isa. It's bad enough I'm violating the beach curfew. We shouldn't even be approaching the navy boat."

"Why ever not? Tell me, what's really going on out there?"

Stewart sighed and then shrugged. "Don't ask and I won't tell, Isa. Just let it be. That's the navy way. You can ask Dr. Sharp all these questions."

With the red light flashing on the NMFS motorboat, Stewart cruised past the two navy patrol boats. The sea was calm this early morning, the spring air fragrant with cedar, brine, and kelp. Isabel breathed in the salt spray, gathering strength.

She was startled when her cell phone vibrated in the pocket of her rain slicker. She considered not answering. But what if it was Marian or a stranding volunteer? When Isabel heard the familiar voice, she couldn't help the wave of warmth that flushed through her body. Thank God Stewart didn't see her reaction. Isabel hoped he wouldn't sense the heat inside her, her heartbeat quickening.

"I know it's early to call . . ." Marshall's voice was solid, as if he stood next to her now. "What's all that noise?"

"Boat engine," Isabel shouted, keenly aware that Stewart was listening to every word. "Where are you?"

"Andrew and I finished up early at the conference." There was a pause. "Found myself here last night at the Ocean Haven Tavern with a bunch of your stranding network volunteers. Looks like they've had another rough night of it—and I'll bet you have, too. Want to take a break and join us for breakfast? "

Isabel said nothing. If she had been alone, she might have met Marshall's inviting tone with her own. But with Stewart listening, all she could say was, "I wish I'd known you were coming back to the coast. Tell the volunteers hello for me."

"What?" Marshall said. "I can hardly hear you. Can you meet me here?"

"This isn't a good time," Isabel said loudly.

Silence. Then Marshall said in a hoarse voice, "Well, I guess I'll catch you next time I'm out on the coast . . ."

"Marshall," she blurted out his name and hoped Stewart wouldn't hear above the engine noise. "I do want to see you again, it's just that I can't . . ."

"Fine," Marshall said too quickly. "I understand."

"No, no, you don't," Isabel pushed on, in spite of Stewart's frown. "I'm with Stewart . . ." She could hear Marshall's dismay in the silence between them. She hurried on. "I did a necropsy on one of the stranded dolphins. It's horrible what we found."

"Where the hell are you exactly?"

"At sea," she shouted.

"Yeah," Marshall said shortly, "me, too."

"Isabel, we're almost there," Stewart snapped.

"Marshall," Isabel said, "I have to go. We're getting too near the navy boat . . ."

199

"Navy boat? Isabel, for God's sake!" Marshall's voice crackled over the cell phone. "What are you trying to do? It's dangerous!"

"I've got to show these necropsy photos to the navy scientist. Looks like their sonar may be the cause of the stranding and . . ."

"I'm coming with you."

"No, we're already there. No time."

"I'll get one of the volunteers to motor me out to the navy boat."

"You can't. It's off-limits."

"It's the ocean, Isabel. It doesn't belong to the navy."

"We're here," Stewart informed her curtly.

"I'm sorry, Marshall. Got to go. Sorry."

"No . . . wait for me!"

"For God's sake," Stewart snapped, "hang up on the guy and pay attention if you really want to get on board!"

Reluctantly Isabel said, "I'll call you back later," and hung up.

Insistently her cell phone vibrated in the pocket of her rain slicker several times before she reluctantly turned it off. As they approached the large navy boat—a onetime destroyer pressed into peacetime service as a research vessel—a voice suddenly halted Stewart and Isabel.

"This vessel is strictly off-limits!" the loudspeaker voice announced.

The boat loomed large above their motorboat. There was a lot of activity on the deck.

"Lieutenant Lester!" Stewart shouted back through his small megaphone. "Request permission to board. We have to talk with Dr. Sharp."

"We?"

"You can't tell them it's me," Isabel cautioned. "After the beach incident, Sharp will never let me near him."

"Federal agent on board," Stewart announced. "Must speak to Dr. Sharp. It's urgent government business."

"Come aboard," the loudspeaker boomed back.

Within minutes several navy ensigns were helping Stewart and Isabel on board. "Dr. Sharp is very busy," a sailor told them in a polite but firm voice.

They were hustled to a makeshift storage shed on the deck, given lukewarm coffee, and ignored for nearly two hours. It was impossible to see anything beyond the shuttered windows and closed door of the tiny shed, but Isabel could hear the shouts of many sailors. She realized that she and Stewart were unobtrusively under guard. The navy could keep them here as long as they liked. Were the sonar tests continuing?

Anxiously Isabel tried to get a sense of the high-tech equipment bleeping and whirring on the deck outside the shed. Her limited hearing maddened her. She was exactly the wrong person for this. Why hadn't she let Marshall come help out, or one of her volunteers? She felt powerless trapped here when perhaps, right now below this boat, the sonar device was droning lethal sound into the sea.

"Stewart," Isabel said, leaning near him, "they'll never let us see Dr. Sharp. We have to demand . . ."

"Enough, Isa," Stewart said. "We did our best . . ."

"No." Isabel started up. "I'm going to find . . ."

With a sigh, Stewart stood and placed a hand on her shoulder. "Okay, okay, I'll see what I can do. But you stay here. Promise?"

Isabel made no promises. She watched her ex-husband walk out onto the deck, noting that he was limping slightly. Damp sea air always made his old knee injury flare up.

Waiting for Stewart, Isabel took copious notes in her pocket note-book—every scrap of relevant conversation, names of equipment, of sailors and technicians. It was not much, it was not heroic, but it was something she could do. Another half hour and Stewart came back with Dr. Sharp by his side. Accompanying Sharp was the burly lieutenant who'd also been on the beach during the stranding.

When Isabel rose, the lieutenant quickly stepped near her and the young scientist.

"It's all right, Lieutenant Lester," Dr. Sharp said. He seemed resigned to seeing Isabel. His eyes were veiled behind thick glasses so that he resembled a computer maven, distracted and driven.

Through the open door of the shed, Isabel tried to track the massive coils of copper wire and snarled black cables of equipment lying on the deck.

"May I talk with you alone, Dr. Sharp?"

The scientist nodded curtly and dismissed both Stewart and

Lieutenant Lester. "But I have only a few minutes before we'll have to ask you to leave my boat."

Isabel noted the authority with which Sharp now claimed the research vessel. No longer was he pretending not to be associated with the navy. But she kept any irritation or urgency from her voice. She summoned all her scientific reserve. Instinctively she knew that this collegial tone—and not an emotional appeal—would be what would touch Dr. Sharp. How many times had she worked with other scientists who, if she betrayed any emotion over an animal's suffering, would promptly dismiss her? "I have some necropsy results here that will interest you."

"Has anyone else seen them?" Dr. Sharp asked quickly.

Isabel said nothing. She would not incriminate Marian, nor did she want to give Sharp the impression that she alone was working on this case. "I have forwarded some of the results to another consulting scientist."

"Who?"

"A peer," she said curtly.

"Who authorized such a necropsy and peer review?" Dr. Sharp demanded.

"I did," Isabel said.

He reached for the file folder Isabel was offering him. At the sight of Isabel's necropsy photos, Dr. Sharp's face betrayed some shock. For a moment, he could say nothing.

"I haven't . . . haven't had time to do a formal necropsy of my own," Dr. Sharp said softly. "Not in the middle of these . . . of my research here on the boat."

It took all her will for Isabel to keep silent. Let the photos and the young cetacean scientist do the work. It was obvious Dr. Sharp had never anticipated such profound trauma to the marine mammals. Perhaps he had even convinced himself that the mass stranding had nothing to do with his acoustic tests. But her evidence was undeniable.

By the sagging of his shoulders and the tremble in his hands when Dr. Sharp lit his pipe, Isabel knew that what he had seen had disturbed him deeply. He was, after all, human. Even the lieutenant, who entered again and briefly glanced at the grisly photo of the shredded ear bone bulla and lacerated dolphin lungs, blanched slightly.

In her softest voice, Isabel began, "Dr. Sharp, I know you never meant to harm . . ."

"Man overboard!" someone shouted, and a commotion started on a lower deck. Isabel tried to step closer to the young scientist to gently touch his elbow, but Sharp was distracted.

"Another trespasser?" he demanded.

"We found this guy in the water alongside the ship, trying to get on board," an ensign shouted. "A civilian motorboat sped away. Must be how he got out here."

Everyone looked to see Marshall being hauled down the deck by several navy personnel. Before they could completely secure him, Marshall slipped out of his scuba tank harness and an ensign's grip. He strode toward Isabel, dragging another young ensign behind him. "Are you all right?" he called. "What's going on here?"

Flustered, Isabel turned to Dr. Sharp. "I'm sorry for the intrusion, but he's with me . . . I guess."

The scientist gave her a wry look. "Obviously." Dr. Sharp closed the folder on her necropsy photos, unlocked a nearby metal box, and slipped the photos inside, snapping the lock shut again. "Arrest this man for trespassing," he barked to the lieutenant, and then he turned away.

Startled, Isabel reached for Dr. Sharp's arm, but he was beyond her now. She spun around to see Marshall being held back from her by Stewart and at least three sailors. "Stewart," she said, trying to keep her voice calm. "You know this isn't right. Let me . . ." But as she walked toward Marshall, the lieutenant pinned her arms behind her back.

"Not so fast," the lieutenant growled. He seemed to take some pleasure in restraining her at last.

Isabel felt a wave of anger. Her body responded now. She didn't have to struggle against the lieutenant's grasp. Instinctively Isabel remembered her t'ai chi teacher telling her, *The very last thing an attacker expects is that you will relax.* With a deep breath, Isabel softened her shoulders. As if this were any morning's practice, she imagined her energy sinking deep down, fathoms deep, to the very bottom of the ocean. She was attached to a power, a magnetic field stronger than her own. *Adhere to the attacker's energy.* She heard her teacher's words as she pulled inward, drawing the burly man ever so slightly off balance. *Change his momentum into your own.*

As the lieutenant gripped her arms, Isabel simply sank down into her standing horse-legs position and, without a shout, raised her arms upward in a powerful arc. *Crane spreads wings,* she heard her teacher say, as if pleased with her movement. *Focus your intent and use your chi like gravity.* As if in a tight orbit around some center on the deck, Isabel spun around inside her attacker's arms and felt his grip loosen. She faced him fully. In that long second she saw the confusion in his clear green eyes, the astonishment in his jaw line, the intelligence in his high brow. He was no enemy. He was doing his duty. Nevertheless, he was stopping her from doing hers.

A calm force not all her own flowed through her. Isabel deflected his wrists as the lieutenant again grabbed for her. *It's a dance,* her teacher always said, *a dance of energies.* And Isabel was leading as she used the man's own attack, channeling it with quick circular blocks to his temple and then a subtle sidestep. *Blue dragon rises from the sea,* her teacher's voice. A final, subtle blur of her hands, a high kick, and Isabel spun free. The lieutenant landed face down, but without force or injury, on the deck. Isabel had cradled his neck and head as he fell.

The man was unharmed, except for his dignity, but instead of going after her again, he shook his head and sat still on the deck. "Okay," he told her and tried to dismiss it all with a snort. "I won't tangle with some god-damn kung fu master!"

Isabel ran across the deck to Marshall, who was grinning widely. "Hey, I thought I was going to rescue you," he said.

"She's going to have to get you out of jail, McGreggor." Stewart cinched Marshall's arms more tightly. "Anybody got handcuffs?"

One of the sailors scrambled in search of cuffs.

"This is just ridiculous." Isabel faced Stewart. "None of us are going to jail. Marshall was just looking out for me."

"Like I do," Stewart said gruffly. "Let's get out of here, Isabel."

Isabel glanced back to see the lieutenant conferring with Dr. Sharp. She felt confusing emotions. Marshall's intrusion had probably ruined any chance of persuading Dr. Sharp to help convince the navy to stop their sonar tests.

She hesitated, not knowing exactly what to do. In that moment, Isabel saw what no one else was noticing.

"Look out!" she shouted as a coil of heavy cable that had lain circling Dr. Sharp's foot suddenly tightened. As if by an unseen hand, the cable quickly dragged the scientist across the deck.

It was Marshall who broke free of Stewart to reach Dr. Sharp before anyone else did. He held on to the man's long legs with all his might, but it was as if the cable were attached to a heavy anchor dropping below. Before Marshall could secure the young scientist, Sharp's body flew up and over the guardrails.

"Man overboard!" a deck officer shouted.

Sailors scattered to their stations, equipment and cords clanking. Chaos.

Then, Isabel noticed, with the precision of a much-practiced drill a group of men launched a lifeboat. But she was even more struck by Lieutenant Lester's urgent order.

"Stop the tests!" he shouted to the men inside the control room full of sonar screens and equipment. "Now!"

Isabel ran over to the guardrails and then looked back at the navy divers on deck struggling into their heavy scuba gear. Precious time, while Dr. Sharp was sinking—he must be unconscious.

"Hurry, damn it," Lieutenant Lester shouted to the rescue crew. "The closer he gets to the source, the more damage . . ." Abruptly the lieutenant stopped, glaring at Isabel and the men standing near her. "This is all your fault."

For the first time Isabel realized that Stewart and Marshall were flanking her. Both men's faces were frozen in expressions of guilt and concern as they scanned the waves sloshing below. It was their argument that had perhaps distracted anyone from noticing the sonar equipment cord tightening around Dr. Sharp's foot.

"Got him!" a diver was yelling from the water.

"Bring him up," Lieutenant Lester commanded. "Be careful."

As an unconscious Sharp was handed over the guardrails to a couple of ship's medics, his bloodied head lolled back and his arms splayed. His tweed suit coat was streaked with seaweed.

"Is he . . . ?" Lieutenant Lester's characteristically hard face was almost as pale as Dr. Sharp's.

"He's alive, sir," one of the navy medics said, examining him on deck. "But there's some injury to the head and one leg broken real bad. Internal injuries maybe."

Isabel stood on her toes to peer over Stewart and Marshall. What she dreaded was indeed there—rivulets of blood from each ear. "It may not be just a head injury," she whispered to the lieutenant, who actually allowed her to take his arm. "Please have the ER check his eardrums and lungs. For God's sake, he's an acoustic scientist, and there may be extensive damage to . . ."

At that the lieutenant straightened and turned to glare at Isabel. "This is strictly classified. If we see any reports of this incident in the news media, we will indeed arrest all of you for criminal trespassing. And because this is an issue of national security, yours would be a military trial conducted in complete secrecy. All civilians off this boat," Lieutenant Lester continued. "Immediately!"

"First, I want to make that arrest, Lieutenant," Stewart spoke up and grabbed again at Marshall's arm. "For malicious trespassing and interfering . . ."

"We won't be pressing charges at this time," Lieutenant Lester muttered and hastily turned away from Stewart as a shout went up from below.

"But Lieutenant," Stewart insisted, "this intruder may have caused harm to Dr. Sharp. Someone needs to be held criminally responsible for any injury."

"We'll handle this ourselves." The lieutenant dismissed Stewart.

Isabel had only enough time to glimpse again the young scientist on the stretcher before a seaman lifted her off the research vessel. He deposited her with unexpected courtesy back onto Stewart's NMFS patrol boat.

Stewart leapt in after her, but when Marshall tried to board, Stewart balked. "Find your own way to shore. How the hell did you get here?"

"Maybe I swam."

"Or maybe one of Isabel's stranding network volunteers brought you.

I *will* arrest him as soon as we get back to the beach. It was Daniel McHalffey, wasn't it?"

"Stop this, Stewart," Isabel said and sat down heavily on a life preserver, head in her hands. "Let Marshall come aboard."

Marshall swung easily onto the motorboat and sat down beside Isabel. He was careful to resist the impulse to wrap his arm around her slumped shoulders.

Isabel turned to him now and said in a low voice, "I asked you not to come out here, Marshall."

Marshall reached out to touch her, but Isabel pulled away. In her eyes there was surprise and hurt. Marshall cursed himself for coming on board, for returning to this beleaguered coast. Every time he got deeply involved with a woman, it was just a disaster.

Stewart jerked on the twin outboard motors and they sped off from the research vessel. Still in his wetsuit, Marshall felt overheated. He unzipped the neoprene.

Marshall tried to catch Isabel's eye. "Please don't blame me for what happened to that guy on the boat. It would have happened anyway."

"Maybe not. The point is, we'll never know whether I would have gotten through to Dr. Sharp, if you hadn't interrupted us." Isabel shook her head slowly. "Now, I just don't know what to do . . . but I have to do something."

Marshall could see dark smudges of exhaustion beneath Isabel's eyes. Why had he come, if only to ruin everything?

At first, he had told himself that he came back to check out the aftermath of the mass stranding. He would drive up the coast to Newport Aquarium afterward and see Mack and Molly again. And he'd dive the fertile Oregon waters, renowned for their octopi and rich plant life. These new photos would make a much-needed addition to his archive, which was more heavily weighted toward coral reefs and tropical undersea life. But halfway to the coast he'd heard of the divers' alert still on for Kiwanda Beach. No diving allowed. At that moment, he should have turned the car around. If he had returned to Portland, he could have caught Andrew and shared the same plane hop to their next diving job in nearby Seattle, then gone on to see Irene in eastern Washington before his flight with Andrew to Africa. Far away. Safe.

But Marshall had not turned back. When he got to the Ocean Haven Tavern, he could no longer lie to himself. He had not come to dive on the Oregon coast; he had come to see Isabel again.

"You're not alone in this, you know, Isabel," he told her now, moving away from her to keep a respectful distance. "Look at all the people still working on the beach and . . . well, I'm here."

Isabel said nothing. She seemed to be struggling with herself. Silence won out.

Marshall was not accustomed to such restraint from a woman. Her doubts about him hurt more than he wanted to admit. Besides, she was right. He had interfered with her plans.

As the motorboat skimmed the mild waves toward shore, Marshall tried not to pay much attention to Isabel. But he could not help noticing that she was still dressed in her pale green scrubs, her worn boat shoes, and blue rain slicker. Her hair was pulled back in a ponytail, and a red lab pencil still jammed in her hair above one ear. In the heavy marine mists, ringlets of wet curls escaped the rubber band and fell down her long neck. Her mouth was slightly open, and for the first time Marshall noticed a small gap between her front teeth.

"I'd make myself mighty scarce when we get to shore, McGreggor." With satisfaction in his voice, Stewart interrupted Marshall's study of his ex-wife.

Isabel sat quietly, her eyes intently focused on the shore.

Marshall moved near her and said sincerely, "I'm really sorry. I was trying to help."

Isabel relented slightly and seemed to lean into him, too. In that moment, Marshall bowed his head and kissed her neck, her curls tasting of salt. Isabel let Marshall kiss her once more before she straightened. Shifting away from him, she said wearily, "Something truly terrible is going on here, Marshall . . ."

"Yeah, there was a hell of a lot of nasty-looking acoustic equipment on that navy boat."

"Water . . . Thunder." Isabel said each word separately, as if it were another language. "It's their new sonar weapon. I think it's causing this terrible stranding . . . all those deaths, the deafness . . ."

She turned to him then, her face full of fear and an unspoken appeal. Marshall moved to again embrace her, but she slipped away from him. Abruptly, she stood up, balancing easily on the rocking boat, and sat down opposite him.

"Marshall," Isabel began in a low voice. Her expression was simply weary.

She seemed disarmingly vulnerable; but Marshall knew better. Isabel's power was immense, and not because she could elude a burly lieutenant and toss him around like a dance partner. Isabel Spinner was someone to be feared because he cared about her. She could throw him far away from her, and he would not get over it. He knew this now. If he had known even yesterday how deep was his attachment to this woman, he would never have come back to see her. Strange, how he had managed to hide this from himself.

There was no judgment in Isabel's voice when she continued. "I meant it when I told you on the phone that this is not a good time, Marshall. There's just too much going on here."

Marshall watched the frantic activity as they neared the beach. More strandings, the volunteers running back and forth among dark, sloped-back shapes thrashing on the sand. The sight sickened him.

"And I can't help at all?" Marshall stopped, seeing Isabel's wan face. Delicate wrinkles that should have been smile lines were etched around her lips.

She could have lied to him, but she did not. Instead, she met his eyes steadily as if she were seeing him for the first—and perhaps last—time.

He shivered. "You see everything about me."

"Not everything," Isabel said softly. "But I do see you, Marshall. I see that I could never really count on you—for long."

"I know I may not live . . ."

"That's not what I meant," Isabel said matter-of-factly. "And you know it."

"You mean I don't really"—he couldn't believe that he again felt compelled to tell Isabel the truth—"devote myself to anyone."

"Have you ever?"

Marshall expected to see disappointment and judgment revealed in her face. Instead, he felt this within himself. And more. Twisting inside his belly was a grief Marshall had never before endured. He was shocked at how physical it was. "No, " he said, his words a choking sound he did not quite recognize. "I haven't."

Before he betrayed himself by weeping, Marshall quickly stood and turned his back on Isabel. For a moment his pulse pounded and he still held a slender woman, hair flowing out from her face as she lay back, trusting him, floating in his arms as tiny dolphins spun waves around them.

So low that Marshall knew Isabel could not hear him, he said, "You, I'll miss—no matter how far down I dive."

"What are you doing, Marshall?" Isabel tried to catch his arm.

"They've stopped the sonar tests for now. I can swim to shore from here."

"No . . . ," Isabel protested. "You don't even have your scuba equipment . . ."

"It's not far," he said. "Take care of yourself, Isabel. I'll stay in touch through Andrew."

"Marshall . . . ," she began and then stopped. Without another word, she sank back down in the boat.

Stewart slowed the motor as Marshall balanced on the edge of the boat.

He dove. Perfectly skimming the water, Marshall took sure strokes. He let a strong swell carry him toward shore. Underwater, he did not know that Isabel called softly, without alarm, with true regret, "Man overboard."

chapter twelve

Deaf, at Last Listening

SITTING AT THE bedside of the man she had once believed was her enemy left Isabel uneasy. She couldn't quite explain why she was spending so many of her lunch hours this week in Alexander Sharp's hospital room. She told Marian that the purpose of her visits was to plead with Sharp to corroborate her evidence of sonar as the probable cause for the stranding deaths. But so far, the young scientist had stonewalled her and would not say if there would be more secret sonar tests off the Oregon coast. Still Isabel made daily visits.

She did not know that just his morning Sharp was given the diagnosis that he would never hear again. But perhaps she suspected. For his part, Sharp was lonely for sound—any sound: the bleep and creak of a dolphin's signature whistle, the walking bass of a humpback's lullaby, the shushing of surf on Kiwanda Beach glimpsed from the window of his hospital room, the night winds off the sea, even the laughter of the nurses, the thwack of sterile gloves, the wooden footfalls of Isabel Spinner's sensible clogs. Once the young man had assumed such sounds would always be there. Just as he assumed he would always be at the top of his field.

Trying to keep any pity from showing, Isabel watched Sharp's pale face, the bandages on each side of his head like snowy ear muffs; patiently, she waited for him to open his eyes. Sharp could not have heard her enter; yet Isabel sensed the scientist knew she was here with him. There was a slight physical pull from him. Isabel felt his despair in the slight dip in her own energy and the warmth between them in this chill hospital room. In repose, the man's bandaged and battered face seemed naked.

Isabel looked away, as if to give him more privacy. Sharp's eyes abruptly fluttered open; they were brimming with unshed tears. "You again."

Isabel smiled and nodded. Then she opened her lunch basket, the one Marian had grudgingly packed for them. By the picnic, Isabel knew that Marian's resistance to sharing anything with this young scientist was bluster. For here was Marian's blueberry pie, curried tuna fish sandwiches, and chips with Marian's homemade salsa. Without a word Isabel unpacked their picnic. Sharp pushed aside his hospital lunch tray with its white peaks of instant potatoes, gray globs of gravy, and bright red gelatin squares.

As was their noontime ritual, Sharp spoke aloud and Isabel responded by typing on his government-issue laptop.

As he picked up the tuna sandwich, he asked, "Dolphin-safe?"

Isabel turned to him—she had started with the chips and salsa. She was surprised to see that he was not making one of his irritating jokes. His face was seized with an emotion he almost mastered.

Instead of leaning forward to comfort him, as she wanted to, Isabel sensed that she must stay very still, even sit back a little.

He bowed his head and murmured, "You still eat tuna?"

After a moment, Isabel leaned over and typed on his laptop, *No, I gave it up.*

"You enviro-nuts don't really believe the dolphins are ever safe, do you?" he snapped.

Isabel sat farther back and did not respond immediately. She opened the freezer bag with the two huge pieces of blueberry pie. "My brother and I sometimes eat dessert first," she said aloud.

"What?" he asked, but his voice was softer. When she still did not answer, the young man shouted, "Can you hear me?"

Isabel nodded and leaned over to type: *Sorry. It was nothing.*

"What did you say?" Sharp was so upset that he almost knocked over his lunch tray.

Labile emotions, the doctor had warned Isabel, explained the shifting and intense mood swings resulting from Sharp's head injury. "Don't overtire him," the doctor had ordered. "Mild head injury—his brain is bruised."

Isabel passed Sharp a piece of pie and smiled. *My brother and I always eat dessert first*, she typed. *It's a Spinner family tradition. Passed down by my grandfather.*

He sighed and nodded. "Blueberry," Sharp said, and his voice was again thoughtful, controlled. "My favorite."

It was the first moment with this man that she had felt somewhat at ease. Mentally, Isabel blessed Marian for her many gifts. They ate together in silence for a while.

But Isabel had so many questions. What was the highest decibel level at which they'd tested whatever acoustic device they had? Marian's Internet research had discovered that anything over 150 decibels caused tissue to rupture in humans. Had the navy really deployed such dangerous acoustic blasts—and so near the beach? She remembered the brief, almost unbearable echo of the stranding dolphin's pain as he thrashed in her arms in the surf. Isabel shuddered to imagine how deafening that sound must have been for a man falling overboard so near the underwater source of the sonar. Having been rescued near the surface, though, perhaps he had been above the worst of the acoustic blast.

"You're not here because you give a damn about me," Sharp suddenly blurted, his voice overloud. "You don't care . . ."

Isabel knew the disorienting echo chamber of one's own skull. You speak words too loudly because you can't hear them, can't modulate the buzz of noise. Everyone else can hear you, but you are buried alive inside a cave of roaring and ringing or—worse yet—distant silence.

"But I do," she said, enunciating so he could read her lips.

"No, you just want to pick my brain. God, I hate it when people say that! Well, go ahead, but my brain's scrambled, and I'm never going to hear a goddamn word you or anybody else says. Ever. So go away!"

Isabel let out a short exclamation. She struggled to control the tumult of emotions and images that her memory summoned: lying in her bunk bed, Stewart leaning close.

"Will I ever hear again?" she asks him, gripping the boy's hand. It's small and rough. She can feel him trembling.

"I don't know, Isa," Stewart says. His lips tremble as she reads them. "No one does."

Isabel rips the white puffs of gauze from her ears, the bandages stained and moist with infection. She cups her swollen, silent ears with her palms and screams.

Nothing. Only the vacuum of sealed air. She screams until Stewart can no longer bear the piercing sounds and covers his ears, too, at last fleeing from her room, as if her sounds are weapons.

And then there is the day that she awakens too early, her sleep interrupted not by the dull light of another deaf day but by a far-off, rhythmic shushing. For a second Isabel thinks it's the familiar and false roaring of ears like dead sea shells that the creatures have long abandoned. She listens to the palpable thud of her heartbeat, the rush of blood. But it's not just her body speaking, it is a greater body of steady surf and curving sand. It is the ancient sound of waves, like that amniotic surf swirling around any newborn. It is farther away than before, and only one ear opens to the waves on her backyard beach. High tide. It is enough.

Another sound now, not at all familiar, a man's muffled voice, his face buried in his hands. What was he saying? Isabel wanted to lean near and tenderly take his hands from his bruised face, cup his ruined ears in her hands. But she sat very still, waiting.

"You can't possibly understand how . . . ," the young man whispered, bent over.

Isabel reached out and took his hand and placed it over her silent ear. "I'm deaf here," she told him and knew that he heard her. Not with his ears. With his pain.

"How?"

Childhood accident, she typed on his laptop. *I had temporary deafness for a while and permanently lost total hearing in one ear.*

It seemed to steady and calm him. "Oh," he said, and let her keep holding his hand. "Oh."

They sat like that for a long time, until he at last gathered himself and withdrew his hand from hers. "Have you . . . ," he began, his face so open, battered. "Have you ever listened to a blue whale?" Sharp suddenly asked. He clicked open an acoustic file on his laptop computer and, though he

could not hear it, turned the volume way up. The hospital room filled
with the haunting and sonorous vocalizations of the largest animal who
ever lived on Earth. Bass tones thundered, then moaned, and sank low
into a rumbling bellow.

Isabel closed her eyes to better hear the blue's fathoms-deep songs.
She remembered her grandfather telling her how he had chanced upon a
migrating blue whale once when he was fishing way off California's
Monterey Bay. "She was a sea god," Grandfather said, "like our ancestors
worshiped. Hell, even other whales must worship those big blues."

"When a blue whale surfaces and blows," Sharp continued, "that blast
of breath is three stories high. It sounds like thunder. A blue whale's blowhole is so huge that a child can crawl through it."

Isabel already knew these astonishing facts about blue whales, but she
was so moved by the scientist's passion and the underwater voices echoing around his hospital room that she did not interrupt his soliloquy.

"I used to listen to blue whales from the research boat in the
Antarctic. That's how the navy found me. They let scientists borrow their
military hydrophone arrays, the ones the navy once used for top secret
tracking of submarines. I would listen all night, recording the blues and
saving their vocalizations right here on my laptop."

Isabel noted the rise and fall of the acoustic recordings on his laptop
screen. It was a visual graph of sound in syncopated reds and blues like
bright geysers. She smiled wistfully and nodded.

"It was like . . . ," Sharp paused and closed his eyes, "like listening to
an alien universe. I thought that one day this underwater world might let
me in, if I could just crack the code."

He told her how the blue whale's perfectly efficient sound vibrations
echo along the deepest ocean canyons so far that it is inconceivable to us.
How the blue whale can echolocate even an underwater abyss, hear and
map its mountains and valleys. Sharp paused and looked up at Isabel.
Again, she noted how much younger than she he seemed. "I wanted to
know how blue whales do that. I wanted to study this greatest of all the
whales. I thought one day I could understand how to chart a sound map
of this world . . . a world we can't see. Except by listening."

The blue whale vocalizations resonated in the room, and Sharp kept his eyes tightly closed. Finally, he opened them. He watched as Isabel listened to the blue whale vocalizations, her gray eyes still and wide, as if to better hear the eerie underwater lament.

Beautiful, Isabel now typed. Leaning over the laptop, her hair haphazardly pulled back in braids, she reminded Sharp of a driven, straight-A graduate student—as he had once been. That was before the navy, before they had read his blue whale research and decided to recruit him as lead scientist to test their new sonar device. He had resisted them at first, even published several papers strongly urging the scientific community to critique and not lend their support to this potentially dangerous acoustics system.

"It's not a weapon," the navy science director had insisted. "It's an acoustic submarine detection system to track silent submarines."

"But I didn't think countries other than the United States had silent submarines," Sharp had said.

"Well, that's true . . . right now. But for how long? These military discoveries have a way of getting into the wrong hands. We have to be prepared." The navy director had paused and then continued, "So we need you, Dr. Sharp, to supervise these tests and their effects on marine life. To determine at what point the acoustic device causes injury and possibly death . . ."

"Are these tests part of an environmental impact statement? Won't the public consider this harassment and a violation of the Marine Mammal Protection Act?" Sharp had to ask, although already he had told himself that, if he didn't do these potentially dangerous sonar tests, some other scientist would. Someone who didn't care about cetaceans as much, someone with less acoustical expertise.

"Oh, we'll get around any EIS," the man had said dismissively. "We can claim it's for national security and get whatever we want." The director had paused then. "But we also need you, Dr. Sharp. No one else has the expertise to supervise this project."

"But you know what the environmentalists are saying," Alexander Sharp had reminded the director. His initial resistance had been strong for so ambitious a young scientist. "Your critics are saying that this is an underwater version of the neutron bomb, this Water Thunder."

"That's not science," the director had snorted. "That's science fiction! You of all people should know better."

"But I *don't* know," Sharp had said with a frown. "None of us really knows what effects this sonar that you want to use will have underwater. It's never been tested. What two hundred and thirty-five decibels, or more, will do . . . could be absolutely hideous."

"Well," the director said, "it will happen underwater. Open sea. Who will notice?"

Sharp had stared blankly at the older man, so ignorant in his understanding of acoustics or underwater marine life. "Anyone who cares about the oceans," Sharp began.

"That's your area of expertise," the director interrupted. "Mine is protecting civilians. And as you know, Dr. Sharp, civilians want to be defended, especially Americans, at all costs. They just don't want to know what the military has to do to make them safe."

The way he said the word *civilians* had reminded Sharp of something, though he would not recognize it until later—lying here in a hospital bed. Only now did he truly hear the contempt in the director's voice. The man's tone was not without a certain patronizing fondness for civilians, but it was clear that he believed that all civilians were part of a lower, less sophisticated culture. Even before Sharp had signed on to work with the navy's new sonar program, he had suspected that what defined intelligence to a military mind was not the ability to create, but the technology and power to destroy.

Sharp had convinced himself that the U.S. Navy was in need of civilizing, of educating. The military mind needed illuminating and expanding, which science could accomplish. He could teach them. But lying now in his hospital bed, Sharp had to ask himself why he ever believed he could change anything. It was he who had been changed.

"Blue whales are the largest creatures on Earth," said Sharp, taking up his monologue again. "Their hearts are the size of a Volkswagen Bug. A man can stand up inside a blue whale artery," he said. He watched Isabel register his voice, though Sharp heard only a humming vibration in his head, the remnants of his hearing. "But you know all this, don't you, Dr. . . . Isabel? And maybe you'll call me Alex—even though I can't hear you."

Isabel nodded. "All right."

"Do you know that some scientists are saying these long-distance vocalizations might be essential for reproduction?" Sharp fell silent and then added in a broken voice, "Love songs."

Isabel sat back, remembering the last time she had seen Marshall in Stewart's NMFS boat before he abruptly dove and swam to shore. Why had she criticized him for boarding the navy ship when he was trying to help her out? Marshall might have come back to the coast as much for her as to assist the stranding network volunteers again. He'd practically said as much. But she hadn't listened. Yes, she was overwhelmed, and yes, she was out of her depth, both professionally and personally. But why had she not welcomed Marshall back? Maybe it was the last thing she'd expected from him. Maybe she didn't know how.

She closed her eyes and listened to the otherworldly love song from the blue whale rumbling along an ocean abyss.

"Isabel," Sharp said in a soft voice, "can't you understand? I just wanted to listen like the great whales do to each other . . ."

Isabel opened her eyes and gazed at the other scientist. He would never believe the indigenous explanation for why the great whales of the world sang. Marian said her elders taught that whales sang along sea bottoms not only to attract a mate but also because their songs had the power to keep the oceans healthy. When blue whales sang, their voices perfectly tuned and restored the powerful *lei* lines, or electromagnetic fields, running through each watery canyon.

That sound could heal, Dr. Sharp would know. Hadn't science invented a crude approximation of dolphin ultrasound, using it to burst open and dissipate kidney stones in the human body? And science used sound to see into human organs and tissue. But would the man ever consider, as Native science believed, that songs continually tuning the Earth might be sound that could also heal?

Isabel remembered Marshall holding his Dall's porpoise and singing an ancient Hawaiian chant—how the song seemed to restore the calf's will to live. She had sung to Marshall, without a trace of self-consciousness, the songs of her own ancestors, also a people of the sea. She resolved to phone Marshall as soon as she left the hospital room. She must call out to him over the distance between them and hope that he would hear her. A mating song.

Quickly leaning over Sharp's computer, Isabel typed in the only language that this scientist might understand, *I know the good work you've done in your field, Alex. I've read your early papers on how sonar affected gray whale migration patterns. You know that sound can heal. It can also kill.*

Isabel looked at Sharp intently. His research on early low-frequency active sonar had shown that when the sonar was tested, gray whales dramatically changed their course. In the navy's own sonar tests, their divers experienced vertigo, nausea, and extreme disorientation at higher levels. Sharp himself had once written, "These navy sonar studies are potentially very dangerous and advance a military agenda in the guise of science."

Isabel added in a blur of fingertips on his laptop, *But I don't understand why you help the navy do this*—she paused—*this horror.*

Sharp read her laptop accusation and sat back in his hospital bed with a sigh. He had once leveled such criticism at the navy. But that was before the navy humbly came to him for advice and education. Before the unrequested state-of-the-art audio computer equipment began arriving at his small Southern California lab; before the National Science Foundation grants he had not applied for came his way; before the urgent requests that he lead the navy acoustics team, even supervise their next sonar tests. Before he said yes.

He wanted to tell Isabel that it was better that he—who loved marine mammals, who had studied them half his life—oversaw these potentially lethal tests; that he had made sure the tests were done right; that he had even tried to conduct tests at the very lowest decibel levels; that he had hoped an environmental impact statement would eventually force the navy to curtail development of this sonar. He wanted to explain to her that he had once believed the navy would learn from him and listen, and that if the tests proved lethal to marine life, the navy would have to stop developing a weapon so destructive it must never be used. But the young scientist saw now with utter certainty that he had only helped to create a weapon that would destroy what he most loved.

Sharp bowed his head and fell silent.

He did not look up when Isabel leaned over and typed quickly, *Dr. Siestina is calling this "an acoustic holocaust."* Isabel sat back and took a breath.

Still Sharp did not look at her.

At last Isabel stood up and gathered her briefcase and the necropsy photos.

"Don't go." Sharp raised his head.

Isabel hesitated and then mouthed the words, "I have to get back to work."

"See you tomorrow?"

Isabel gazed down at Alexander Sharp with what he believed was a passionate impatience. He admired that about her. Isabel Spinner judged him as he now secretly blamed himself. But perhaps her judgment was not without some sympathy. After all, she was a scientist, too, accustomed to doing things most ordinary people found inexplicable or even reprehensible.

"Well," Sharp blurted out, "you cut open dead animals." His words made her stop and turn back to him. He had the strangest feeling that he was not talking out loud, but was instead speaking to her from another place within him. And because he couldn't hear his own words, he could now perhaps say anything—even what was so burdening his mind. "How many people, even animal lovers, would really understand your forensics work is *devotion?*"

Isabel threw back her head and laughed so heartily that Sharp could almost hear it, could see the air shimmering with the vibration of her laughter. Isabel sat down again beside him and typed rapidly, *Not many!*

"Listen," he said, his eyes feverish. "I convinced myself that I could teach the navy. That I could educate them about how dangerous this sonar is if used without proper protocol and limits. They came to me asking for help. I knew that, without my expertise, it would be a bloody disaster!"

Isabel gave him a long, level look that was not unkind. And then she leaned over to type the words *You believed you could control them?*

Sharp nodded and struggled to meet her eyes. Then he did something that startled them both. He leaned over his laptop and he wept while

Isabel sat very still. Finally he looked up. "What do you want me to do?"

Intently, she typed, *Will they test again off our coast?* She saw Sharp hesitate and frown, looking down at his hands. She touched his shoulder instead of calling his name. *Please,* she typed, *please tell me.*

He knew enough not to speak aloud, lest the deputy sheriff that Stewart had posted outside his hospital room overhear. Instead he simply typed it to her: *Yes, the navy will test again this weekend, Sunday at 3 A.M. They intend to raise the decibel level to 235. It's never been tested that high, and they need to assess the damage.* Sharp stopped typing a moment, adjusted his glasses, and then continued, head bent. *At that higher decibel level, it's also lethal to humans. That's why they've issued another divers' alert and closed off the beach.*

Thank you, Isabel typed. *We will do everything we can to stop it. Will you help us?*

The man's nod was almost imperceptible, but then he typed, *There's something else you should know.* He paused to look at Isabel, and his expression was so full of fear that it softened her. Staring at her in silence, Sharp simply shook his head slowly from side to side. Then he leaned over and typed, *Navy divers are reporting that there are many more carcasses at sea. Whales and dolphins. Hundreds dead. But out of sight. Those you pushed back into the sea were only temporary survivors.*

"I know," Isabel said out loud. "But some survived . . ."

Those animals farthest from the source of the sonar, Sharp typed.

Suddenly Isabel had a piercing memory of watching Marshall gently holding aloft the Dall's porpoise calf as she took its vital signs. Clasping her own hands tightly together, Isabel studied Dr. Sharp.

Somehow he had dislodged his bandages, and small spots of blood stained the white gauze cupping his ears.

"I'm so sorry," Isabel said.

Then with a sterile towelette that she always carried in her purse in case she came upon a wounded animal, she tenderly removed the gauze and cleaned the blood from his raw ears. As she did, Isabel hummed in the low, steady voice she often used to calm terrified creatures—a fox on the road hit by a car, an orphaned seal pup, a broken-winged eagle.

Alexander Sharp could only sense the vibration of her humming. Her hands were light, hardly a touch at all. But it was enough to soothe him more than any of the sedatives the medical staff had given him. She asked nothing except that he stay very still and let himself be cleansed, let his deaf ears receive something other than sound—the silken rustle of touch.

chapter thirteen

Aquatic Apes

So, YOU LIKE my sister?" Andrew asked Marshall as he prepared to fall, oxygen tank first, into the cold waters of Seattle's Elliott Bay. "Or was it our beautiful Oregon coast that kept you so long?"

Marshall hesitated. He was running for his life from a woman who had basically dismissed him. Even so, Isabel had left several messages on his cell phone. She was asking to see him again, but Marshall didn't know if he could risk another rejection from her. Her weary face creased with a disappointed frown; her refusal to plead with him, like other women, to stay with her; her frank assessment of his behavior—no wonder he had dived down into the safety of the sea and not returned her calls. With Isabel, he found himself saying things he hadn't meant to reveal. He'd wait until he had a better grip on himself, several months or so. Hell, maybe he'd be dead by then; that would solve everything. Or, if this new heart was still strong and he still hadn't rejected it, he would be far away, in Africa. Andrew would probably call his sister from Africa, so Marshall would say a quick hello and make some excuse about not getting back to Isabel sooner. The cardiologist had said transplants should give themselves at least a year to stabilize before making any big decisions. "For you," he'd said, "every day is an unexpected gift."

"Your sister basically told me to get lost," Marshall shrugged.

"Yeah, sometimes Isabel can say just the wrong thing," Andrew admitted. Perching on the side of the research boat, he fiddled with his face mask, spraying the defogger and cleaning the lens. "And so can you." He shot

Marshall a grin before continuing. "Once when I was still in high school and Isabel came home from medical school, I let her talk me into a double date for my prom. I think she was hoping I'd keep Stewart Salk at bay."

"That guy's a piece of work." Marshall pulled on his fluorescent green flippers and hefted his heavy underwater camera. On the surface, this camera gear was so heavy he hated lugging it around. But they would need the macro lens and wide-angle lens, the special underwater housing, strobe, and flashlights for this difficult underwater cave shot. "What did Isabel ever see in Stewart?" Good. He had managed exactly the right tone—casual, disinterested.

Andrew shrugged. "Stewart stays at home."

"Small-town boy."

"Right." Andrew tested his mouthpiece and released a blast of air from his regulator. "Anyway, that prom. All I wanted was some necking in the backseat with my date on the way home—God, was she gorgeous! But no, Isabel has to start in about how local fishermen were scapegoating marine mammals and blaming them for the salmon crash. What a disaster! My date practically slammed the car door on me. Not a single kiss. All she did was inform Isabel, who, of course, was driving, 'Don't you blame fishermen! We gotta eat.' Course her Dad ran the town's most successful fishing trawler."

"But Isabel was right," Marshall couldn't help but say.

"That's the problem. Isabel is always right. Do you know how irritating that is for a younger brother?" Andrew stared at Marshall. "And maybe for any guy who falls for her."

"Look, I helped your sister with the stranding and screwed things up for her on the navy boat." Marshall held up his gloved hands. "It was a mess, like I told you. That's all."

"You two argued?" Andrew asked insistently.

"Yeah, whatever. We argued," Marshall snapped. "Are we ever going to get to this dive?"

Andrew nodded. But right before he adjusted his mask, Marshall saw another look of disappointment on a familiar face. What was it with this family? Did they practice that disapproving frown in the mirror? Had they inherited it? Without another word, Andrew fell backward into the emerald chill of Elliott Bay.

Marshall was relieved that any continuation of their conversation would have to take place underwater. Andrew was no good at sign language. As the two men dropped down through the clear depths, Marshall let off a stream of bubbles. Sticky, translucent tentacles of a pulsing moon jellyfish parachuted past him.

Where is she? Andrew signed as he emerged from a rock sculpture formed by pink hydrocoral. *Where's U-R-S-U-L-A?*

Ursula was the name given a giant Pacific octopus captured as a juvenile by a diver off Fox Island and then reared by the Seattle Aquarium. Because she had an imperious personality, the octopus was named after the sea witch Ursula in the Disney film *The Little Mermaid.* Ursula frequently changed moods and her color, which ranged from luminous white to scarlet. Her stunning color changes, along with her species' capacity for learning and remembering, made Ursula a local celebrity and attracted large crowds. Schoolchildren made special field trips to the aquarium to marvel at Ursula's antics. They could hardly believe this creature had pale blue blood and three hearts, that the largest giant Pacific octopus weighed six hundred pounds and had an arm span of thirty feet. After almost two years, Ursula had grown old enough to mate, and so the aquarium released her back into the wild.

Two weeks earlier, a media frenzy had accompanied Ursula's release. Coaxed with a delicious herring smeared along her tank wall, Ursula was convinced to crawl from the safety of her rocky den into a barrel, which was promptly loaded onto a cart. Ceremoniously the three-year-old octopus was wheeled down the dock to the water and slipped into Elliott Bay. Hundreds cheered as the television cameras rolled. Once underwater, Ursula had stretched out her tentacles to slide down a piling. As she drifted down, she turned a deep crimson, her eight arms engaged in an octopus ballet of scent, touch, and taste. She was home. On the sea bottom, she changed her colors again, taking on a mottled red-and-white pattern to match the scarlet nudibranchs, pale sand, and rocky reefs around her. Ursula had settled under the end of a barnacled log.

Now the postrelease documentation began, as Marshall and Andrew, hired by the aquarium, set out to search for Ursula's den. Had she survived and perhaps even attracted a consort male? Octopi previously had made homes in this jagged rock pile forty feet beneath the aquarium, where the two men began their search. Would Ursula still be here?

Marshall looked into the den midden, with its piles of red rock and kelp crab shells. Here was a good sign, he thought. The octopus den had recently been cleaned out, and the crab shell pieces seemed fresh. This meant that, if this octopus were Ursula, she was hunting on her own and feeding herself. But where was she hiding?

Balancing at about forty feet down, Marshall wedged his feet against the constant pulse and pull of the bay's currents. He held up two large herring and waited for the octopus to spy him. If this were Ursula's den, she would come to him. For over two years, she had allowed herself to be fed and touched by the devoted aquarium staff. If this were a wild octopus, Marshall could wait forever with herring and never be approached.

Out of the corner of his mask, Marshall saw Andrew, at a discreet distance, position the strobe light. For a moment, it was easy to imagine how a marine creature might react to these awkward, gear-laden divers with their flashing light and huge eye-lenses, the whirring noise of Andrew's video camera—it was enough to make anyone want to hide out. With all his own dangling photography equipment, it took great physical effort for Marshall to keep himself still and not look menacing to a small octopus.

Drifting near the cave, he relaxed. He always felt most alive and yet meditative in these timeless moments underwater. His mind drifted as if he were held in the greater heart of the sea.

Between worlds and memories, Marshall twirled in slow motion, caught up in a brief cyclone of starry flounders and their blue-yellow rings of flickering scales. Above him a swaying forest of bull kelp filtered faint sunlight into watery shafts, pale prisms of silt and seawater. Marshall's mind still wandered. He moved his arms in a wide arc and scattered the fish, smiling. He was free again, clear of any messy entanglements. Even someone with Isabel Spinner's confounded appeal couldn't reach him underwater. And Andrew was busy videographing patterns made by the spun black shells of moon snails embedded in the sea bottom.

For a precious half hour of oxygen, Marshall floated, rocked by the currents as he awaited signs of Ursula. A speckled brown-and-white tentacle reached out of the rocky den. A keen octopus eye fixed on Marshall. The eye of this wily invertebrate was as focused and well developed as a camera lens. Was this Ursula? Marshall willed himself to be unobtrusive, emotionally neutral. Ursula swiftly emerged and, with a snap of her hard beak, snatched a herring from Marshall's outstretched hand. He smiled and signed to Andrew, *U-R-S-U-L-A!*

How had the octopus fared these past two weeks in the wild? Marshall wondered. Was there a mate hiding nearby, watching Marshall as he peered into the cave searching for Ursula?

Out of the corner of his eye, Marshall saw Andrew signaling to him that their oxygen was running low. Soon they would have to surface. Not yet. Marshall moved in closer to the craggy, crab-shell-strewn rocky den. Gently he laid more herring at the den's opening and watched with a grin as a long tentacle touched the fish, suckers smelling and sensing that here was easy, delicious prey. In seconds, the herring disappeared.

Perhaps Ursula was curious or even a little lonely for humans, having not yet found a mate or laid her seventy thousand eggs to hatch a new brood, for she again reached out one of her eight arms, this time wrapping it around Marshall's gloved hand. The suction-powered disks delicately glided along his arm and then seemed to dance atop his head. Those sensitive suckers, over two hundred of them, were like a combination of fingers and tongues tasting and feeling him at the same time.

What did he taste like to this octopus? Neoprene and salt, peppermint defogger and pungent herring? At only thirty pounds, Ursula did not yet outweigh Marshall. Still, he had a moment's trepidation as her tentacles expertly explored the camera equipment dangling from his weight belt and vest. Underwater, in her element, this man was no more than a curious discovery. Attached to him were bright bangles and shining metal jewelry, the kind of objects that an octopus delightedly stockpiled. Octopus dens were full of abalone shells, shards of sapphire-blue glass, and other precious found objects.

Nimbly, Ursula used her tentacle to tear a loose metal zipper pull from Marshall's vest. With her one huge, rectangular pupil, she studied the gleaming treasure. Using her sharp black beak, she tried to break open the metal zipper pull as it if were a crab shell. As she floated so near Marshall, arms undulating up and down with the rhythmic pulse of the sea, Ursula's sentience was more palpable and present to Marshall than before. Taking full possession of the bounty stolen from this human diver, Ursula wrapped one curious and long arm entirely around the man's body.

Marshall was very still, floating, aware that here was one of the sea's most intelligent creatures—some scientists said more acute than any house cat. Between octopus tentacles, he saw Andrew's strobe light flashing, camera spinning loudly. Such an irritating noise. But he and Ursula *were* the picture.

As Ursula held him, Marshall suddenly sensed that he must strip off all his gear. It had nothing to do with the documentary Andrew was shooting. It was simply what the octopus wanted. How did Marshall know this? He just did.

Ursula kept one arm wrapped around Marshall's waist. She was like a weight belt, holding them down as he carefully shed his Nikon camera. He wedged his camera bag and all its attachments between two seaweed-strewn stones, careful not to disturb a clinging scarlet starfish. He slipped on the seaweed, but Ursula's tentacle held him steady. Marshall was tempted to take off his oxygen tank and free dive. But he was too deep.

Without all his ungainly gear, Marshall might as well have been naked here in this watery womb. He could accept this strange undersea embrace, as he once had surrendered to a broken heart at the bottom of the sea.

Suddenly the image of Isabel Spinner floated into his mind. She was strong like this octopus, she was wild in her own way, and she had a hold on him that Marshall couldn't escape. Did he want to? No, this image, fathoms deep, filled him with such longing that his body relaxed all the way down to his flippers. Registering this with her entwined tentacle, Ursula's long body flushed the deep crimson red of pleasure.

He felt suction and pressure along his legs and torso as Ursula's arms now gracefully wrapped around him—and then the rectangular pupil floated inches from his mask. His chest expanded, yellow blotches floating before his eyes. But this time Marshall did not lose consciousness. No blackout. No dream. This time, Marshall clearly remembered:

He is crouched in a tiny metal box, with bars blocking his view. Animals shrieking. Everywhere is the stench of fear, feces, urine, and days-old food. Where is his family? Hara and her son? Groggily he hurls himself against the bars and then he stops, frozen by the sight of his Hara. She is stretched out, her lean arms manacled to a metal table, and she is screaming.

But he cannot get through the bars to help her. Instead, he can only lash out at the man in a mask who opens his cage and thrusts a needle into his neck. He can only struggle, scream, and then slowly fall prey to a paralyzing injection. Blackness and floating as if in a great river. Swift currents carry him. He is held very carefully—as if he is, only now, valuable.

Then bright lights overhead. His heart is beating strongly again. But he is not the same. He is not on a surgical table or in a tiny steel cage, yet he is alive, conscious. He is somehow inside another's body. Man-animal. He cannot get out. Over time he finds that he can get out when the man dreams or is floating and forgets himself. Like now. Here is another animal. Another kind of mask. He can see everything now. But it is liquid.

How can he get away from the prison of this man's body to find Hara? If he can only make this man see what he sees, and feel what he feels, he might find his family again. They have stolen his body, but not his heart. Not his memory.

Fathoms deep, Marshall remembered the intelligent face, a long primate body stretched out on a steel table. *Hara,* he signed her name. Marshall closed his eyes. Cold deep in his bones. Heat in his heart. The words he once rejected when others spoke them now wafted through Marshall's mind and he shuddered: *I am a transplant. I acknowledge the sacrifice of the dead.*

Ursula felt the man-animal's vulnerability and fear and responded with a swift change in her skin. All along her arms and bell-like body, she glowed ghostly white. Filling her pale mantle with seawater, she squeezed it out though her siphon and powerfully propelled away from this man.

Marshall shook his head and tried to reach out for Ursula again, but the octopus released an inky jet that bloomed into a black cloud swirling around him. In the darkness, Marshall could not see sea bottom or surface. The propulsion of Ursula's retreat sent a small pressure wave that spun him into a backward somersault. He tucked his legs to his chest, tumbling slowly.

It was Andrew who stopped his confused, slow-motion somersaults across the sandy bottom. Chortling bubbles of laughter and breath rose up from Andrew as he grabbed Marshall by his weight belt and steadied him.

Ursula's already in love, Andrew signed with a grin.

Then Andrew saw Marshall's ashen face inside his mask. *What happened?* Andrew signed, all humor gone.

Surface, Marshall signaled to Andrew. *Out of air.*

Marshall knew Andrew was not buying his story of an oxygen tank dangerously low on air. Hypoxia, hallucinations. But Andrew didn't press for any further explanation. Marshall thought of the eerie beauty of Ursula. His metal zipper pull was now among the shining treasures in her den.

"Maybe you shouldn't be diving right now," was all Andrew said as they sat at dinner that night at a waterfront restaurant on Elliott Bay.

"I'll do the diving in Africa," Marshall retorted, "without you."

"And be the one to discover the missing-link fossil? No way!"

"Order for us, will you? I've got to make a quick call."

"Tell my sister hello." Andrew's good humor returned and he smiled knowingly.

"Nope, not Isabel." Marshall tried to make light of it. "Another woman."

At a pay phone on the weathered dock, Marshall had to shout so Irene could hear him over the summer ferryboat traffic. He had chosen not to use his cell phone because he didn't want Irene to have that number. Having it would mean she could reach him anywhere, any time she wanted. But she had given Marshall her cell phone number, which he had not used until now, preferring the distance of e-mail.

"Hello, Irene," he said.

"Hello, sailor!" Irene's voice was warm. "What's up, and where in the world are you? I hope just across the mountains from me."

"I can't stand it anymore. I've got to tell someone."

"I'm glad it's me, Marshall."

"Yes, yes, yes, but listen." For one more moment, Marshall hesitated. "I didn't just lose my heart, Irene; I think I'm losing my goddamn mind."

"Well, it's no wonder, after what I saw in those horrible photos of the stranding you sent me." Irene was quiet and then said, "Good for you, Marshall."

"You don't have to cheer me on," Marshall snapped, "like some sort of new convert. It was something I could do. Photos. It's *all* I can do," he emphasized. "So don't get any ideas that I've . . . come over to your side. I just thought your . . . underground contacts might have some information on the stranding. There's a federal wildlife forensics pathologist out here on the coast who seems to think it's navy sonar that's killing those whales and dolphins. Know anything about that?"

"Yes, a lot, in fact. It's not underground anymore, Marshall. It's all over the Internet. International scientists protesting, American marine mammal biologists from the Defense Department on the take big-time. Mass strandings off Greece and the Bahamas. Doesn't stop the navy . . ." Irene paused. "So, are you still planning to visit me over here in Ellensburg at the institute? Come on, you promised . . ."

"I don't know . . ." The prospect of seeing more primates both alarmed and compelled him.

"The chimps here are the only ones who've ever loved my cooking, especially my pasta primavera."

It was enough to dream about baboons, quite another thing to have to engage with primates again. "No, that's all right. I'll catch you another trip."

"But you won't, Marshall." Irene's tone was suddenly very serious. "I'm going . . . going away for a while. You won't be able to find me. I'll have to find you."

"What . . . ?" Marshall stopped. The thought that he might not be able to talk to Irene, to reach out to her as he was doing now, deeply troubled him.

"You'll miss me," Irene said. It was not a question.

"How long will you be . . . underground?" It sounded like something a gopher, not a human being, would do. It sounded silly. Yet it might be dangerous. Would Irene be harmed? It must be something illegal. Marshall didn't want to know. Yet he asked, "Does it involve trespassing? Primate labs?"

"I really can't say. You don't want to know, remember?"

"I . . . I do want to know." Marshall felt his heart beating erratically. Any illusion that he was in control of his own life seemed to be fading.

He wanted to tell her everything—the memories, the visions. And then, to his great surprise, he did.

Marshall was aware of the pop and snap of syncopated static on their phone line, of the patient commuters awaiting the Bainbridge Island car ferry. He fell silent, taking in the rows of idle cars. People sat in them reading, chatting, catching a nap with their car seats tilted back. A typical Seattle evening commute, the humble willows, the jubilation of Japanese maples, and even a few scarlet-barked madrona trees reaching out from side streets and apartment terraces. The salty breeze off the Salish Sea stirred changing alders and swayed lithe bamboo. It was a city of passionate yearlong gardens refreshed by moist gray mists, a city that also belonged to the water, living by tides and mists and mysteries—like a moody octopus at the bottom of a ferry piling, filling her den with shiny gems she'd stolen from men. It was an ordinary August night.

But nothing about him was ordinary anymore.

"I can't even function until I get to the bottom of this," Marshall blurted. "It's getting in the way of my work, my diving. I . . . I think maybe you're right," Marshall at last finished, breathless. "We're . . . we're changed."

"Yes," she said, "changed."

Leaning against the restaurant's weathered wood dock beside the ferry terminal, Marshall at last told Irene about Hara. *Silken, shaggy brow and eyes that never let go of him. A long arm that groomed with care in an unrelenting sun. Her acceptance after such a long friendship. Her steel cage.*

The young woman had been so quiet that Marshall thought he had lost her. Suddenly he could picture Irene's impish face, the freckles across her cheeks that had sprinkled onto her forehead and arms and, after her diving lessons in Hawaii, along her legs. Irene would have a long life; she would make a difference in the world. Would he? Had he ever?

"Marshall," she said softly. "Your heart is remembering for you."

"Can you help me? Can you help me maybe track my new heart's . . . family? There's a medical research lab near the hospital in Portland . . ."

"Yes, I'll help, but you'll have to do your part, too. Agreed?"

He hesitated. How had he reached this point? Why couldn't he just be like those ferry commuters, routinely sailing from one sure shore to the next? Nothing illegal. Nothing weird or too far out of his control.

"Listen, Marshall, we can't really talk about this on the phone. I've got some ideas. But you'll have to come see me." Irene lowered her voice. "And if you give me a day, I can do some . . . research for you."

"Thanks. I really appreciate that."

What he was asking of her might be illegal. Irene would have to go through her underground Animal Liberation Lifeline channels to help him. Maybe she could track the movements of lab animals—which Hara seemed to have become—used for medical research. But at least he could set his heart at rest about whether the baboon matriarch and her family were still alive. And if they were—then what?

For a moment, Marshall closed his eyes. A foghorn from the arriving ferry echoed along the wooden dock. Vibrations from the cars rolling from dock to backwashing ferryboat thudded beneath Marshall's boots. He could not tell whether the dock or his own body was shuddering. Maybe he shouldn't do this. Look what happened the last time he had tried to get involved. *Just get on the plane for Africa this weekend. Don't look back. Dive.*

"Marshall?"

"I'm here," he said wearily.

"Yes, Marshall, I think you are."

"Are what?"

"Here," Irene said. "Finally here."

When Marshall asked Andrew to join him in visiting Ellensburg's famous Chimpanzee and Human Communication Institute, he had pitched the trip as a lark to satisfy an old childhood curiosity—and a new, post-transplant interest—in primates. Andrew was so accustomed to his older sister's passion for science and other animals that he didn't question Marshall's brief detour after their Seattle diving assignment.

"It'll be fun," Marshall told Andrew now, as they drove the lush back roads of the Cascade Highway. "It'll also prime us for more aquatic ape research."

As he drove, Andrew glanced at the bright blur of salmonberries and pale yellow poplars already changing colors along the roadside. At higher altitudes these hints of fall had eclipsed the splendor of the short mountain summer.

Marshall gazed out the car window at the passing landscape. "I'm so used to undersea gardens," he said, "I don't know much about terrestrial plants." From habit, he reached for his small Nikon and snapped several shots. It occurred to him suddenly that, in the time since his transplant, he'd spent more time on land than on water. Maybe it was his imagination, but his heart's post-transplant recuperation on dry land had left him with an uneasy sensation of heaviness in his bones. It was as if his very marrow were denser, his skeleton contracted. Never before had Marshall felt his body structure and movements to be more primate-like.

"It's a good thing we're doing more of our fossil research in Africa soon," Marshall told Andrew. "I guess I'm feeling more like an aquatic ape now than merely a mammal who's choosing to go back to the oceans."

"Well, if we have to be landlocked, this is the place," Andrew said, nodding at a vast alpine meadow.

All the way up and over Snoqualmie Pass, the two men drove in the comfort and camaraderie of shared silence. Marshall photographed the great cedars, and as they descended the pass, there was an abrupt, dramatic drop in size and density of the abundant fir trees. Here was sage land, as arid as the high deserts of South Dakota or Wyoming. As they eased into the irrigated Yakima Valley, the sparse landscape gave way to hay and alfalfa.

"Here it is." Marshall pointed to the exit for Ellensburg and Central Washington University's Chimpanzee and Human Communication Institute. After a mile or two, as Andrew pulled into the institute's entrance, Marshall was almost startled to realize he had no idea how he was going to introduce Irene to Andrew. Friend? Fellow transplant?

He might have known the young woman would introduce herself.

"Irene Feinstein," she said, shaking Andrew's hand first. "I volunteer here. So, you're the diving buddy who helped save Marshall's life?"

Andrew smiled and glanced over at Marshall. "And you're the only woman Marshall ever phones back."

"Lucky me." Irene made a face. She turned to Marshall. "You look great for a dead man."

"Thanks a lot," he said.

As Irene embraced him, Marshall felt a moment's pleasure in their reunion. He stood back and appreciatively studied the young woman. She was lovelier than he remembered.

Irene noted Marshall's approving nod and explained, "Color by Audrey Hepburn. I'm in my elegant waif stage."

Companionably, the young woman took Marshall's arm as the three of them waited for a group of tourists, students, and visitors to gather for the "Chimposium."

"Okay, everyone," Irene instructed the visitors in a commanding voice that Marshall did not recognize in her. "Please speak quietly and respect the animals as you enter."

As Andrew and the others walked ahead into the facility, Irene held Marshall back. "Listen," she whispered. "We've been able to track the matriarch of the troop we think was captured with your baboon. Hara? Those baboons are still in the labs at Roseland Research in Portland, near where you got your new heart. Certainly didn't take much detective work on our part," she chided him. "Hara is still in Portland at the medical lab. Anybody could have found that out—if they had really looked."

"What?" Suddenly light-headed, Marshall almost stumbled. "Hara is still there? Alive?"

"Yes. That's probably why your sensations were so strong when you were in Portland. You were really near her." Irene held him steady. "Hey, you okay?"

"Sure about all this?" he managed to say. He could hardly breathe.

"Certain. One of our undercover lab workers has been watching all the sales and transfers between primate medical research labs. Roseland also has the space chimps and that new one we're hoping to rescue—the baby rhesus monkey."

"So, you're going to break into Roseland?"

"Yeah, so here's your part to help out the cause. Take some documentary photos."

Marshall stalled for time. He could not seem to get hold of himself. Had he unconsciously been moving toward this moment ever since he first returned to Portland? Had his heart known more than his mind that he would come to this? What was it Irene had once told him—something about the ancient Egyptians discarding the brain as worthless after death, but ritually preparing the sacred heart in a jar with the royal mummy? Egyptians believed a soul needed its heart for all eternity. "What baby rhesus are you talking about?"

Images again flooded his mind. *Grassland, an infant baboon easily astride a matriarch's cinnamon-colored back. Metal bars, and an unconscious Hara splayed out on a steel table.*

"Honestly, Marshall, don't you ever read newspapers? Or have you been underwater all this time? You know, the Roseland rhesus monkey. Scientists spliced his DNA together with a jellyfish gene. That designer baby monkey glows in the dark. In a couple of years—if the jellyfish gene gets passed to his offspring—this poor little monkey will father a new race of genetically altered primates that . . ." Irene grabbed Marshall's arm in alarm. "What's wrong with you? You're drenched in sweat!"

It took all Marshall's strength to detach from her. He felt sick. He had forgotten his pills again. Reaching into his jacket, he swallowed a dose of cyclosporine. "Nothing. My meds may be off."

"Tell me about it," Irene said. "I get so sick of all these pills. The chimps like to imitate me popping them."

Then she said, "It's time for me to lead a tour," as a small busload of elementary schoolchildren crowded into the building for a guided observation of the famous chimpanzee Washoe and her family.

Marshall read the educational display while Irene corralled the children. Washoe was a former space chimp, who, like all the original chimpanzees in the space program, had served her country in the 1960s as one of the first astronauts. Some of the chimps had originally been taken as infants from their mothers in Africa and shipped to America to be trained as "chimponauts." These chimpanzees had been sealed in compression chambers to test the limits of endurance for zero gravity; they had been whirled in centrifuges and strapped onto deceleration sleds as if they were crash-test dummies. Finally, the best-trained chimps were shot into outer space before any human astronauts.

But later, in the 1970s, when the space race involved only human astronauts, the U.S. Air Force decided their chimpanzees were unnecessary surplus. More than a hundred space chimps were offered up for bids to toxicology labs that would use the chimpanzees in their medical experiments. A nationwide campaign to protest this treatment of the space chimps led to a long court battle with animal rights activists. Twenty-one animals, including seven of the original space chimps, were lucky enough to find shelter in a Florida primate sanctuary and other private refuges. But the other eighty or so were sold to research labs, including Roseland Research outside Portland.

Washoe was one of the lucky few. A captive-born space chimp, she was transferred to a teaching university lab. Under the guidance of the primatologist Dr. Roger Fouts, the young chimp had startled the scientific world by learning American Sign Language. For thirty years she had communicated with humans and now talked in signs with other chimps who had learned ASL. For several generations the chimps had passed on the visual language to their own offspring as part of chimpanzee culture.

Irene's manner abruptly shifted when she noted something odd about the milling schoolchildren. They were very, very quiet. Many of them were excitedly talking to one another, but with their hands. "Oh, they're deaf," Irene said.

Irene led everyone into the spacious building that featured a three-story-high, open-air mesh roof. The interior was landscaped with lush green savannah grasses and a large climbing structure that moved like a real tree. Casually twirling inside a tire swing, one of the chimpanzees eyed the visitors with interest. An older male in the community began displaying, pant-hooting and patting his strong chest.

Irene spoke and the schoolchildren's teacher translated her words into sign language. "Humans don't enter the chimpanzees' home except to clean, make repairs, and give medical care," she said. "We want Washoe's family to live in a society free from our demands or intrusion."

The deaf children were riveted on their teacher's every visual word and her expressive face. They all nodded, except one child who seemed distracted, gazing straight up at the lights as if mesmerized. Unlike his classmates, this boy did not sign but instead kept snapping his fingers with a frantic *pop-pop-pop*.

Washoe was comfortably situated high up in the spacious "canopy" of fire hoses designed to simulate a high rain forest. Ignoring the commotion below, she rested on steel mesh that hung like a hammock; she was deeply absorbed in the pages of a battered *National Geographic*. In a private monologue, Washoe was signing to herself as she flipped through the magazine's pages, pausing every now and then to ponder a picture.

Irene explained, "Washoe was raised like a human infant. She ate at the dinner table, wore baby clothes, was toilet trained, and played with dolls. Our director here at the institute, Roger Fouts, was one of Washoe's earliest companions and researchers." Irene paused to let the translator-teacher explain, and then continued, "Washoe learned ASL just as any human child would. Chimpanzees use language and tools—these signs of culture tell us that these primates are very self-aware." Here Irene stopped. She smiled at the schoolchildren, who could barely contain their own pleasure and excitement at seeing the chimpanzees sitting together grooming each other. Sometimes the chimps would pant-hoot or make other noises the children couldn't hear; other times, the chimps would sign to each other.

It thrilled the children to recognize the chimps talking in familiar ASL. They soon lost interest in Irene's lecture and began crowding against the viewing glass, signing to the chimps. *Come here. We see you.* But the chimps either hadn't noticed them yet or chose to ignore the silent children with their flying fingers.

With a shrug and a grin, Irene turned back to continue the lecture for Marshall and Andrew. "Until the chimpanzees proved they could not only communicate but also use one of our own human languages, ASL, science had dismissed them as 'thoughtless brutes.' For a long time we believed that humans were the only species capable of using symbols and language. But Washoe and other signing chimps—and Koko and other signing gorillas—have disproved that theory. Now we have to ask: 'What does it mean that other primates think, feel emotions, and can even *talk* with us? What does it mean that they ask us about death? That they can now tell us how it feels to be sad or lose someone they love?" Irene paused and then rushed on, "For example, researchers have discovered that Michael, a second-generation signing gorilla living with Koko, has memories of having witnessed his parents' deaths at the hands of poachers. He can tell his keepers the story of witnessing them being killed. He still has bad dreams about it."

Irene turned to Marshall, but he was no longer beside her. Instead, he was with the deaf children, squatting down on his knees and intently watching their faces. Marshall was also talking with his hands, as expertly and animatedly as any of the deaf children.

Andrew leaned near Irene and asked, "What's Marshall saying? He always signs too fast for me when we're underwater. Can you translate?"

"Well, I've only been studying ASL awhile," Irene said, "and I never dreamed Marshall knew ASL. The guy's a mystery. Okay, now Marshall is asking the kids why that one little boy over there is not joining in, the one snapping his fingers." Irene listened carefully with her eyes and then added, "The kids are telling him, 'He's not in this world with us yet.'"

Irene smiled. "Oh, I get it. The kids are saying the boy's autistic and just starting to learn ASL." She nodded and watched a while longer, then told Andrew, "You know, Roger Fouts was one of the first to recognize that autistic kids couldn't process auditory and visual information at the same time. But he saw that autistic kids had really good motor control and they could also do sophisticated movements with their hands. Why not teach autistic kids ASL? You know, so much of the early work with deaf people focused on forcing them to speak. Just like scientists kept trying to get apes to talk, even though they don't have the proper larynx for human speech. But a visual language like ASL let us discover just how smart autistic kids and apes really are. Look at them!"

Irene paused to take pleasure in all the signed conversations, to listen in on a few and nod appreciatively. Then she continued, "So Fouts and others discovered that, once the autistic children began signing, they also began to speak aloud for the first time. You know, this proves that Darwin was right. Our human language did evolve from animal communication.

First we gestured, then we talked." Irene looked up and gave Andrew a sly smile. "Some of us—like our friend Marshall—are still evolving."

Andrew threw back his head and gave out a hearty laugh. At the noise, two of the chimps stopped their grooming, glanced over at the humans, and then ran over to the glass barrier and the deaf schoolchildren. The glass may have physically separated chimpanzees and children, but it was no real barrier. As the chimps' leathery fingers deftly reached out, all the children crowded together to watch these hands that seemed so familiar, so human. With these hands, the chimps began to talk.

Who that? signed one of the most self-assured chimps to one of the small girls. This eighteen-year-old chimp had been born in a medical research lab, but instead of spending a lifetime in a tiny cage, Loulis had been chosen as an infant by Fouts to become an adopted son of Washoe, now the matriarch of this complex society.

Me Christine, the girl signed. *Who you?*

Me Loulis. The young chimp's fingers were delicate. *You got candy? Coca-Cola? Fruit?*

My mom says not good for me! Christine signed back with a woeful shrug. *You got mom?*

Mom Washoe, the chimp signed with a thumb to his heart and a small rapid circle.

You happy here? Christine asked earnestly, her hands sculpting the air.

The chimp paused and gazed straight into the girl's eyes for a long moment. Then simply signed, *No bad here. Good food. Good us.*

Marshall knelt down beside the little girl, quietly observing as she continued her conversation with Loulis. They talked together as if they were becoming fast friends. Watching Christine and Loulis, Marshall felt himself relaxing. The last time he had felt such peace was in the aquarium lying next to Isabel as she slept, her breathing steady and soft.

The chimps and children continued their dialogue, and Marshall glanced over at Irene. She had slipped her arm through Andrew's, and they were lost in conversation. As Andrew listened, his expression took on an uncharacteristic gravity. What was Irene telling him? Surely she wouldn't confide in Andrew anything about her undercover work to rescue lab animals? Or Marshall's request for help in finding Hara? Surely

Andrew would never condone such a thing. Yet by the tilt of his head and the intensity with which he listened to Irene, Andrew's face showed a fierce concern.

As Marshall sat on his haunches, watching the children and chimpanzees talk, the thought rose up from his belly, *She's really alive. Hara is alive.* He could try to help rescue her and maybe even bring her home to Africa.

And then, as if he had never recognized the fact, Marshall knew that *he* was also completely alive. His heart—his broken, borrowed heart—was happy. He could hear it: *A-live. A life. Our life.*

chapter fourteen

Room 66X

THE CINNAMON-COLORED matriarch had not made a sound when they took the infant from her after two months. Here, in the lab at Roseland Research, Hara had learned that any resistance was severely punished. The lab veterinarian had strapped Hara to a steel table to deliver a baby directly from her belly.

Hara had been one of the first baboons in her troop to be housed in cages marked "Nursery Unit. Sterile." Unlike the powerful troop leader, Namib, and the others, she had not yet been moved from the nursery unit because of her pregnancy, cesarean section, and nursing. But now that they had taken her infant, it would soon be time for her to join Namib in room 66X.

Several weeks earlier, Namib had disappeared behind the locked door of room 66X. Sometimes Hara heard him shrieking for her. These were the same frantic screams Hara had heard from still another room, where they took the young baboon she had claimed as part of their family. Sol. He too had cried out for her. Then Sol was gone. So many of the family had disappeared. Hara remembered them all, especially those she had adopted and named.

Room 66X was a chill, sterile lab of steel cages measuring five feet by five feet by seven feet. Lighting was regulated every twelve hours, the air exchanged every four minutes by whirring extractor fans. Double rows of cages were labeled Z400 through Z425. Every cage held a huddled primate. Dazed by suffering, the twenty-five animals were still not beyond terror.

The baboons cringed whenever a lab tech peered through the steel bars into their dim cages. They flattened themselves against the backs of the cages, some shivering violently, others wracked by muscle spasms. Several doubled over, clutching their stomachs, vomiting. Many of the baboons were juveniles sitting forlornly in their own feces. Metal-wire stitches zigzagged across their bodies, with blood and pus seeping from precise, purposeful wounds.

How many of these baboons still remembered the sweet, open grasslands of their native African savannah, the community curled up together at night on their sleeping-rock cliffs, the sunlit days spent grooming and playing with their families as the matriarchs kept watch? How many of these juveniles had been born here under fluorescent lights? After several months spent clinging to their mothers' soft fur, how many had been separated into these solitary cages—awaiting a transplant from another animal they would never see alive? These cross-species heart, liver, and kidney transplants the baboons' bodies would immediately reject as alien. But the massive amounts of immunosuppressant drugs would forbid their bodies' natural defense systems and force them to accept a foreign organ.

Room 66X was the xenotransplantation lab. Here pig organs were transplanted into baboons used as human surrogates—experiments scientists claimed would one day be perfected in direct pig-to-human organ transplants. The longest a baboon had ever survived a transplanted pig heart or liver was thirty-nine days. The average survival rate was seven days. All the baboons died or were euthanized after these transplant experiments.

In room 66X, Namib was not caged. Instead, the large baboon lay strapped down on a steel operating table with his great arms and long legs splayed out, cuffed in iron manacles. Attached to the bulging blood vessels in Namib's neck was a pig's heart swollen three times its normal size. This borrowed, swollen red organ pumped visibly. Even though manacled, Namib could cradle this pig heart attached to his own neck artery. He held the alien organ as if each thud of the heart hurt him. His manacled hands could touch, but not tear away, the other heart.

When Marshall entered this room marked No Admittance, Namib did not move one muscle. Marshall felt paralyzed, as well. Could he really go through with this? Andrew and Irene and the ALL activists were on other floors attempting to rescue the space chimps and the genetically altered rhesus monkey.

For a moment, Marshall was afraid he might cry out at the sight of this creature cradling another animal's beating heart to his own neck. Marshall let out a long, ragged breath and steadied himself against a counter as his heart pounded. He felt light-headed, nauseated. No. He backed away. It was too much. He just couldn't bear this.

It was one thing to promise Irene that he'd do his part to document these animal experiments from the inside. It was another to come face-to-face with such suffering. But none of the others who had quietly broken into the lab today, when most of the Roseland staff was attending a company picnic, had Marshall's photography skills. Without his images, no one on the outside would really believe what went on here. The other ALL activists, mostly kids in their late twenties and true believers, depended on him.

And what about his hopes of finding Hara here? The careful ALL undercover work, the sacrifices of these young people—he couldn't let them down. Not to mention Andrew. Marshall had tried everything to convince Andrew that his taking part in the ALL rescue was wrong. It wasn't Andrew's fight; he would only be in the way. Worse yet, Isabel might blame Marshall for involving her brother in illegal activism. He knew she was already profoundly disappointed in him, which was why he still could not return her calls. What if he had called her and again had been compelled to tell her the truth—this time about what he and Andrew and Irene had planned? Any leak would endanger them all.

Andrew agreed that neither of them should call his sister until the rescue was over. But he had swept aside Marshall's concerns about Isabel's judgment. "You don't know my sister very well. If we get caught doing this, she'll not only visit us in jail, she'll organize her stranding network and bust us out like beached whales."

"But this has nothing to do with you, Andrew—or your sister."

"You're right. It has everything to do with *you*."

"So, why . . . ?"

"Because," Andrew said, exasperated, "anything to do with you, Marsh, has to do with people who care about you."

Marshall could think of nothing else to say. This was what he had always avoided—the blurred boundaries of love and obligation. But that was before his transplant. Marshall saw his life as a before and after: there were the years when his own nature had repeatedly failed him and others; and then there was this post-transplant life, in which he had another heart, stronger in every way—one that drove him to reach out to others. Some people were born with this desire to give back something to the world and the people who nurtured them. These young people in ALL, for example. So many of them were like Irene. They had hope; they believed that other lives, even nonhuman, mattered as much as their own.

Marshall wasn't sure he could help make the world more humane. He wasn't convinced that everybody can make a difference. But he was sure that he had a job to do, something he was good at. Raising his Nikon, he focused his entire being inside the viewfinder.

With each click of his camera, the baboon flinched.

After he had exhausted a roll of film, Marshall kept his distance from this baboon. He did not know what was more horrible—the sight of the baboon or the fact that somehow he recognized the animal. Suddenly Marshall even knew his name—Namib, after the mysterious wet desert of Africa. How did he know this?

Familiar savannah and an all-powerful Namib grooming Hara, hoping she might mate with him again. He is watching from above on the sleeping rocks, a craggy stone perch. He is not jealous. He is cautious. This older male is high-ranking, like Hara, and he has barely tolerated the new male baboon in the midst of Hara's family. Often Namib has threatened, but he has never attacked.

Just as suddenly as it had come, the memory was gone, replaced by the artificial breathing of the lab's chill and sterile air conditioning. Marshall forced himself to stare down at this fellow creature strapped to a steel table, alien heart throbbing at his throat. It was so like another memory—Marshall's own—of gazing down at a steel operating table with a man splayed out, his chest cavity open, waiting.

"Easy," he told the baboon now and stepped closer.

Drugs had dulled the once-mighty baboon's brown eyes. But there was still enough intelligence in those eyes to pierce Marshall's.

As if pulled by gravity toward Namib, Marshall bowed his head. "What can I do?" he asked, as if Namib might understand his words. "Is . . . is she here? Hara?"

It seemed to take every fiber of his strength, but Namib shrieked, baring his fangs.

Marshall's heart expanded, ached, raced so fast that it was as if he were running from a lion across hot savannah. He felt a powerful surge of his own energy, his pulse pounding in his ears. An image of Hara in a cage alone, biting at her own wrists.

"Namib," Marshall said and at last touched the creature's shaggy shoulder. "Where?"

The once so fearsome baboon looked up into Marshall's eyes, his silken brow creased with pain. His elegant, long snout was now prematurely white. Namib's eyes were swollen but still keen. It was like gazing into the eyes of another human being. And there was something else recognizable in those eyes. A plea.

Marshall hesitated only a moment before he pulled out his pocketknife. Then, with one quick slash, he cut free the throbbing pig's heart from Namib's wizened neck. He had no key to unlock the hand and foot shackles that bound Namib to the steel table, but he could rest the flat of his warm hand on the great baboon's sunken chest, listening to the weak beat within.

Gratitude in Namib's eyes. And an echo of his long-ago fierceness. Marshall felt his own heart surge with strength as he obeyed the baboon who had once been their leader, their protector.

Marshall reached for the syringe that Irene had forced upon him before they broke into the lab. "It's a fatal dose of mercy," Irene had said. "When there's no hope of rescue."

Carefully Marshall found a shrunken vein in the baboon's manacled wrist and slowly released the drug into Namib's body. One by one, the primate's fingers unclenched. His fists fell open; his eyes fixed, then gently glazed over. One last sigh from his much-stitched chest—and he was free.

Marshall leaned down, resting his forehead on Namib's brow. The door to room 66X abruptly flew open and a young man in a white lab jacket ran in.

The veterinarian halted when he saw this intruder leaning over the research baboon.

"Hey, stop!" the vet cried. There was no authority in his voice. Only fear.

Marshall slowly looked up at the vet. "No," he said evenly. "You stop." Turning back to Namib, Marshall laid a hand one moment longer on the quiet chest.

Backing up, the young vet stood warily in the doorway until others might come to his aid. "We're saving lives here."

"You're killers," Marshall said. And with one backward look at the large baboon, he ran out a side door to a hallway.

Down a winding hall with video monitors—shut off by Andrew, Irene, and the ALL activists—Marshall ran. He was lost. How would he ever find his way back to the others?

"Marshall!" A familiar voice.

It was Andrew. "We've got some of the space chimps already loaded in the van."

"Only some of them?" Marshall asked.

Andrew nodded. "According to the records our undercover hacker studied before we got here, half the animals have already died from experiments. And there's a female Irene had to euthanize. She was carrying a dead fetus in her womb—looked like it's been rotting inside for a while." Andrew grimaced. "Terrible . . ."

Marshall turned away. "How many space chimps rescued?"

"We got only seven of them. But all the animals we're rescuing are healthy. The records show they haven't yet been injected with any diseases. They can join the others at the sanctuary. Did you find her . . . your matriarch?"

"She's downstairs, I think, in the nursery." Marshall turned to go.

Andrew tried to catch his arm. "You know that for sure? We've got to get the hell out of here!"

"Okay. You get Irene and the others out of here and out to the van. Now. I'm going down to the nursery floor."

"But you'll get caught!"

"I've got to try. Don't wait too long for me." Marshall nudged him. "Go on. Save the animals you can."

The walls of the Nursery Unit were sterile white, but there was a different sound. Not the chill whirring of room 66X, but instead the chattering of tiny, pink-eared infants—baboons, chimpanzees, rhesus monkeys—most in separate cages. A few of the infant baboons were in a playpen with plastic animal toys that squeaked when squeezed.

Marshall stopped, catching his breath. Which infant was Hara's? And where was she, if not with her infant? He did not know what to do. Surely the young vet had sounded the alarm by now. Thank God that most of the staff was gone. The ALL activists had told Marshall that Roseland was leery about calling in outside law enforcement for any reason. Inevitably, stories of what went on inside the lab leaked to the press after outsiders got a good look around. So maybe he would have to deal only with in-house security.

But if Marshall were to have any chance of rescuing Hara, he must search the floor until he found her. Still, he lingered. The little ones gawked at him curiously, their dark eyes and eyebrows quizzical. So much life in such a place of death.

He wanted to touch them, to take one of these beautiful babies in his arms at least once. Never in his life had Marshall wanted a child. Now, he wanted to carry all these infants to safety. Even though they were not human. Even though they were not his kind.

What was he thinking? He must find Hara now. But where—in which of the many rooms on this floor? He didn't know if he could bear to find Hara stretched out on an operating table like Namib. Better to take the living with him than get distracted by the dead.

Making clucking and other comforting sounds with his tongue, Marshall picked up one of the infant baboons. Immediately, the little one clasped her arms around Marshall's neck, flattening her small body against the man's chest as she might when carried by a friendly adult in her troop.

Marshall's heart responded with a leap of pleasure. Then he turned and ran with the infant clinging to him. Down the hall, he searched desperately, trying to figure out which room still held Hara. All of a sudden he stopped and stood completely still, feeling the weight of the infant, listening to his own strong pulse.

Could his heart really find its way to Hara? He heard a shriek behind him. It was not a baboon, but the pant-hooting of a chimpanzee. Still, Marshall followed the cries. Passing through a door to a small lab room, he was surprised to find wizened hands reaching out and signing to him. How had these chimpanzees learned ASL? Marshall remembered Irene telling him that some of the animals who ended up in these medical labs had come from university programs in which they had been taught ASL. Often when the university programs lost funding, they had to sell their signing chimps to medical labs. So here these "educated" chimpanzees lived, desperately trying to talk a human language to lab workers who couldn't understand them.

Help! a row of caged chimpanzees signed over and over. *Man. Help.*

Out? one of the elderly male chimps signaled through the bars. *Key?*

Marshall closed his eyes. If it had not been for the tiny baboon clinging to his chest, he might have sat down here and just given up.

Instead his hands talked. *Baboon. Mother. Where?* And then he signed, *Hara?*

The elderly chimpanzee studied Marshall as if he had all the time in the world. And so he did. This chimp wasn't going anywhere. In those ancient brown eyes, Marshall recognized reasoning and even calculation. Watching this other primate making a plan was like looking back through the eons to a time when a human, chimplike ancestor might have shown this exact expression, this light in his eyes as he plotted his escape from an overpowering predator.

Me. Out? the old chimpanzee signed.

Could Marshall keep his promise if he said yes? He too had to calculate. He could carry this infant and, he hoped, Hara. But he couldn't carry this old chimp as well to safety. *You. Me. Run?* Marshall signed back.

Pant-hooting, the old chimpanzee jumped up and down in his cage. *Me. Run. Run. Run!* His fingers flew.

Holding the infant baboon against his chest, Marshall reached out and paused at the latch to the cage. He pointed to the infant. *Mother? Here?*

The elderly chimp nodded eagerly. *Me. Show.*

Without another sign, Marshall unlatched the old chimp's cage and was surprised at how agile the old male was as he swung out and down to the white-tiled floor. *Come,* the chimp signed.

As they ran, Marshall felt the surge of physical power in his legs, his arms, how young and healthy his heart was—almost too strong for his body. Running after the elderly chimp, whose limp barely slowed him down, Marshall felt a moment's raw exultation.

With his lean arms, the old chimp thrust open the swinging doors to another nursery room. A dozen infant chimpanzees in a large pen leapt and pant-hooted in a frenzy of greeting—and, for some, fear. A few baboons were hiding behind a tower made of old tires. They screeched to Marshall's infant, who clung more closely to his chest.

Had the chimp misguided him? Marshall suspected as much when he saw the old male lift up the tiniest chimpanzee with so much tenderness he might have been a mother.

In his bowlegged walk, the old male crossed to Marshall, the tiny chimp in his arms. *Me. Fred.* He signed his name slowly several times, to make sure that Marshall understood. *Baby. Me. Man, baby . . . Go!*

Me. Marsh. Marshall signed, giving up any hope of finding Hara. At least he and the old male could do some good here for the infants. *Yes. Us. Babies. Go!*

But then a cry rose from his infant baboon, who leapt from Marshall's arms and scampered over to a cage in the very back.

A shriek from inside. An arm—strong but bitten at the wrists—reached out and fiercely pulled the infant against the bars. Pant-hooting, baboon shrieks, his infant's excited chatter.

Marshall peered inside the cage. Long, elegant slope of cinnamon-colored snout. Eyes that held his. Blood rushed to his head, hope surged through his arms, and Marshall ripped the cage door open.

Hara leapt out, not at him, but for the infant that was somehow also Marshall's. She swept up the tiny creature and settled her to ride easily on her back. Marshall watched as the matriarch with her infant frantically circled the white lab, all the other primates screaming, jumping up and down in their cages.

He stood absolutely still, watching the magnificent baboon leap, looking for an escape. When she had exhausted herself, Marshall very carefully eased toward her. She could kill him with her razor-sharp teeth; she could knock him down with one powerful arm.

But Hara did not. She waited, watching Marshall under a brow furrowed and wary. She allowed him to come closer and closer. Her infant chattered, reaching out to the man while keeping hold of Hara.

Marshall was astonished. Why did the infant still want anything to do with him? Maybe he was the first human who had ever approached the infant without a mask and needles. Or—it was a crazy idea—could it possibly be that both the infant and Hara somehow recognized him? What he carried of them inside his body?

And then Marshall did something astonishing. He slowly reached out a finger and traced the Cesarean scar on Hara's belly. The infant and the old male chimp curiously watched all this. Then Marshall carefully opened his shirt to reveal a vertical scar from sternum to navel. Fred reached up and touched the man's chest, hooting softly.

Marshall's scar was better healed than Hara's, but it was from the same kind of knife the lab poachers had used on her swollen belly. Hara met his eyes steadily. Intelligence. Again, acceptance.

Nodding, Marshall said one word. "Sol." Then he switched on the cell phone to speed-dial Irene and the others, whom he hoped were still outside in a van hidden behind the lab among the trees.

"Marshall! Where the hell are you?" Irene asked. "We can't wait any longer."

"Wait for us," he whispered.

"You found her!"

"I'm bringing the whole damn family!" Before Irene could protest, Marshall said, "Side gate B," and hung up.

Infants leapt and screeched around him. He grabbed up two— another baby baboon and an underweight baby chimp. Hara could carry her own. And Fred had his infant chimp under one grizzled arm. Pulling another clinging chimp away from his ankle, Marshall said sadly, "Sorry, little guy..."

Then Marshall ran with them—fleet Hara with her daughter and Fred with his tiny chimp, all at his side. Marshall's two infants held on, shrieking as if this were a joy ride. Though they fled along winding, white laboratory hallways and not across some hot savannah, they were escaping the predator together. They were never more endangered; they were never freer.

chapter fifteen

Family Cottage

IF I DIDN'T KNOW you better, I'd say you were speeding," Marian said as Isabel drove them along the winding switchbacks toward her beach cottage.

"Okay, okay," Isabel muttered. "I'll slow down."

Though she told herself she was calm, Isabel noticed a slight nausea in her stomach, the bitter taste of adrenalin. Was she really going to follow Alexander Sharp's carefully typed e-mail directions, drawings, and photos and attempt anything as dangerous and illegal as dismantling the navy research vessel's sonar equipment before the tests began again early tomorrow? Daniel McHalffey had agreed to meet Isabel at her beach cottage tonight. She couldn't believe anyone except Marian would join her in this desperate action. Isabel would never have asked Daniel if she had still been able to dive below the navy boat and disengage the acoustic speakers by herself.

According to Dr. Sharp, it was a simple task. But getting down to the sonar device undetected was the real feat. Even in the photos that Sharp had shown Isabel, the sonar had looked menacing. Its black steel casing— an array of eighteen underwater sonar speakers—resembled a giant hand-gun or pneumatic drill.

"It can blast up to two hundred and thirty-five decibels," Sharp had cautioned Isabel. "Like standing right next to a twin-engine F-15 fighter jet at takeoff."

But you must have warned the navy that human and cetacean eardrums will rupture at such extreme acoustic levels, Isabel had typed on the scientist's laptop.

"Listen." Sharp had sat straight up in his hospital bed. "The navy swore up and down to me that they would never test the sonar at its highest range."

"And what were they testing it at when you lost your hearing?"

Sharp didn't have to read Isabel's lips. He understood the question. "That's the first thing I demanded to know after . . . after what Lieutenant Lester calls the 'incident.' " The young scientist had lowered his eyes and cupped his ears with his palms, as if he might still protect himself. "One hundred and ninety decibels," he said very softly.

Isabel had not moved to comfort him. She had discovered that her presence, her quiet witness, brought Sharp more solace than her compassion. So it had surprised her when the man reached out and took her hand in his. It was a soft, elegant hand—a hand that perhaps had played the piano when Sharp was a child and that later tapped computer keys with the same syncopated skill and devotion. It was not the hand or the touch of someone who had ever meant to do such harm. And yet, her beach lay strewn with the sea's dead.

"And tomorrow morning . . . ?" Isabel had shaped the words clearly.

"Testing at the upper limits." Sharp's voice broke. "It will be . . . horrible." He fell silent. Silence was where he lived now.

As she slowed to navigate a narrow switchback, Isabel glanced down at Kiwanda Beach, where weary stranding network volunteers were still cleaning up carcasses. The National Marine Fisheries Service still had its divers' alert in effect from last weekend. When Isabel had called Stewart to tell him she feared renewed military testing and more strandings, he'd refused to give her any more information.

"Ask your new boyfriend for help," he'd said hotly. "Maybe he can get you into even more trouble."

"I'm sorry, Stewart, I never meant for that to happen. Besides," she added, "Marshall's gone. He won't be back."

"Yeah, well, we all have a way of coming back to you, Isa. And I almost lost my job because of it. If you know what's good for you, you won't do anything silly. Don't be a hero." When Isabel said nothing, he added, "Remember what the lieutenant told you about going to the press," he said. "The navy will press formal charges against you and Marshall for criminal trespassing if you breathe a word about any of this to the media. Besides, you're a federal employee. The navy is on your side."

Isabel wondered then if Stewart could be trusted. Since she'd been visiting Dr. Sharp in the hospital, Stewart had seemed overly suspicious and watchful of her. Had he or the feds tapped into Dr. Sharp's e-mail or hers? Would Stewart ever betray her? Isabel refused to believe that he could. He was just jealous and hurt, not vengeful.

As she drove, Isabel turned to Marian with a nervous smile. "I don't know what I'd do without you, Marian." She reached across the seat and patted her friend's shoulder. "Are there any rules left that I *haven't* broken?"

"I can think of a few," Marian said. "Are you going to murder anybody? If so, I can only do illegal autopsies on animals."

In spite of herself, Isabel laughed. "No, no murders, I promise."

As they drove the last familiar curves to her beach cottage, Isabel was quiet. The truth was that she was profoundly worried about taking this step. All her life she had wanted to help animals, and her work as a forensic pathologist gave her the satisfaction of seeing those who did harm brought to some kind of justice. But this was crossing a line that Isabel had never imagined before. She could end up losing her job or, worse yet, in jail. What help could she give the animals then? And could she really bear the responsibility of seeing her friends suffer simply because of their loyalty to her?

"Marian," Isabel said firmly as she glanced across at her friend. In her red rain slicker and baseball cap stitched with a scarlet salmon, Marian looked suddenly younger. Perhaps fear made one seem more vulnerable. "You shouldn't be part of this anymore," Isabel decided. "Not for me. Not for anything. It's not worth it. I'm going to drop you at the Ocean Haven." The bar and grill was around the next curve.

"If I live that long," Marian commented as Isabel careened around a switchback.

"Sorry."

"Forgiven. But do slow down, dear. I really won't forgive you if we both go over a cliff." Marian grinned.

Isabel slowed her truck. She pulled over on the slender shoulder and turned off her headlights. In the darkness, there was the imposing bright weight of a half moon above and, far out at sea, the navy research vessel. In five hours, if Sharp's information was correct, the navy would again test its deadly sonar.

Isabel reached out and took Marian's hand. These were working hands that rescued animals, worked in the lab, and planted extravagant flower gardens. "I'm asking you, Marian," Isabel pleaded, "not to do this. I can't lose you."

Marian dropped her bantering tone. "You won't lose me."

"I'm so used to Andrew being . . . well, missing. He hasn't returned my phone calls for days. He's probably in Africa by now with . . ." Isabel stopped. "With Marshall." She didn't add that Marshall had also not returned any of her calls. Marian had, of course, intuited that. "If anything happened to you, it would be like . . ." Isabel hesitated. "Like being an orphan."

"If anything happened to me," Marian swore to her, "my family would never let you be alone." She sat back and managed a smile. "In fact, the concept of solitude is utterly foreign in my family."

"I mean it, Marian," Isabel insisted. "Swear to me that you'll take no part in this, that you'll stay on shore and help us by staying hidden. Out of the way. Out of danger."

Marian was quiet a long time. She seemed to be memorizing her friend's unkempt hair and delicate face. Isabel's slender European face was not one that Marian had ever expected to love. How much more generous and familiar were the wide faces of her Oskeena family. And yet here Isabel was, her best friend, someone she counted as family. But, would history now repeat itself—as had happened with all her people, would people and animals be given little chance against the military?

Marian at last made a promise. "I swear that I'll stay as far out of this as I can. But I won't stand by and watch you get hurt."

"I'm not doing the diving," Isabel said grimly. "Daniel's the brave one here. I'm just driving Grandfather's old boat."

They turned onto the gravel road to Isabel's beach cottage. High atop a grassy bluff overlooking the Pacific, the cottage still had the moss her grandfather had planted atop the roof shingles to stop all the leaks. As they arrived in a sputter of gravel, Isabel noted Daniel's van parked near the cottage.

Just then, the Spinner cottage door swung open and Andrew Spinner strode out. As Isabel got out of her truck, he swept her up in a strong embrace. "Isabel, don't be mad at me. We don't have much time," he said.

Isabel was so stunned to see her brother that she let him lift her several feet off the ground. What was he doing here at the cottage? He was supposed to be a world away. But here he was, with Silkie happily following at his heels.

"Some watchdog you are," Isabel scolded Silkie as her brother gripped her more tightly. "Why haven't you returned any of my calls, Andrew?"

"I can explain everything, but you'll know as soon as you walk inside. Isa, listen, I never meant to get this involved. It's just that Marshall needed help and . . ."

"Marshall?" Isabel demanded. "Is he here, too?"

It was the last thing Isabel expected, and yet she was not completely surprised that Marshall was waiting inside her beach cottage. Hadn't she once invited him to share her bed? Hadn't she known, without believing it, that he would return to her? A tumult of emotions—happiness that Marshall was here, dismay that it was on a night when she could least afford any intrusion, and dread that Marshall might again try to interfere and land them all in real trouble. The man had the worst timing of anyone she'd ever met. "Put me down, Andrew!"

Her brother set Isabel down easily, as if she weighed no more than his long-lasting rebreather tanks. The rebreather tanks had taken both Andrew and Marshall deeper than ever before, permitting them to descend down through the indigo world of pink and opal jellyfish, of invertebrates who made their own light. Down to that twilight zone where all colors disappeared into a blackness broken only by blizzards of tiny organisms like marine snow, the detritus that gives sea creatures life.

As Isabel headed toward her cottage, Andrew held her back. "Isabel, there's . . . there's a lot of . . . well, you'll see." Then he led her into the cottage as if revealing to her a surprise party in her honor. "Everyone's here," he informed her awkwardly.

Isabel crossed the threshold and gasped. She could hardly believe the scene. There were strangers—animals and one human—in the familiar crannies of her small cottage. On tables and chairs, several cages sat wide open. Resting together on the Chinese throw rugs were two ancient chimps. A strange young woman was balancing an infant chimpanzee on one arm, while an elder chimpanzee held a blue plastic baby bottle to the young one's hungry mouth. The nursing infant's baby whiskers trembled, his eyes glancing between the young woman and the older chimp feeding him.

"The baby is Sinclair," Irene said, "and my assistant adoptive parent here is Fred, the famous Air Force veteran chimponaut. Fred has survived outer space and electroshock therapy." The young freckle-faced woman seemed absurdly proud. Isabel noted a turquoise stud piercing her nose. "And I'm Irene Feinstein."

"Oh, my God," Marian burst out. She pushed into the cottage past Isabel and stared around at the chimpanzees. "It's the Roseland break-in. Space chimps rescued. I heard about it on the radio."

"Yeah. They probably wouldn't have called the police if we hadn't also taken their precious jellyfish monkey. I'm afraid a lab tech identified me and at least got a good look at Marshall. Enough for someone like your ex-husband to put out an all-points bulletin on both of us," Andrew admitted and flinched under his sister's stare.

"So you're fugitives. And you came here?" Isabel asked in disbelief. "They'll expect you to come to me, Andrew."

"We had nowhere else to hide for tonight, Isa," Andrew explained. "Some of the other ALL activists used the break-in van to drive the other rescued primates to safety. We're setting up an underground railroad for these animals so we can also get them down to . . ."

"ALL?"

"Animal Liberation Lifeline," Irene explained.

Isabel felt dizzy. It was too much, her brother getting caught up in a primate lab break-in, her own ridiculous plans to try to dismantle military equipment. What was she thinking? What were they all thinking?

"We truly thank you for this sanctuary," Irene added, a little tentatively.

"This is not your sanctuary," Isabel snapped. She turned to glare at

Andrew. She couldn't help but notice that Silkie was licking Fred's face and bowing down to ask for more play. "This is my home. The only reason you're here is that my brother seems to have suddenly remembered that this is his home too."

"Don't be too hard on them, Isabel." The familiar voice came from behind her.

She turned quickly to see the man who sat almost out of sight at her small kitchen table. Though his clothes were rumpled and his hair unkempt—those black curls strangely lank—Marshall's expression was calm. Isabel would never have imagined he could be this self-possessed or engaged.

Next to him, sitting on the table as if a sentry, was one of the most magnificent creatures Isabel had ever seen. She was a mature female baboon, her brow a ledge of golden-brown fur that lent the deep, inset eyes a dark glow. There was maternal concern and piercing intelligence in those eyes. Isabel looked down to see a tiny baboon in Marshall's lap. Red ears almost comically large and sticking straight out from each side of a tiny face, the infant baboon seemed human, vulnerable, and worried. Isabel could not help but stride across the living room and bend down on both knees to assure the infant baboon that she was no threat. "Shhhh," she said softly, as if seal-sitting on her beach. "It's all right."

Isabel's voice seemed to reassure the infant, who promptly scampered up his mother's strong shoulders, clinging to handfuls of matted hair.

"Hara," was all Marshall said.

Hearing the name Marshall always called her, the matriarch baboon turned around to the man and let herself be groomed by him. With a delicate hand, he preened and pulled at the dense fur along her arms.

Isabel knew without Marshall having to tell her. Hara must somehow be connected to Marshall's baboon heart. Was she from the same troop? Did baboons mate for life? Isabel's chest tightened as if she had just run across a vast space, in vain. Struggling with her own feelings, Isabel backed away a respectful distance from the matriarch baboon and her infant.

"Were they harmed in the lab?" Adopting what she hoped was a professional tone, as if this were another animal she must rescue, Isabel continued, "Were they infected with HIV or any live virus?"

"Not yet. The lab records on that were meticulous," Marshall answered. "But we had to . . . ," Marshall paused, a shadow crossing his eyes, "euthanize some of the others."

"I understand," Isabel said, recognizing the pain in Marshall's face. Suddenly he seemed weary, his composure fading. She could only imagine what he had seen. Isabel had read about the controversial xeno-transplantation experiments at Roseland; and after Marshall's transplant, she'd researched more on the Internet, finding the famous "Diaries of Despair"—graphic photos and exposés on animal abuse, mostly published in the British press. Turning back to the magnificent, wary Hara, Isabel asked, "What happened to her wrists? Will she let me examine her?"

"I don't know," Marshall said. "Hara allows only me to come near her and her baby."

"She recognizes you," Isabel said simply. For the first time, she met Marshall's dark eyes. They seemed to at once draw her in and hold her at a distance. But it wasn't ambivalence that she read in Marshall's eyes; it was the fierce attachment of grief and loyalty. "Yes," Marshall said softly, "I think she does."

His place surely was with Hara now. He was her sanctuary. In the short time this man likely had left, he must be with those who needed him most. And who was to say that Marshall did not most need the solace of such a fiercely trusting creature? It was the first time Isabel believed this man capable of devotion. She softened and smiled at Marshall. He was a good man; he might stay with someone. But not her.

"Hara is very beautiful," Isabel could say at last, and mean it. In that moment, she completely relinquished Marshall to the matriarch. Isabel had learned long ago how to say goodbye to those she loved most.

"I'm sorry about all this, Isabel," Marshall told her, nodding to the assorted animals and humans inside her cottage.

Before she could respond, Isabel noticed someone else in the kitchen. He was quietly feeding a tiny rhesus monkey from a plastic baby bottle. It was Daniel McHalffey holding a newborn monkey with huge eyes and a pale and delicate nose and mouth. Most striking were the newborn's tiny hands with perfectly humanlike fingers, each nail an eerie red, as if painted with bright polish.

"So this is the famous baby monkey with jellyfish genes?" It was Marian, appearing without a sound behind Isabel. "They spliced and inserted jellyfish DNA into a virus," she explained, "and then infected several hundred monkey eggs with that virus. They fertilized the eggs, implanted dozens of embryos, and voilà—of the babies born, only this lucky one has the extra gene. Think what they'll do soon with us humans . . ."

For a moment more, Isabel studied the newborn rhesus, his fingers gripping the baby bottle as he gazed up at Daniel and nursed. Always ready to lend a hand, Daniel was the one person whom Isabel could always count on to show up at a stranding.

In his red plaid shirt, his spectacles slipping down his slender nose, Daniel looked oddly at ease with the newborn monkey. Grinning up at Isabel, he asked in a soft, husky voice, "You want to hold him?"

Overwhelmed, Isabel sat down heavily at the kitchen table. "Not right now, thanks." For a moment, she sat staring vacantly at her cabinets, bewildered. Then she straightened. Stay focused. If Daniel was here, then Andrew and Marshall probably knew all about her plans to try and stop the navy's tests later tonight.

Andrew joined them in the kitchen and leaned his long body against the stove. "Daniel here tells me that you've got some crazy notion of trying to stop the undersea sonar tests tonight. Isabel, you can't really be serious. Your plan is way more dangerous than anything we've done!"

"That's debatable," Isabel told her brother. "But it's all right. We've got Daniel here and a few of the other stranding network volunteers to help us out. One of the navy scientists has told me exactly how to disarm the sonar and stop the tests."

"You can't dive, Isabel!" Andrew sputtered furiously. "What in God's name are you thinking?"

She turned to her brother and fully met his anger. "I guess I'm thinking what you're thinking." Her voice was steady and insistent. "Crazy notions must run in our family."

Andrew walked over and pulled his sister up into an unexpected embrace. At first she resisted her brother, out of sheer frustration and fear for him, for both of them, for everyone here in the shelter of this family cottage. It was too much—trying to save these doomed animals, loving the wrong people. Andrew held her so tightly that Isabel could hardly breathe. Suddenly she remembered a scene right here in Grandfather Spinner's kitchen. How many years ago was it now?

A seven-year-old Andrew had strolled in, his face bronzed, his hair streaked with sun, to find his sister leaning intently over the cracked Formica of their kitchen table. Spread before her was her book project, *Noah's Lost Ark*. With her watercolors, Isabel had painted every extinct animal she could research—from dodo bird to broad-billed parrot to Tasmanian wolf.

"*You're* the dodo," her little brother had hooted. "Come outside and play. There are seals down in Silkie's Cave. Low tide. Maybe we'll find another sealskin."

"No," Isabel had told Andrew crossly and pushed him away. She hadn't recognized then the disappointment and hurt in her brother's face. "I'm busy." She had turned back to her huge homemade book of extinctions.

"Busy with what?"

"Big, important things!" she'd snapped and again thrust him away from the table.

"Dead things!" her brother protested. "They're not important."

"Oh, I guess our parents aren't important, either, are they?" She'd whirled on him. "They're never coming back, Andrew. Never."

He'd stared hard at her, with all the longing of an orphaned child. "But Grandpa says that they're silkies . . ."

"That's just a made-up story."

He reached for her and knocked over Isabel's ceramic glue pot. A golden glob smeared across her book.

"Go stick to somebody else!" Isabel shouted. In a flash, she dipped her brush in the slow spill and streaked both her brother's arms with translucent glue. Shocked, he looked up at her and then ran out of the room stumbling and sobbing.

Now as Andrew held Isabel in his arms, she had to wonder: Was that day in this kitchen when he'd decided he had no home with her? Her brother had traveled a world away. Had she sent him on that journey?

Isabel leaned fully into him and wrapped her arms around his back. Andrew was so tall. How had he grown so much taller than she?

"I'm so glad you're here," she said, laying her head on his shoulder. "Home."

Andrew breathed, "Me too." He rested his chin on the top of her head.

"By the way," the young woman with the freckles dusting her flushed cheeks said as she entered the kitchen, "I'd like to help out tonight, if you'll let me."

As Andrew released his sister, Isabel turned to Irene. "Thanks, really, but it's just too risky . . ."

"All my life, I wanted to be a marine biologist," Irene said with some wistfulness. "Marshall gave me diving lessons in Hawaii. I can . . ."

"Oh, no, you don't!" Marshall suddenly spoke up, the alarm in his voice startling Hara. She tilted her head back and let out a piercing shriek, which made her infant hide in her dense fur. Marshall had his hands full soothing the matriarch and infant.

"Oh, yes, I do! You can't stop me. I'm too damn healthy now."

"Maybe Marshall's right." Isabel considered the young woman with the short, haphazard haircut.

Irene seemed scrawny and yet mutinously determined. Isabel could read the lack of muscle tone in her arms, the slight bow to her skinny legs, as if she were too long bedridden. She was the last person who should be diving tonight, but Isabel sensed it would be impossible to keep Irene out of the water. "Are you a transplant, too?"

"Not like Marshall, but yup," Irene said, "a pig's valve."

"Our grandfather had one of those," Isabel said softly.

"Complicated, isn't it?" Irene grinned. "Andrew's told me a lot about you—and your work. I admire what you do."

"And now that you're so damn healthy again," Isabel said, smiling, "are you going to become a marine biologist?"

"Nope. I found out that biology is just the study of life. Science has absolutely nothing to do with the love of life. Besides, aren't some marine biologists the same scientists who are helping the navy to conduct these horrible sonar tests? What kind of death wish is that?"

"Some biologists. Others are fighting it." Isabel liked this odd young woman. Perhaps if she were younger, Isabel might have adopted the same kind of radical activism. After all, humans were the only species with a death wish. It could destroy the Earth—and all its creatures. "We don't love life as much as the animals do," Isabel said, offering Irene a cup of tea.

If they'd had all the time in the world, Isabel would have engaged Irene further, asked about her life and how she had come to this decision to cross the line, break laws—all for the animals. Glancing at Irene's narrow shoulders, the delicate brow and hazel eyes, Isabel would have taken her for a scholar, not an activist. At some point, Irene had made a choice to break the law and rescue animals. What had been the turning point?

Was it when the girl had seen evidence of too much suffering? Like the hemorrhaged brain and ears and other organs shredded by sound that Isabel and Marian had stared down at during the necropsy? Or like the terrified eyes of a dying dolphin whose newborn would never nurse or swim in synch with that sleek body? Every person here had perhaps experienced that turning point when what they witnessed had propelled them into unknown territory—a realm of the heart in which human life and culture were not the only measures, when human minds and human suffering were not the only ones that mattered. They had crossed over and were no longer alone.

Gazing around her cottage at the gathering of primates—Marshall grooming his Hara, Daniel nursing a baby rhesus monkey whose fingers opened and closed in rhythm to his sucking, Marian and Irene fussing over and feeding a newborn chimp from a baby food jar of winter squash—Isabel at last met her brother's eyes. Sipping peppermint tea, Andrew sat down at the kitchen table to review Dr. Sharp's studies on sonar, which Isabel had earlier given to Daniel. Her brother looked so much like their father. He had the same sun-blasted red beard and hazel eyes; he was fair like Father and as nomadic. But unlike their parents, her brother had come home to her, to this strange, extended family. Isabel's eyes welled up with an unexpected happiness.

"Okay, listen up, everybody." Andrew straightened in his kitchen chair and spoke with an authority that Isabel didn't recognize. "If we're going to get anything done tonight, we have to act fast."

"Actually," Marian interrupted, "we have to do two things at once—

get these animals to safety and stop the military from blasting sonar into the ocean again."

"Okay, what do you suggest?" Andrew asked. "How can we do all this?"

Isabel was adamant. "Daniel was wrong to tell you about the sonar testing," she said. "You and Marshall have too much to reckon with as it is. Everyone will be searching for you. You'll be no help to us at all."

"So what's your big idea?" Andrew demanded. "You and Marian are going to stop this sonar all by yourself tonight?"

"I told you we've called some other volunteers we can trust," Isabel said sensibly, as if this would be the end of the subject.

"But who can you trust like your own brother?"

Isabel would have none of it. "Andrew, you can use the cottage tonight until it's safe to move these animals to a shelter."

"Maybe we should take the animals out by boat," he answered. "You'd be surprised how many fishermen sympathize with laboratory animals. They know what it feels like to be at the mercy of the government and scientists with no scruples."

"There's too much going on at sea tonight for you to escape by water," Isabel argued. "With the navy testing, the whole area for miles around is full of military and NMFS boats. You'll never get through. We'll be lucky if we even make it out to the navy boat."

"Yeah, so how are you getting the whaler out there?"

"The navy has hired local people to patrol the coast here." Isabel had to smile. "People like Daniel and other stranding network volunteers."

Andrew nodded. "Okay, okay. So how are we getting these animals out of here?"

"One if by sea, two if by land," Marian teased. "Isn't that something like what your Paul Revere said?"

Isabel was irritated at her friend's levity when so much was at stake. She was about to say something testy when she realized Marian was right. One of them would have to drive the animals to safety. And that someone would have to be a trusted local, a woman whom Lawasskin officials would never expect to harbor criminals.

"I'm invisible," Marian said simply. "There aren't many Indian animal rights activists anymore. They got killed off with the buffalo." Marian nodded to Irene. "I'll take the animals out of here."

"There's a sympathetic primate sanctuary in northern California," Irene said. "They're ready to help. We just have to get the animals down there."

Andrew spoke up. "Marian's right. No one will stop her."

"Once we can get the animals to the Mendocino coast sanctuary, other ALL members will get Hara back to Africa," Irene said. "We've already set it up with a California activist who's also an international exporter. And the space chimps are going to an underground sanctuary in New Mexico. We'll keep the rhesus monkey safely hidden for a long time, so that he can live out his life in peace and not have to father a new breed of genetically altered creatures."

Marshall had been unnaturally silent throughout this exchange. He seemed completely absorbed now in grooming Hara's shoulders. Isabel wondered if Marshall might talk some sense into Andrew. Then again, if he began talking, Marshall might make things even worse. After all, Isabel thought, look what he had talked Andrew into already.

"We destroyed a lot of the genetic research in the Roseland lab," Irene continued with satisfaction. "Of course," she sighed, "they'll probably just replicate it in some other lab."

Before Isabel could respond, Marian began calling one of her cousins to help her drive the animals down the coast. Irene and Daniel would join Andrew in a newly revised plan for disarming the sonar equipment. Isabel looked over at Marshall. "Can't you talk some sense into Irene and Andrew?"

"You're not a diver, Isabel," was all Marshall would say.

"But I can damn well drive a motorboat and . . ."

"Isabel," Andrew said firmly, "we need both you and Marshall to stay on shore for backup . . . in case something goes wrong. Daniel, Irene, and I can take the whaler out to the navy boat. We'll do the diving and disengage the sonar before the tests. Then we'll signal and meet you back at Silkie's Cave. We'll wait there until tomorrow, when someone can take us out by water to some halfway house where we can stay until all this blows over."

"Not a good plan, Andrew," Marshall said and, for the first time, left Hara's side. He crossed the kitchen and laid a hand on Andrew's shoulder. "You really need me underwater with you."

"No," Andrew gave him a sad look. "I can't be worried about you when we're diving this time, Marsh. If something happens to you, I can't . . ."

Marshall looked down and then nodded. He turned to Isabel and said quietly, "We'll stay on shore."

"You can keep one of the rebreather tanks in the cave," Andrew added. "In case we need backup."

"Will do."

Isabel's shoulders sagged. Things were getting so far out of her control that she could barely keep it all straight anymore. With a sinking sense of inertia unfamiliar to her, she sat down at the kitchen table. She took some comfort in gazing at the beautiful Hara and her baby now nursing contentedly, those bright eyes fixed on Isabel. For a time, as the words of the others washed over her, Isabel returned the steady, trusting gaze of the infant baboon. She marveled at the clear intelligence shining in Hara's eyes.

"Isabel . . ." Marshall's hand was light on her arm. "It's decided. Give us those photos and diagrams Sharp sent you that show exactly how to disengage the underwater sonar device."

"Here." Isabel handed him another folder that she'd gotten from Sharp. She watched as Andrew studied the seemingly simple plans to disarm the sonar equipment rigged at the bottom of the navy ship.

"Okay," Andrew said, "here's what we've got to do . . ."

Marshall returned to sit by Hara, still at her post on the table, and listened as Andrew outlined his plan, with tense interjections from his sister. But his mind was not fully focused on his diving buddy. Hara delighted in pulling out the kinked strands of Marshall's curly hair. Her fingers, so humanlike, were more agile than any human hands Marshall had ever allowed to touch his hair. There was a new openness in the way he offered himself to Hara, a lack of self-consciousness, a generosity in his surrender to this proud matriarch. Hara knew her place, and her power.

After two days with Hara, hiding in safe houses near Portland,

Marshall had begun to understand the etiquette of grooming. As if by some sense of equality, Hara would stop pulling and straightening the strands of his unruly hair and simply turn her shaggy back. This was her signal that it was Marshall's turn to groom her. At first he was awkward, and then the preening ritual felt more natural. Marshall also discovered that if he played fondly with her infant daughter, this softened and relaxed Hara. It delighted him. The infant was a small, furry bundle of energy and dependence. When Marshall held her, the baby baboon made snuffling sounds of contentment and fell immediately into the dreamy gaze exchanged between all parents and infants. It was the look of pure love, the look of primate affection. And it didn't matter that they were two different species gazing at each other. The exchange was an ancient devotion, the promise of a parent or guardian to an infant: *You are mine. I claim and protect you. You belong with me.*

Hara would watch contentedly as Marshall held and sweetly groomed her daughter. What surprised him was how comfortable he felt near Hara. She had a world and a mind of her own. She was not easily frightened or anxious, like many of the chimpanzees, especially the space chimps, who'd hollered and pant-hooted inside the van as it lumbered over every pothole in Portland.

Sitting here beside Hara, Marshall felt a peacefulness descending on him that was complete, as if he were not here at all, but far away on a sunny savannah, looking down at the world from the safety of his sleeping cliff. Marshall turned his attention to Isabel. She was leaning over the table, one arm lightly embracing her brother as the group went over the plans for dismantling the sonar device one last time.

From this distance it was easy to recognize how devoted the sister and brother were to each other, though they were always apart. Marshall could see how the Spinners must have looked as children, here in this same kitchen—Andrew the planner of great beach adventures and Isabel the one who always got distracted by an abandoned seal or other sea creature who needed her rescuing. She was an orphan who adopted other animals so that she would not be alone; Andrew was a wanderer always searching at sea for the parents he had lost. Had they ever found in each other their lost family? Had they ever realized it was each other they longed for most?

There was something in Isabel's posture that Marshall had not recognized until now; it was a stance both competent and despairing. There was strength in her shoulders and spine, in the lean body of a woman who spent much of her time outdoors. A serious martial artist. But her chest was slightly pulled inward, hidden, as if anticipating an attack. Marshall wondered if anyone had hurt Isabel as much as her family.

Women like Isabel didn't remarry once disappointed. They worked late at labs or hospitals or shelters for abused animals or women; they took the whole world on their backs and rarely received any credit. They were not heroes or famous or even acknowledged. They were, however, survivors; and because of them, those who were never meant to survive, did.

He would not do Isabel any more harm. He would not abandon her tonight. Instead he would help her; and then he would let her go on with her long, good life. This much he could do for her, as the best way of showing his—his what? Perhaps he could name it this once, to himself. His love.

"Okay, everybody . . ." Andrew straightened and his sister's arm fell away from him. When he clapped his hands, several of the young chimpanzees mimicked him. "Let's get going."

Marshall stood and for a moment rested his hand on Hara's strong back. Then he crossed into the living room and bent down on his knees in front of the eldest chimpanzee. He talked directly to Fred, using sign language.

Go ride, he signed. This chimp was proficient in ASL; his eardrums had been shattered in an Air Force test to determine the highest decibel level that primate ears could endure. Marshall pointed to Marian, who came over to clasp Fred's willing, outstretched hand. *Happy ride.* Marshall signed. *Good house.*

Then Marshall strode back into the kitchen to Hara and began speaking to her in a soft voice. He also used rudimentary sign language, which he'd been teaching his matriarch over the past several days.

Hara registered his voice more like a murmuring breeze across a vast open space. But there was no space between them, no chasm, only closeness. Pulling her infant daughter more tightly against her breast, Hara let Marshall lead her back to her large cage. Inside, she gazed out at all of them calmly and then turned a steady eye on Marshall.

As everyone took up their duties, Andrew and Marshall gathered up their diving equipment. Daniel was reminding Irene about how to use her oxygen tank.

Outside the cottage, Marian gave Isabel a brief embrace before swinging herself up into Daniel's van. "So, Isa, I'm keeping my promise to stay safe. That means you have to promise that you'll stay on shore, like Andrew said. It's our beach."

"Yes," Isabel said with a sad smile and laid her palm against her friend's cheek. "Our home."

After helping load all the primates into the van, Marshall hung back while Marian and Isabel said goodbye. As Marian was carefully backing down the gravel driveway, Marshall walked alongside and advised her, "Hara is the leader of all the other primates. If you earn her trust, the others will follow."

"I understand strong matriarchies," Marian assured him with a frown.

As she pulled away from the familiar beach cottage, Marian saw Marshall reaching out an arm to pull Isabel toward him. Instead of yielding to his touch, Isabel briskly walked ahead of him to help her brother with the rebreather tanks.

"Oh, Isabel." Marian shook her head as she drove away. "It's doomed. *He's* doomed."

Marian set her mind on the journey. She glanced at the baby rhesus monkey on the passenger seat. He lay curled in a fetal position in a basket cushioned with one of Grandfather Spinner's soft and frayed red fisherman's sweater. In this darkness, the newborn faintly glowed. Or maybe it was the moon. Sorrowfully soothing him into sleep, Marian sang the chants taught by her people—ancient and vulnerable as the sea.

chapter sixteen

Silkie's Cave

THE MIST-SHROUDED BEACH was much more familiar than the man, yet Isabel let herself be pulled down toward the ocean through the rocky sea stacks as if by an undertow. Andrew had already launched Grandfather's boat and was moving into position beyond the thrashing, moonlit surf. There he would rendezvous with the local people the navy had hired to patrol the coast—people, including Daniel, who also happened to be stranding network volunteers.

Isabel watched the water. Almost high tide, she thought, and the bright half moon of late April. Not the best elements for subterfuge.

"Give me your hand." Marshall reached to help Isabel navigate a particularly stony path in their descent into Silkie's Cave.

"You should be following me, Marshall. I know the way."

Marshall turned back to her, his face full of what Isabel considered inappropriate good humor, as if they were simply out here on a lark together. "I have," he said. "I've been following you since we met."

"No, " Isabel corrected him, "you've been running away from me since we met."

Marshall smiled and said nothing. The moonlight flashed off his uneven teeth. As he crawled through a narrow crevice in the sea stack, he held Isabel's hand lightly, with no sense of possessiveness or force.

At high tide, most of her secret childhood cave would be underwater, but until then there would be enough space for them to hide. It was almost midnight. At 3 A.M. the sonar tests would begin. Isabel was sure of the test time because Dr. Sharp had told her the Coast Guard was allow-ing regularly scheduled freighter traffic only until 3 A.M. There would be a window of opportunity for the navy to renew their sonar tests with no interference from ship traffic between 3 and 5 A.M. As soon as Andrew, Irene, and Daniel had disabled the sonar device beneath the navy's research boat and were certain they had not been detected, Andrew would signal to Isabel that all was clear. It had been decided that Daniel and Irene would make a preliminary short dive to be sure the device was indeed where Dr. Sharp had said it was. Then Andrew, the most experi-enced diver, equipped with his long-lasting rebreather tank, would dive down and disengage the acoustic speakers.

Isabel glanced at her watch. Still three hours until the sound tests began. Nothing to do but wait. She checked her old rowboat hidden inside Silkie's Cave. Yes, it seemed sturdy enough for motoring out to Andrew in case of an emergency. Marshall scrambled back up the stony path to the top of the sea stack, where he had stowed the rest of his rebreather gear and a small outboard engine. Once back down in Silkie's Cave, he methodically checked and double-checked the diving equipment. "Just in case," he said, and then climbed back up for the motor.

A moment later, when Andrew called on his cell phone, the ascending ring ricocheted spookily in the cavern. "There's a supply ship alongside the navy boat. As soon as it leaves, we'll move in closer," Andrew whis-pered. "So far, so good."

Over the phone, Isabel could hear the slap and slop of water. "You can all still bail out," Isabel said softly. Suddenly the young woman, Daniel, and her little brother seemed like children attempting an adult's job. "In fact," Isabel blurted, her heart pounding, "in fact, I really think you should."

"Don't worry about us, Isabel." Andrew hesitated and then lowered his voice. "Grandfather would be proud . . ."

A deep chill shivered up Isabel's spine. An urgent intuition overcame her. "Get away from there, Andrew. Now!"

But there was only static in response. Had Andrew heard her? Had the navy overheard them? Deciding not to risk calling her brother, Isabel sat very still in Silkie's Cave and said a quick prayer for everyone's safety.

She didn't feel fear so much as dread. She trembled, but Isabel couldn't know if this was a premonition.

Marshall's return eased her from her dark reverie. He set down the small outboard motor with a groan. "Andrew tells me that when you two were kids, you once found a sealskin right here in this cave. You thought it was magic."

"This is an odd time to be thinking of that."

"No, it's not. Like most magical things, it needs a complicated setup. Andrew set this up." Marshall grinned and wiped the sweat from his face. "You and me here together." Expertly, he attached the outboard motor to the old rowboat at the mouth of the cave. Though it was late summer, the strong night wind off Kiwanda Beach was chill.

"I hate to break it to you, Marshall." Isabel couldn't help but smile. "There's nothing magical about you and me."

"No? A man who finally follows his heart—and it isn't even actually his? A woman who thinks she's all alone, abandoned, when everybody loves her and would risk anything for her?"

Silently, Isabel sat cross-legged watching Marshall as he stripped down to his skivvies without a shred of self-consciousness—a diver at work.

Pulling on one leg of his wetsuit, he met Isabel's eyes and smiled. "Andrew doesn't realize that it's really more dangerous for you and me here on shore."

For a moment, Isabel considered Marshall's remark. Love, for each of them, was dangerous. Hadn't it drowned her parents? Hadn't it driven Isabel and Marshall both to commit crimes? And what else would it make her do? Isabel wondered. She shoved that question way down, along with the dread and the trembling. Watching Marshall's broad shoulders and graceful economy of movement, Isabel realized that not all her shivering was from fear.

She turned her eyes, and her desire, away from Marshall. But still, she imagined him pulling on the thin, sleek neoprene wetsuit like a man who had only momentarily shed his water-skin to stay on shore with her.

Looking back at him, Isabel noticed a golden glint from the chain on Marshall's naked chest. Her ammonite fossil hung there against the raised ridges of his long scar. "Last time I saw that, it was at the bottom of a fish tank," Isabel said, her voice very soft.

"You didn't think I realized how much of yourself you were giving me—how precious it was?" When she said nothing, simply bowed her head, Marshall added, "Isabel, I can't do this."

"Me, neither," Isabel said.

He seemed to be struggling for breath. He sank to both knees, his chest still bare, half his wetsuit sagging behind him in the sand instead of pulled tight across his shoulders. "I mean, Isabel," Marshall breathed, "I can't make love to you again in my wetsuit."

"It's not a good time." Isabel tucked her knees up beneath her chin.

"It never is." Marshall smiled almost sadly. "Love is never convenient."

Kneeling in the sand, Marshall pulled at his neoprene boots, tearing them off his feet as if the second skin were somehow burning him alive. Isabel watched Marshall steadily as he pulled and tugged at the wetsuit, peeling it down over his buttocks and then sitting in a spray of sand to slip the black suit down around his ankles.

She moved gracefully toward him. "Let me help you."

And he was free. Marshall had never felt so unburdened of his heavy gear, the skin that always fit too tightly except underwater. He watched as Isabel pulled off her own clothing and then stepped toward him. High tide eased nearer to Silkie's Cave, but Isabel and Marshall ignored the rising waves. Her arms were as light and supple as seaweed surrounding him. In cold, fertile waters like those along this Northwest Coast, Marshall would often tread water, holding on to the tallest canopy of kelp forest as an anchor. Isabel was his living, swaying anchor now as she draped herself over him, her body slightly longer than his.

This difference in body length made Isabel laugh a little. As if to reassert his authority, Marshall rolled her over several times until both their bodies were coated with fine, wet sand.

"Is this where you brought all your sweethearts when you were learning to make love?" Marshall asked. He took her ear lightly between his teeth, kissing the intricate whorls of skin.

"No," she said, her breathing quickening. "This cave belongs to the seals. At high tide, it's underwater."

"Then let's drown together," Marshall murmured and kissed her lips, his tongue tentative and sweet.

Though she heard his words, though her mind told her that this was the kind of thinking that had doomed her own drowned parents, Isabel's body did not listen to her command to stop, to ease out from beneath Marshall.

When Marshall kissed her breasts, his tongue teasing them into tense pleasure, when he gently touched the salty rivulet between her thighs, when he stroked her belly in tingling circles, everything in Isabel's body rose up to meet and draw him inside. Marshall moved with the same rhythm and pulse, as the waves now splashed higher and higher on the beach.

Isabel had often watched harbor seals twirling together in a sensuous ballet, the waves lifting them. Their small, dark heads at the water's surface suggested the underwater embrace of slick bodies. *Seals also come ashore to mate.* This was all she could think as Marshall raised up on his elbows, still moving inside her, to gaze into her eyes. His black hair was coated with sand, his brow troubled, the dark pools of his eyes like obsidian. What she saw in his face both broke and opened Isabel's heart. He was hers. He would not live long.

"I will always come back to you, Isabel," he told her. His breathing thickened, and she could feel the beating of his heart echo in her own chest. "No matter how far away I go, I'll come back to you."

"How do you know I won't come to you?" Isabel asked. She rose up and lifted his weight. In one quick movement, she was on top of him. Now Isabel could move effortlessly in a slow dance on his body.

It delighted him. Marshall let Isabel's rhythm become his. She moved and floated above him like flotsam from a shipwreck. Strange and surprisingly domestic things might wash up on shore after a storm at sea: waterlogged photo albums, a copper lamp shade, a child's rocking horse, a teakwood bed stand carved with hummingbirds. Marshall knew that even if shipwrecked, he and Isabel would always wash up on the same beach. They belonged together. The laws of nature, the absolute certainties of tides, the gravitational pull of the moon would salvage them together.

As high tide began to claim the hollow stone intricacies of Silkie's

Cave, Marshall felt as if he swirled within Isabel's body, finding even those places she had not yet explored herself, seeping into every inner curve and hidden chamber, the way water always seeks its own level, its sure, slow, and world-shaping way.

As Isabel rolled over to take him on top of her, clasping his buttocks with both legs, she held him very still. For just this moment, Isabel understood her own parents' bodies entwined like seaweed in death. It had always seemed unnatural to her, even horrible, this fatal grip on each other, if not on life. But with Marshall still inside her, their bodies now spent, limbs smelling of salt and sweat, the dense green pungency of kelp beneath them, Isabel forgave her mother and father not only for dying but also for holding on so hard to each other.

She understood because this was the way Isabel kept her legs wrapped around Marshall, even knowing the tide was too high and they must leave their cave. She turned her head, knowing that she should see Andrew's flashlight—*All clear*—like a fallen star on the waves. But there was no flashlight signal saying that the dive below the navy ship was a success. What was the delay? How could she and Marshall have done such a thing when so many other lives were at stake? But still Isabel could not move. Marshall seemed to be sleeping; his breathing was even.

"Took me all these years . . ."

"For what?" she asked.

"To get it," he murmured. "But maybe it takes everybody their whole lives to figure it out . . ."

Isabel shifted beneath Marshall's weight and the wet sand sank deeper. She said nothing, waiting.

Marshall seemed to struggle with himself and then relaxed. "I mean, to finally find out that the love of my life is . . ." He hesitated.

"Is what?"

"Not only my life . . . but others."

Inside Silkie's Cave, waves entered and flowed toward them, foam washing over their bare feet. It was cold. Still, they did not move.

Isabel stretched her full length, listening to the steady surf one more moment. Lifting up, she tenderly kissed Marshall, this man who now had her heart, too. "What time is it?"

Marshall glanced at his underwater watch. "Almost 1:30," he said.

"We should climb up on the sea stack so we can see Andrew's signal better. He should give us the all clear soon."

"Right." Marshall disentangled his body from Isabel's and sat up. Sand coated his back and hers. He brushed off the wet granules and quickly pulled on his wetsuit.

"What do you think is keeping them?" Isabel asked, putting on her clothes.

"Don't know." Marshall hefted a rebreather tank into the rowboat. "I'll get things ready in case I need to get out there fast."

Isabel nodded. "The tide's rising. We should get a signal from them soon."

"Maybe I should head out there now."

"No, let's climb up top—there's a passage through the rock from inside the cave—it's our old lookout."

They scrambled up through the craggy sea stack tunnel that had been hers and Andrew's childhood hide-and-seek refuge. Climbing took all her strength, but at last Isabel was on top of the sea stack, looking down at the powerful, moonlit surf cascading against rocks. Marshall was right behind her. With her binoculars, Isabel scanned the waves, awaiting the crucial signal from Andrew's boat. In an emergency, Andrew could always risk calling his sister on the cell phone. Suddenly Isabel remembered, "Oh, God, I left my satchel with the cell phone down in the cave."

"I'll get it," Marshall said and was gone before she could protest.

Cursing her own forgetfulness, Isabel again peered through her binoculars, studying the brightly lit navy boat about five miles off shore. She watched anxiously for some signal. Nothing. She leaned against a boulder, vaguely aware that, above, the constellations Cassiopeia and Orion shone like luminous maps. What was taking Marshall so long?

A movement startled Isabel. Below on Kiwanda Beach someone was running. A knot of people rapidly approached. Isabel trained her binoculars on one of them. By the slight limp and skip of his left leg, she knew that it was Stewart Salk. She had been with Stewart when he'd fallen and crushed his knee while climbing these same rocks years ago.

This sea stack, with its stony face and mists, was one of the few parts of her childhood Isabel had ever shared with her ex-husband; and it had caused him injury, as if even the stone denied Stewart entrance into Isabel's secrets, her hideaways. For just one moment more, Isabel allowed herself to imagine that this eerie race below was not dangerous, that it had nothing to do with their subterfuge. But when Isabel trained her binoculars on the figure running ahead of Stewart's group, leading them away from the cave and her lookout, Isabel gasped. It was Marshall, rebreather tank bouncing against his wetsuit.

Then Isabel heard a bullhorn. It was a familiar voice, one that she had always trusted. "Just give up, McGreggor." It was Maggie Salk's voice over the bullhorn. Maggie had planted herself on the beach and was shouting, "You and Andrew Spinner are already wanted for trespassing and criminal mischief in the Roseland break-in. And what you're attempting now is terribly dangerous. There's a divers' alert on."

Marshall did not stop running.

"No harm will come to you," Maggie continued. "If you just surrender, no one else will get hurt, either."

Did Maggie know of their plans to sabotage the sonar tests? Is that what she was talking about? Isabel stood up. Should she call out to Maggie and try to stop this all right now?

Stewart was gaining on Marshall, who was weighed down by his diving equipment. "Stewart!" Maggie bellowed to her son. "Let the sheriff handle this. You're not the whole damn posse."

Stewart did not fall back with the others, but instead stopped and drew out his gun. Pointing it straight up in the air, Stewart fired a warning shot.

Maggie Salk pleaded, "For God's sake, son, this guy is just some animal rights nut. And he's unarmed. What the hell are you doing?"

Isabel glanced at the illumined numbers on her waterproof watch—almost 2 A.M. The sonar tests had not started yet. So why wasn't Marshall escaping in her old rowboat and joining Andrew at sea? That was their backup plan if something went awry. Marshall would be able to escape by sea in the boat, and he had an extra rebreather tank should Andrew or the other divers need one. Was this some heroic idea to save her? She could save herself, especially from Stewart.

"Marshall!" Isabel waved her arms, screaming. Did anyone hear her?

She remembered her flashlight and turned it on, hoping someone might look up and notice her flailing beam.

She had to do something. Isabel slipped down the tunnel in the sea stack to another lookout point she'd often used when she and her brother played pirate and princess as children. Standing on a far ledge, Isabel at last saw Andrew's repetitive flashlight signals.

Trouble, Andrew signaled. *Trouble.*

Her brother seemed so far away. He could not help them. Nor she him. Her cell phone was likely lost now in the high tide inside Silkie's Cave.

Isabel flashed her light at Andrew. Three short bursts of light. *Trouble,* she signaled to him.

It was the extent of their language of lights. All Isabel could do now was watch as the people ran on the beach below, weaving among the tall, stone stacks. She knew each monolith by name: there was Castle Rock, the Emperor, and Sea Witch. And this sea stack that had sheltered her so many years, this was called Seal Rock. As Marshall led them away from Silkie's Cave, Isabel saw Stewart almost stumble.

Isabel suddenly decided what she must do. Scrambling up again to the beach side of the sea stack, she looked down at the running figures. "Stewart!" she screamed. "Stop this! *Now!*"

And he did. For just one moment, Stewart Salk halted and looked up at Isabel.

In the moonlight, Isabel could see his face, familiar and sad.

"Come down!" he cried.

Only a few yards ahead of him, Marshall picked up his pace, his primate heart pumping the powerful blood to his strong legs as he ran away from Isabel and Seal Rock.

From her high perch, Isabel saw a sudden sneaker wave rise up to break over the two men in unpredictable fury, pulling them in.

Underwater, both men must have tumbled head over heels until the slow circling of the undertow took them down together. It was what everyone who lived on this beach dreaded. This sudden, overwhelming wave.

"God, no!" It was Maggie screaming for her son.

Isabel slid down the sea stack tunnel, not caring that the stone tore at her hands and knees. She had never descended the labyrinth of rock and cavern so quickly. By the time she stumbled into Silkie's Cave, by the time she took a deep breath and swam underwater the entire length of the cave, out through the mouth, and far into the surf, Isabel knew it was too late.

From the water, there was no sign of either man. Shivering, knowing she had less than fifteen minutes before hypothermia set into her own body's core, Isabel spun around in the roiling waves and looked for Marshall and Stewart in the surf. But all she saw was Andrew's light flashing farther out at sea.

Trouble.

Silence. It was as if Isabel had always been alone. If she did not want to drown, she must swim to shore. For a moment she hesitated. Is that what her mother had felt in the waves; is this why she had wrapped her arms around her husband and drowned? Isabel's bare legs tingled with a rising numbness and her teeth chattered, her core body warmth quickly ebbing. Turning to shore, she swam desperately.

As she did, she saw another shape nearby and screamed out, "Marshall! Over here!"

But this was no human. It was a dolphin. Perhaps the creature would save her, swim her to shore, as dolphins often did with drowning people. But this dolphin was on its side. As Isabel swam toward the sleek creature, a sob rose up in her already aching lungs. She reached out one hand for the supple skin of the silver-gray dolphin. Isabel pulled the creature toward her like a life preserver and floated a moment, breathless.

Then she saw the dark, unblinking eye. Wide open, glazing over, blood pooling in the socket. "Oh, God, no!" Isabel breathed.

It was supposed to be an hour or more until the sonar tests began. And yet here was terrible evidence that they had already begun. When? Ducking briefly under the cold waves, Isabel heard now the far-off, metallic pinging of underwater blasts like piercing squeals. Inside she felt a faint resonance, a painful, dizzying ache and throb like a whole-body migraine. It left her weak, struggling to stay afloat. Marshall must have heard the high-pitched sonar even above the water. He couldn't take her boat out to sea and risk getting any closer to such lethal sound. No wonder Andrew's signals from near the navy's ship were so frantic. She was five miles away from the source of the sonar, and still she felt the sickening pressure waves in her body and ears. What must be happening to those nearer the dangerous blasts? Isabel remembered Alexander Sharp's body being carried up from the water and, in her lab, the sight of the dolphin's lungs and brain and ears.

Panicked now, Isabel clung to the floating dolphin. She fought back nausea and aching chills in her own bones. She believed that she was far enough from the ship and the sonar's source to escape serious injury. But she prayed for Andrew, Irene, and Daniel. Perhaps they had not yet dived into dangerous waters. And Marshall, where was he? Why was this sonar blaring underwater more than an hour earlier than scheduled? Had someone warned the navy of their intended sabotage?

Stewart. Stewart must have warned the navy to start the tests early. Had Stewart somehow gotten wind of the stranding network's plans to dismantle the sonar? But Isabel could not believe that Stewart would do anything to hurt her. Did he even know she was involved?

Chilled now beyond numbness, Isabel treaded water, desperately holding on to the dead dolphin's dorsal fin, her legs exhausted. Had the sneaker wave knocked Stewart and Marshall unconscious? Were they drowning nearby and she couldn't find them?

Exhausted and freezing, Isabel finally pulled herself on top of the dolphin and used its body as a small float to paddle to shore. Lying belly to belly with the animal, she stroked the water with all the strength left in her arms. Her legs felt paralyzed with hypothermia.

As Isabel reached shore, she saw a trail of white headlights and flashing red emergency lights along the bluffs overlooking the beach. Overhead thrummed a helicopter with the brilliant shining eye of a searchlight scanning the water.

Maggie was running toward Isabel, coming close enough now to recognize her. "Isa," she cried out, "do you see my boy?"

Isabel pulled herself upright, shivering violently. She could barely stand. A long trail of bull kelp tripped her in the high surf. But she kept her balance as Maggie ran up to her.

Then she realized to her horror that she was not alone in this thrashing surf. There were already other bodies stranding beside her. Cold beyond her endurance, Isabel staggered through the turgid surf toward the dark shapes rolling on the sand. So many. Not all sea creatures.

Some of them were human. Some of these broken and sound-blasted and blood-soaked bodies that the sea had borne toward shore, Isabel knew.

Epilogue

It's pure happiness," Marian said. "You'll remember how it feels again someday, too, Isabel."

Ear-splitting exultant whistles, bleeps, and rapid-fire clicks and squeals as Mack and Molly called out to each other. Today on Kiwanda Beach, the stranding network volunteers would release the calves in the hope that they were strong enough to survive and find their own family pods. If not, they would always have each other.

In the truck, held securely in their carrying slings inside two sloshing tanks, Mack and Molly rested, submerged except for blowholes and backs. So their sensitive skin did not get sunburned, so their body temperatures remained stable, Marian and Isabel tenderly bathed each calf in chilly water, as if giving a child a sponge bath.

They made one last check of vital signs before the Newport Aquarium truck rumbled to a stop on the wet sand, where the volunteers would lift the slings and carefully carry each calf back into its home waters.

It was Molly that Isabel was most concerned about, because she had sustained some permanent inner ear damage. But it was not enough to condemn her to a lifetime of captivity, in which her own echolocations would bounce off cement tank walls in a useless cacophony. Molly was more likely to die of depression if kept in the aquarium than of predation in the open ocean—especially since they were releasing the healthy Mack. In the wild, his help would compensate for Molly's injuries, much the way Silkie guided half-deaf Isabel through her world.

A bolt of nausea, and Isabel tried to steady herself so the calves didn't sense her emotions. But there it was again, the overwhelming sneaker wave of pain that for the past two weeks had been threatening to drown Isabel, just as the undertow had taken Stewart and Marshall. Just as the sonar tests had taken Irene and Daniel and most likely her brother, as well as many more whales and dolphins. Isabel could not believe how physical this grief was, its dull ache suddenly rising up to a pitch of pain that left her breathless, dizzy, and even nauseated.

"Sadness is always so physical with you," Marian had noted as Isabel went through her days like a sleepwalker, only to be seized suddenly with trembling, nausea, shortness of breath, and loss of balance. "How else would you know you're still alive?"

"And they're not," Isabel managed to say, her heart too full, pounding.

But today's release of Mack and Molly would be a respite from her mourning. Or at least she must disguise it so that the calves might sense only her pleasure in returning them to their home waters. Dribbling ice water over Molly's back with a sponge to soothe her, Isabel tried to smile. "Mack will be right beside you. And out there in the wild, Moll, you'll get a little stronger every day," she promised.

And perhaps so would she. But Isabel knew she would never completely recover from this loss. Just as she had forever lost half her hearing, Isabel had now lost half of herself—her brother, Andrew. She was truly an orphan.

Then there was Marshall. What she lost when the wave took him would always be a mystery. Isabel saw her days stretch out before her: She would sit on her beach alone, except for the occasional company of a stranded seal pup; she would continue her forensics work and find sanctuary in the daily, comforting routines of her life. Holidays she would celebrate with Marian's engaging, generous family. Out of loneliness or kindness, she might have affairs with men who were sweet-natured nomads like her brother; but she would never meet Marshall again—the man with whom she might have made a perfect empathic pair. Yet even in her solitude, she would not be pathetic or bitter. Isabel would have the lifelong constancy of her ocean and all its abundant life. She would remain active and reliable, knowing that her work in the world made a difference.

It would be a good life. After she passed on, she would be truly missed.

Molly startled; her blood pressure shot up as she suddenly tried to turn her head sideways in the sling to gaze up at Isabel. There was alarm in her unblinking eyes.

"Easy, girl, easy," Isabel said in her softest voice, running a tender hand along Molly's sleek wet skin.

"That's the problem with being part of our empathic pair," Marian said and patted Mack's flanks. "You're never alone with your worries." Marian reached over with her other hand and shook Isabel gently. "Or your happiness. Come on, Isa, just forget for as long as it takes to let these babies go home. We can't send them off carrying our sadness."

Isabel nodded and inwardly shook off her despair. In a low alto voice, she began to sing into Molly's tiny pinprick of a good ear. It was her silkie song, but it always calmed Molly:

Storm born, their babes
See first the winter sun. . . .

Give them sweet life
Until their day is done.

Isabel filled her mind with the remembered joy of releasing Merlin only last week—the seal pup who, under the care of their sanctuary volunteers, had put on sixty pounds and was now a strapping, strong-willed juvenile. As they had carried him into the surf, he had barely glanced back at the human family that had briefly been his. Nor did he surface to fix on the compass point formed by that group of people so that he might better navigate his return. Isabel and many other sanctuary volunteers had nursed him around the clock, had donned the seal-mother rubber outfits so that the pup would not imprint on humans—and this was their reward. The healthy seal pup was not interested, never would be interested, in humans on shore. Perhaps a fleeting memory of other eyes reflecting his—that's what might remain in his mind. His rescuers were already a memory; they might someday figure in a faint dream as he slept in the sanctuary of a kelp bed.

But with Mack and Molly it was different. They were more vulnerable to attachment and might again seek out the company of humans. This memory and bond would be the greatest risk to the calves' survival. It was why all the stranding network volunteers had slowly weaned Mack and Molly away from human companionship—so their cetacean bond would become the strongest. It had been weeks since Isabel had allowed herself to touch or be this close to the calves. From behind glass aquarium walls, she had shared their pleasure, their excitement, as they sensed their release this last week. Perhaps they were telepathic, as some researchers believed?

But now in the truck bed, right before letting them go, Isabel ran her hands along Molly's smooth, cool skin and could not help but think of Marshall. Was he really dead—drowned with Stewart by the massive wave? Or had he somehow made it safely out to Grandfather's boat? If so, why hadn't either Andrew or Marshall made contact with her? Surely they would not let her suffer, believing them dead? There was only one explanation. Everyone she had ever loved, except Marian, was gone.

As the volunteers clambered aboard the aquarium's truck to begin the delicate job of lowering the calves into waiting arms for the short transit to the surf, Isabel glanced up at the green cliffs above the beach. Of course they would be there, government and military personnel. Since the deaths two weeks ago of more than thirty marine mammals and three humans, the town of Lawasskin had been taken over by what the townspeople grumbled was a militia of federal and state officials. Some were investigating the claim that the U.S. Navy had tested its sonar equipment at high decibel levels. Other officials were in town to attempt to cover up what had flared into an international event, with Nova Scotia, Greece, and the Bahamas formally accusing NATO and the U.S. government of secretly deploying this lethal sonar off their own shores as well.

Now that human death was involved, few would defend the military or the sonar. The sacrifice of NMFS enforcement official Stewart Salk was a matter of pride to the people of Lawasskin. Rumors circulated that Salk was one of the brave handful of underground Animal Liberation Lifeline activists who had given their lives trying to stop the navy's tests. Who could have suspected that Stewart Salk had that kind of heroism in him?

"I just can't set the whole damn town straight on this," Maggie Salk had told Isabel last week as the two women made funeral plans for Stewart. "People believe only what they want. And I can't tell them the truth." Maggie stopped, shaking her head. She pushed the blackberry cobbler away from her, half-eaten, and reached for the bottle of Scotch that Isabel had also brought her.

The two women sat in silence in Maggie's kitchen, the biggest room in her ramshackle beach house.

"No one who really knows what happened would forgive Stewart." His mother paused. "Don't know that I'll ever be able to forgive my own son."

"You will."

The older woman reached out a hand to take Isabel's. "Will you?" Maggie's green eyes, so like her son's, were bloodshot and puffy. Even so, she was still beautiful, still the only real mother Isabel had left. "Stewart didn't mean this, Isabel," Maggie said. "Yes, he told the navy that some local people were going to try and stop their tests. That was just plain mean on his part. Thought he was losing you to all these outsiders. But my son would never, ever harm you, Isabel."

"I know."

"If Stewart had just come to me before going to the navy . . . I'd have . . . oh, hell!" Maggie looked at Isabel in bewilderment. "Who would ever have thought those bastards would just go ahead and divert boat traffic and then blast away ahead of time? How could they risk . . . ?" Maggie fell silent, staring down at the haphazard crisscross of pie crust lattice.

"I can never make cobbler like you, Maggie," Isabel said softly.

"This is goddamn blue-ribbon cobbler." Maggie drained her glass of Scotch and poured another. "But you did forget the tapioca so the filling could set up."

"I did." Isabel reached over and wrapped her mother-in-law in her arms.

Maggie had asked Isabel to fill out official missing persons reports for Andrew and Marshall. Quietly Isabel also mourned Stewart. Her ex-husband had a horrifying death. Caught off-guard in the sneaker wave, Stewart had been slammed against a rocky snag in the surf. Then his limp body was turned over and over and over like a stone abraded by water. At last he was thrown back on the beach, like flotsam. Of course, a sneaker wave might have taken him at any time on this unpredictable beach. But

Isabel blamed herself for all the human deaths. What had she been thinking? Could she ever forgive herself?

Every time Isabel remembered those three human bodies that lay on the beach until the emergency teams could reach them, she shuddered. Dolphins had lain thrashing and dead everywhere, and alongside them lay a twisted, gangly Daniel still grasping a frail, freckle-faced young woman. Ears streaming blood, eyes startled open as if awestruck, Irene and Daniel no longer looked like mortals. They were creatures of the sea.

Though Maggie Salk had wanted a quiet funeral for her son, many activists, including ALL members, thronged Stewart's memorial service; the next day, they staged a protest rally at the double memorial service for Daniel and Irene. A stranger to the town, Irene, too, was nonetheless considered a local hero. Someone from ALL had posted throughout the town a photo of her taken in Hawaii—a young woman grinning into the camera, obviously proud of the weight of a scuba tank on her slender shoulders, her expression at once buoyant and a little unsure. Marshall must have taken this photo. Every time Isabel saw it tacked on the bulletin board at her wildlife sanctuary, she had to turn away.

Isabel had attended all the funerals, even though they turned into media events and environmental protest rallies, even though FBI undercover agents tried to fit in with the mourners, both to identify ALL members and fugitives and to search the crowd for some sign of Andrew Spinner and Marshall McGreggor. The two were still wanted for questioning in the Roseland lab break-in. Isabel suspected that her phone and e-mail were tapped, in case the two were somehow still alive and tried to contact her.

At his insistence, Isabel had accompanied Dr. Alexander Sharp to Portland for a hasty official gathering of congressional members flown in from Washington, D.C., to investigate this disaster, what the U.S. Navy insisted was simply "a regrettable incident, an accident." But speaking and answering the typed questions of Congress members, Dr. Sharp told them and the world another story: a story of what he had betrayed and what he had lost, of a naval mind that saw the oceans not as an ecosystem but only as "a backdrop against which to wage war."

After testifying, he said to Isabel, "This won't stop their sonar. Nothing will. The military always finds a reason to use its new weapons."

"People will stop it," Isabel said firmly, "ordinary people."

In fact, seven major environmental groups were bringing suit against the navy to stop the development of this sonar, which it had planned to deploy in over 80 percent of the world's oceans.

Once home, Isabel had taken a two-week leave from her forensics work. She spent most of her time on the beach with Silkie and told everyone she was seal-sitting, though no one mentioned that there had been only one orphaned seal pup this month. Isabel's one consolation was Marian, who had returned safely with her cousin from transporting Hara, the space chimps, and the other animals to the Mendocino underground primate sanctuary, only to find Lawasskin turned upside down. Together, the friends went through the motions of daily life; together, they waited for word of Marshall and Andrew.

"Slowly . . . slowly . . . yes!" Marian said now as several volunteers lifted Mack from his canvas carrying sling and held him between them as if he might break. As they lowered him into the sea, Marian said, "Now, little Molly. She's more agitated."

Mack let out a burst of clicks, keeping very still in the many arms. His sounds soothed Molly, who then let Marian and Isabel lift her from her tank, with only one frightened thwack of her tail flukes against Isabel's cheek. It left a red welt on her face.

"I'm okay," Isabel said. "Don't drop her, Marian."

"No one's worrying about you right now, Isa. Isn't it a relief?" She leaned over and hummed into Molly's ear, a low chant that had the effect of mesmerizing the calf.

Many hands reached up to the truck bed to take hold of the dolphin calf with the wary eyes. Why should she trust these outstretched human hands when she had been weaned so thoroughly these past weeks?

But the open ocean and Mack were calling for her, and though air was only half Molly's element, she must somehow allow herself to be hoisted up, held aloft in these ungainly arms—so much more awkward than fins, so much less evolved, so unpredictable, changing everything they touched.

"Molly . . . sweet Molly. May you never be alone, may you always be well and wild . . . ," Marian crooned after she and Isabel leapt down from the truck and together lowered Molly into the surf. Molly liked Marian's voice more than the taller woman's, whose eyes were so often full of saltwater, whose stomach gases held sadness and turmoil. For Isabel, Molly felt grave concern, but not enough to turn from the sea.

Nearby, Mack called. A quick inhale and Molly submerged her small body so she could listen for the far-off ricochet of signature whistles, not her own. Her mother had died on this beach, but what was left of her pod was perhaps not far away. They would welcome her.

And here was Mack, right next to her, his pectoral fin stroking along her small flank, his brown eye urging her—*Come, come . . .*

One mighty little thrust of her tail flukes and Molly shot free of human hands, spiraling through this dangerous, loving ocean. No walls. Only the green massage of kelp forest swaying, a burst of barracuda, and a harmless dog shark below. Dive down, arch of spine, fluke propelling her upward to blow together with Mack, to soar and barely skim the waves, to breathe in fast and then splash down in perfect synch.

In the shelter of Mack's pectoral fin, tucking around her so they swam at a speed they had never experienced in the tank, Molly veered straight out to sea. If they passed this way again, they would stay far from this beach. But they would remember it.

The next weekend, Isabel showed up at the forensics lab after Marian called her in to help out with a routine necropsy. Isabel was a little irritated at Marian's request, but also somewhat relieved to return to her familiar regimen. She feared that the lab might have been bugged by navy personnel, who had decided that Isabel must be one of the undercover ringleaders of ALL. There were rumors that the federal government might even terminate her job at the wildlife lab. Even though the navy itself was under a relentless investigation, they made obvious their surveillance of Isabel Spinner.

Setting her thermos of coffee on a desk overflowing with work and unopened mail, Isabel sighed and sat down.

"Thanks for coming in, dear." Marian poured herself a cup of Isabel's coffee. "At least I can help you sort your mail."

Isabel turned her attention to her nuclear microscope, under which she was studying a butterfly wing believed to be from one of the Amazon's most endangered species. An eighty-two-year-old man had been apprehended in Los Angeles International Airport smuggling rare rain forest orchids, brilliant orange and red feathers from poached parrots, and dead butterflies in his underwear as he tried to pass through U.S. Customs undetected. A bloodhound trained to sniff out drugs had shown noticeable interest in the old man's clothing—in the panoply of endangered animal and plant species inside.

"Lunch?" Marian suddenly asked Isabel and indifferently tossed a small package atop her crowded desk.

"I just got here," Isabel murmured.

"You're hungry." Marian's voice carried electricity that Isabel felt run through her own body. "You're starving."

In surprise, Isabel looked up from her microscope. Marian's eyes shifted slightly to the package waiting on Isabel's desk. Tightly tied in twine and postmarked Kenya, it was indistinguishable from the other pieces of mail. Carefully Isabel picked up the brown package with its badly typed label. Probably a warden wanting their lab to help track down bush-meat poachers who were killing wildlife as quickly as the logging trucks slashed new roads.

Still, her heart was thumping loudly. Slowly Isabel untied the string. Inside was a battered foreign postcard. A picture taken as if underwater, it was so blurry. Nevertheless, Isabel could make out the uneven ledges of a rocky cliff overlooking a wide savannah. Sleeping as if they had not a care in the world was a troop of guinea baboons, several females and infants drowsing in the brilliant sunlight, their long limbs wrapped around one another. One baboon stood out among them all, holding her infant. A healthy halo of light gleamed around her. A matriarch. A Madonna.

With her fingers trembling, Isabel carefully opened the tissue paper surrounding two intertwined strands of hair. One was the reddish, thick hair of a primate. The other hair—a black, curly strand—was obviously human. A jolt of joy ran like lightning up and down her spine as Isabel forced herself to resist the urge to smell the hair, hold it to her face as if she could summon the whole person back to her—the way she identified an entire animal, genus and species, from one tiny, forsaken part.

Glancing at Marian, Isabel did not smile. She could not allow herself to show her relief and happiness. But she knew Marian felt it, too. She could tell this in the faintest nod from her friend, in the way Marian reached down to take out a small red bag of tobacco and say a silent prayer, as she often did before they began their work to save other animals.

Only then could Isabel turn the postcard over and read, her eyes brimming:

We're very pleased with an old man's boat
and the rebreather equipment that allowed us
to stay afloat and underwater for so long.
Looking here in Africa for a fossil record many
believed lost. But so sad for all those also lost
at sea.

It was her brother's beloved scrawl, and it concluded:

Can you please identify these two animal
specimens? Possibly evidence of an aquatic ape?
Endangered, yes. But we're hoping that, with
reintroduction and some habitat protection,
they will live on a long time together.

Come—do the research.

Author's Note

THE SCIENCE in *Animal Heart*—including xenotransplantation and the use of a new military sonar—is factual and reflected in real-world current events. This novel is inspired by my love for our oceans and marine life and my concerns about the threats posed to them by some of these new scientific technologies.

The U.S. Navy's use of mid-to-low-frequency active sonar has especially troubled me. In 1998, I wrote my first of many articles about this sonar—"War Games in a Whale Nursery." Since that time, there have been mass strandings of marine mammals linked to such sonar tests from Greece to the Canary Islands. And in March 2000, there was a stranding of whales off the Bahamas, for which the navy belatedly admitted its sonar was the probable cause—only after official necropsies showed that the cetaceans had suffered hemorrhages in their jaws, inner ears, and brains.

After the navy tested its sonar in my home Pacific Northwest waters in the spring of 2003, thirteen harbor porpoises stranded. Newspapers reported the deaths and the scientists' questions: Did these animals beach themselves to escape the painful acoustic blasts—sounds so loud they were heard above water by whale watchers twenty miles from the navy ship? Did the noise send the panicked cetaceans into dives so deep that they ran out of air, then surfaced too quickly, suffering a form of the bends? Or does the sonar disorient, deafen, and cause hemorrhaging due to traumatic "sonic pressure insult"?

This high-intensity sonar is like "acoustic bullets," says orca expert Ken Balcomb, "like having a nail driven into your head and it stays there."

New, international research now confirms the lethal link between military sonar and necropsy evidence of decompression sickness in marine mammal deaths. A U.S. federal court has taken an important step in limiting the navy's far-reaching, low-frequency sonar, when the navy had originally planned to use it in all the world's oceans. But a new environmental exemption for the military will probably undermine this judicial limit, and mid-frequency sonar—like that responsible for the fatal Bahamas and Canary Islands strandings—is still being used by NATO and the U.S. military throughout the world.

I believe that it's not just scientists or government agencies that will finally halt or limit this dangerous underwater technology. It's also up to us—everyday people and grassroots organizations. If you wish to make our seas safe for all life, please contact Orca Network (www.orcanetwork.org), Natural Resources Defense Council (www.nrdc.org), Ocean Mammal Institute (www.oceanmammalinst.org), SeaFlow (www.seaflow.org), or Ocean Futures (www.oceanfutures.org).

—Brenda Peterson
Seattle, Washington
www.literati.net/Peterson